A Re
Beauty

Luc held out his sword, tip lowered to show his inclination to mercy. "You are my prisoner. Take me to Lord Balfour, so that I may accept his surrender."

Soft laughter met his demand. "That is impossible."

"For your sake, it had best not be. I would meet the man who cost me good soldiers, and I would meet him now, or it will go hardly with you and all in your hall."

After a moment of taut silence, the girl shrugged her shoulders. Golden hair rippled down her back. "I have no desire to see more lives forfeit because of my failure. If you wish to be taken to my father, I will take you."

She turned, head held high. Luc followed her down the narrow weed-choked path, to a small stone cairn tucked beneath a leafy bower of new trees. Brushing a strand of loose hair from her face, she met his gaze and swept out an arm to indicate the pile of stones. "Lord Balfour awaits your demands, Sir Knight."

Luc stared at her mocking face, the slight smile twisting her lips. "How long has he been dead?"

"Eighteen moons have waxed and waned since Balfour joined his fathers."

"Then you will tell me who is lord in his place. I want the man who has rebelled against William and refused my demands to surrender, the man who is responsible for commanding the battle to defend Wulfrun."

Draping her slender body against the stone cairn, the girl's mocking gaze did not leave his face. "That person is before you, Norman. Do your worst."

ALSO BY JULIANA GARNETT

The Quest

The Magic

Juliana Garnett

THE VOW

BANTAM BOOKS

New York Toronto London

Sydney Auckland

THE VOW

A Bantam Fanfare Book / February 1998

ISBN-0-553-57626-7

Published simultaneously in the United States and Canada

Bantam Books are published by Bantam Books, a division of Bantam DoubledayDell Publishing Group, Inc. Its trademark, consisting of the words "Bantam Books" and the portrayal of a rooster, is Registered in U.S. Patent and Trademark Office and in other countries. Marca Registrada. Bantam Books, 1540 Broadway, New York, New York 10036.

PRINTED IN THE UNITED STATES OF AMERICA

OPM 10 9 8 7 6 5 4 3 2 1

To Clive Harris and Jane Harris Merola, who were kind enough to help me with my research, and who have the marvelous good fortune to be Rita's children. It's most helpful having such excellent researchers who don't mind overseas calls and runs to the local bookstores to find out about castles and kings . . . In the future, I promise to try to remember the exact time difference between England and America.

To Beth Hezel, who so kindly posed for the photos of my idea of Ceara, I want to say thanks. And another thanks for your kind care of Sheba. You make her trips to the vet's office much nicer!

And to Chris Adair, another avid reader of English history. Thanks for the loan of your research materials.

The maid of woven tresses
Smote the fierce hearted
with bloodstained blade.

Judith, from BEOWULF
Ninth Century

The Vow

Prologue

May, 1067

"If you are too cowardly to defy the Normans, I will go to fight in your place."

The words hung in the suddenly still air like drawn swords: a challenge. All motion and conversation ceased; eyes turned toward the slender blond woman standing in the center of the hall. She stood steadfast, chin firm, ice-blue gaze steady beneath a sweep of insolently long brown lashes. No errant thrum of lute or lyre by careless minstrel, no casual comment, could be heard in the hall awash with light from lamp and torch. Those perched on benches or leaning against stone walls seemed to hold their collective breath. Ceara, daughter to the Saxon lord of Wulfridge, waited with nervous defiance for her father's reply.

Some would like to see her fall, she knew well enough. Fah, she did not care what they thought. Their anticipation was as pungent as the sharp scents of burning pine knots and oil lamps. But all that mattered to her now was vengeance and pride—for 'twas all she had left.

Wulfric is dead, and with him have gone laughter and hope. . . .

She saw rage in the pinpoint flames that lit Lord Balfour's

bright blue eyes. She did not look away. Their gazes were almost level, for she was as tall as most men—even the Norman foes who raped their lands.

Ceara lifted her chin and her long, loose hair drifted over a bared shoulder, cool and soft against her skin. The gunna and kirtle she wore were her own style—pagan some said, though not usually the men who eyed her shortened attire with sly appreciation. Lecherous fools. Around her waist, instead of a gold-linked or woven girdle, she wore a sword; no mere eating dagger, but a lethal Roman gladius—taken, the tale went, by a long-dead Celtic ancestor from a legionnaire. The weapon had been handed down through her family for hundreds of years. And she could use it most agilely, so that no man dared approach her without good reason.

A sword clinked against stone. Someone coughed, and a slight mutter was quickly silenced. Drifts of smoke lazed across the hall, carried by an errant breeze that stirred flame and bright woven wall hangings indiscriminately. Light from a flickering torch gilded her father's hair with silver and played across his craggy features. Had he always had such deep creases in his face?

"I swore an oath to William." Lord Balfour's aged voice had the hoarse sound of a grindstone. "I do not forswear my oaths."

"Oaths given under duress are not meant to be kept."

"And what would a woman know of fealty?" His mouth twisted in an ironic smile that brought heat to Ceara's cheeks.

"More than most men, I daresay, though 'tis not a woman's lot to decide her own fate." She dragged in a deep breath that tasted of smoke and incense and the residue of a thousand evening meals, her cold gaze riveted on her father though her heart had begun to thump against her ribs. "Must it always come to this with us? Can you not listen to *my* counsel as you did to Wulfric's?"

Balfour leaned forward. "Nay. I cannot. You are not Wulfric. He is dead, and I am left with a daughter who is more willful than obedient. You have barely sixteen winters to you, Ceara.

Surely, you did not think *you* could replace Wulfric's wise counsel."

The softly spoken words fell on her like harsh blows. As she answered, her own voice shook slightly, but she steadied it with fierce resolve, her nails digging deeply into the palms of her hands. "Nay, of course I cannot. Wulfric is—was—a man, while I am only a witless female, meant to sit at cooking pots and looms instead of war councils."

"Aye, but you seem to have forgotten that."

"Nay, not for a moment have I forgotten how you wish to keep me in a corner, unnoticed and unheard. Yet in days of old, women's voices were heeded as well as the men's. Now, the Normans have done more damage than the Romans or even the Vikings. They have laid waste to the entire country and made us into curs groveling at their heels, yet you prate of fealty to their bastard king as if it is a matter of honor to lay down our arms and do his bidding like tamelings!"

When she paused, anger making her tremble as if with a chill, her father lifted a hand to beckon two of his thralls forward. They flanked her swiftly. Her chin lifted at this insult, but she made no move to flee.

"You will be escorted to your chamber until you have reconsidered your hasty words," Balfour said coolly, but flames lit his eyes with the heat of a hundred torches.

Ceara met his gaze steadily. Cowards. All of them. Including Balfour, though he was her father and lord of their lands. *Wulfric would never have yielded. . . .* Yea, but Wulfric was gone, she reminded herself. And by all that was sacred, no man would force her to swear a loyalty she did not feel.

Raking the two thralls with a scathing glance, Ceara crossed her arms over her chest. Her mocking smile stretched into a taut grimace. "I shall grow old and withered in my chamber before I will consider yielding to the bastard duke of Normandy."

Fine white lines etched Balfour's eyes as he glowered at her; he turned suddenly on his heel and moved away. He wore the tunic and fur-lined robes of a baron—a Saxon lord—though since the coming of the Normans, the fur was not as thick, the robes increasingly threadbare. Balfour crossed the beautiful tiled floor slowly, the once vibrant pattern of moon and stars beneath his feet now faded. He stepped onto the dais to take his customary seat in the high-backed stone chair made comfortable with bolsters of stuffed feathers and fur.

"You are insolent, my daughter."

Ceara allowed a faint smile to touch her mouth. "Yea, my lord, I learned insolence at your knee. But you know I am right as well as insolent."

Balfour studied her narrowly. "You would have me flee to Malcolm for succor? I am to yield to the king of the Scots what the Norman king has not yet taken? What, then, is the difference, I ask you?"

"The difference is couched in your own words—'tis better to give freely than to be taken from."

Balfour leaned forward, his words a soft hiss between tight lips. "To use your own words—never."

"Then you doom us to—"

"Nay! If I deal fairly with King William, he will deal fairly with me. Wulfridge needs a man who is as fierce as a wolf to hold it against invaders, not a she-wolf who snaps and snarls at every wind. Now go. Think of all that could be lost with hasty action just to further foolish vengeance."

Balfour dismissed her with a slight jerk of his head. Stinging from his sharp words, Ceara whirled about on a sandaled foot. Her loose hair swung around her shoulders and against her waist as she paused a few feet from the dais and snapped her fingers. "Sheba, to me."

Lying in a half crouch nearby, a huge white wolf-bitch rose in a lithe movement, the gold-brown eyes watchful. No one moved as Ceara quit the hall, the white wolf at her heels and her escorts trailing behind.

Ceara felt their eyes on her as she walked the length of the hall with measured tread, continuing through the colonnaded Roman archways to the long corridor that led to her chamber. Ivy climbed the outside walls of the corridor, poking spiny green fingers inside open windows. As she passed, she plucked a three-lobed leaf for good luck and tucked it into the leather sword belt circling her waist.

Her hand went to the pendant that hung around her neck, a legacy from her mother, with glowing amber stone and intricately wrought silver. Her only ornament. The only thing of value she had left since the Normans had come, save pride and self-reliance. Yea, the lady of Wulfridge had left her daughter a legacy of spirit that would not wane in the face of hardship or danger, and it was that, she thought, that pricked her father most.

When Lady Aelfreda died, she'd taken the light from her husband's eyes. Ceara had watched helplessly, raging against the fates that had taken her mother and left her father a changed man. But it had changed her as well.

Once, she had been close to her father, his beloved princess, always at his heels or his side, adoring and adored. Now she felt so alone, isolated from everyone save Sheba. The wolf-bitch was all that remained to her of unconditional love and loyalty.

Behind her, Sheba's huge paws padded over stone with faint clicking sounds from her claws. The thralls stayed a healthy distance from the wolf-bitch, a respect well earned when an unwise individual once dared lay a hand on the shaggy head. The bite had been deep, the lesson swift.

Ceara smiled. Aye, 'twas true that she was like the wolf-bitch that most named her, but she wore the epithet proudly. It was a glorious compliment to be called after the lithe, fierce beast. And they were like, in that neither tolerated fools nor cowards gladly. The mere scent of fear was enough to raise her hackles, and Ceara was filled with anger that her father cared more for his hide than his honor.

A chill swept over her, and Ceara spun on her heel in the

open doorway of her chamber. Her escorts jerked to a halt and eyed her warily. She lifted a brow. "As even you oafish clods can see, I am safely arrived. Go back to my father's hall, and to the buxom wenches who may want your pathetic company."

One of the thralls shot her a glance of resentment. "You've an evil tongue, my lady, for all that you are so fair. 'Tis said you are consort to the Dark One, and I am most like to believe it myself."

Ceara's brow lowered at the man's harsh tone. Sheba came to stand protectively at her side, the thick white fur ruffling beneath the fingers of her mistress's left hand. The animal sensed her tension, and she saw the thrall's eyes flick downward nervously. Now she smiled. "Believe it, Hardred. I whisper with the old ones of the trees of a night. I dance with the demons beneath the sacred oaks, and I can rid myself of paltry men like you with a mere snap of my fingers."

Lifting one hand, she snapped her thumb and finger together and Sheba crouched, a low growl emanating from her throat. Hardred took a hasty backward step, then another, keeping one hand on his sword hilt, and both eyes on the wolf.

"You are evil," he choked out, "both of you!"

Hardred stumbled into the other thrall as they both quit the dimly lit corridor. Ceara listened to the sound of their swift retreat with satisfaction. Fools. She had nothing but contempt for them. Yet fools were all that were left since King Harold lost to the bastard duke and so many good men died with him. Only a few served Balfour now, when once there had been many brave warriors filling the halls. She turned restlessly, unable to bear thinking of those days.

A small lamp of precious oil burned fitfully on the low table near the rope bed she had slept in since she was a small child. No fish oil was used for fuel in her lamp, for it stank and filled the room with foul smoke. She opened the shutters that covered her windows and breathed in air spiced with the beckoning promise of the sea. The draft stirred the *wahrift,* the bright-colored medley of woven stuff decorating the wall. Soon it would be spring, and the land would put forth new life, tiny green shoots rising from the sleeping fields. Where would she be then?

Sheba nudged her hand, whining low in her throat, a question and reminder. Ceara closed the shutters and turned away from the window. A small slab of meat, round of cheese, and half loaf of flat bread lay on a wooden platter, and beside it was a carved pewter flagon of mead. She poured the rich liquid into a small cup. Then she tossed Sheba a chunk of the mutton, which the wolf downed in a single gulp. Ceara smiled slightly.

"Greedy gut."

Sheba's tongue lolled from one side of her mouth, carelessly, happily, and her eyes were bright and watchful, darting to the remaining meat, then back to Ceara with a hopeful blink.

Ceara knelt, and stroked the soft fur gently, her mouth close to the wolf's ear. "We've only the two of us, cony, to fight against William. What shall we do without Wulfric? By all that's holy, whatever shall we do without him?" She buried her face in the thick white coat as Sheba aimed an anxious swipe at her cheek.

The future stretched before her with dark promise. There was little hope of survival for the vanquished. But she had made a vow that she would never yield willingly to the enemy, and she meant to keep it, though it cost her all.

Part I

Chapter One

Yorkshire, England
October, 1069

"CURSE THE OLD man for his treachery." William, duke of Normandy and king of England, leveled a fierce glare at the quivering messenger. Rage blazed in his dark eyes, and the thick shelf of his brows lowered into a thunderous scowl, but he was too well schooled to relinquish control in front of a servant. "How many men with Sir Simon were killed?"

The messenger swallowed hard. "Near four score, sire. And the horses taken, those that were still fit."

"Great plunder for the Saxon rebel, I warrant." William drew in a harsh breath and glanced past the messenger. Tall and commanding, the king was imposing even when pleased. William's mouth worked, and deep lines carved grooves on each side of his thin lips. "What think you of this new rebellion, Louvat?"

Luc Louvat shrugged. "I think the foolish Saxon needs to be taught a lesson, as it is certain Sir Simon has just learned one."

William's laugh was curt. "Yes, it is true that Sir Simon must indeed be rung the severity of the lesson taught him by Saxon rebels. Lord Balfour de Wulfridge swore an oath of fealty to me, and until now, has abided by it. For him to rise up against me when I have all of York brewing like boiling eels is either careful planning or cursed fortune."

Luc smiled slightly. "All know you make your own fortune, sire. It has been said that you could turn water to wine if any mortal man can."

"Blasphemy, Louvat. Bide your tongue."

But a faint smile lurked in William's eyes and at the corners of his mouth, and Luc knew he was not wholly displeased by the remark.

William dismissed the nervous messenger and moved to a table bearing flagons of wine and bowls of fruit. He chose a ripe pear. A chill breeze insinuated itself between chinks in the newly erected wooden walls of the castle, but the king seemed not to feel it as he regarded Luc thoughtfully. "I am beset on all sides. An entire garrison and two castles have been destroyed by these cursed Yorkshiremen. Now the rebellion in the north gnaws at my patience. I dare not allow the Saxons even a moment's control when they are so close to the northern barbarians. It would breed more trouble were they to have time to reinforce their numbers." He bit into the pear, and juice dripped over his fingers unnoticed as he frowned into empty space. After a moment he turned back to Luc with the suggestion of a smile on his face. "Wulfridge is said to be a fertile land close to the sea, though peopled with churls that comprehend little. This Lord Balfour is old, and his numbers few. I am amazed they were able to best Sir Simon, but perhaps he grew careless. I need a reliable knight to bring Wulfridge to heel."

Luc did not reply. He waited, knowing that when the king was ready to continue, he would. But he shifted uneasily, not at all certain he liked the direction of William's thought. It was bad enough riding with William to retake castles that had been conquered before; he had no desire to join Sir Simon in the northern reaches of this barbaric land. There was little of England he liked, and indeed, he would not be here at all if not for the fact that he could no longer remain in Normandy.

William took another bite of pear before saying, "It is fitting that you be the knight to crush the rebellious Saxon of Wulfridge, as even your translated names are like."

Louvat—young wolf—a name given him by William when the king was still only a duke; a jest at the time, for Luc's father had referred to him as a wolf cub still wet behind the ears. The epithet had been humiliating at first, but he'd grown used to it over time. Now it was his only name, for he had no other left to him.

"Yes, sire." He nodded stiffly.

"You speak their language, and that alone is a great advantage. The Northumbrian earls have fled York for the moment and the Danes have gone to their ships in the Humber River, but there is a new revolt near Stafford. By the Holy Rood! I will see this country burned to ashes before I allow the Saxons to rise and take it back." He frowned down at the crushed pear core in his hand. "Cospatric and Edgar have fled to the Scots king for succor, but if Lord Balfour unites with these earls, their forces could give me much trouble. I want the old Saxon rebel alive and brought to me in chains. I need to make of him an example."

William's smile did not diminish the threat of his final comment, and Luc bowed. "I will leave at first light, beau sire."

"Your success will be well rewarded. Bring me Lord Balfour, and I will deed you his lands and title."

Luc stared at William. "Sire? Am I to understand you mean me to have the lands of Wulfridge?"

"Only if you can take them," the king said dryly.

"But Sir Simon—"

"Failed me." William's voice was inflexible. "And not for the first time. I do not countenance the inadequacy of my commanders for long. It would be a twofold lesson to deed these lands to you, I think. A reminder to Norman as well as Saxon that a worthy man makes his own fortune. Do you accept?"

There was no question of refusal. Never had Luc thought to gain so much in William's service, not after the debacle of his past.

Drawing in a deep breath that tasted of hope for the first time in four years, Luc met the king's gaze directly. "I will bring you the lord of Wulfridge in chains, sire, and put down the rebellion in your name."

"I expect it, Louvat."

But it was not until later, when Luc had readied his men and gathered supplies for the march north, that he acknowledged the opportunity beyond the king's promise. It was Robert de Brionne, his friend of many years, who broached the subject, coming to him in the gloom of the stables with grinning satisfaction.

"So you are soon to be lord. Will I needs bend the knee to you?" He gave a deep bow.

Luc cuffed him lightly on the shoulder. "Only if you are willing, my friend."

Robert's grin faded as he straightened and nodded solemnly. "I am most willing. You deserve this, Luc."

"I have not yet taken Wulfridge, Robert."

"You will. You have given the king loyal service in Normandy and now England, and it is time that he reward you for it."

Luc shrugged. "It is only of late that I am free of the past. To have been given lands before would give rise to too much speculation, and I did not want that taint upon me as well as—"

When he didn't finish, Robert nodded gently and said, "This will crush all rumors about you, Luc. It will give you back all that was taken from you. No longer will you be a landless knight, but an earl in your own right."

It was true. "When I return with the rebel baron in chains, we will celebrate my success, Robert."

"Ah, would that I were going with you."

Luc grinned. "The king would not spare you, and you know it well. Besides, too many lovely ladies would have empty beds were you to go with me."

"Ah, so true." Robert kissed the tips of his fingers in a sweeping flourish. "I could not bear to disappoint them, so I will stay here to hold the castle for the king, with deep regrets for not being able to witness your conquest of the foolish Saxon who has dared defy William."

"This lord of Wulfridge will rue the day he attempted to take one of William's holdings. It is his undoing."

Robert looked up at Luc's banner, a black wolf on a red field. "I pity him."

"SIR SIMON IS dead."

Luc stared at his captain. Sweat smeared Remy's face, seeping from beneath the nose guard of his conical helmet to drip from his chin. "We have lost," Remy added miserably, and gestured toward Wulfridge's stone walls with the tip of his sword. "We are undone."

"No, we are not." Luc's denial was so fierce, his burly captain took a stumbling backward step. "No clumsy Saxon warrior can vanquish trained Norman soldiers, Remy. We will withdraw our men from the fight but not the battle. Give the order to retreat to the wood and regroup. And, Captain Remy—do not speak to me of defeat again."

At Luc's crisp orders, Remy's face creased with relief. "At once, Sir Luc."

"I will join you shortly."

When Remy silently nodded and retreated, Luc reined his mount, Drago, around to study the forbidding stone walls that rose from the limestone cliff. Since the Norman retreat, the Saxons had melted away, no doubt to savor their triumph. Luc swore softly. Curse them, he would not yield, would not allow this old lord to make a fool of him. Sir Simon's failure was not his.

Wulfridge *was* a surprise, however. He had expected to find the familiar wooden fortress with stockade walls and clustered buildings, not this impenetrable stone edifice with gates tightly shut, iron overlaying wood making it resistant to fire arrows. Not once had these gates opened, yet men had appeared outside the walls to engage Sir Simon's troops and just as easily seemed to disappear into a thick mist that clung stubbornly to the ground.

Luc shook his head. There seemed to be no style to the structure, yet he could see carved niches among the irregular crown of jagged rocks that provided the defenders with arrow notches. Moss and lichen greened the stones, and ancient ornamentation pocked the walls with intricately carved Celtic knots. For a great distance around the castle, trees had been leveled to afford an easy view of an enemy's approach. This was a well-planned stronghold that reminded him of ancient Roman forts. On the way north they had passed long stretches of earth and stone wall, built centuries before and undulating across the land like the gray bones of a giant serpent: further evidence of the Roman occupation.

And here, near the boundary of the land of the Scots, Wulfridge perched like a predatory beast atop a promontory that dropped steeply into the churning froth of the North Sea. High, chalky cliffs afforded no hope of invasion from the sea side. Already, a half dozen of his men had bogged down in the marshy ground, with horses sunk hock-deep. They were fortunate that more were not hindered.

The Saxon lord had the element of entrenched forces on his side: a fortress that was nigh impregnable. Even if a stout enough tree could be felled and brought to use as a battering ram against the wooden doors, the ascent was too steep to wield it effectively. Luc set his jaw grimly. These cursed defenders must think themselves invincible, shut up in their stone fortress to rain down arrows on the foe at their leisure. Infuriatingly, it seemed true enough.

He rode the castle perimeter slowly, just out of arrow range. Grass studded the sandy ground in places, and small patches of thicket sprung up in waving barriers that unnerved Drago. When an undulating branch came too close to his line of vision, the stallion shook his head in a metallic jangle of bridle bits and trappings. The thick mane whipped across Luc's face as Drago's hooves sank into the sand with a rasping sound. Cursing, Luc urged the sweating destrier to more solid ground.

He reined in the horse on a scrabble of rock, and leaned to pat the animal's damp neck. "For shame, Drago, to let a few leaves frighten you. Or is it because they are Saxon leaves?"

The horse snorted. A seabird wheeled overhead with a keening cry, a dark sweep against the brittle blue of the sky. Luc straightened in his saddle, suddenly feeling as if he were being watched. Nothing moved along the castle walls above or below, save the beat of tall grasses against stone. A shadow flickered over the ground, but a glance upward revealed only the circling seabird. Faint now, its eerie cry spiraled toward the water, almost lost in the thunder of surf and whine of sea winds.

The same sea winds beat against Luc's face and spit sand into his eyes. As he brushed the sand from his lashes, he heard the cry again, mocking this time, and louder. His head tilted back so that his gaze scoured the very top of the steep stone walls.

There with feet braced apart and sword lifted high in a gesture of defiance, a youth had stepped out onto the jagged parapet. Sunlight glinted from his steel and buckler in blinding splinters that danced across Luc's face. Drago pranced sideways, snorting and tossing his head so that the whip of his jet mane caught Luc across the face again. He swore and held tightly to horse and control as the unmistakable sound of laughter drifted down from the walls.

"Norman dog," the boy challenged in the Saxon tongue, "did you come to fight or flee?"

Silent, Luc stared up at the bold youth. Scant armor covered the boy's chest and shoulders, and a short tunic ended at midthigh, in the style of ancient Roman attire. Laced boots rose almost to his knees, but the rest of his legs were unprotected. Luc smiled grimly. If all the warriors were clad thus, victory would be certain once he gained entry.

Nudging Drago forward, Luc ignored the youth. Wind and surf drowned out any further challenges, but the encounter had reinforced his determination to seize Wulfridge. Perhaps Sir Simon had lost, but he would not. Nor did he intend to be defeated as the Norman forces at York had been a month before.

Another such Norman defeat could weaken William's hold on England. And besides, it was not only lands and a title Luc sought to gain by beating back these rebellious Saxons: it was vindication.

He urged Drago forward. The land sloped sharply upward there, around a curve of sand and grassy hummock. The destrier clambered up the bank, froth dripping from his mouth and foaming his muscled neck despite the sharp bite of the sea wind. His huge hooves sank deep into the sand before finally gaining purchase on more solid rock, muscled flanks bunching beneath the weight of armed knight and trappings.

When they reached the top of the hill, Luc rewarded the sweating stallion with a murmured word and pat on the neck. As he bent forward, a humming that sounded like the path of a large honeybee sped close by his neck, and he heard the solid crack of an arrowhead glancing off rock. Drago skittered to one side, and Luc had to rein him in hard as he glanced up at the castle again. Archers had appeared on the high walls where the youth had stood, and the sky was suddenly dark with flying arrows.

Luc spurred Drago down from the rock in a scramble of hooves against limestone. With arrows hissing around him, he ducked feathered barbs to move just out of range again. Frustrated, he studied the fortress. There had to be a chink in Wulfridge's defenses. Long stretches of ancient wall formed fortified ramparts with no sign of door or window in the uneven stones. Scattered weeds, bushes, and clumps of grass laced the rock-cluttered footings. But there was no sign of weakness.

He halted Drago at the sharp edge of chalk cliff out of arrow range, cursing softly. The sun beat down, bright for early November. The volley of arrows had ceased. He squinted against the glare, thought about removing his helmet and decided not to. His mail chinked softly as he threw an arm across his forehead to shade his face. A glitter caught his eye when he did and he paused, one arm still across his face. Somewhere in the expanse of stone, sunlight glinted from metal. Perhaps it was not unusual, in a wall studded with twisted shapes and carved in ancient Celtic knots, but a memory teased him. Years ago, playing among the ruins of a similar fortress, he had seen just this kind of ornamentation in the primitive stonework. And in the whorls and grooves of rock he had accidentally discovered a very old lock—made of metal that winked in the sun from its hiding place. It had taken him a month to master the secret of unlocking it. But he *had* mastered the secret.

Now his narrowed eyes picked out the same kind of ornamentation in these rock walls. And tucked cleverly into the rocks, almost imperceptible unless you knew where to look, was a door. A small postern door built into a crevice and half-hidden by a waving clump of sea grass.

Luc grinned. He lowered his arms and looked out to sea. Now, there was a chance for success.

FIRST LIGHT WAS still only a faint glow on the horizon, limning the seam of sky and sea with a misty gleam as Luc took a small troop of seasoned soldiers to the door he had found the day before.

They moved quietly, with only the barest armor to cover them, so no chink of mail or weapon would betray their presence. It took longer than it should have for Luc to get his bearings in the slippery murk and finally he dismounted and made his way by running a hand along the sheer stone wall until he collided with a small obstruction: the lock that secured the small postern door.

With bare fingers, he slid a thin metal pick into the mechanism, feeling his way until he heard the familiar click of the tumblers. The iron was cool and slippery and every sound seemed to echo in the early morning stillness. Suddenly the lock separated with a grating sound, falling free of the hasp. He heaved open the door.

Inside, he and a dozen of his men swarmed over an open bailey. The small force of Saxon sentries was quickly outnumbered. Luc took in the rambling walls covered in ivy and the colonnades rising in delicate arches. For a moment he felt as if he'd stumbled into an ancient Roman villa, but then the alarm was given and that impression was quickly eclipsed by the very real Saxon resistance overrunning the walls with raised weapons and unbridled screams.

The fighting was fierce, for the Saxons defended their home against the invaders with desperate determination, but soon the well-armed and armored Normans beat them back. When the front gates were opened, victory was assured as the rest of Luc's men poured inside. The cacophony drowned out every thought but the driving need to vanquish the foe as Luc found himself locked in ferocious hand-to-hand combat.

The battle raged into a central courtyard marked by crumbling evidence of neglect. A ruined fountain lay dry save for the blood of those who fell into it, and tumbled stones made hazardous footing for the unwary. The pitched fighting was over quickly. Those Saxons that were not killed and were still able to flee abandoned the stone and tile halls with a rapidity Luc found as amusing as he did cowardly. It had been the same at Senlac

Hill, when trained Norman knights fell upon the Saxon rabble and sent them scattering into the dusk like frightened geese. Yet now was not the time to worry about those who had fled into the forests of the mainland. There were other, more important matters.

He beckoned Remy to him, and his captain arrived red-faced and breathing hard. Luc gestured to the wounded of both sides. "Tend our men first. Do your best by the others, for Saxons will be needed to till these lands. I will spare those that swear fealty to me and to William. But now I would find the old lord of Wulfridge."

Remy swept the cluttered courtyard with a dark gaze. "One of the prisoners says their leader has taken refuge in a stone chamber on the east. Shall we rout him?"

"I will see to that, while you tend the captives and wounded." Luc summoned several men, and together they moved toward the stone chamber Remy indicated. It was set in a thick grove of midsize trees, an ordinary storehouse from the appearance of it, with only one door. No doubt, the lord of Wulfridge took refuge there rather than relinquish his fief to the conqueror. Luc's mouth curled into a smile of contempt. Victory tasted sweet. Wulfridge was his.

"Balfour de Wulfridge," he shouted into the sudden quiet left by the end of the battle, "come out and yield your arms. The day is lost to you, but not your life. If you will lay down your weapons, you may accompany me to the king to present your defense."

The English words faded into silence, but there was no answer from the storehouse. A leaf fell, twisting in an unsettled current of air, drifting to the hard-packed dirt beside a gnarled tree root. Luc waited, then repeated his demand. Silence.

Losing patience, Luc moved toward the door. Suddenly a Saxon warrior appeared in the darkened opening, brandishing a Roman short sword in one hand and a round shield in the other. Luc stopped in midstride. It was the tall youth from the walls who had taunted him the day before.

The boy's Roman sword whistled through the air, as menacing and tempting as his cold Saxon taunt: "Come, Norman, test my skill if you dare."

"I do not fight children," Luc growled back in English. "Not even boasting boys with swords bigger than they. Move aside, and call out Lord Balfour."

"Ah, but I am here in Balfour's place, Norman." The sword swung through the air, and the boy leaped agilely atop a fallen tree to balance on the broad trunk. "He is my father—will I not do?"

Luc eyed the youth. Garbed in ancient armor of brass chest plates, an apron of brass-studded leather, and leather boots laced to the knee, he managed to look like a Roman gladiator instead of a Saxon warrior.

Luc's patience waned. "Do not play the fool. Take me to your father. The battle is done, as you must know, and you are lost."

"Nay, Norman, it is not lost until I yield." Moving more swiftly than Luc anticipated, the youth leaped forward. The tip of the Roman sword caught Luc across the bicep in a swinging slash that could have cost him his sword arm if he had not reacted with his warrior's instinct.

Luc parried the blow and thrust at his foe, grunting in surprise at the ferocity of the answering attack. He should have expected it, should have sensed the desperation behind the bravado. But he did not. To Luc's astonished chagrin, the youth slid deftly beneath his guard and thrust the Roman sword's tip against his throat. Luc stilled instantly.

The ice-blue eyes piercing him across the blade's length held no mercy, only grim determination mixed with exultation. "Yield, Norman."

"And if I do not?"

"You will die."

The blade pressed more firmly, obstructing Luc's air passage. Little fool—surely this witless Saxon must know how swiftly he would die should he be reckless enough to slay Luc.

"Call off your dogs, Norman," the youth said coolly when two knights started toward them with drawn weapons. "Or suffer the consequences."

Luc put up a warning hand, and the knights stopped a short distance away.

"Zut alors!"

"Quel con, ce mec!"

The curses of Luc's Norman knights were harsh, but none dared move for fear of earning their leader his death. While they may not have understood the language Luc and the Saxon youth spoke, they clearly grasped the danger. Not even the strongest mail could deflect the tip of a hefty sword driven forcefully into his throat. For the moment, Luc's mail coif cushioned the prodding intent. Yet if he so much as lifted his sword, no doubt the Saxon would skewer him like a capon. Luc felt a fool and worse for not giving this boy the same wary regard he would have given a seasoned soldier. His inattention might yet cost him his life. His gaze dropped to the short length of Roman sword.

Soft, mocking laughter curled the air between them, and the sword blade vibrated ever so slightly as the Saxon gripped the hilt with both hands to steady it. Luc's muscles tensed.

"Would you earn your death so swiftly, young Saxon? For that is what 'twill be if you kill me."

"My life is well worth the loss of a Norman knight, I think."

"I doubt your father would agree." For a moment he thought his verbal dart had found its mark as the Saxon's light eyes clouded, then with a soft oath, the blade dug more deeply into Luc's mail. A warm trickle of blood bathed his throat beneath the chain.

"My father and I have not always agreed, Norman. And so

it has come to this—I have you at the point of my sword. Would I purchase my own life with a cowardly surrender?"

The voice lowered, painfully hoarse, and now Luc saw the fatigue in the face beneath the helmet, the faint bluish circles under the eyes, and the grim twist of a curiously vulnerable mouth. Ah, this lad was too young to go to war, though no doubt not much younger than Luc had been when he had first gone into battle.

And it was that knowledge that gave Luc the edge, his experience and years of training that had kept him still now allowed him to gauge his opponent. His opening came swiftly, more swiftly than he hoped, as the Saxon continued to stare at him. The sword shifted slightly as bare, slender hands tightened on the hefty hilt. Holding up even the short sword would be wearying to an untried youth.

Luc gave a sudden backward twist of his body, evading a surprised thrust as he swept his own blade upward in a lightning-quick move, catching the boy's sword hilt with the tip of his blade. Driving forward, he turned his wrist, snagging the Saxon's weapon and sending it sailing through the air. The youth's sword clattered to the ground several feet away, resting against a knobby oak root curled among the fallen leaves.

Now came the moment of truth, and Luc intended to send this young pup running for his father. Pressing his sword tip against the boy's armored chest, he snapped an order to his men to search the stone chamber. To his captive he said, "Yield or die, Saxon."

"May you suffer the pox, Norman swine."

The Saxon words came out between gasps for air, and beneath the smooth metal helmet, hot blue eyes narrowed with purpose. A gray light glinted in the boy's hand and gave Luc an instant's warning. Swiftly he twisted to one side, and the dagger the youth had thrown dug deep into the trunk of the oak behind him, vibrating with the force of its flight.

Furious now, Luc moved with swift resolution that caught

the boy off guard. Striking him across the chest, Luc pressed him to the ground with his greater weight, tempted to slit the whelp's throat for the trouble he had caused. Only his obvious youth saved him. Did these rebels never admit defeat? Foolish, to resist when the outcome was obvious, yet they always did.

Straddling the boy, Luc pinned him to the ground with his knees, and using the tip of his dagger, slit the leather strap that held the boy's helmet fast. He pulled it away roughly—but scowled when a cloud of wheat-gold hair tumbled free. A plague upon these Saxons who wore their hair long as a woman's, refusing to cut it even at William's order.

"Mayhap I should trim this hair as well as your throat, Saxon whelp," he muttered as he tossed the helmet aside. "You can wear the Norman mode this season."

"Kill me and be done with witless prattle!" Blue eyes glared at him, and the slender body beneath Luc's knees trembled violently.

"Oh, no," Luc snarled when the boy twisted his head to one side, and he reached out to tangle a fist in the long mane, jerking hard. "You will face the fate you have brought upon you this day."

"May the demons take you back where you belong."

Buckling beneath him, the youth struggled to dislodge him. Luc laughed contemptuously. "Nay, 'tis not likely that a puny creature such as yourself can unseat me. You're as scrawny as a starved cockerel, and not near as strong. If not for your armor, you'd be no bigger than a suckling."

Luc surged to his feet and pulled the defeated youth up with him, one hand still wrapped in the thick mass of hair. Frowning, his eyes narrowed at the slight weight of him. He turned the boy to study his comely face, the lush mouth and long-lashed eyes that refused to meet his. . . . An awful suspicion ignited, and he grasped the softly rounded chin in his other fist, holding hard.

A flush stained the high cheekbones as Luc tilted his captive's face toward the gray light that sifted through the heavy oak limbs shading the courtyard. Deliberately, Luc shifted his hand lower, over throat and shoulder, the backs of his fingers skimming over the round brass plates of ancient chest armor to the webbing between. Wide eyes held his in a steady gaze, not blinking even when Luc slid his hand beneath the armor to touch the linen sherte beneath. His exploring hand found what he suspected, and he swore softly.

Luc stared at his adversary, his fury fading into amazement. It was not possible . . . but the evidence filled his palm, soft and tempting, and unmistakably rounded. He slowly drew his hand from beneath the armor, his voice rough:

"You are no stripling lad."

The girl's eyebrow arched in feigned surprise, and her full mouth curled into a scornful smile. "Your intellect is superior to your prowess on the field of battle, Sir Knight. Bested by a mere maid—how will your reputation fare in William's court now?"

"Be 'ware of whose temper you prod—and keep in mind that 'tis my dagger at your throat this time. Your battle is lost."

"I could not forget. Not with my father's men dead all around me." Bitterness tinged her husky voice as her gaze skimmed the scene around them, and her blue eyes darkened with pain. For the first time, he noticed that blood dripped from a shallow cut on her forehead.

Luc sheathed his dagger and picked up his sword, holding it out with lowered tip to indicate his inclination to mercy. "You are my hostage. Take me to your lord, so that I may accept his surrender."

Soft laughter met his demand. "That is impossible."

"For your sake, it had best not be." Luc's words were clipped. "I deal harshly with those who refuse my commands."

"You and William are cut from the same cloth, then."

"Do not whine to me of ill treatment. Complain instead to your father, who took William's oath only to break it. 'Twould have been better had he not taken it at all than to dishonor his sworn word. At least then he could have kept the king's respect."

"The bastard duke of Normandy deserves no respect. Nay, and Lord Balfour never broke a sworn bond in his life, so do not speak ill of him now."

Impatient, Luc shook his head. "You bandy words, when 'tis Balfour who should offer his own defense. I would meet the man responsible for the deaths of good men, and I would meet him now. Take me to Lord Balfour immediately, or it will go harshly with you and all in your hall."

After a moment of taut silence, the girl shrugged her shoulders. A gust of wind teased the golden hair that rippled down her back and over her arms. A faint smile played on her lips. If not for her obvious female attributes he might still think her a young lad, for the timbre of her voice was low and rich. "Since you insist, brave knight, I will take you to him."

She turned, head held high, to indicate the narrow path leading away from the vault. She possessed the confident grace of a young doe, a wild creature standing in the midst of the tangled trees and stones. When Luc did not move immediately, she glanced back over her shoulder at him. Her voice purred, sultry and provocative.

"Poor Norman knight—do you fear treachery? If I thought 'twould serve me, I would lead you into a trap, but I know you are right and the battle is lost."

"It is not fear of treachery that delays me, but kindness that bids me warn you not to play me false, or you will soon regret it."

Her response was a throaty laugh and eloquent shrug of one shoulder as she said, " 'Tis traitors who fear treachery most, I think."

"My lord," Remy spoke up quietly, "do not go alone. I do not trust her."

"Nor I, Remy. Search the grounds, then join me. I do not

think there are enough Saxons left to spring a trap, but neither do I put faith in them blindly."

Luc followed the maid down a narrow, weed-choked path to a small stone cairn tucked beneath a bower of young trees. There she swung around to face him with an unreadable expression on her lovely features. He came to an abrupt halt, glancing about the deserted grove. Fallen leaves cluttered the ground and rustled dryly beneath their feet, and the musty smell of death permeated the air around them.

"What is this, *demoiselle*? A ruse to delay me while your father escapes?"

Her soft laugh sounded more bitter than amused. "Nay, he has already escaped invading Normans. But you are welcome to follow him. Indeed, I pray that you do." When he scowled and took a step toward her, she swept out an arm to indicate the pile of stones. "Lord Balfour awaits your company, Sir Knight."

Luc stared at her mocking face, the slight smile twisting her lips, and suddenly he understood.

"How long has the lord been dead?"

"Three moons have waxed and waned since Balfour joined his fathers."

"Then you will tell me who is lord in his place. I want the man responsible for the death of Sir Simon, and this rebellion against William."

Draping her slender body against the stone cairn, the girl's gaze did not leave his face. "That person is before you, Norman. Do your worst."

Chapter Two

It was over. All her plans, her hopes—gone. If she had not stopped to help Rudd—but that was irrelevant. She could not have left a frightened, injured boy to face the Normans alone—as she was doing now.

Despite her show of defiance, Ceara was more terrified than she had ever been in her life. Yet she would not give this tall, brutal knight the satisfaction of knowing he made her feel so vulnerable. It was all she could do to keep her voice calm, her chin proudly lifted, and her gaze steady under his ruthless glare.

"Tell me," the Norman knight repeated, his dark eyes intense, "who inherited Wulfridge?"

He had asked the question of her twice already, apparently unable to believe that she—a mere female—would be able to lead the men who had defeated Norman knights. She lifted a brow. "Why do you care, Norman? Wulfridge is yours now by right of conquest."

"Aye, and I would know who else would rise up to try and take it from me," he growled.

"Are you so fearful, then? You, a brave Norman?"

Angry sparks diffused the darkness in eyes she had thought

pure black. Her barb had found its mark. Ah, so he was not as invulnerable as he seemed. Yet this knight wore only a mail coif and leather tunic as armor, as if contemptuous of the Saxon warriors he'd fought so savagely. She had seen him earlier in the courtyard, laying about him with wicked slashes that took men down in a wide swath. It was then she recognized the man she had taunted from the walls, the leader of this Norman rabble.

Standing before him now, she fought the wave of despair that threatened to undo her. Accustomed to tall men, she was yet overpowered by the height of this knight. He was taller than most, and broader of shoulder, yet it was not his height that had defeated her. Beneath his leather tunic was lean, powerful muscle and skillful efficiency that had rendered her appallingly inadequate. All her practice and skill had not won the day for her, though she had come closer than she ever dreamed. It was a small victory—but one to savor: the memory of how she had briefly held a Norman knight at the point of her sword. If not for the dreadful weakness in her exhausted limbs, perhaps she would have yet triumphed. . . . But it was done, and she must answer to this dread foe with her life and liberty, and that of her people.

A curious crumbling at the back of her knees threatened to send her sprawling, but she steeled herself with stubborn determination. She would not quail before these Normans, would not shame her lineage by showing weakness to the enemy.

They stood beneath the trees around her father's grave, and fall leaves fluttered from almost bare branches with a rustling sound like old bones, covering the ground at their feet. Fitting, that the death of the season marked the death of Wulfridge.

Looking away from him, Ceara cleared her throat and focused on the low stone wall that the Romans had built so long ago. A cold gust of wind blew against her face and bare arms, smelling of sea tang and faraway places she would never see.

"The legacy is mine, Norman."

"Impossible. No woman alone inherits land and title."

Her gaze swerved back to him. "No? When my father died of mortal wounds inflicted by Normans at Senlac Hill, the title and lands came to me. It is our way. In days of old, women fought alongside men."

"If your father died of wounds inflicted at Hastings, he took a long time about it, little Saxon."

The mocking reply continued to ignore her claim, and her chin lifted. "Aye, so he did. Lord Balfour suffered greatly at Norman hands."

"And you have sworn to avenge him."

"Perhaps." She couldn't help a bitter smile. "Do you think that is why I raised an army? Why I do not tolerate Norman swine rooting on my lands? Ah, you are a petty man, for all that you are cunning, Norman."

"Am I." It was more statement than query, and the thin curve of his mouth was without humor. He shifted, and his dark eyes were so piercing she looked away when he said, "But I can recognize vengeance, even cloaked in the guise of fidelity."

Ceara stiffened with irritation. How did this Norman cur speak the Saxon tongue so well? Most Normans spoke only French, disdaining as too barbaric the native tongue of the country they had conquered. Managing a calm she did not feel, she met his gaze steadily. " 'Tis indeed loyalty that prods me. Perhaps to Wulfridge more than my country, but for reasons a barbaric Norman would never understand."

"Would I not?" He straightened from his lazy stance and turned to beckon to the men who had joined them in the clearing. Switching back to Norman French, he bade the men, "Search thoroughly for the Saxon warlord, as the old lord is dead. They must be hiding their new leader."

Ceara looked down to hide the anger in her eyes. Did he think her so foolish that she would not bother to learn the language of the enemy? From beneath her long lashes, she surveyed this knight standing with his feet braced wide apart and leaning with casual confidence on the hilt of his long sword. He looked much too sure of himself—as if she had not bested him in front of his men.

"Nay," she said loudly in English, "you would not understand loyalty to a legacy. Your understanding seems limited to the heritage of the sword, and not even that very skillfully. I know of no *Saxon* warrior who has e'er had my blade at his throat so quickly."

For an instant, she thought she had gone too far. The Norman turned toward her, and in his grim visage she saw a ruthless intent that made her stumble back a step against the stones of Balfour's cairn. Jagged edges of rock dug into her armored back and scraped against her bare thighs. The knight closed the space between them, so near now that his breath stirred a loose tendril of her hair where it lay against her cheek. His voice was soft:

"Do you bide your tongue, *demoiselle*. There are among my men those who understand your language, and might take it amiss should they overhear your boast."

"Do you deny it?" She leaned back against the cairn and crossed her arms over her chest to hide her angry trembling. She felt the Norman's gaze rove over her, dark and speculative behind the nose guard of his metal helmet.

Something like amusement flickered for a moment on his face, and he shook his head slowly. "Nay, I do not deny that you bested me. But look you who has the advantage now. I will not be reminded again of your brief good fortune in catching me off guard."

"I thought it was more skill than luck that—" she halted. The humor in his eyes had vanished, and she was unwilling to press him. If fortune was with her there would be another time.

One of the Norman soldiers approached them then, a burly man with a young face and old eyes. His manner was respectful but not submissive, and he waited until he had his leader's attention before he spoke.

"We searched the storehouse and secured the grounds, Sir Luc."

"Ah, Captain Remy, tell me what you found."

The captain hesitated, his eyes flicking to Ceara before returning to the knight. "We found a small boy hiding under a pile of hides in the storehouse. After some coaxing, he told us that the old lord's daughter led the uprising, sir—my lord. Her name is Lady Ceara."

She almost laughed at his mangled pronunciation of her name, the Frankish lisp obliterating the *r* instead of emphasizing it. Sir Luc was not so ignorant, and flashed her a thoughtful glance as he repeated her name more properly.

"*Keera* is it? And the lady is alleged to have led men in battle? I do not think so. It is either a ruse to allow the true leader to escape or a plan to confuse us, Remy. See if you can get the truth from these stubborn Saxons."

Remy grinned, his craggy features relaxing. "I will discover the truth. It does not take much to frighten Saxons, sir—my lord."

"Do not exert yourself over proper titles, Remy. It will be as difficult for me to grow accustomed to the new rank as it will be for you. And until William confirms it, I am not yet the new lord of Wulfridge."

"The king keeps his word, and you have kept yours by taking the fortress and subduing the rebels. The documents are only a formality."

Ceara stood stiffly. She dared not betray her understanding of their tongue, but it was growing increasingly difficult not to voice her outrage. Poor Rudd. She had hoped they would not find him, but the Normans had been thorough. He was only twelve—easily frightened, as this captain had so contemptuously remarked. Surely they would not harm him, but they spoke so casually of "subduing the rebels." The men they had subdued had names, families, lives of their own. Did that matter to them?

Nay, it did not, she answered her own question bitterly. Not to conquering warriors who thought only of victory, not what these lands meant to those who loved them. Most of England lay raped and charred beneath the Norman boot, a wasteland where fertile moors and forests had once lain. Little had been spared, and entire villages had died of starvation that first winter after the Norman invasion. Even monasteries had been razed, priests murdered. Wulfridge now risked the same fate, as she had known from the start. It was the gamble she had taken for freedom from the Norman yoke.

All for naught.

"Do you walk willingly with me, or would you have your people see you dragged?" Sir Luc was asking, and Ceara recovered from her rumination with a startled jerk.

"I am a Celtic princess. I do not need to be dragged to my death like a bullock at Samhain, Norman."

His lips curled slightly. "No one spoke of death. Yet."

Despite her growing fear, she kept her voice cool and steady: "I am already acquainted with Norman justice. Do you visit it upon small boys as harshly as you do women?"

"If it is deserved." His gaze was keen. "If you speak of the boy you were hiding in the storehouse, he is safe. And will be as long as he obeys. It is a lesson you might consider, *demoiselle*, to keep you safe from harm."

"Do not think to deceive me with honeyed words, for I know your intent."

"I think you do not," was the soft reply, and he lifted his sword to indicate the direction of the hall. "Saxon royalty should precede even a Norman knight, so you may walk ahead of me, princess."

A hot flush warmed her cheeks. He was mocking her, of course. She suppressed the impulse to defy him, even in this, and held her head high as she walked past him. She half expected to feel the sharp nudge of a sword in her back.

Her entire body ached, bruised and bloodied, drained from the strenuous exertions of the day's battle, and she walked slowly. *I cannot display weakness,* she thought raggedly, *not in front of Normans, and certainly not in front of my own people. Wulfric, you should be here now . . . you would know what to do, how to keep these Normans from destroying us. . . .*

She stumbled over a broken stone and caught herself, using the distraction to wipe an angry tear from her eye. Wulfric would never give advice again, would never come to her with laughter in his eyes, teasing her and enraging her at times, but always there. He was gone forever. They were all gone. If only her father had listened to her before it was too late. But he had not. He kept his sworn oath to the end, and it had destroyed them all.

But she had made a vow of her own. . . .

THE HALL WAS littered with dead bodies and Norman soldiers. Ceara steeled herself. Familiar faces glazed with the mask of death must be ignored, for it would give her enemies another weapon to use against her.

Yet it was more difficult than she anticipated. Even the unarmed and defenseless had been killed. An elderly servant sprawled just inside the door, his sightless eyes staring up at the high ceiling and blackened beams of the hall. She looked away.

Behind her, Sir Luc prodded her forward with the flat of his sword. "Advance to the dais, *demoiselle*. I would have you near me."

Ceara jerked forward. The reply she meant to be light and mocking came out in a choked snarl: "I did not think you would grow enamored of me so quickly, Norman."

"You nurture false hopes, *demoiselle*."

" 'Tis you who nurtures false hopes if you think to hold what you have slain so many to take! Justice will win out, and you will reap the fruits of murder that you have sown, vile Norman, I swear it!"

His hand closed on her bare arm, fingers digging deep to cut off her accusations.

"Do not be misled by my gentle nature. I will not long suffer your barbed words." The cold menace in his voice chilled Ceara to the bone, but somehow it allowed her to regain her composure.

She suffered Luc to push her to the dais where Lord Balfour had once held sway. His heavy hand pressed her down to the tiled lip of the platform, but she resisted just enough to signal her continued rebellion before she sank to the floor. Only then did she realize how utterly bone-weary she was, how her limbs shook with fatigue. The days had been long, the nights short and sleepless.

Ceara watched numbly as Norman soldiers moved the dead bodies from the hall, detaching herself from the painful sight and the knowledge that Wulfridge was no longer hers to command.

Shattered wooden benches and tables were removed, torn wall hangings pulled down, the floor swept clean of debris. Ceara did not speak, made no protest even when her armor was demanded of her, but yielded it up silently. Clad only in a short tunic, she sat on the cold floor and watched as the Normans stripped everything. The woven Saxon *wahrift* that decorated the walls were removed with little regard for their brightly colored beauty, leaving the stone beneath barren and cold.

One soldier asked Sir Luc about clean rushes as none could be found. Gesturing at the floor, the Norman complained in nasal French, "These barbaric Saxons do not even know how to cover a floor decently, my lord."

Ceara bristled in silent disgust. Rushes. In *her* hall, covering the exquisite beauty of the ancient tile floors! Blind ass, he was too intent upon destruction to see the masterpieces that had endured through the ages. It confirmed her belief that all Normans were barbaric and crude.

But Luc surprised her. "No, Alain, do not cover these floors. It would be a pity to hide such craftsmanship and beauty with straw."

"Not use rushes?" Alain frowned slightly, then glanced up at Ceara with a swift scrutiny that made her uneasy. He had half-lidded hazel eyes and a face that many may have called handsome, yet made her think of a coiled serpent. But his smile was bland, his manner cordial as he inclined his head deferentially. "As you wish, Sir Luc—my lord. What then shall we use to cover the floors?"

"Our feet." Luc waved a hand in impatient dismissal, and observed tartly that he should not be bothered with petty housekeeping details. "Inform Captain Remy that he is to oversee the distribution of duties, since it was his failure to control his men that caused the deaths of unarmed servants."

"At once, my lord." Alain backed away, but not so quickly that Ceara missed the gleam of triumph in his eyes. Could there be strife among these Normans?

She wanted to smile in satisfaction, but dared not—not yet, when keeping her understanding from the Normans might still win her freedom. So she kept her head down, her attention on her folded hands, clenched together so tightly that her knuckles grew white with strain as her home was transformed into a Norman abode.

When Ceara could bear to look up at the hall again—completely changed now, with furniture moved and familiar hangings gone—she recognized Hardred, one of her father's thralls, being pressed into service by the Normans. While she had never liked him, she could not help a feeling of pity that he was now a slave to Norman whims. Just as she was. . . .

She shuddered and Luc leaned forward, his mouth close to her ear as he murmured in English that soon a fire would be built to warm them. His breath was heated against her cheek, his presence much too near, too immediate, so that she found it difficult to reply, or even to breathe. Did he think a few kind words would replace the deeds of the day? Impossible. And she refused to acknowledge his pretense of courtesy.

After a moment of stubborn silence, he laughed softly. "Ah,

little Saxon," he said in French, "you are as fierce as the men of your land, but you are now brought to hand, as a tamed gyrfalcon. Your wings have been clipped, but you will not admit to defeat . . . perhaps it will not be so boring a journey as I had thought, delivering a rebel to William in chains. And perhaps you may yet find that being conquered is not all that you fear."

Chains? Ceara tensed, that word standing apart from the others, ringing ominously in her brain. She was to be *chained.* Hatred sparked anew. Did they think to humiliate her? She would not have it. She would fight him, escape or die rather than be presented to the Norman king weighed down in chains and shame.

Was it not shame enough to be forced to sit at the feet of the enemy in her own hall? The hall where she had played as a child under her parents' loving eyes? And well this man must know it, for he kept her here as a prize to display before her own people as well as his. She was branded now, tarred with the brush of defeat.

And I will escape, she vowed silently, her fingers curling into such tight fists that her hands began to ache. Yes, she would flee into the forest beyond Wulfridge if given the slightest chance, retrieve her beloved wolf and leave this land behind. Wulfridge was no longer hers, would soon be swallowed up by the Norman horde and become unfamiliar. Ah, everything she had done was wrong, save for sending Sheba away to safety. But how safe would the animal remain with Normans prowling fen and wood? They slaughtered everything, these savage invaders, leaving nothing alive for the use of Saxon inhabitants. Not even elderly servants were spared, and certainly not those who defied them with sword and hatred. If she did not escape, she would die as well.

It seemed an eternity before Luc leaned back and away from her, though he kept a hand on her shoulder, his fingers toying with her loose hair. Did he never tire? He had not yet sat down, but stood behind her like an avenging angel while his men kept Saxon prisoners at work clearing the hall.

Ceara did not betray the turmoil inside her by word or gesture, yet it gnawed at her while she sat silently at the Norman's feet. Time lagged endlessly. Nor did she betray her distress when Saxon captives were brought before Sir Luc weighed down in heavy chains. The men, bloodied and yet hostile, were offered a choice between swearing fealty to him and to William, or death.

"Know you," Luc warned, "that if you swear to me, you will keep your oath or suffer the consequences. I do not tolerate treachery, and would respect a man more for the unwelcome truth than a false oath."

The silence that fell over the hall was oppressive, rife with foreboding. Ceara held her breath, mutely pleading with each man not to yield to the Norman foe.

But she was disappointed, as each man bent the knee to Sir Luc and swore fealty to him and to William, swearing to ply arms only for the Norman rulers. Not one abstained, not even Kerwin, the grizzled captain who had been her father's finest commander.

"You have made wise decisions this day," Luc said to the grim-faced Saxons. "I have need of good men to serve me, and will see you rewarded justly for loyal service. Go now and have your chains removed and your heads shorn to the Norman mode, so that all will know of your free choice."

Ceara closed her eyes, sick at heart. This, then, was the end.

The sickness stayed with her long after the men were led away. They would return to homes and families, while she was to face her fate alone. But had she not known this from the first? Yea, she had known when she took up the reins of command and convinced Balfour's men to follow his daughter that she risked more than they did if she failed.

At last Luc took his seat, and a table was dragged to the dais and laid with platters of meat, bread, and cheese, as well as flagons of ale. She did not touch the trencher that was placed before her, but stared with such pointed disdain at Luc when he bade her eat that he did not persist.

"Rebellious Saxon. Starve yourself if it pleases you, then."

A small smile touched the corners of his mouth, and she was struck by how much younger he seemed then. Without his helmet and coif, she could see that his dark hair was longer than most Normans', with tousled locks covering his ears and almost brushing against his broad shoulders. Strong black brows soared over his inky eyes like hawk wings, and a rough stubble of beard shadow darkened his cheeks and jaw. Despite a thin scar at the corner of one brow, and another along the square line of his jaw, he was a well-favored man. Yet he was still Norman—still the enemy—and thus detestable to her eyes.

Her disdain did not have the unsettling effect on him that she would have liked. Instead he seemed to find amusement in her aloof silence, and took advantage of any opportunity to goad her with comments made to Captain Remy in English, so she would be certain to comprehend. But she understood the game, and controlled her temper with an immense effort.

Torches burned low, pungent sparks flickering to the tile floor as the Normans ate and drank, celebrating their victory over the Saxons now being forced to serve them. Most of those pressed into service were young and untrained, and looked terrified as they stumbled clumsily about in a desperate attempt to satisfy the victors. Acrid smoke from green wood filled the hall in drifting layers and stung the back of her throat. The smell of burnt meat mingled with the stench of unwashed bodies and spilled ale. What tables were not shattered had been set up along the length of the hall, and wooden benches flanked the long oaken slabs. The enemy filled Wulfridge's hall with laughter and boasts and the retelling of their victory until Ceara wanted to cover her ears with her hands. Stark pride was the only tether that kept her bound to the Norman at her side. She would not give him the satisfaction of admitting her longing to flee, so sat stiffly with her head held high.

But exhaustion left her almost reeling. She longed for her bed, yet dreaded the coming night. Already, she had seen the few women of the household disappear, and could only imagine their fates at the hands of these rough men. No less would be her fate, she was certain. Luc had kept a hand on her all evening, playing with her hair and occasionally stroking her cheek with the backs of his fingers, as if she already belonged to him. Unnerving in itself, but coupled with the knowledge of what was surely to come, it was almost enough to undo her.

The moment came far too soon. He rose to his feet, a careless hand still on her shoulder. His fingers pressed into her flesh. "Come, *demoiselle*. I would seek rest this eve, for the morrow comes early. You may show me to a bed."

Stubbornness and fear kept her seated, and tension made her tongue sharp. " 'Tis customary for dogs to sleep at the door, Norman. Seek your rest there."

"Do you intend to join me?" His tone was mild, but his fingers dug into her shoulder painfully. "You may once have been the lady here, but Wulfridge is no longer yours to command. Lest you wish to sleep on stone yourself, you will show me to a soft bed instead of a cold portal."

She managed a shrug that did not dislodge his grip. "Wulfridge has long been mine to command, and I prefer my own chamber."

"Foolish little pagan. If you test me, it will be to your discomfort, for my patience is near gone and I will deal with you harshly. Now rise. I do not intend to quarrel with you in front of the entire hall. I have more pleasant pursuits in mind for this eve."

Ceara stiffened. The last was spoken loudly enough for her people to hear, his clear English carrying the length of the hall. She glanced up. Dismay flickered on familiar Saxon faces, while the Normans looked smug at her plight. Captain Remy had the temerity to laugh, a grin creasing his face, and he lifted his cup in a salute to his lord.

Reckless fury surged through her, and she forced a serene smile as she obediently rose in a graceful movement. Even as she stood, at last, on a level surface with Luc, he was much taller than she. Yet she would not be intimidated. Not for his satisfaction, nor the entertainment of his men.

She pushed back a loose strand of her hair as she met Luc's dark eyes with a steady gaze, then deliberately lifted her voice so that all still remaining in the hall could hear: "Yea, you may very well have taken the hall, Norman, but you have not conquered all. As to *pleasant pursuits*, my lineage is pure and I will not willingly suffer the touch of a Norman bastard."

It was a taunt, such as those he had been pricking her with all evening, but she saw at once this barb was swift and true. Captain Remy slammed down his cup and growled an oath, and there was an uneasy stirring among the Normans before a heavy silence fell.

In the sudden quiet, the sputtering of torches sounded overloud to her ears, as did the wild thud of her heart pounding in her chest. Hot flame leaped in Luc's eyes; his brows lowered like swooping hawks, and his fury was visible in the strained white lines on each side of his mouth.

Luc's hands flashed out to grab her upper arms and lift her, dangling her above the floor. It was not an easy task, for she was no small woman, and no man had been able to thus handle her since she was but a green girl. Ceara realized with increasing alarm that she had gone too far, but it was too late to retract her words even if pride would allow it.

"Saxon bitch," he snarled softly, "be 'ware of whose temper you prod with reckless words, for I am not known for tenderness to women."

The warning was evident in the fierce grip of his hands and the baleful gleam in his eyes. It was so quiet around them that she could hear the scrape of booted feet shifting uncomfortably on the tile floor, and the faint clink of chain mail as Norman knights moved to get a better view.

Bitterly, she recognized that to further flaunt her defiance would only earn her more humiliation than she had yet suffered. So she nodded curtly, a short jerk of her chin to acknowledge his warning. His grip did not loosen. A muscle twitched in his jaw, and his dark eyes were narrowed and smoky with rage.

Ceara managed not to whimper when he finally released her even as she fell with a jarring thud to the floor, nor did she try to evade him when he curled his fingers around her left wrist in a painfully tight grip and dragged her abruptly from the dais. She had a blurred vision of gaping faces as she was drawn past Norman and Saxon observers. One face stood out, the pale, freckled features of young Rudd watching in horror as his lady was pulled past him. She tried to reassure the boy with her eyes, but was dragged by so quickly she barely had time to fling him a glance.

She stumbled and barely saved herself from going to one knee, but Luc paid her no heed, striding relentlessly on. Her feet skimmed over the hard tile floor in a staggering run at his heels, and she felt foolish and frightened at the same time. He drew her past the armed guards at the hall doors and into the long corridor.

It was empty here, the silence stifling. Their footsteps echoed eerily on the stone. Holy Mary and all the saints—did he mean to kill her for the insult? She must remain calm, must keep her wits about her or she was doomed.

Yet all her wits vanished when he swung open the door to an empty chamber and flung her inside in a smooth swing of one arm, releasing her at the last moment so that she flew like a bound bird toward the rope bed against one wall. She landed half on the edge of the bed, half on the floor, rocking back to stare up at him through the loose net of her hair. He loomed over her, dark and menacing—a threat and a promise, terrifying in his rage.

Ceara swallowed the impulse to cry out for mercy. There

would be no mercy from this Norman, 'twas plain. He glared down at her, tucking his thumbs into the wide leather belt around his waist, his brows crowding pitiless black eyes.

Though Luc did not raise his voice, anger vibrated in his words with grim intensity: "Now you will learn who is master of this hall."

Chapter Three

CEARA STARED UP at him with wide eyes shadowed by hatred and fear. Her chest heaved with the quick, soft breaths of a hunted fox as she clung to the bed in a half crouch. A brass lamp filled the room with foul-smelling light, and clouded the air with oppressive gloom.

Luc struggled for control, but fury pricked him hard. All evening he had watched her, his growing admiration for her refusal to yield in the face of overpowering odds mixing with irritation that she refused to recognize his hard-won right to be lord. If not for her insult, he may yet have inclined himself to leniency.

Norman bastard.

So he was, and it cut deep that even this pagan Saxon could see it. It was as if there were a visible mark on him, some sign that all could see that branded him as a bastard son, worthless save as battle fodder. Even his father had said it, though it had been years ago. So long now it would have been forgotten by most, but not by the son at whom it had been directed. No, those spiteful words had cut him deeply, a mortal wound he'd once thought. Yet he lived. How powerful words could be, uttered with contempt, or joy, or yearning—more powerful even than action. They had a greater power to heal than the most skilled medicines. And a greater power to hurt than a sword.

Yet William's promise had given him what nothing else had—what none would take from him, not even his father's contempt. Or perfidy.

Traitor . . .

It was that word that had brought down his father, and would bring down many more foolish enough to defy William. Like this rebellious Saxon staring up at him so mutinously, her hatred a palpable thing between them.

He drew in a deep breath and held out his hand. "Rise, *demoiselle*."

When she gave a contemptuous shake of her head that sent a clutter of pale hair into her eyes and cascading around her shoulders, his tight hold on control wavered.

"Rise," he repeated in a soft snarl. She did not move, but remained in her half crouch like a feral beast, a she-cat with wary eyes, poised for flight—or attack. How long did she think she could defy him without reprisal?

Bending, he yanked her up from the floor, holding hard when she tried to wriggle free. He caught her chin in one fist.

"Nay, do not think to flee. You are well snared, and must yield to me whither you will it or no."

"Never!"

His grip tightened. White splotches appeared on her pale skin where his fingers pressed. "Yea, vixen—you will. You will swear to me, and swear to William, or your life may well be forfeit. Do not think the king will hesitate to see you undone, for he is not a kind man."

"There is no need to tell me that—he is Norman, is he not?"

"And you think all Normans to be unkind."

"Can you deny it?"

Luc almost smiled. "Nay. Nor would I want to. Kindness is a weakness when dealing with Saxons who forswear oaths."

Ice-blue eyes turned even frostier, a hard-winter freeze that chilled him even as he forced her head back to look up at him. Her lips were trembling, and his gaze was inexplicably drawn to her mouth. Lush lips parted, revealing white teeth gritted in a faint snarl. It was a bristling show of defiance, like that of a startled kitten.

Luc released her chin and studied her until her creamy skin flushed with color, and her dark brown lashes lowered to veil wide eyes glittering with hostility. Even scratched and bruised, she was lovely. Earlier, with the unmistakable curve of her breast against his palm, his body had responded with a predictable tightening of his groin. It had been annoying that he would react so to a woman who had tried to kill him, though not very surprising. The heat of battle sent the blood surging, as did the heat of a female caress.

"Yield," he said roughly, irritated further by his arousal. "Yield to me, *demoiselle*."

In that moment, he didn't know if he meant her to surrender to his authority, or to surrender her body. Never had he dealt with a Saxon woman with her long legs bare and tempting. And without her armor, her slender curves were easily discerned beneath the simple tunic that ended just above her knees; sandals laced to midcalf and leather bindings wrapped around bare legs and feet only emphasized her shapeliness. She was enticing in a primitive fashion, and he had seen more than one of his men eye her with lustful curiosity during the evening. It had prompted him to sit beside her with his hand on her shoulder or tangled in her hair, stating his ownership of her by the occasional touch on her cheek.

Now she rebuffed him with a contemptuous curl of her lips, the jerk of her chin upward, and the scathing rake of her glare—as if she knew well that he was not what he pretended:

not new lord of this estate, but a son made bastard by his own father, spurned by his own blood.

Impulsively, his fingers twisted in the cloth of her tunic and he dragged her hard against him, driven to crush her rejection and the mockery in her eyes. Alarm quickly replaced her contempt, and his mouth curled in a satisfied grimace.

"Yea, well should you fear me. I've no patience for stubborn Saxons too foolish to yield when there is no other choice."

Her fisted hands pushed futilely against his chest, and she struggled desperately in his grip. " 'Tis all Saxons have done since your cursed king set foot in our land—yield lands and pride and even our lives to William the Bastard and his marauding knights. Allegiance is expected, but must I yield my maidenhead, as well, to satisfy Norman justice?"

Behind her panting defiance he recognized fear. She expected to be raped. Tempting, he admitted, but he had no intention of obliging her. He preferred his women warm and willing, not biting, scratching, and exhausting a man so that any chance of pleasure was destroyed. But why tell her that when it would be to his advantage to leave her quivering in apprehension?

"Une pucelle?" He laughed softly and shifted back to English. "Even if you are truly virgin, you value yourself too highly to think your maidenhead is adequate payment for the damage you have caused." She hissed at him, trying to pull free, but he held her fast. "Nay, do not think to escape me. When I want you, I will take you. For now, your oath will serve my needs."

Her eyes were sharp as daggers as she glared up at him. "I will not swear to you or to William—and you will have to kill me before you can take me."

"Will I? You cannot even free yourself from my hold. Can you thwart me from doing whatever I will?"

"Aye—"

Provoked as much by some obscure emotion as by her tart challenge, Luc curled one hand into her hair to pull her head back, tilting her face upward. Panic clouded her eyes.

"You said you wanted only my oath—"

"Aye, and I also said I would take you when I want you, princess."

"Don't call me that! Curse you—" The words came out in a husky, strangled sob. "Don't ever call me that again. . . ."

Her knee came up in a slashing jerk, and he barely avoided the blow. His hand splayed against the small of her back to press her close against him. He could feel her muscles knotting beneath his palm. His lips slanted across her mouth in a punishing kiss, and the blood began to beat hot and swift through his veins. It was a contest of wills that he meant to win, but by the Rood! he began to wonder if he had underestimated the effect she had on him. He had bedded his share of women in the past, but not like this one. None had ever bested him at anything. Most of the women of his experience were rather pale, simpering creatures who grated on his nerves with sighing professions of everlasting love, exhausting him with their expectations.

Not this one. She was fire and ice, defiance and hatred, a contradiction and a challenge that would stir any man. Still, he did not expect the potency of his response to her, a raging need that clouded the memory of other women.

Jésu, her mouth was soft, honey-sweet and as hot as the fire that raged through him. His entire body was a throbbing ache. He wanted her. He wanted to push her down to the waiting bed and spread her beneath him, plunge inside her toward that sweet release that only a woman could give him. Yet he would not, and he knew it even as he kissed her into limp submission, felt her weight sag in his arms and her body drape into that curious boneless compliance that oft preceded a woman's surrender.

Only then did Luc lift his head and allow her to take a stumbling backward step away from him. Hot color stained her high cheekbones, yet her lips were strangely bloodless, her eyes like wide blue bruises beneath straight brows. She was trembling, and she put her arms around her body as if chilled.

In a shaky voice, she snapped: "I see Normans are as bestial as they are reputed to be."

"So we are. And you will see just how bestial I can be if you do not swear to me as your new lord, *demoiselle*." Slowly, he began to unbuckle the wide leather belt around his waist.

"You . . . you would not!"

"Better leather than steel, but do not deceive yourself into believing that I would withhold my hand from delivering Norman justice where it is warranted."

"Justice, or tyranny?"

When he said nothing, but looped the length of leather belt in his hands, her crimson flush deepened and she looked away from him, biting her lower lip between her teeth.

The silence dragged between them for a long moment before Ceara looked at him again, her expression mutinous but her voice subdued. "It seems that you are right—I cannot stay your hand. And though it galls me, I concede that you fought well and fairly against us. Wulfridge is now yours to command."

Her capitulation was too sudden and too evasive to be believed. Luc said nothing, waiting with lifted brows, slapping the looped belt against his open palm.

Ceara's shoulders lifted in a slight shrug. "It must ring false to you, my lord. I understand. But I am so weary, and now that it is over, I have little to gain by earning your hatred. It would be better to have your amity than your enmity, I think."

"A wise decision. To what do I owe this sudden—if incomplete—change of heart?"

"Fear."

The blunt admission was unexpected, and he grinned. "Fear of what I may do, or fear of what you may do, *demoiselle*?"

Her mouth tightened, and she shot him an irritated glance from beneath her lashes. "You are crude indeed, sir. Do not flatter yourself that I will fling myself into your arms with abandon. I merely thought to oblige you in appreciation for your mercy earlier today."

"Mercy . . . *My* mercy?"

"Yea, my lord. As you *escorted* me from the hall, I saw the boy that was hidden earlier in the storeroom. Rudd is unharmed."

"I have no reason to harm children. Or women who do not attack me with sword or dagger."

Another flash of irritation crossed her face, and she took a deep breath. "Yea, so I see. Do not misunderstand me—I do not profess love and devotion, only gratitude."

It was Luc's turn to be irritated. "I do not want your gratitude."

"No?" She looked up, blinking innocently. "What else do you want from me, my lord?"

It was a dangerous question. If not for his heavy leather tunic, it would be obvious what he wanted from her, or what his body wanted. And why not? She was lovely, soft-skinned and desirable in her short garments, her long legs drawing his gaze again and again—until he forced himself to look away. A man's admission of his desire was a potent weapon in a woman's hands.

"Your oath of loyalty will be enough for now, *demoiselle*."

Silence fell, lengthening until she cleared her throat. "Can I trust that?"

" 'Tis you who flatter yourself. Do you think me so enamored of you I cannot restrain myself? I assure you, I am not a green youth about to lose control. I prefer a woman who knows how to be a woman, not a half-clad warrior wielding a sword and mouthing threats. You are safe enough, I warrant."

It was a lie, and he knew it even as he said it. He should never have touched her. His body was taut as a bowstring and thrumming with need. What would William say if he did as he wanted to do? An act of war was an act of war, but the king had strict rules of conduct. She was a political hostage. If he took her, he may well have to answer to William for it.

Ceara had gone even paler, and lines of strain formed

brackets around her mouth as she stared at him. "I suppose you kiss all your enemies as you did me, then."

"Only those foolish enough to play the seductress so clumsily."

"Norman swine, do you think for a moment that I would truly attempt seduction with one such as you?"

Luc's hands were on her so swiftly she had no time to evade him, and she gasped when his fingers dug harshly into the tender skin of her wrists. "Bide your tongue," he said with soft menace. "I weary of this carping."

He released her with a slight shove, and watched as she straightened and stalked to the farthest corner of the dimly lit room. She pressed her back against the wall and watched him warily, as if he might yet use a whip or sword to punish her. Well she might be wary, for he was tired of her sharp tongue. It cut as deeply as a dagger.

He gazed at her moodily until his squire arrived with Luc's chain mail. A boy was with him, a towheaded, freckle-faced youngster wearing the short tunic of a peasant. Alain swept out an arm to indicate the boy. "I brought this lad with me, Sir Luc, as he seems to be a likely prospect to instruct. Scrawny, but quick of wit and obedient."

"That will be a welcome change. Obedience is in short supply here." Straightening, Luc tossed the leather belt onto a small table, and wryly noted the boy's quick glance from the belt to his bruised mistress. Little could be done that servants would miss, and no doubt the tale would be all over Wulfridge by the morrow that the new lord had beaten the Saxon maid who had dared draw steel against him. The error would certainly do no harm, and might even be to his benefit.

"Bring me a length of chain, Alain," he instructed when his mail was laid out. "I have need to bind a she-wolf this night."

The squire glanced at Ceara curiously, his expression altering when she drew in a hissing breath. Though they spoke in

French, the girl's face had gone even paler than before, as if she understood them.

Alain smirked, but his voice betrayed nothing when he asked if Luc required a guard for the maid. "Or perhaps she should be chained in a cell, my lord?"

Luc shook his head. "No. This will suffice for tonight. What the—here, boy, get away from that."

At the harsh command in English, the boy with Alain immediately dropped Luc's heavy hauberk, and it thudded to the floor with a solid clank. Trembling, he stared at his feet until Luc told him in a milder tone to tidy up the chamber, as it had been badly used.

Turning back to Alain, Luc frowned with weariness as the boy scurried to obey. "On the morrow, set clerks to inventorying the goods still usable, so that I will know what to tell William about Wulfridge's value. It may be better to raze this fortress and build a new castle on the site than use it in its present condition."

At that, the girl made a small, choked sound, and Luc turned to look at her. "Do I disturb you?" he asked in Norman French, but she only stared at him, eyes filled with turbulent emotion that could mean anything. He watched her carefully. Did she perceive more than she feigned? It was unlikely, but not impossible. Educated priests roamed England freely, and there was a priory on Holy Island off the northern coast. For a fee, the good fathers would impart their knowledge most willingly to the young men of a household, though he'd never known of an educated Saxon daughter. Still, Lord Balfour was rumored to have been an independent man, with his own ideas of propriety.

"My lord?" Alain's query interrupted Luc's reflection and he turned to the squire, grimacing at the fact that she could so easily distract him.

Alain repeated his question. "Is there anything else you require?"

"Yes, Alain. Send me wine, warm water to wash, and thick

blankets, along with the chains. And take that boy with you. He's too frightened to be of much use this eve."

"At once, my lord." Alain grasped the boy by the shoulder, startling a squeak from him, and propelled him toward the door. "I will fetch your needs myself," Alain said as he shut the door softly behind him.

Clad now in only sherte and chausses, Luc shrugged free of the linen garment he wore beneath his leather tunic. He grimaced. Sword cuts from the day's fight made the garment stick to him where the blood had dried, ripping his skin as he removed it. Ceara watched, her unblinking gaze riveted on him as he tossed the sherte on the narrow rope bed. She did not look away, even when his hands moved to the cross-garters that held up his chausses. He began to untie them with swift efficiency. Apparently, she had no qualms about watching him disrobe.

"Do you watch for your entertainment, or for mine, *demoiselle*?"

She ignored his mockery and shrugged, crossing her scratched, bruised legs at the ankle. "You would not be the first man I've seen unclothed."

"No? Yet you claim to be virgin."

"Just because I've eyes in my head, does not mean I have oats for brains," she retorted with a derisive snort. "Do I seem so simple as to yield to temptation at the mere sight of a man? I've seen nothing to recommend the male body, for all that men are prone to boast of their prowess."

Luc did not bother to refute her, shrugging as he stepped out of his chausses and moved to the large brass brazier where coals had burned down to gray ash. Only a faint warmth still emanated from the brazier as he stripped away his loincloth.

Despite her professed scorn, Ceara averted her gaze, staring at the floor. He grinned, rubbing his hands up and down his bare arms to warm himself. It was all a bluff, of course, her claim that she had seen naked men before. The hectic color in her cheeks betrayed her.

"Foolish wench. Did you not consider that it would be very easy to discover the truth? A meaningless lie, as it is of no matter to me if you are virgin or sullied. It may well matter to William, however, as the king may yet believe it advantageous to make you a favorable marriage to a man of his choosing."

Her head jerked up. "He would not!"

"Do not fret unduly. His other choice may be the sword. Which would you prefer? Or need I ask?"

Her mouth set in a grim line, and the color leached from her face. Luc wondered if William would find her as irritating as he did. If she were foolish enough to act with the king as she had with him, it would go very badly for her. Useless, of course, to tell her that. She would only distrust his motives.

Alain returned alone, bringing wine, warm water, and a length of chain. "There is no soap to be found, my lord. Doubtless, these Saxon dogs never bathe, and our baggage is scattered about so carelessly that I could not find our own supply."

"No matter, Alain. Warm water will do to wash away the worst of the grime." Luc poured himself a goblet of wine, then began to wash before the water grew cold. He was aware of Ceara sitting in the far corner. Her head was tilted back against the wall, cushioned by her bright hair and exposing the clean line of her throat. She stared up at the ceiling as if fascinated by smoke-blackened beams and cobwebs. Her long bare legs were drawn up almost to her chest, pinioned by her crossed arms. Slender calves and thighs gleamed with pale luminosity. The short hem of her tunic scarcely covered her female virtues. She should have looked ragged and pathetic with her rent garments and tangled mane of hair, but she did not. The display of long limbs and shadowed mysteries lent instead an air of sensuality that was as disturbing as it was arousing.

And he did not seem to be the only one affected: keen interest lit his squire's eyes as Alain checked Luc's armor for breaks, his glances straying again and again to the Saxon hostage. "What do you intend to do with her, my liege?"

"What I vowed to do when it was thought it was Balfour who had rebelled. I will take the rebel to the king as he commanded me." Luc's eyes narrowed slightly at Alain's rapt interest in Ceara, but the squire was too engrossed with the maid to notice.

"And until then, my liege? She is very beautiful, and only a hostage now, for all that she was once lady of this hall." Alain's intent gaze continued to linger on Ceara far longer than necessary. "The king may give her in marriage, do you not think?"

"It is possible. Do you aspire to wed the she-wolf?"

Alain laughed, but there was an odd note in his voice. "Stranger things have happened, even to a man of my station. And she seems not to be so willful as she was before."

"Do not be deceived. The maid has a tongue sharp as a carter's blade. Be wary she does not wound you with it." When the squire shrugged in an expansive gesture of indifference, Luc said softly, "The maid is not for you, Alain."

Alain flashed him a startled glance, and his face reddened. "My liege—"

"She is to go to William, and it is for the king to decide her fate, not for you or I to belabor the point at such a late hour."

Luc's brusque tone said much more than his words, and Alain was far from stupid. "You are right, of course, my lord. It is late and my tongue is clumsy with weariness. Forgive my impertinence."

Annoyed by his reaction to the squire's interest in the girl, Luc nodded curtly. "We are both weary and on edge. A full night's sleep will remedy much."

With a swift efficiency that betrayed his anxiety to depart, Alain cleaned Luc's armor and set aright the small chamber. Luc finished washing, scrubbing his face, arms, and chest with a dripping cloth to remove the sweat and blood of the day from his skin. When he was through, Alain silently handed him a square of cloth warmed at the brazier with which to dry himself.

The squire's unusual deference only reminded Luc of Alain's interest in the maid, and he snatched the cloth more forcefully than necessary. "You play the part of obedient servant well," Luc muttered.

"As you wish, my lord. Is there anything else, my lord?"

Luc wrapped the damp cloth around his waist. "Yes. Chain her to the bed, and throw some of the warmest skins on the floor for her use. I would sleep what few hours are left to me without worry of having my throat cut."

Surprise flared in Alain's eyes. "As you will, my lord." He complied swiftly, pulling Ceara to her feet, ignoring her sullen glare as he fastened a length of chain around her waist, then secured it to the foot of the sturdy wooden bed.

Luc poured more wine and sipped it in preoccupied silence. When Alain hesitated, Luc stared pointedly at the door. "I bid you rest well, Alain. Shut the door after you."

"Good night, my lord." Alain crossed the room, turning back at the portal. "Sleep well." He bowed stiffly and the door closed behind him with a soft thud.

Luc glanced at the pile of furs. Ceara had burrowed into them so that only the bright mass of her hair showed above the mound of pelts. Frowning, he poured himself more wine, enough to warm him but not enough to dull his senses. Like King William, he was not fond of hearty drink or the effects it had on those foolish enough to indulge too freely.

Alain had placed parchment and writing instruments on the table by the flagon of wine, but Luc found himself too weary to make a report of the day's activities. He would call a scribe to him in the morning, and have him detail the necessary information while he made ready for his journey. If William was still at Stafford, Luc would have much farther to travel, and he did not relish the thought. Weariness rode him hard, and the wine coursed warmly through his blood, relaxing him at last. He tilted his head and drained his cup, then set it atop the table.

Removing the damp cloth from around his waist, he tossed

it onto a small, three-legged stool and turned toward the bed. Ceara was sitting up in the hillock of fur pelts, watching him. When he paused, she rose to her knees in a soft clink of chains. Hazy light filtered over her, gilding her shoulders in a rose-gold sheen. She was naked. No tunic draped her slender body, nor did shadows conceal the thrust of bare breasts.

Riveted, Luc stared at her. His belly clenched in a tight knot. She was lovely, tempting him with the sudden need to reach out and touch her, to skim his hands over the deep pink rosettes that rode the high crest of her breasts, to tease them into taut peaks with his tongue . . . despite his own nudity and the brisk chill in the air, he was suddenly sweating. Involuntarily, his eyes dropped lower. Bruises had blossomed on her arms and thighs, tokens of Norman regard, but it was the shadowed juncture of her legs that held his gaze much too long.

Silent and unmoving, she watched him. A fey maid with pagan eyes and tempting curves, sweet-faced and hell-bent, as dangerous in combat as in captivity. . . .

Belatedly, he realized that there are some reactions near impossible for a man to control. To his chagrin, his naked body had betrayed him.

Ceara's gaze dropped to his loins. She smiled, a slow sensual curving of her mouth until the dimples on each side of her lips grew deep. In a husky voice, she purred, "Ah, so even Normans know how to rise to the occasion, I see. . . ."

Chapter Four

Luc stared at her without moving, his body revealing his desire but his face revealing nothing. Ceara waited with trembling determination. If she was to be bartered to a man, it would be under her own terms, not those of a Norman king. And while she detested the means, she had few options left to her. William would likely marry her off. This man would hold Wulfridge. If she could bind Luc to her, she would not lose her rightful legacy. It was chancy, but the ultimate prize would be worth the risk.

Cool air prickled her skin, and the strained silence was as heavy as the chains around her waist. She knew that Luc was right. She was no seductress, though it galled her to hear that he found her unappealing. Never before had she attempted this; indeed, her experience with desire had not been to lure men, but to keep them at the sharp end of her dagger. How did she proceed? She felt every bit as inexperienced as she was, and more than a little embarrassed. As the silence dragged, she flushed so hot the chill went unnoticed.

It grew increasingly difficult to keep her eyes from straying to ascertain if his desire was flagging. Why did Luc not respond?

Say something? Or move? But he just stood there holding her gaze, his expression unfathomable.

When he finally stirred, it was to close the distance between them in two long strides and jerk her up. The chain bit into her skin, and piled furs fell away to puddle at her feet and tickle her bare ankles. Luc's voice was low and savage.

"Do not think to play me that way, *demoiselle.* I have long dallied at the lists of love and know well how to parry your foolish attempts to draw me into a honeyed trap."

Embarrassment and despair knifed through her. His rejection was as frustrating as it was humiliating. If she had to change tactics, she would, but she knew what must be done to keep both Wulfridge and her life. Later, once she was again lady of the hall, she would find a way to rid herself of this arrogant Norman. But until then . . .

"You misread me, my lord."

"How is it possible to misread this?" His hand shifted to sweep down the slope of her body, lingering on the swell of her breast in a slow caress. A thrumming ache made her nipple tighten to a taut peak that he teased with his thumb and finger until she could barely hear his muttered words: "Nay, I think it unlikely I would misread your intentions."

Sounding strangled even to herself, she said as coolly as she could, "Yet you have managed it."

"I think not. You would not be the first damsel to so seek to entice me."

Anger edged her laughter, and she moved slightly so that his hand fell away from her breast. The heat of his touch lingered, and there was still an annoying throb in the pit of her stomach. "Arrogant Norman. Nurse your dreams if you must, but do not involve me in them."

" 'Tis you who have involved yourself by this play of straws, *demoiselle.*"

She shrugged casually. "I admit I chose an unfortunate moment to make a jest at your expense, but I do not share your apparent conviction that I am enamored of you, my lord."

A muscle leaped in his jaw at her quietly scornful words. "A jest? Mock me at your own risk, Ceara."

She put a hand on his bare chest, fingertips gliding through the dark hair with a feathery touch. "I do not mock you. I meant only to lighten the mood, for I saw that you—reacted—unexpectedly. I sleep unclothed. Since you did not hide your body from me, I assumed that you cared naught for modesty. Do not think me too forward, lord, for it was truly a mistake."

Yea, a great mistake if it costs me Wulfridge. . . .

For a short, sizzling moment, Luc did not move. He stared into her eyes with intense concentration, then said abruptly, "It is not yet certain who has made the mistake, but you are now warned. I do not forgive deception easily."

"I do not lie, my lord."

His derisive snort was evidence of his differing opinion. "See that you do not."

Ceara did not reply to that, for it was obvious to her that Luc would only make more threats, blustering like a lion with a sore paw. He had yet to make good on any of them, though she knew he would not hesitate to retaliate harshly if truly necessary. This man was more complicated than she had considered. Few men would restrain themselves on principle when they were obviously aroused, yet he had done so.

Luc turned away from her, his attention fiercely directed to the parchment and ink on the table. "Get back to the bed before I decide to take Alain's advice and chain you in a cell, *demoiselle*. And cover yourself."

It seemed wise not to comment, and she moved silently to the pile of furs and wool and burrowed beneath them. Her fingers curled around the smooth, comforting hilt of a dagger hidden beneath a scrap of blanket. Clever Rudd, to so deftly steal the weapon and slide it to her unnoticed. She felt better knowing that if the worst should happen she had protection, but knew that once drawn, the dagger would have to be used. It would be a last resort.

Studiously ignoring her, Luc came to bed, and his weight made the ropes creak loudly. He was so close she could almost feel the heat of his body. Close enough that if she chose, she could slit his throat in the night. He thought himself safe. She smiled. What would the arrogant Norman say if he knew she held his very own dagger close to her bosom? How invincible would he think himself then?

Tossing and turning, the sweet oblivion of slumber eluded her long into the night. The lamp guttered and died before she sank into exhausted sleep, and even then she was beset with troubling dreams that left her restless.

DAWN CAME MUCH too early. The fair-haired Norman squire came to wake his lord with a swift knock at the chamber door. Luc rolled over with a creaking protest of the bed ropes and gave his permission to enter. Alain sidled inside, his gaze moving quickly to where Ceara still lay curled among the pelts. She did not like him. There was a sly quality to the squire, a guile that set ill with her, and she made no bones about her dislike.

"The men await you in the hall, my lord. Shall I help you dress?" Alain closed the door softly.

Luc swung his legs over the side of the bed and stood in a smooth uncoiling of his muscular body. Uneasy at his close proximity, Ceara watched through her lashes as Luc stretched with lazy grace. Taut muscles banded his chest and roped his flat belly, and his legs were long and sinewed. Sleep-tousled black hair lent him the oddly appealing appearance of youth, straggling over his forehead and around his hard face, softening it. Yet his eyes belied any illusion of tenderness—ebony orbs beneath a thick bristle of black lashes, aloof and cold as if he had not held her in his arms and kissed her with unmistakable desire the night before. She could not be wrong about that. His body had not lied. Now he ignored her as if she were a piece of furniture, unworthy of notice. It was daunting to think he could ignore even his own needs. He was more dangerous than she had guessed. Men of principle always were.

While Luc moved across the room to dress, Alain came near her under the pretense of airing the rope bed. His sharp eyes sought her out, and his gaze lingered overlong on the bare skin of her shoulder that lay exposed above a wool blanket. He bent close as if to remove the bedcovers, his voice low as he whispered to her in his native French:

"Il ne fait pas bon avoir affaire à lui, demoiselle. Vous êtes bon vous! À ces mots—"

Ceara pulled the pelts up to her chin and curled her fingers tightly around the hilt of the hidden dagger. She stared at him in blank silence. Did he think her stupid enough to fall for such an obvious ruse? She would not. And she knew well enough that Luc was a dangerous man to meddle with, so this ambitious squire need not think his warning would endear him to her. Nor would his declaration of admiration, for she saw through that as well. Foolish squire, to think she would be so credulous as to view him with tender regard for mouthing a few insincere words.

"Leave that, Alain," Luc ordered from the table, "and send for the scribe. I've need of his skills this morn so that William may know the worth of this demesne to him." He'd spoken in English, an apparent oversight, for he glanced up and repeated it in French with a shrug to excuse his lapse.

Alain moved away reluctantly, but not before he took a moment to feign inspection of her chains, an act that gave him the opportunity to brush his hands against the bare skin of her leg. Ceara lashed out with one foot, catching him hard enough against his thigh to make him grunt in pain. A scowl creased his brow and his hazel eyes narrowed with anger, but he did not betray himself to Luc.

Norman curs, they were all alike. Treacherous, sly, rapacious, and lustful. None had yet changed her opinion of them. Not even Luc's self-denial had greatly altered her estimation of his character, for it was too easy to prate of principles when one had none. Since the Normans had first set foot on English soil, they had valued nothing but destruction. It would hardly change now, nor would one man be likely to be so very different from those before him. No, if Wulfridge was to survive with its glory intact, she would have to save it. Nothing would be too great a sacrifice to accomplish her ends.

MORNING MIST CRAWLED through the courtyard in silent ribbons, glistening on stone and wood and the steaming hides of restive horses. Pearlescent dampness shrouded the walls of the castle and muffled the sound of men and animals. A salty tang was in the air, smelling of the sea.

Luc waited for Alain to bring Drago to him, impatient now that all was ready. He would deliver his hostage to the king and collect his reward for it, and put the past behind him. No more would he be just a hedge knight, his sword for hire to whatever power wished to pay, condemned to wander with no home of his own. Now perhaps some of his bitterness would dissipate. Robert was right: it was past time for it.

A gust of wind stirred tendrils of fog into swirling eddies that momentarily eclipsed the main door to the hall, and when it cleared, he saw Ceara standing beneath an arched entrance. Despite the turmoil of the past day, she remained composed, looking mystical and elegant garbed in a long blue kirtle, boots, and hooded mantle of dyed red wool.

Where was the pagan princess of hours past? The woman who had knelt before him clad only in lamplight and enchantment?

Vanished now, exiled by this lovely, remote creature gazing about the courtyard as if she still owned it, as if she was the lady and Luc the interloper. Provoked by some nameless emotion, he walked toward her. She turned to watch him, her eyes unreadable yet drawing him closer. A current of air lifted the edge of her mantle in a graceful swirl. Beneath the outer garment, she wore a pendant, and it gleamed with soft luster against the blue material of her kirtle. Exquisite silver coils formed the familiar knotwork of the Celts, and an amber stone cradled in the middle was richly lucent and textured. It was not an extremely valuable piece, but one that should have caught the eyes of men searching for jewelry.

Beneath her wary gaze, he reached out to lift the heavy ornament in his palm. The backs of his fingers brushed against her breasts, and she drew in a sharp breath. As he held the pendant, he felt the quickening beat of her heart beneath his hand.

"A lovely piece, *demoiselle*. How did it escape the notice of my men?" It was not an idle question. By William's own command, every item of value in England was to be counted and reported.

Ceara's fingers were cool as she closed them protectively around both his palm and the pendant. "God was with me, my lord. This belonged to my mother, and is all I have left of her."

"Yet you wear it where all can see. Do you not fear that we brutish Normans will take it from you?"

She ignored his mockery with a faint smile. "If 'tis what you wish, there would be little I could do to halt you. I am at your mercy, my lord."

Luc snorted. "You have never been at any man's mercy, I think."

Her smile deepened. Her gentle fragrance teased him, and beneath the curved shadow of her lashes, her eyes were as deep and placid as the waters of a lake, drawing him in. There was knowledge in their depths, mystical secrets of times gone by, an age-old wisdom that reminded him of things best forgotten: elusive enchantment, silent promises, creamy skin turned rose-gold by lamplight, and the disquieting waver of his resolve. For an instant, he felt as if he were drowning, inexorably pulled beneath the surface of her eyes.

Then behind her in the mist a figure moved, shattering the haze of scent and shadow, and he released the pendant abruptly. A mailed soldier emerged from the archway, no doubt the guard he had earlier ordered to tend her while she made ready to journey to the king, but it was not a man he recognized.

"What is your name, soldier?"

"Giles, my lord. Of Caen. I was one of Sir Simon's men, and was with him when he was killed. Alain de Montbray bade me be the lady's guard, as I have knowledge of her tongue."

"My squire is most efficient, I see. Giles, see you that the lady is mounted and kept close to you. I would not have harm come to her, nor would I find it pleasant to explain to the king why she was not delivered to him as promised. If that should come about, it is to you I will direct the king's questions. Is that understood?"

Giles shifted uneasily and nodded. "I understand, my lord. I shall not allow her to come to harm, nor allow her to escape."

"Good. I see that we are alike in our purposes. You will be well rewarded for a job finely done." It was unnecessary to repeat the rewards of failure. Facing a furious king was not a task any sane man would relish, especially when that monarch was William. The king was terrible in his rages, ruthless in his purposes, and few men escaped his wrath lightly. Yet for all the ease with which he could leave a man quaking in his boots, William was possessed of a strong sense of justice. Luc had long admired him, since the time William was only duke of Normandy, and he was still an earl's cast-off son. It seemed decades ago, when in truth it had only been five years. But it was a long time to a man with little but the bitter dregs of disappointment for his daily fare.

No longer. Through his own efforts, he had won lands and title, and these he would defend to the end of his strength. No man could take them away from him once William deeded them, none but the king himself. And that would not happen as long as Luc remained steadfast. Unlike his father.

"My lord, your mount is ready."

Just behind Alain was the horse steward, his fists tightly gripping Drago's halter and lead lines. The temperamental stallion pranced nervously at the end of his tether.

"He is fresh this morn, my lord," the steward said, panting. "I can barely keep him from breaking loose."

"He will settle in. Like the rest of us, Drago must learn to pace himself."

The steward grinned, his weathered face almost splitting at the seams. "I have rarely noticed you taking a slow pace, my lord."

"That is for old men like you, Paul." Luc's jest earned a chuckle from the steward, for at twenty-six he was younger than his lord by more than five years.

Alain held out a brimming horn of ale, and Luc drained it quickly, then mounted the edgy destrier. He reined Drago in with a firm hand and looked down at his squire, who had retreated to a safe distance from the lethal hooves.

"Captain Remy is in command while I am gone. See that he has what is necessary until my return."

"I had hoped you would change your mind and allow me to accompany you, my lord."

"I do not intend to be gone that long, Alain, and I need you here. Remy's talent with soldiers is needed to hold Wulfridge, and your talent with servants is needed to make it livable."

Alain ducked his head, but not before Luc caught the sulky disappointment in his face. The squire was willful, but adept. He had been with Luc for three years, sent to him by a deseisined father as squire, for it was all that was left open to a young man without funds or prospects. At the time, it had seemed fitting to

Luc, a landless squire for a landless knight, both adrift in a ruthless world. Now there would be opportunity for both, if Alain would see past his resentment to the possibilities ahead.

The squire murmured his compliance and wishes for a speedy journey, looking up with a tight smile. "I will see to Wulfridge as if it were my own, my lord."

"Prudent men are always rewarded well, Alain. It is a truth that I am more inclined to believe in now."

THE GROUP LEFT Wulfridge castle and took the narrow, crumbling road that led from the promontory to the marshes beyond. It was cold and damp, and the mist was heavy as the troop settled into a steady pace. They forded the river at a shallow point near a sandy wash, then clambered up the steep banks and entered a shadowed wood where little light penetrated the ancient trees and brush. It was silent here, save for the steady clop of hooves and incessant jangle of bridles and spurs.

Luc resisted the temptation to seek out Ceara the first day, but rode at the head of the troop without looking back. Giles would tend her needs, and soon he would be rid of her. He knew he must leave it up to William to decide her fate, but at odd moments a vision of her wide blue eyes flashed before him in silent reproach. There was a part of him that admired her stubborn courage, and was astonished at her effrontery in donning battle gear and taking up a sword against him. That she had beat him in battle and single combat was as admirable as it was annoying. He anticipated many a jest at his expense when William's court discovered it, as they surely would. In fact, *that* juicy bit of news would most likely reach William long before he did. Bad news winged swiftly, while good news plodded afoot.

His great destrier settled into a steady rhythm on the narrow, rough track that passed for a road in this northern region. The frequent passage of carts had formed two ruts that straddled a thin line of frost-killed grass. Much of the road was washed away by rains, or gutted by huge holes that still held slushy puddles of brown water. When they at last broke from the forest into open land, the mist still blanketed the soggy moors stretching beyond the road on both sides. Gray skies melded with the dull gray mist to form a nearly seamless landscape. The dismal view made him long for the sunnier climes of France where he had spent so many years.

But England was his home now, and what had France and Normandy given him but bitter shame? Nothing. It was here he would make his new life, seize the promise that had once been his and make it manifest.

"My lord?"

Luc half turned, lifting a brow when he recognized Giles approaching. The man-at-arms was slightly flushed, and looked uncomfortable when he drew his mount alongside his leader.

"Yes, Giles, what is it?"

"It is the lady, my lord."

A glance reassured Luc that Ceara was still with them, mounted on a fat gray mare that looked sulky at the brisk pace. The lady looked just as sulky, her mouth pressed in a taut line and her eyes mutinous. He looked back at Giles. "What about the lady?"

"She is . . . uncooperative, my lord."

"Uncooperative." Luc stared at Giles so long that the man-at-arms lowered his gaze and shifted uneasily in his saddle. "How is it you wish for her to cooperate?"

Giles cleared his throat nervously. "She will not obey when I tell her not to rein back her mount to a slower pace. It is very difficult to keep my horse apace with the rest if I must be constantly slapping hers on the rump." Giles scowled, his eyes flashing with ire. "The lady informed me that she does not have to keep up, that it is my duty to guard her, not drag her down the road."

"Did she now?" Luc suppressed a smile. "Then it is clear to

me that you must take matters firmly into your own hands, Giles."

"But, my lord, she is very willful. When I tried to take the reins from her, she slapped me across the face with them. My cheek bled for near a mile."

There was, indeed, a red welt across Gile's cheek, crusted with dried blood. Indignation glittered in the young man's eyes, mixed with frustration.

"Giles, when I bade you watch the lady, I did not say you must suffer insult at her hands. Take her reins and lead her horse, and if she resists, inform her that it is better you who takes them than me."

Triumph replaced the frustration in Giles's face. "At once, my lord. And with great pleasure."

Luc watched with interest as Giles reined his mount around and returned to Ceara, and found it difficult to restrain his laughter when she sweetly relinquished her reins before the man-at-arms could even speak. It must have greatly diminished Giles's satisfaction not to be able to convey the veiled threat he had been authorized to use.

Looking past Giles, Ceara met Luc's eyes with an innocent lift of one brow, as if she could not comprehend the man-at-arm's ire. A clever wench, bold and saucy, cool and poised even with a dagger at her throat. She had the courage of a man, yet the mysterious moods and caprices that marked her actions were as incomprehensible to him as any woman's.

Strangely, it was not her defiance that nettled him as much as her compliance. Her inexplicable shift from snarling hatred to breathless yielding had nonplussed him most. He could deal with resistance handily, but her surrender had nearly undone him. His hard-won restraint had caused him a restless night and left his temper unreliable. Even now, he could visualize her naked body as if she were before him, the tempting allure of her sweet curves a prodding reminder that it had been overlong since he had been with a woman. When he reached William's court, he would rectify that lack as soon as discreetly possible.

As the day wore on, the morning mist finally lifted, and it grew lighter as the sun appeared from behind scudding clouds. With a gentle warmth filtering down over fields and road, the air grew pleasantly crisp. In a welcome contrast to the gloom of mist and cloud, the shafts of hazy light brightened the landscape and Luc's mood. He felt as if he had the world in his fist.

On the second night they made camp at dusk near the banks of the Wansbeck River. A thick wood stretched beyond the river, providing ample fuel for the fires. After the arduous day's ride over miles of rough terrain, the prospect of a warm fire was an agreeable one. The wind was from the northeast, cold and damp and smelling faintly of salt though they were miles from the sea by now. It seeped through mail and clothing with icy fingers, and fires sprung up on the banks as soon as the men could gather wood and light them.

Guards were posted around the camp at intervals, while others set about picketing horses, cleaning their gear, and preparing food for the evening meal. Luc cleaned his own gear as his squire had remained at Wulfridge, then knelt close to a fire to warm his bare hands. His mail gauntlets provided protection from sword but not the cold, and the heat slowly eased his cramping fingers.

Ceara watched him silently. He had avoided her until now, leaving her in the care of Giles, who had looked so harried and miserable that Luc had finally relented long enough to order Ceara left in his charge for a time. She was wrapped in her long wool cloak, the hood over her bright hair as she huddled against the wind. The flames reflected in her eyes made them gleam like rare jewels.

"Where do we go, my lord?" Her sudden question was so casual that he knew she had dwelt on it for some time before asking. Most likely, since they had left Wulfridge the day before. He shrugged.

"To the king."

"Do you think me a lackwit? I am fully aware of the purpose for this journey, but not the destination. Is the king at Winchester?"

Amused, Luc shook his head. "No, he is not. What would it matter to you where we find the king? His whereabouts will hardly affect his decision as to your fate."

She shifted, and held her hands out to the flames. The edges of her cloak parted, and the amber stone dangling against her breast glittered in the firelight. "I did not think it would, my lord. It's just that I have never been to Winchester."

"Ah." Luc studied her in the flickering glow. "A pity you must take to travel in this manner, then."

Her eyes flashed, and she bent her head so that the hood of her cloak cast a deep shadow across her face. "Just so, my lord. I cannot think what came over me."

"Can you not?" Highly amused now, Luc rubbed his hands together briskly and asked, "Why did you break your sworn oath to the king? William does not take treason lightly."

"Nor do I." Her head jerked up, and her eyes were slightly narrowed. "But I never swore an oath of fealty to William."

"Your father did."

"My father and I did not always agree. He hoped the king would be just."

"And you have found William not to be?"

"Hardly just, to have helpless serfs slaughtered, their huts set afire and kine stolen, I think. But then, I am not Norman, so my views may be different than William's or Sir Simon's."

"Is that how your father died, *demoiselle*? Fighting Sir Simon?"

She expelled a heavy breath that made the flames dance. "I have told you time and again—*I* set the men against Sir Simon. When he came to Wulfridge to demand that I surrender the castle and all that it contained, I refused." She shrugged. "In retaliation, he burned villages and serfs, and ravaged the lands. He thought because I was a woman, I would be frightened into yielding."

"Instead you called up an army."

"Yea, and they fought well, every one of them." Her voice quivered, and she lapsed into silence for a moment before adding softly, "They were all good men, but few were soldiers. Many of our fighting men were slain when the Danes attacked a fortnight before Sir Simon arrived. All we had left were serfs and a few vassals."

"Perhaps you should have thought of that before you pressed them into service."

"Would you have me meekly yield up what is mine? Nay, I would not, not to Sir Simon, and not to you. You are like, in that you are both arrogant and insatiable."

"You should have considered negotiation. Not even arrogant, insatiable men enjoy losing good men and horses."

"I offered Sir Simon a truce when he first came to Wulfridge. He did not take it."

Luc fell silent. It had the ring of truth to it, for he had known of Sir Simon, a pompous knight with a reputation for cruelty. After a moment, he looked up at her again, frowning. "What kind of truce did you offer?"

"What difference does that make? He slew the messenger I sent him, and returned poor Edric's ears to me with a letter demanding unconditional surrender. Until then, I had offered only token resistance, for I listened to other counsel. But when my advisers saw Sir Simon's reply, no one could argue that he would be merciful."

"If what you say is true, Ceara, then the king will make amends. But if you lie, he will be ruthless."

"And do you think the king would believe anything I might say?" She shook her head incredulously. "He will not."

"You may be surprised."

"I long ago ceased to be surprised by the nature of man, so I doubt seriously that your king can astonish me." She bent her head to concentrate on the folds of her cloak, as if they were the most important thing in the world.

Luc regarded her with reluctant compassion, an emotion that was as startling as it was aggravating. Beneath her prickly surface there was an innate dignity and hidden gentleness. The invisible armor she wore was thick enough to deflect pity and compassion from most, but there were moments in which she let down her guard. Like now, staring morosely into the flames, her tender years evident as she clung tightly to the edges of her cloak. It could not be easy for her, yet she refused to retreat, refused to swear a fealty she did not espouse. Her honor, alone, made her admirable to him. He had his fill of those too quick to swear, too quick to deceive.

It occurred to him as he watched her that perhaps he was becoming too involved with her. And when she glanced up at him with wide eyes and a tremulous smile that made his belly tighten, he knew it for certain.

Chapter Five

SPARKS FLEW UP from the fire as a log burned through with a snapping sound. In the distance, a wolf howled, its desolate cry shivering through the night. Ceara's head jerked up, and she half rose to her feet.

"It is only a wolf," Luc reassured her. "It will not come too close to our fires. They avoid man for the most part."

"And who said animals were dumb beasts?" Ceara replied in a shaky voice. Her hands trembled as she wrapped them in her cloak. Luc would not have expected this fierce little Saxon to be afraid of a wolf's cry in the night, not the same woman who had defied Sir Simon to his teeth, and offered Luc a challenge in every breath. He was almost beginning to regret the necessity of taking her to the king.

It shouldn't matter to him what happened to her, he reminded himself. But in these fearsome times it was hard for a man to keep his wits about him and remain steadfast, and for a woman to do so was even more surprising. If it was true that she had held Wulfridge against the Danes, it was an astounding feat.

"Why did word not come to William that Lord Balfour had

died?" he asked after a moment, and she turned to him with an odd look in her eyes.

"Why? 'Tis obvious, I would think."

"To you, perhaps. But I am slow. Tell me the reason."

A faint smile curved her mouth. "I swore our vassals to secrecy. Do you think I wanted to be used as a pawn? If Earls Cospatric or Edgar learned of my father's death, they would be as like to seize Wulfridge as William. When I explained it thus to Balfour's loyal vassals, they understood well enough what was at risk. Our numbers were so few after Hastings that only William's sanction had saved my father from the Scots and Danes who coveted our holdings." She shrugged. "When the time finally came when I must choose fox or weasel, I chose the least likely to ravage the lands. It seems I was mistaken."

"Not so. William would never have sent me to seize Wulfridge had you not attacked Sir Simon."

"I would not have attacked Sir Simon had he not slain my messenger, an unarmed boy of only fifteen!"

Luc frowned. He disliked complexities of this nature, for it was never simple to discover who lied. Sir Simon was dead, but there were those still alive who could tell another side to the tale, and Luc determined that he would discover the truth before he delivered this hostage to William. If she lied, she would reap the reward of her perfidy. If she did not, he would plead her cause, though he doubted she would thank him for it.

Ceara's eyes were watchful as she stared into the shadows beyond the campfires. When Luc rose to his feet, she leaped up as well, eyes mirroring the dwindling light.

"Grant me permission to tend my needs in private, my lord."

Her terse request made him hesitate. To allow her to wander alone in the wood was to invite trouble, yet there was no other woman to accompany her. Giles had relinquished temporary custody of her to Luc with obvious relief—but now he must be recalled.

"I grant you leave to tend your needs privately, but must require that you be shackled to your guard by means of a long tether, *demoiselle*."

Bright splotches of color stained her cheeks, and her eyes flashed. "Yea, I had forgotten how nervous you Normans can be in the face of such a fearsome foe as an unarmed woman, my lord. Pray, forgive my oversight and call to me the quaking guard who has plagued me with endless complaints since we left Wulfridge behind."

"There are moments you sorely test my patience, Ceara. It might be to your advantage to see both sides of the coin at times."

"All I see are two sides of a Norman coin, and neither side is pleasing to me." She held her cloak more tightly around her as the wind caught one edge and lifted it. "It is near dark. I would prefer to go while there is yet light enough not to fall down a ravine. Unless it is your goal to rid yourself of me in that manner?"

"Were I trying to rid myself of you, the sword would be more swift and less uncertain, *demoiselle*. Do not tempt me."

Luc beckoned Giles to him, and did not miss the quick glance of dislike he directed at Ceara. Unsurprising, as she surely had bedeviled the man-at-arms most unmercifully.

"When the lady has no further need of you, Giles, I would speak with you," he added after instructing him to bind her to him tightly. "Bring her back to the fire so that she may eat while we converse."

"As you wish, my lord."

By the time they returned, dark had fallen and torches lit the camp. Giles wore the expression of a man greatly harassed, and his lips were taut with anger. As usual, Ceara was coolly composed, and took a seat by the fire as if naught were amiss. When she began to pick at her food with blithe unconcern for the two men watching her, Luc led Giles to one side.

"I vow, my lord," Giles burst out in French, "she has a

tongue sharp as a blade! It does not matter what is done or not done, it is not to her liking, and her words cut a man like a sword."

"I agree that she is a bit difficult. Yet she is a woman, Giles, and a hostage. You must not allow her to bully you."

"Allow?" The word came out in a strangled croak. "I would have to kill her to stop her."

"That is not an option. Your task is to guard her so that no harm comes to her, and if you must endure hardship, you will have to deal with it as best you can. In fact, I did not wish to talk to you about the lady, but about Sir Simon. You were his man, were you not?"

Giles nodded rather sullenly. "For two years, since before we left Normandy."

"Tell me about Sir Simon's arrival at Wulfridge."

"What is it you wish to know, my lord?"

"Why were you there?"

Giles looked puzzled. "Sir Simon was bade by the king to survey and record this region of Northumbria, and to determine the intent of the barons here."

"Were there records made?"

"I would not know that, my lord. Sir Simon's clerk would be better qualified to answer that question. I do know that no inventory was made, as we were refused entry."

"Did Sir Simon negotiate with the lady to be admitted to Wulfridge?"

Giles shifted uneasily from one foot to the other. He glanced about the camp, then back at Luc. "Sir Simon was not possessed of tact, my lord. He disliked negotiations and much preferred the language of the sword. He oft said it removed the necessity of lengthy conversation."

"And did he slay a messenger sent out from Wulfridge, and cut off his ears, as I have been told?"

Reddening, Giles nodded slowly. "The messenger brought

a plea for time instead of immediate surrender, and that was Sir Simon's reply."

So Ceara had not lied. Not about that.

"You may rejoin your comrades now, Giles. I will see to the lady for the night."

Giles's relief was obvious, and he left quickly, as if afraid Luc might change his mind. The men rolled up in blankets beneath trees and small shelters of brush and limbs, but a tent had been set up for Luc's use. He smiled to see it. How quickly circumstances changed, for only a short time before he had been one of the men shivering by the fire. Now he had a tent, position, and the respect that was given a man as lord.

At the moment the tent was the most important reward, and he moved toward it. The limber walls shivered in the press of wind, stretched taut by ropes and poles. A light burned inside, a steady inviting glow.

Luc paused by the fire and held out his hand to Ceara. She stared at it warily for a moment, then rose slowly to her feet. When he did not move, she took a deep breath and gingerly placed her hand in his. He closed his fingers around her palm. "Join me in the tent, my lady."

"Do you dare risk being alone with me, my lord? I might be dangerous."

Luc laughed softly at her testy tone. "You are most definitely dangerous. But I am a man who loves a challenge, unlike poor Giles. You have terrified the man."

"Good. He is a spineless cur. I doubt he has ever used his sword for anything other than shaving, for he is as clumsy a cow as ever I have seen."

"Nevertheless, you will cease tormenting him."

"Why? It amuses me. And I have done nothing to him, save point out a few of his weaknesses. He will be a better man for it. You should thank me."

"No doubt the king himself will wish to show his appreciation for your philanthropy, but I am not so inclined." His hand tightened around her fingers in a gentle warning. "It would be to your best interests to heed my advice, *demoiselle*."

"That is debatable, but I will take it under consideration since you have asked so nicely."

Tension underscored her words, and Luc paused beneath the sputtering light of a pine torch to look at her more closely. The hood shadowed her face, but there was a quivering agitation about her that struck him.

"What is it you fear, *demoiselle*?"

"I fear nothing."

The words came quickly, much too quickly, an abrupt denial that did not ring true. His gaze sharpened. Something had unnerved her, and he did not think it was her precarious situation with the king. Did she fear being alone with him in the tent? No, not after the events of two nights before when she had all but flung herself at him. It could not be that.

"As you say, my lady. Here, step into my tent. It is much warmer out of the wind."

As he spoke he urged her toward the open tent flap with firm patience, and after a last brief resistance, she stepped just inside and stopped. It was only when he entered behind her, his body forcing her forward a step, that she moved farther inside. She turned toward him, looking as if she were poised for flight.

"I prefer sleeping outside, my lord."

"Your preference is not mine, however. There are cushions, blankets, and a skin of wine here. It would be foolish to sleep outside when it is much warmer in the tent." When she stared at him unmoving, he lifted a brow. "Do you fear I will force myself on you?"

She made a rude noise and shrugged as she began to unfasten the brooch that closed her cloak at her throat. "That is hardly one of my great concerns, my lord."

Annoyed that she would treat it so lightly, he demanded with a sharp edge to his voice, "Do you think me incapable?"

Her fingers stilled on the silver cloak pin, and she looked

up at him with a faint smile. "I am not so advanced in age that I have forgotten how . . . *capable* . . . you were on the night before last, my lord. Nor am I so blind that I could not see the size of your capabilities."

Luc stared at her, chagrined at the hot flush he could feel rising up his throat and face. "*Bon Dieu*—you dare to remind me . . . *Jésu!* Have you no shame?"

"Perhaps you have forgotten, but I was not the one who disrobed first. Is it shame only if it is not the man's idea?"

For the life of him, he could not think of a worthy response. His hands clenched and unclenched at his sides, and after a moment Ceara shrugged out of her cloak as if he were not standing there in furious, choked silence. She draped the wool garment over a small stool and moved to warm her hands at a brass brazier filled with glowing coals.

Curse her, she was so cool now, when only a moment before she had displayed such uneasiness. A changeling, with mercurial moods that always left him feeling as if he had made a misstep. It was not a familiar sensation, nor one that he relished.

"There are blankets on the floor for your use," he said abruptly. "Give me your word you will not attempt escape, and I will not bind you."

Her head came up, eyes wide and shadowed as she stared at him. The silence stretched. The wind gusted against the tent walls with a thumping sound, and the faint howl of a wolf rent the night air, closer than before.

Ceara blew out a small breath and smiled faintly. "Do not trust me, my lord, for if the chance should come, I fear that I would do what I felt I must."

He had not really expected her to promise, but it was irritating that she would not yield in even this small thing. If she would not swear to this, it was unlikely that she would swear to William. And that monarch would not take her refusal lightly.

Grimly, Luc bound her right wrist with a stout length of rope, and fastened the other end to the wooden frame of the cot erected for his use. Alone, it would never hold her, but with his weight in the cot, she would not escape.

With deliberate silence, he examined the reports his scribe had prepared for William, ignoring Ceara. If he had thought to annoy her, it seemed that she was pleased to be ignored, for she said nothing, lying upon the pile of blankets in silent contemplation of the tent ceiling. He read the neatly penned reports for some time, then glanced up.

Ceara lay in repose, her eyes closed and her hands crossed over her chest as if laid upon a funeral bier. His lips twitched with wry humor. She was either overly dramatic or hoped that he would find her dismissal of him deflating. Even more deflating was the fact that she was right. If ever there was a woman who could shake his confidence, this might be the one.

Praise God that he would not have to deal with her much longer. Once matters were set aright with William, the king would no doubt find her a suitable husband and send her off to some remote part of England where she would be of little danger to anyone, including herself.

Rising from the small, hard stool, he stretched to ease his cramped muscles, then moved to the narrow cot and lay upon it fully clothed. Morning would come much too quickly. If William were not back at York, he would have to travel on to Stafford to find him, or worse—Winchester. It would take overlong, when he was anxious to get back to Wulfridge and set about making the land profitable.

It did not escape him that if not for the stubborn courage of the girl lying so close, Wulfridge might yet be in the hands of the Saxons and he would still be a landless knight. What fate took from one, it oft gave to another.

He turned in his cot to look at Ceara in the faint glow of the lamp. She looked lovely and serene, almost vulnerable. For a moment he regretted the necessity of what he must do. But then he steeled himself. It was the way of things.

Outside, the wolf howled again, and he heard the uneasy

snorting of the horses. Then came the sound of men cursing, and a rattle of steel. The men were nervous and on guard. It was not a good night for Saxon wolves to be about.

THE LAMP GUTTERED and died. Ceara was tensely aware of Luc as she listened to his breathing slip into the even rhythm of slumber. It had seemed as if he would never tire. She was still trying to decide what to do when the mournful wail of a wolf mingled with the rising wind outside.

Slowly, Ceara slid the stolen dagger from beneath her long skirts, breathing a silent prayer of gratitude that she had been bound with a rope instead of a chain. Since they had left Wulfridge, she carried the dagger fastened to her thigh with a garter. Now with her left hand, she sawed clumsily at the thick rope binding her to the cot, careful not to tug so hard that it would jostle the frame. Curse him for tying her right hand instead of her left. It made this twice as difficult.

When she finally felt the rope fibers fray and part, she seized the freed end and wrapped it carefully around a heavy pelt. If he felt for her in the dark, he would find the rope anchored by weight instead of hanging loose.

She fumbled for her cloak in the deep shadows lightened only by the torchlight from outside the tent, pulling it clumsily about her neck. There would be time later to fasten it properly. Now she was propelled by urgency. Stealthily, her progress accompanied by the pounding of her heart, she crawled to the closed flap of the tent. A sliver of light was barely visible between the flap and floor, and with trembling fingers she managed to unfasten the buckle holding it shut. As she lifted the heavy flap, cold air whisked over her face through the narrow gap. It smelled of smoke.

Sprawled flat on her stomach, she wriggled beneath the stiff, oiled hide. Fallen leaves and dirt scraped her bare palms, and her legs tangled in the long folds of her skirt so that she had to hike it up above her knees.

Once free of the tent, she glanced up warily. Soldiers lay near dying fires and beneath brush shelters, still and quiet. The guards were posted in a circle around the camp at staggered intervals, and she paused to get her bearings. Already, she could hear the faint clink of mail and swords, and knew that they were restive. The wolf, no doubt. Guards would definitely be posted with the horses, and she must avoid going near the line where they were picketed. Fleeing on foot would hardly be easy, but she knew this country much better than did the Normans.

Newcastle was not too distant. She and Wulfric had visited the city on numerous occasions. It had been a treat for her to go to market there, and once they had traveled east of the town to an ancient priory to visit old Father Waltheof, who had instructed them in languages, sciences, and history when they were young. Wulfric had gone on to higher education, but as a female, her further education had been in matters of the house. An unhappy decision that had resulted in her first real rebellion. The result of which had been Wulfric's secret promise to teach her to use a sword. And it was a promise he had made good on until her mother discovered them practicing in the outer courtyard one afternoon. Ah, the furor that had ensued!

What would her mother say if she could see her now? Lady Aelfreda would most certainly disapprove of some of the things she had done, but Ceara could not believe her mother would disapprove of this. Not after all that had happened. And besides, she had not given him her word.

Keeping to the shadows, Ceara edged around the tent toward the river. Her knees were shaking, and she knew that disaster loomed if she were caught. But she must flee before the wolf reached camp. It was Sheba. No other wolf had that little break, the sorrowful sound like a child's sob in the midst of the lingering howl. It was only a matter of time before the wolf found her. And what would the Normans do then? Past experience had proven to her that few men were rational in the face of a snarling wolf. She could not be sure that she could keep Sheba from being harmed.

The wind was much colder by the river, blowing over the water and riffling tall grasses in a swishing sound that made her look over her shoulder. Her feet sank into the boggy ground, and water drenched her boots. She pulled one foot free with a sucking sound, and lifted her leg high to place it on firmer ground. It was so dark, with no moon to light the area: a mixed blessing. If she could not see, perhaps no one could see her.

Holding up the hem of her cloak and kirtle, she slogged along the riverbank away from the Norman camp. If Sheba was close, the wolf would be able to pick up her scent.

When she could no longer see the light from the campfires, Ceara paused, breathing hard. Then she whistled, a soft low sound like a night bird. But the only sounds in response were wind in the trees overhead, the clacking of empty branches, and the tumble of water over rocks. Her lips were dry. She wet them with the tip of her tongue and tried again.

This time, an excited yip came from close by. Straining to see through the trees and darkness, she could only make out a landscape of dark blues and dense black shapes.

Then something struck her hard between the shoulder blades with such force that she sprawled facedown amid the high weeds and twisted tree roots. She cried out involuntarily—and then realized it was Sheba, the rapturous swipes of a wet tongue on the back of her neck, cheek, and hand ample confirmation. She tried to roll over, but Sheba settled atop her in wolfish ecstasy, whining and pawing at her mistress, quivering with a blend of excitement and anxiety.

"Sheba, off . . . Sheba—*no*!"

In her pleasure, the wolf yapped like a dog, high-pitched yips stretching into vibrating moans that became howls. Suddenly terrified the noise would alert the Normans, Ceara summoned her strength and rolled over, grasping Sheba around the neck and pulling her head down to muffle the sounds. The wolf was delighted with this new game, and jerked from her hold to bound away, crouching with her front paws extended and her rear in the air. The elegant plume of her tail swished in excitement, a white flag against the black shadows surrounding them.

"Oh, Sheba, no," Ceara moaned, but the animal would not be quieted. She pranced about, throwing back her head with howls of joy that the long separation was ended.

Ceara stumbled to her knees, and Sheba pounced, huge paws knocking her backward. Normally, this would have instigated another round of play, but now Ceara gripped Sheba in a desperately tight clasp, and in her sternest voice said, "Be still!"

Sheba responded by licking her from chin to brow, still wriggling with wolfish delight. But at least she was quiet. Holding on to the animal, Ceara lurched to her feet and stood a moment, listening. No alarm had been given, no hue and cry raised. Perhaps there was hope yet.

Using her dagger, she sliced a strip of cloth from her cloak and wrapped it around Sheba's neck. It held the wolf now that she had grown calmer, and Ceara took a moment to kneel and press her face against Sheba's.

"Good girl, Sheba. Ah, I'd like to know how you found me, cony, but I'm glad you did. Come along."

"Come" was familiar, and Sheba aimed another loving swipe of her tongue, rising on her hind legs to drape her paws over Ceara's shoulders as she had done since she was a pup. It knocked Ceara slightly off balance, and she flung out a hand to steady herself against the ground.

As she did, Sheba jerked away with a snarl. Startled, Ceara heard nothing else until a voice said from the shadows, "Be calm, and I will slay the beast."

Luc. And he thought—

"No!" Ceara lunged for Sheba, who had gone into the low stalking position she used before she attacked. The wolf's throaty growl rose into the air as she eluded her mistress. "Sheba—to me!"

The snapped command was all she could think to do, with Luc separating from the darker shadows around him, dull light glittering along the sharp edge of his drawn sword. The wolf she could stop, but Luc listened to no one.

He came forward with lifted sword, and Sheba did not retreat. The wolf stood in front of Ceara, her snarls growing louder and fiercer. But against the sword, she had little chance, and it was apparent that she would not leave her mistress.

"My lord, please . . . do not kill her. . . ." Ceara's plea was almost a sob, but Luc paused. Kneeling on the ground, she put her arms around Sheba and tried to control the agitated wolf.

Stroking her, whispering soothing words in one breath and broken pleas in the other, Ceara held tightly to her beloved pet.

"You plead for a wolf?"

"Yea, my lord, I do. She is my pet. I do not know how she found me, but she is here . . . please, my lord. Do not slay her. She is all I have left of Wulfric."

Silence greeted her. It grew long before Luc asked abruptly, "Who is Wulfric?"

She closed her eyes. Why had she mentioned him? This Norman would never understand. Not a man like him, so full of confidence and arrogant virility.

But Luc would not be stayed, and demanded more harshly: "Who is Wulfric?"

Ceara opened her eyes, and stood slowly, keeping one hand on the wolf still crouched warily between them.

"My husband."

Chapter Six

"It seems, my lady," Luc managed to say calmly, "that you are as full of lies as you are tricks. You swore you were virgin, yet now you say you are married."

She shook her head, and her pale hair gleamed softly in the faint blue light. "Nay, lord. Wulfric is dead."

"A fine distinction." He eyed the wolf a moment, the white beast whose howls had put the entire camp in chaos. Two horses had broken free and fled into the night, and his men were forced to go after them—putting them in unnecessary danger in unfamiliar territory.

Taking a step back, he gestured with his sword. "Do you have a way of containing the beast? If you do not, I will be forced to slay it."

"Aye, my lord. I do. A leather belt would hold her—"

"As you no doubt can see, I did not pause to don my usual garments and armor. Use something else." A cold wind blew through his thin sherte and linen chausses. He hefted his naked blade in his hand, impatient and angry and oddly grieved that she had so boldly lied to him, and that he had been fool enough to believe her.

"I beg pardon, my lord. I . . . did not notice. I have a strip of cloth somewhere close." She dropped to her hands and knees and felt around on the ground. The wolf continued to eye him warily and make low threatening noises that did nothing to contribute to his good temper. Just when he was ready to bring up his sword, Ceara straightened.

"I found it. She will not harm you, my lord, not if I tell her not to. I swear it." Crouched beside the beast, her face and hair a pale haze in the dim light, Ceara stared up at him as she slid the cloth strip around the wolf's neck and crooned soothing sounds that could only lead him to believe that she was not at all certain the wolf would not attack.

"Do not be misled," he said harshly. "I may yet slay the beast. It matters not if she is your pet if she attacks my horses or men."

"She will not, I swear—"

"Your sworn word does not carry the weight it might have earlier, *demoiselle*."

His clipped response silenced her immediately, and Ceara bent her head to finish restraining the wolf. When she was finished, she rose slowly to her feet and with great dignity and poise she said, "Shall I walk ahead of you, my lord?"

"At sword point." He hefted his weapon and she strode past him, half dragging the reluctant wolf.

Their arrival in camp brought instant pandemonium, and Luc bellowed an order for his men to fall into file. Grumbling, they lined up in various stages of undress, eyeing the wolf.

"It is a tame wolf, by the lady's account, so I do not want it yet destroyed." Luc heard Ceara's muffled sound of distress, but did not even glance toward her. "I want two volunteers to fashion a cage for the beast, built of sturdy wood that will keep it confined."

"A cage!" Ceara burst out, for the English and French words were the same. "She is not to be kept in a cage—"

He turned to her. "If you want her alive, she will be caged. It is your choice, my lady."

After a short pause, she nodded shortly. "Of course, my lord. A cage will keep your poor men safe enough, I think."

"Do not try my patience, for I think your wolf will regret it more than you," he said softly, and her anxious gaze flicked up to him. Light from the recently stoked fire slanted across her face so that he could see the impact of his words. He was satisfied that she believed him.

"Yea, lord. I understand."

"A bit late, I think." Luc turned away sharply and beckoned to the two men who had reluctantly stepped forward. "Build the cage quickly, and place it on one of the carts. I want nothing to impede our swift progress to the king."

"As you wish, my lord." The speaker hesitated, and glanced at the wolf nervously. Sheba obliged him by showing her teeth in a fearsome snarl that made him take two steps back and turn to Luc, his face white. "Must we also put the wolf into the cage?"

"The lady will do that. For now, bring me a stout length of chain to bind the animal."

He half expected another protest from Ceara, but she said nothing when he bade her chain the wolf to a thick tree and added, "If it flees, I will send men to kill it."

Still silent, she nodded and knelt beside the animal, whispering to it and stroking the huge head. In the firelight, he could see that the wolf was almost entirely white, save for faint streaks of brown along the back and on the tips of the ears. In contrast to her matted fur, the tail was thick and bushy, a graceful fan that swished back and forth as Ceara spoke. To his irritated surprise, the wolf lavished a sloppy tongue across her face, then threw back its head and emitted a long, gurgling howl. Immediately, the horses began to shrill frantically, and he heard his men cursing.

"If you wish for a swift fate, my lady, you will encourage the animal in that madness."

"She cannot help it. She's a wolf. Wolves howl."

"I will not have my horses running all over northern England because you cannot control your pet. Either silence the beast, or my sword will."

Urgency thickened her voice as Ceara took the wolf's head between her hands and gave it a slight shake. "Stop it, Sheba. Be still. Be *still*!"

The wolf hung its head, ears splayed to the sides. Despite his reservations and his anger, Luc could not help being somewhat bemused by the relationship between Ceara and this savage beast her husband had given her.

Wulfric . . . her husband. . . .

"Leave the beast, now, my lady. We must discuss a certain matter."

She looked up at him and took a deep breath. "Yea, my lord, we must. May I beg a morsel for Sheba? She's so thin, she must not have eaten for days."

"I suppose a well-fed wolf is less dangerous." Even while he gave the order for a joint of mutton left from their evening meal to be tossed to the wolf, he wondered why he had not just slain it. It would be much less trouble. Yet it was obvious this creature meant a great deal to Ceara, and nothing else had brought her to her knees. If a wolf could accomplish what he could not, then it might well be worth the trouble, after all.

With great reluctance, Ceara left the wolf and walked to the tent, her feet dragging. The hem of her cloak hung at an odd angle, and the pretty blue kirtle she wore was wet and stained, torn in two places. Even her boots were ruined.

Once inside, Ceara moved swiftly to the far wall and turned to glare at him, grim and wide-eyed with apprehension. Her arms were crossed over her chest, and her chin was lifted in a gesture he'd come to recognize, while her mouth was set in a taut, stubborn line.

He did not delay. "You have tried to play me for a fool, my lady. That does not set well with me."

"My lord—"

He put up a hand to forestall her excuses. "Do not bother concocting another wild tale. It is not me that you will have to tell. But you had best invent another, more plausible tale for the king, for he will not so easily swallow such a lie."

"It is no lie. You never asked if I was married."

Caught between incredulity and anger, Luc stared at her. "Perhaps you have told so many lies you've forgotten this one, but you said plainly that you were virgin. Normally, a damsel does not remain virgin after marriage, unless Saxons have found a new way to circumvent that."

"No, my lord, but—"

Anger overrode restraint, and Luc was in front of her in two strides, grabbing her by the upper arms to give her a vicious shake. "If you dare tell me some ridiculous tale of virginity after bedding, I will not be responsible for what I do."

His rough handling had whipped the hair into her eyes, and the look she gave him through the bright tangled strands was dark with defiance. "It's true."

"Jésu!" Because he was so near to losing control, he released her with a shove, sending her stumbling backward. "Tell me this—how long were you wed before he died?"

"That is not the point, my lord, for you see—"

"How long, my lady?"

At the menace in his tone, she snapped, "Three years."

"Three years." He repeated the words slowly, clasping his hands behind his back to keep from wrapping them around her deceitful neck. "Yet you expect me to believe that he did not bed you."

"I did not say we did not share a bed, only that—"

"By all the saints, if you finish that sentence I will make you sorry." He inhaled deeply, but the rage that had been building up in him since she had blurted out her husband's name did not fade. "This, of course, explains many things that puzzled me," he said when he could speak calmly. "Few untried maids are so casual about a man's body as you were. Or as casual about their own. I should not have been surprised by your offer or—"

He broke off, raking her mutinous face with a slow, assessing gaze before saying softly, "But perhaps I have misjudged. Since you were so willing before, my lady, I see no reason to delay. I intended to avail myself of the favors of *une putain* when I reached York, but why wait? After all, you are here and it has been a long time."

Clad only in his chausses, boots, and linen sherte, it would not take him long to disrobe, and he eyed her startled face with bleak satisfaction. "What? No coy pretense? No bold acceptance? Which are you, Ceara of Wulfridge, whore or maid?"

She watched him uncertainly, her eyes moving to his bare chest as he tossed aside his linen sherte, then back to his face when his hands dropped to the cross-garters that held up his chausses.

"You would not dare—"

"Oh, yes, Ceara, I would most certainly dare." Holding her gaze, he untied his chausses and let them drop to the floor, then kicked free of his boots. "Come along, wench. Disrobe for me, as you did last time. I wish to see what I have bartered for."

"Bartered!" The word came out in an explosive rasp. "I am no bread loaf to be haggled over!"

"True. But neither are you the virgin you pretended to be. One more man can hardly make a difference to you, and since 'tis you who began this game, I shall be the one to end it. Now remove your clothing."

She flung up a hand when he tucked his thumbs into the waist of his loincloth, her mouth trembling a little. "Do not pursue this further, my lord. There is something I must explain—"

"No. No more lies." In a swift motion, he removed his loincloth and cast it aside to stand boldly before her. Ceara stood as if frozen. He had been such a fool, refusing to take her because she was an untried maid. How she must have laughed at him. But she would not laugh now. Now, he intended to humble her. Her shame would be small penance for the trouble she had caused him, for the past two nights when he had lain awake and restless, his body afire with need for her, the memory of her unclad curves and sultry promise scalding him.

"Well?" he demanded. "Do you not wish to disrobe for me? Please, go slowly, *ma biche*, as I wish to savor the moment. Ofttimes, the anticipation will enhance the act, much as fine wine is best when it has aged."

"Do not speak of me as if I am a course for your table."

"Ah, but are you not? Come. Begin, my lady, for I am growing impatient."

With trembling fingers, she at last began to draw up her skirts. His gaze shifted to the long expanse of her bare leg as the hem rose higher and higher above the tops of her boots. She bent slightly from the waist, hair falling forward in a tangled curtain that momentarily blocked his view, and when she straightened, he saw the dagger in her fist. Not just any dagger—but his dagger, the one he had not been able to find before leaving Wulfridge. Alain had wasted much time searching for it before admitting that it was lost. Luc grew still, his voice harsh.

"Do not be foolish, Ceara."

"It is you who are foolish if you think I intend to undress and spread myself at your demand, Norman." The dagger quivered slightly in her grip. "What I do of my own accord is my affair, but I will not be told I must allow you to . . . to—" She drew in a sharp breath. "I will not be used like a common whore."

"That is your choice, my lady. I also have a choice." He calmly crossed his arms over his chest, and lifted a brow with studied indifference. "Poor Sheba. It would be a shame to have to kill the wolf because of your lies, do you not think?"

Not even the rosy glow of the lamp could add color to her

suddenly bloodless face, and she made a small, choked sound. "Nay . . . you would not."

He shrugged. "That is your choice."

"You will not harm her if I yield?"

"When I give my word, 'tis kept. Unlike even those few Saxons who profess honesty."

The dagger wavered, and with a sound of defeat, she threw it hard across the tent. It struck the far wall and clattered atop a small wooden chest. "Curse you. Curse you. . . ." The final word ended on a strangled note as she began to unfasten the pin at her throat.

Then the red cloak crumpled to a puddle at her feet. Luc waited. Defiantly, she tugged fiercely at the side laces of her kirtle, tossing it atop the cloak when it came free. Clad now in her undergarment, the longer gunna that reached to her ankles—she faced him with obvious contempt. It should have affected him, but it did not. She had already proven herself to be a liar. And he did not want to examine his motives too closely. Her trespass had surely freed him from the strictures that bade him not to persecute a captive.

"Does it not matter to you that I am unwilling?" Ceara flung at him as she shrugged out of the gunna, her words muffled by a length of linen.

Luc did not reply. Clad now only in lamplight and her boots, Ceara briefly held the gunna to her breast, then with slow deliberation, let it slide the length of her body to join her other garments. She was more lovely than even his fevered dreams recalled. The high, proud thrust of her breasts was firmly round, crowned with taut peaks of deep rose hue. Slender waist, gently curved hips, and a softly mounded belly tapered to slim thighs and shapely calves that disappeared into the tops of her cuffed leather boots.

Luc forgot his intention to humble her. He could not have resisted the urge to move to her, trace the rosy peaks of her breasts with his finger, then weigh the fullness in his palm. She drew in a sharp breath and closed her eyes, quivering.

"You are afraid, *ma belle*? You have nothing to fear from me. I do not want a quaking maiden, but a woman well versed in love." He raked his thumb across her nipple and she shivered. "See, it is not so bad to yield, even if only for the moment."

At that her lashes lifted and she shot him an accusing glance that spoke volumes. "I have not yielded. I am being forced."

"No, it is your choice."

"Yea, if I would lose my beloved pet, I could refuse. You know I will not."

"Then see? 'Tis your choice, as I said." Before she could protest again, he bent his head to her breast, tasting skin that smelled of lavender and smoke. Against the cushioned swell of her breast, he murmured, "You have much to learn about bartering one thing against the other, *ma belle*."

She was soft and smooth beneath his palms as he slid his hands over the ribbed expanse and down to her waist, to cup her hips and pull her against him. A soft moan vibrated in the back of her throat, an echo of the wolf's earlier cry. A curling tendril of blond hair slithered over her shoulder to tickle his cheek, and he lifted his head to gaze down at her. The throbbing ache in his loins grew more intense as she put the heels of her hands against his chest to lean back and away, her hips pushing into him as she sought his gaze.

"You mistake the moment if you think I barter, my lord." Her naked flesh pressed seductively against his, and his body responded.

"Then this is a surrender?" Half suspecting a trick and unwilling to face further struggle, his arms tightened around her unresisting body.

"Nay . . . a tactical retreat, perhaps."

The blood thundered through his veins as she traced an imaginary path over his chest with her fingertip, then blew softly on his skin. Luc could wait no longer. He pushed her back toward the narrow cot, half carrying her when she suddenly went boneless. Her long lithe form draped gracefully from his arms, an enticing blend of erotic sensation and intriguing resistance.

"Your battle is lost, *ma chérie*," he breathed against the sweet curve of her throat and shoulder, and felt her shuddering sigh.

"Is it?" Her arms had curled around his neck when he lifted her, reflexively he'd thought, but now they tightened. He bent his head back to look down at her. A provocative smile curved her mouth, and the sweep of her lashes lowered, teasing. In her soft, husky voice, she murmured, "Beware of claiming victory too soon, my lord, for you may yet wonder who has won after all."

Driven by both need and determination, Luc dismissed her words as another bluff. She was as full of them as a forest was trees, one coming right after the other in an unending litany. Yet nothing mattered now except the moment and the woman, the urgency of his desire and her sudden capitulation.

Aflame now, he took her down to the cot with his weight, his hungry mouth covering her parted lips with a fervor he had never known could exist. This was no detached lust, but an encompassing, mindless need that smothered everything but the burning desire to make her his.

Kissing her closed eyes, her moist mouth, and the arch of her throat, he wedged his knees between her thighs and moved them apart, urgency riding him so hard he could think only of release. Rose petal-soft skin lured him to caress her everywhere—the enticing curve of her breasts and dip of her belly, the pale glossy threads on her woman's mound, and the arousing, damp heat between her thighs.

Ceara moaned. Her breath came in harsh pants, and she twisted restlessly beneath him as he lavished attention on her lush curves. When his mouth closed over the tight peak of her nipple she cried out, grasping him by the upper arms to hold tightly. With his hand stroking her soft mound and his mouth moving from one breast to the other, he paused to lave the scented valley between with his tongue, and she responded with urgent little noises that spurred his own desire.

Murmuring French endearments in a thick, rasping voice, Luc lowered his body on hers to sheathe himself in her warmth, his weight resting on his bent arms. She arched upward, hips meeting his slow thrust even while a soft cry escaped her and her fingers dragged down his bare arms.

Ah, she was so tight and hot, so exquisite that for a moment he did not comprehend the message behind her sudden, sharp cry of pain. Yet even as he drove into her again, he realized the significance, and immediately went still. With his head down, the muscles in his arms shaking with reaction and strain, he tried to speak and couldn't.

Slowly, he pushed himself up and lifted his head to stare down at her pale face incredulously. So it was true. She had not lied about this, at least.

His voice a muffled croak, he finally rasped, "Damn you—you are a virgin."

"Nay, my lord, I *was* a virgin. . . ."

Chapter Seven

LUC LAY ON his back with his forearm thrown across his brow, staring up at the tent's ceiling. His jaw was set, and his dark eyes were carefully blank. "Tell me," he said coldly, "why a wife wed three years would still be virgin."

Ceara did not reply. She couldn't. The raw shock of their recent encounter had left her limp, with frayed emotions that threatened to dissolve into a flood of tears. Inexplicably, she wanted to press her face into Luc's chest and feel him hold her. Inexplicably, he had pulled her to him without being asked, tenderly stroking the hair from her misted face and muttering in French that he had made a damned mistake.

Her urge to weep was entirely expected, she supposed, but a weakness she detested. The evening's events left her shaken and uncertain of herself, or what she might do.

How could she have lost control with this man? But she had. Once her anger faded, she realized this was exactly what she had wanted from him. Easy enough then, to play the part of a whore, to undress slowly and deliberately, to entice him with her smile and eyes. His body had already betrayed his desire, but she had not expected her body to do likewise.

For she had found herself responding in a way she'd never dreamed. The exquisite sensations of his hands on her body, his mouth on her breasts, and his fingers sliding over the aching center of her had ignited an explosive response that whirled her into mindless oblivion. Until that sharp, stabbing pain had wrung a shocked cry from her, she had forgotten herself that she was still virgin.

After that, the lovely haze of fiery need had melted under Luc's recriminations as he rolled off her and to one side. Night air quickly cooled steamy skin, and it was Luc who leaned over to throw the covers over them.

Ceara worried the blanket's tattered edge between her fingers and tried not to look at him, but the urge to peer at him from beneath her lashes was irresistible. They still lay on the narrow cot, bodies pressed against each other, though Luc had his arms thrown back over his head. A magnificent creature, really, with his hard-muscled body and beguiling kisses. *Madness, to think of that now. . . .* She edged away from him with an agitated mutter, and he put a hand on her shoulder to hold her.

"It is not a difficult question, Ceara. Answer me. With the truth, if you value all that is dear to you."

She didn't need further explanation of that ominous threat this time, and shrugged before answering, "Wulfric and I grew up together. He was fostered by my father after his parents were killed in a Danish raid when we were both small children. I thought of him as my brother."

"I won't mention the vague laws of the church about consanguinity at this point, but it's something to consider once you meet with the king. Do you have a natural brother?"

"No. My father always longed for a son, but my mother was . . . frail. I was all she could give him for an heir, and he would not do as some other man might have done and go to another woman. He loved my mother dearly. . . ." Her voice trailed into pained silence while she composed herself.

"Am I to believe that you lived together as brother and sister, as adults as well as children?"

" 'Tis the truth." She cleared her throat. "For years Wulfric and I played together, studied together—there was a monk who stayed a time at Wulfridge, and taught us lessons in Greek and Latin, as well as history." Her mouth twisted wryly. "As a female, of course my studies were not taken seriously. Wulfric excelled in everything, but he was best at military strategy. He and my father would plot campaigns well into the night, always imaginary, as Wulfric was yet a boy. Yet those imaginary battles were enough that Balfour recognized him as a brilliant strategist. It was that, I think, that endeared him to my father. More than the fact that his inherited lands were vast and adjoined our estate."

"Ah, so Balfour married you to him and increased his holdings. But why a foster brother? Why not one of his stronger vassals? Wulfric's lands could not have been that vast."

She turned and met Luc's gaze. "I would have none of them, and my father knew that. He despaired of ever making me a suitable match, for you see, it was rumored that I could be rather . . . difficult."

"Je n'en suis pas surpris." Some of the tension eased from Luc's eyes, and the suggestion of a smile tugged at one corner of his mouth. "But obviously you did not object to wedding Wulfric."

"I was very young, just twelve at the time, and thought only of the way Wulfric and I would always be together. Matters of the flesh did not occur to me, and because Wulfric was older and loved me, he waited. He refused to consummate the marriage. At the time, I thought my age was the only reason."

Luc frowned slightly. "I take that to mean there was another reason he did not consummate."

"Yes." She hesitated. The memory was still painful to her, still made her cheeks hot with remembered anguish and trembling guilt. But she could not tell Luc that, could not tell him how she had disappointed brave Wulfric. Or how she had always loved him—though not in the way he wished. He'd known it, too well, with sadness in his fine eyes and the wistful curve of his mouth. . . . *I know you will never love me as I do you, Ceara, but that is all right. Just love me the best you can, and it will be enough.* . . . But it had not been enough. Not enough to keep him alive.

Ceara chose her words carefully. "I always thought Wulfric the most beautiful boy in the world, and he was. When we were children, it did not matter that he was not very tall, but as I grew taller I saw that he did not, and his body became twisted with a wasting disease." Here she faltered, and unshed tears thickened her voice. "He was so brave. I never heard him complain, even though there were those who scorned him. He never gave them the satisfaction of acknowledging his pain. Ah, he was so fine, with a face like an angel. Eyes the blue-green of jewels and fine hair the color of moonlight . . . when he died my father said he was just too pure and noble to remain in this world."

"So he did not die in battle."

She tried to laugh, but the sound was strangled. "Oh, but he did. It was the Danes . . . they came in their long ships, gliding up the coast to ravage the countryside. My father was away—trouble with the Scots to the north—and Wulfric insisted upon leading men to protect Wulfridge. He planned a brilliant strategy, dividing our forces and tricking them into chasing our men toward a wooded glen where he waited with more warriors . . . but it was there that he fell, slain with a sword in his hand as he had always said he wanted. And his plan worked—our men were able to turn back the invaders and save Wulfridge."

She tried to draw in a deep breath, but her throat ached and she felt as if a huge stone were crushing her chest. Even now, after four long years, grief had the power to undo her. For she knew as surely as if she had held the sword, she had killed him. His inability to consummate their marriage had been his destruction. After that, he had sought death eagerly, sought his redemption as a valiant warrior. And died for it. If it had not been for her . . .

As the silence stretched between them, she began to wish she had not confided in this man. After all, he was the enemy, was he not? Why had she blurted out her heart's ache?

Slowly, Luc said, "Your husband sounds like a noble man, as your father said. Not every man is able to die as he wishes. It was a blessing for him."

Ceara wished she felt the same. But Wulfric's death had left so huge a void in her life that it was still impossible for her to see it that way. She was too selfish. That was what Kyna, her old nurse, had said.

"Every day he was in pain, yet you wanted him here only for you," Kyna scolded. "Did you not care that 'twas an agony for him to rise of a morn, or to dress, or to pretend that he was well so you would be happy? Ah, selfish child, one day you will grow up and realize that real love is not based on how someone else makes you happy, but how happy you make each other."

"I made Wulfric happy!" she cried, but Kyna scoffed.

"Yea, I always noted how pleased he looked when you insisted he accompany you on long rides, or treks over fen and moor with that dangerous wolf he gave you—yet you never saw it."

It was appalling to realize Kyna was right, and for weeks after she'd been inconsolable. And then had come the grief, then anger, then blame. In a desperate attempt to seek solace, she had visited an old crone in a hut down by the sea. There, she had sat upon a woven mat of grass and let the winds blow her hair into tangles as she watched the crone throw the Runes. But this time the prophecy stones did not answer her questions about the future—or the past, for the crone was bent more on prophecy than answering her anguished questions. *"The wolf will bring great grief and strife to the land, but after there will come peace for a time, and with it—love. Great love, m'lady, and the lifelong loyalty of a wolf will be yours. . . ."*

Ridiculous prophecy, but uncannily accurate in some ways. William of Normandy had come, ravaging the country like a wolf though most men called him the lion, and grief and strife had come with him. But the time of peace had not arrived, though it had been over three years since William landed near Hastings at Pevensey and slew Harold on Senlac Hill. Long years, years of terror and apprehension, and still no sign of peace. Save for the loyalty of her wolf, the prophecy was empty.

CEARA TRIED NOT to look at Luc. He rode at the head of the line, beneath the banner carried by his standard bearer, and she gazed at it resentfully. Already he had created his baronial arms, and a black wolf fluttered on a red field, proclaiming him lord of Wulfridge. A new standard, a new day, a new lord. What would become of her?

It was midafternoon, and the town of York lay just ahead. So much could happen, and though Luc seemed to think William would be merciful once he heard of Sir Simon's provocation, she had none of his faith.

Of William she knew only what she had seen along the journey from Wulfridge: Once thriving villages lay in charred ruins, surrounded by black-stubbled fields and the bones of slaughtered cattle lying in massive heaps that bespoke the Norman definition of mercy. Glimpses of the population were few, as any who saw the approach of Norman knights fled for their lives. It grieved and infuriated her that so many had suffered so much.

As if sensing her reaction, Luc kept his distance. It was Giles who received the brunt of her anger, his leering smirks and suggestive comments pushing her to release her pent-up fury.

"Norman swine," she hissed when he demanded she keep her mount at a pace with the rest, "do not speak to me of haste. Nor more of your apish friend Alain. I have no regard for him, so do not tell me of his affection for me."

Giles's jaw set, and behind the metal nose guard of his helm, his gray eyes were flinty. "I told Alain he was mad, but he would have me give you his message. A pity Sir Simon did not slay you instead of the messenger."

"He had not the courage to do that," she retorted with narrowed eyes. "Just as you have not mettle enough to deal with a woman, but must run to Sir Luc at every chance. I vow, within the hour you will be whining to him of your ill treatment at my hands, and how I abuse you."

Giles tightened his hold on one end of the chains about her waist, lifting them with a slight, threatening clink. "If I were Sir Luc, instead of binding you with these chains, I would have you riding in that cage with the wolf, for the two of you are like."

"You are not half—nay, one quarter—the man Sir Luc is, so do not prate to me of what you would do. No doubt you would be trembling beneath a hawthorn hedge at the very thought of facing Sheba."

"Sheba." Scorn dripped from the word. "A noble name for a scruffy, ill-kempt beast. Sir Luc should have slain it at once. It makes the horses nervous."

"You mean it makes *you* nervous." Ceara gripped her reins tightly in both hands to keep from slapping Giles with them. Luc had warned her she must not strike the soldier again.

Luc. Sir Luc. *Lord* Luc. Aye, he would be lord of Wulfridge once William granted him the lands as he had promised. And she would have no claim on a stone of it, nor a blade of grass, nor even a clod of dirt. The land that had been in her family since the time of the Romans would belong to an invader. Danes, Scots, and Vikings had been repelled time and again, and now the Normans had succeeded.

Giles nudged his mount close, until he was level with Ceara and his face was just inches from hers. "When you reach the king, he will give you your just reward, I hope. And I will see that Alain receives the message you sent him. You will lose all, *putain*."

Luc's stern warning forgotten, Ceara slashed out, catching the man-at-arms hard across his mouth with the straight edge of her palm. The blow caught him by surprise and he reeled backward. As his spurs grazed his mount's sides, the startled beast sprang forward with a shrill whinny of alarm. Dropping the end of Ceara's chain, Giles grabbed for his reins and let out a bellow of dismay that spurred his horse even faster. She watched with grim satisfaction as the floundering soldier tried to regain his balance and control of his horse, half on, half off the beast, one rein dragging as the panicked animal fled down the narrow path in a thundering rush of hooves and damp earth.

It was vengeance enough that Giles looked the fool, and she kept her mount at an even pace, watching with feigned innocence when Luc turned in his saddle to see the cause of the commotion behind him. He glanced immediately from Giles to her, the expression on his face relaying his irritation.

Turning his mount, Luc rode past Giles—who by this time had managed to right himself and control his horse—reaching Ceara much too quickly. "What have you done to him this time, or need I ask?"

She shrugged. "The reports of fine Norman horsemanship are greatly exaggerated, I believe. Giles is an excellent example of how one should not believe rumors."

"You try my patience, Ceara."

Though his tone was level, it held an edge of controlled anger that left her uneasy. She switched to another tactic. "I most humbly beg your pardon, my lord. I was provoked by Giles to reckless behavior. He called me a whore, and that privilege I reserve for you."

Behind her words lay a double-edged sword, as she well knew. Luc had declared her inviolate to his men, and for one of them to overstep the boundaries required action. Yet had he not set her up as a whore? Every man in camp must have heard their struggle that night in the tent, heard the cry that would be correctly interpreted. And worse—by insulting a lady under Luc's protection, Giles had insulted Luc. What sweet vengeance.

Luc's face reflected his immediate grasp of both the insult and the violation of his authority. But there was no time for her to savor her triumph, for he leaned from his huge destrier to snatch her horse's reins and the end of the chain dangling from her waist.

"We will discuss this with Giles when we reach York. Until then, you will ride at my side, and I do not think you foolish enough to try with me the tricks you've played with him."

"You do not know the whole of it, my lord."

"I will soon enough. If you think to try my patience, you have succeeded. Enjoy the fruits of your labors, *demoiselle*."

The wealth of anger in his words was enough to keep her wisely silent, even when they passed Giles and Luc snapped an order for him to fall into rank. "See if you can manage your horse better than you can an unarmed woman," he added in scathing French. "And pray that you did not ignore my commands, as she claims."

"Dieu m'en garde. . . ." Giles's protest came out in a choked moan that Luc ignored, and the man-at-arms flashed Ceara a furious look that none could misinterpret.

Ceara thought that honest hatred was much better than his pretense of friendly conspiracy, his whispered words repeated from the squire Alain that left her filled with loathing and disquiet. At least now she would no longer have to counter his vague suggestions, nor suffer his resentment for her well-placed contempt. He was a worm, just like the squire who had assigned him to guard her, and she trusted neither of them. Had Giles not been Sir Simon's man? Yea, and no doubt he too thought that Saxons were to be used and discarded at will, like old shoes.

Ceara gripped the high pommel of her saddle, uneasy at Luc's swift pace. He did not look at her, but held tightly to her reins so that the fat little gray mare had to work hard to keep up with the longer strides of the huge black destrier he rode. Even when they reached the front of the line, Luc slowed his pace just enough so that the mare no longer sounded winded.

A brisk breeze was blowing, chilling her cheeks and exposed hands and tugging at the loose edges of her cloak. She tucked one edge of the material beneath her knee, keeping a hand firmly on the pommel so that she did not tumble from the saddle, and then secured the other edge. It kept her cloak from blowing wildly behind her, and kept her legs warmer. Though as she rode astride like a man, her skirts now came up almost to her knees.

There was a sharp tug around her waist from the chain and she looked up to see Luc staring at her. His dark eyes regarded her with something akin to conjecture. Her heart thumped against her ribs. Would he admit to his attraction for her and agree to take her to wife? If her eavesdropping was a guarantee, he was not wedded and she would eagerly agree to marry him if Wulfridge was the prize. Of course, it was no longer her dowry, but to be assured that she could return to her home. . . .

Luc looked forward again, and released his tight hold on the chain so that it did not pull on her. Ceara chewed her lower lip, clinging to the saddle and wishing she knew what to say. God help her, she was as attracted to him as he was to her. If he was anyone but a Norman—but that was foolish. He was what he was, just as she was what she was. He had told her plainly that lust meant nothing more to him than release, even when the woman was virgin.

Though he had not touched her since, nor betrayed by word or glance that he wanted her, she knew differently. He had already broken his own rule to have her, and despite what he vowed, there was an invisible bond between them, a tension as charged as a lightning bolt. She felt it as palpably as she felt the jolting pace of the mare she rode.

Time was closing fast upon her. She must make Luc admit his desire for her before he delivered her to the king, and she might yet see Wulfridge again. But if he would not, another plan had come to her in the early hours before the sun rose.

She glanced at him, studying his dark profile and rigid pose. He was still angry, of course. That was hardly conducive to achieving her goal. But at least she was riding with him now instead of Giles, a distinct improvement. If only she were one of those women adept at flirtation, with lowered lashes and winsome smile, the cajolery that seemed to come so naturally to some but eluded her understanding. It was not in her nature to be vague, for she was better suited to directness. Still. She must find a way to charm him, or at the least disarm him.

"My lord? A moment please . . . my cloak has become tangled and I am like to fall. . . ."

Luc swiveled to cast a frowning glance toward her. He eased the pace as Ceara indicated the cloak tucked beneath her leg. "It does not seem so dire as to dismount you, *demoiselle*."

"But I can hardly keep my balance, as both sides are caught . . . please assist me, my lord."

Leaning from his mount, Luc grasped the edge of her cloak and gave it a sharp tug that freed the red wool. The hem of her blue kirtle had ridden up to expose her leg and thigh. His hand lingered, eyes riveted on the sweep of bare flesh. She did not attempt to push down her skirt, but pretended interest in the clasp holding her cloak at the throat. The horses' pace had slowed to a walk. Luc slowly straightened, removing his hand as he glanced up at her face.

Ceara smiled and lifted her shoulders in a helpless shrug. "The pin has jammed on my cloak, and is sticking me. Do you mind, my lord?"

Luc's mouth thinned, but he silently halted the horses and leaned forward to repin the brooch. "If your cloak causes you this much trouble, perhaps you should remove it," he muttered, but there was no anger in his voice. His large hands fumbled with the pin for several moments. Soldiers passed them on the narrow road, directed onward with a jerk of Luc's head.

"Bon Dieu!" he grumbled. "I am not a lady's maid. The pin seems to be bent—ah, I have it."

He fastened the pin and straightened, hands grazing the swell of her breasts as he smoothed the cloak. He stilled, eyes flashing up to her face, then dropped his hands.

"God's mercy for your kindness, my lord." She smiled, but did not attempt to flutter her lashes. He would see through that ruse right away. "I do not deserve your kindness when I have caused you so much trouble."

"True." His brow lifted. "But I think that Giles also is to blame for the dissension."

"I fear that is true, my lord. He—"

"Not now. As I said, I will learn the truth when we reach York."

Her disappointment must have shown, for he laughed softly and leaned close again, taking up her mare's reins. "If this was to sway me to your side, *demoiselle,* all it has done is remind me how soft your skin is, and how you taste of lavender."

She managed not to show her delight, but feigned a resigned shrug. "You are much too clever for me, my lord."

"You should have realized by now that I am well accustomed to the teasing tricks of a woman."

As they eased back into the line of soldiers, Ceara regarded him curiously. "You must have known many women, my lord."

"Not as you mean." His voice hardened, and a muscle leaped in his lean jaw. "The women of my acquaintance are for one purpose only."

"No fond memories of mother or sister? No first love?"

The look he sent her was cold and hostile. "None."

Taken aback, Ceara retreated to silence. There was a wealth of undertones in that one word and she did not care to examine them too closely. It could only hurt her purpose to remind him of unpleasant companions at this time. So she managed a faltering smile, a shrug of one shoulder, and a flash of bare leg as she daintily arranged the folds of her skirts. It did not go unnoticed.

Luc angled a glance in her direction before turning to stare straight ahead again. There was a tense set to his shoulders and a taut slant to his mouth that could mean anything, and Ceara wondered if she had made a misstep again. It was possible.

When they reached a bend in the road, Luc broke from the ranks and rode to the front, bringing Ceara with him. She glanced back once to reassure herself that the cart bearing Sheba was still with them, and glimpsed the supine form of the white wolf behind wooden bars. The glimpse of her loyal friend imprisoned renewed her determination to win back Wulfridge and a semblance of her former life.

Her hands trembled slightly. The closer they drew to York, the nearer they came to the moment when her fate would be decided. Yet how could she win Luc's assistance when every step she made was wrong? It was agonizingly clear that he did not intend to wed anyone—much less the woman who had held his men at bay, then put her sword to his throat when he gained entry to the castle.

Distress brought tears to her eyes, and she bent as if to tie a boot lace so none would see her weakness. Under guise of straightening her cloak, she surreptitiously wiped away a shameful tear. Stupid to weep for what could not be changed, futile to wail for what could not be won.

When she straightened, she saw the outline of York beyond broad fields. Her chest tightened as they drew closer. Blackened, charred hulks thrust skyward, and when they entered the city, she saw the remains of a more recent fire. Tumbled stones lined the streets, and splintered wood with jagged, scorched edges pointed upward. A desolate scene that not even the few untouched houses could lessen.

She could not keep the bitterness from her voice as she remarked that not even prosperous cities were safe from Norman depredations. "But perhaps Normans find more value in burned wood than live merchants," she added angrily.

Luc gave her a narrowed glance. "I suggest that you do not

remind the king of how York came to be burned, my fine Saxon lady, or you may wish you had been silent."

Too late, she remembered the tales of Saxon earls rising up and seizing York, of Norman troops setting a blaze to storehouses that spread to the town, then dying in desperate battle outside the city gates. Yea, William would be loath to be reminded of that loss, she was certain, but the Saxon victory was for naught. Normans still held England, still held York, and though many had died, there was ample evidence that the townsmen of York had lost most.

Pinched faces stared at the soldiers riding through the narrow streets, some of them small children so thin they resembled the bare branches of willow trees. A pathetic reminder of what war could bring to both sides.

Yet there was rebuilding as well, the smell of new-cut timber and the sound of workmen. Atop an earthen mound above the city a new castle stood where the old one had been, with raw wood walls and sturdy ramparts protecting it. As they drew close, her stomach churned with apprehension and a sense of loss. Perhaps the king was not there. It was possible. He could be at Winchester, or London, or even in Normandy by now. Delay was her only hope for success. She needed time to sway Luc to her cause, time to persuade him that Wulfridge would fare better with a familiar mistress to supervise the people.

Luc urged the horses to a faster pace. Hooves clattered on cobbled stones, sounding like thunder to her ears.

Ceara glanced up when Luc exclaimed with satisfaction, "The king's banner flies—he is here."

Hope faded as she saw the waving banner of the Normandy lion, red against white, snapping atop a wooden tower in the late afternoon light. As she watched, the sun came out from behind a cloud and the red lion seemed to come alive, glowing like blood against a white field, ravenous.

Her heart sank, and she sat her mount numbly as they rode through a guarded gate and into the castle grounds. Perched atop a high mound of dirt the Normans called a *motte*, the castle dominated the site. Around the earthen mound were wooden walls. The outer courtyard teemed with activity, and Ceara clung to her horse with both hands as Luc dismounted into a knot of well-wishers. He still held the reins of her mare in one hand and turned casually to greet those around him, ignoring Ceara as if she were of no importance.

"Word came that you were successful, my lord," a tall, handsome man said in French, cuffing Luc lightly on the arm. "I suppose I must bow and scrape now."

"I would like to see that, Robert."

"I am certain you would." The dark-haired man named Robert shifted his gaze to where Ceara stiffly sat the gray mare. One brow rose, and he eyed the chains around her waist with obvious amusement. "No, no, Luc, you have erred. You're supposed to bring back the old lord in chains, not his nubile daughter!"

Luc glanced at Ceara. "If you knew this one's temper you would not say that."

Grinning, Robert shrugged. "Ah, she is so lovely that her temper should not matter. But what of Lady Amélie?"

Ceara's blood chilled, and she suddenly felt as if there were a huge stone in her throat. She tried not to look, tried not to betray that she understood them, but it was almost too difficult, especially when Luc laughed softly.

"The lovely Amélie means as much to me as ever she did, Robert, you know that."

Ceara blinked. She should have guessed. He may not be wed, but he was promised. His denials meant nothing. He was as all men were, faithful only when his loved one was a foot away and keeping an eye on him. Why had she not remembered their true nature?

"Luc! Luc!"

The high female voice rose above the babble of stewards and soldiers, and Luc half turned as a small woman with shining dark hair and a piquant face flung herself at him. He caught her in his arms, muttering something as she curled her arms around his neck and drew his head down for a kiss. Laughter rose, and men applauded as the kiss deepened, but Ceara could only stare with rising anguish. It didn't help that Luc was the one who broke away, firmly removing the woman's arms from around his neck, his voice slightly rough.

"Not now, Amélie."

Amélie.

The courtyard blurred, and for a horrified moment, Ceara thought she would burst into tears. The sudden ringing of church bells was almost deafening. But hadn't they passed a burned church? How could the bells be ringing so loudly? They would not stop clanging, a thousand at once, while around her everything went from blurred to dim, then to nothing at all. There was the oddest sensation of falling before she was enveloped by a soft, dark cloud.

Chapter Eight

THRUSTING AMÉLIE AWAY, Luc barely caught Ceara before she struck the hard ground by Drago's hooves. The huge destrier was already nervous with so many people around, and might very well slash Ceara to ribbons before he could be stopped.

"Take my horse," Luc bellowed, and someone quickly took the reins to lead the agitated mount away. Half kneeling, Luc cradled Ceara's limp form gently in his arms. Her head lolled to one side, and her eyes were closed, long lashes shadowing cheeks that looked much too pale. She made a soft, pitiful sound as he held her.

Kneeling beside him, Robert quickly checked for broken bones, his hand as swift and certain as any surgeon's. He looked up with a smile and a shrug. "She seems fine to me. Save for a few bruises here and there, I see no sign of serious injury."

Luc raked a hand through his hair and blew out an exasperated breath. "She has eaten very little in the past three days. I could have forced her, but forcing Ceara to do anything she doesn't want to do is like forcing the king."

"Ah, a formidable woman. How intriguing." Robert's brow

lifted with curiosity. "So, my lord Luc, just why are you traveling with this formidable young woman?"

"She is my hostage."

Luc's terse comment should have been enough to warn Robert, but his friend's curiosity was as boundless as it was unwise. "Hostage? This lovely maid? You jest."

Through his teeth, Luc snarled, "I do not jest. This is the leader of the Saxon revolt, and if I do not deliver her to the king, I may just as well have not gone to Wulfridge at all. Now move from my path, Robert, for she is in obvious need of rest and food—and fresh air."

Some of Luc's worry and anger penetrated Robert's amusement, and he nodded and rose to his feet to move people away, shouting that they must allow Lord Luc through to the castle.

To one side, Amélie waited, her large green eyes dark with suspicion, her brow furrowed. When Luc started past her, she stepped in front of him. "What does this mean, Luc? You have brought back a . . . a woman as hostage?"

Ignoring her question, Luc snapped, "Where can I take her for privacy and rest?"

"If she is your hostage, I suggest the guardhouse," Amélie returned tartly, but at Luc's glare added in a sulky tone, "There is a room just off the entry that has cushions for the ladies."

As he started for the castle steps, Amélie came after him, lifting her skirts daintily in one hand, almost on her toes to get a good look at the woman in his arms. It was Robert who distracted her, tactfully pointing out that it hardly looked proper for her to be running after Luc and his Saxon hostage like a rude peasant.

"Unless it is your wont to look foolish, Lady Amélie?"

"You know it is not!" Amélie drew in a deep breath and looked pointedly at Robert's hand on her arm, which he removed as promptly as if bitten. "You are too forward, sir. Tell Lord Luc that I will await him in the anteroom of the hall."

"Of course, my lady." Robert swept her a deep bow that

held more than a hint of mockery, and Amélie gazed at him so coldly he affected a mock shiver. "You freeze me with your icy heart, beautiful lady. Do not be so cruel."

"Do not be so impertinent. I will tell my cousin, and you will be properly punished."

"Queen Maud went back to Normandy for a time. Will you go there to tell her?"

Amélie's eyes narrowed to hostile chips, and her lovely mouth contorted into an ugly grimace. "No, you imbecile, I will send a messenger. Be wary, Robert de Brionne. You do not want to make of me an enemy."

Spreading his hand on his chest over his heart, Robert shook his head with feigned horror. "God's mercy on us all, Lady Amélie! I would not want to be enemies with the woman who had suddenly decided that Luc Louvat is finally good enough to marry now that he has won a title. . . ."

Amélie's hiss sounded like an angry cat, and Robert looked past her to see Luc disappear up the steps and into the castle. He abandoned his game now that his goal was won.

"Excuse me, my lady. I suddenly recalled some duties I must attend."

Robert left her standing in the courtyard and found Luc in a small anteroom off the great hall. It still smelled of new wood and pitch, but was made comfortable with cushions and low couches for ladies to recline upon. On one of these lay the Saxon hostage, still wearing chains, her face as pale as new milk.

"Who is she, Luc?"

Luc did not turn from loosening the laces of the girl's dress. "Find Giles. He has the key to these cursed chains, and I must remove them."

"Giles . . . ?"

"One of Sir Simon's men. A man-at-arms in my troop."

Luc still did not look up, and there was an urgency to his tone and movements that seeped through Robert's first amusement to render him thoughtful. Could it be that his friend had fond feelings for the maid he called hostage? It would seem so, for he cradled her tenderly in his hands, no small feat if one recalled Luc's past interactions with women. And Robert recalled them well.

"I'll go at once," Robert said quickly when Luc looked over his shoulder. He snapped his fingers. "Giles. Sir Simon's man. Key."

"Imbecile—"

"Careful, Luc. I shall begin to think there might be some truth to that title if it is applied to me too often." Robert left swiftly, before Luc could do more than shoot an angry look toward him. He had tweaked his friend enough for now. There was always later. It should be most entertaining to discover why Luc had left to chain a rebel, yet returned with a lovely maid instead. *Most* entertaining, indeed.

LUC'S TEMPER WAS not improved by Robert's subtle mockery. Nor was it likely to improve. Before the day was over, he would have to face William and present his case—or more correctly, Ceara's case. He did not expect a pleasant interview. Nor did he expect Ceara's cooperation.

When Ceara awoke, blinking vaguely, she was sullen and reserved. Brushing away his hand, she sat up with an abrupt wariness that set him back on his heels beside the stuffed cushion where she lay.

"Leave me alone."

Luc frowned at her harsh rejection. She was hardly appreciative of his efforts. "I could have left you in the dirt for Drago to cut to pieces with his hooves, but there would not be enough left of you to take to the king."

Still sullen, she flicked a glance up at him from beneath heavy lids, her mouth tucked into such a tight frown that deep dimples grooved her cheeks. "Is that a complaint? I thought 'twould suit you."

"If it would, I would not have gone to so much trouble to get you here alive and unharmed."

"Aye, so you would have me believe."

"Annoying brat—I have no reason to lie to you. Nor do I have reason to help you. Before you tweak me too greatly, you might think of that."

Spreading her fingers over her face, she pushed her small nose into the palm of her hand with a soft sound of distress. "My head hurts . . . did I hit it?"

"No. I caught you before you struck the ground."

She peeped at him from between two fingers. "You were the one who caught me?"

"Aye, who do you think?"

"I do not know." She shrugged and her hand dropped from her face to her lap. "All I remember are ringing church bells."

"There were no bells. Your hunger has made you faint. You will eat, then make yourself presentable. There is no reason for you to go before the king looking like a common wench."

Her delicate brow lifted in a high arch. "No? Yet is that not how the king already views me? I am a nithing to him. He will not care how I look, only that I am the rebel who dared defy him." She drew in a ragged breath. "I am well aware of William's views on rebellion, and you cannot say he will be merciful. Not when he lost one of his knights and over four score men and horses."

"I grant you four score men and horses are a loss, but not near as grievous as the loss of nine hundred men here only two months ago. Your brief triumph pales in the face of that other, little though you may countenance it."

His faint mockery made her eyes flash. "Aye, your defeat of Wulfridge will please him, but 'tis you he will favor, not the one who held out against him. Do not prate to me of mercy from a king who has wasted my country. He will have none, I assure you."

"No man can predict what the king will say of a matter until he says it." Luc rose to his feet and gestured impatiently for her to rise from the cushions. "But be assured, my lady, if you present to him a defiant face, you will reap what you have sown. My suggestion is that you swear fealty to him at once, and throw yourself on his mercy. He is not unjust. When he learns of Sir Simon's disregard for his orders, I doubt he will be grieved as to that knight's loss."

" 'Tis not Sir Simon's loss he will mourn, but the waste of time and resources. He will rejoice at gaining Wulfridge, and most like be pleased that my defiance earned him another estate. But that does not mean that he will allow it to go unpunished. It would set a bad precedent."

Luc couldn't help grinning at her perceptive retort. "You know the king better than you should, my lady. Too bad you did not act upon your knowledge earlier. It could have saved you much."

"Nothing would have saved me. I was caught between two devils."

"Yea, but now it is this devil who has you, and you must swear to me and to William if you value your life."

Blue eyes darkened, and she looked away from him toward the floor where bars of sunlight and shadow marked a small mat. "I cannot."

"Do not be a fool, Ceara. You cannot win. This is the king we're discussing, not some bloodless puppet who can be swayed by a smile or a bribe."

"You do not understand why I—"

"Curse you, I do not need to understand." He gripped her hard by the arms, giving her a rough shake that sent bright blond hair tumbling into her eyes and over her shoulder. "I offer you a way to survive. If you have any sense, you will think on what I have said. Do you wish to die? To have your people punished and even your wolf slain?"

A soft cry wrenched from her. "You will free Sheba, will you not, my lord? Do not let her suffer for my mistakes."

"No." Luc watched her eyes widen and her face go pale, but did not relent. 'I will not save her. It is up to you to do so. Swear to the king, Ceara, and no matter what he decides, I will see that your wolf is set free in the distant countryside. But you must swear fealty to William and to me, or I will let the wolf die."

He released her arms and Ceara stepped back, tumbling to the cushion again to put her head into the cradle of her palms. After a moment, she looked up, her voice bitter and weary.

"I will swear. For Sheba's life, I will swear. 'Tis a hard pact you have offered, my lord."

"It is the only way, Ceara. Now come, I will see that you have food and proper garments to meet the king. After that, your freedom and life are in your own hands."

"Why do you care if I live?" she demanded, refusing his outstretched hand as she pushed to her feet.

Her question took him by surprise. For a moment he did not reply, but stared down at her, frowning. Then he shrugged. "You were a worthwhile adversary. You fought well and bravely to defend your home. A worthy foe deserves a chance to repent."

"And if I do not repent?"

Luc's jaw tightened. "Then you will suffer severe consequences. I suggest that you consider whatever you say very carefully."

He called for a guard, giving him orders to see to the lady's welfare with food and clean garments fit to be seen by the king. "But watch her close," he added, "or you will answer to William."

The guard nodded and there was grim comprehension in the gaze Ceara gave Luc as she passed. He stood at the door to watch them go down the short corridor, then disappear around a corner. When he turned back, Robert had approached with Giles at his side.

"I found him, Luc, but he has no key, I fear."

Giles was tight-lipped, his knuckles white around the hilt of his sword as he faced Luc. "It is lost, my lord. Somewhere on the road—no doubt, when the lady struck me and caused my horse to bolt."

Robert smothered a snort of laughter, and quickly turned his face away. Luc ignored him.

"Then find another key, Giles. The lady must be made presentable for the king. Unless, of course, you wish to explain to him how the key was lost . . . ?"

Giles paled and bobbed his head. "Yes, of course, my lord, I will find another key. Or have the locksmith forge one. I will see that it is done quickly."

"I knew you would not fail me. And later, we will discuss the disturbance between you and the lady."

"Yes, my lord. As you say, my lord."

Robert leaned one shoulder against the wall as Giles departed, and regarded Luc with a thoughtfully raised eyebrow. "There goes an unhappy man, I would say."

"You would be right. He is responsible for the key."

"And you for the lady."

Luc turned to look at him with rising irritation. "Say what you want to say or ask what you want to ask, Robert, but no more of these cursed obscure comments."

"Ah, so I shall."

Robert grinned, and for a moment Luc could not be irritated with him. It was always this way with Brionne, the sly wit and supreme self-confidence. It was those qualities that had first appealed to Luc so long ago. He should not curse him for them now. But Robert had a way of pricking him that could be much too close for comfort.

"Say it then, Robert. I am in need of food and clean garments before I meet with William."

Clapping a friendly arm around Luc's shoulders, Robert turned him down the corridor. "We shall talk along the way. I find myself quite curious as to your interest in this chained lady, and would hear why it is necessary for you to so bind your female conquests."

Luc shook his head. "She is not my conquest. It is her lands that I conquered, not the lady. The lady is—not yet conquered."

"Even more intriguing. Come to my chambers, and I will give you good wine and meat, and share my meager wardrobe."

Luc eyed him dubiously. Robert was almost as tall as he, but slim as a birch rod. "It has been a long time since we were able to share clothing."

"Yes, but a loose tunic can cover a multitude of sins with the right belt. Have you increased your girth that much, old friend?"

Luc grinned. "If you want answers to the questions you are so determined to ask, you had best be courteous."

"Ah, did I offend? I most humbly beg your pardon." Robert steered him into a small chamber with one window high on the opposite wall over a narrow bed. It was empty of furniture save for a table and some stools. Several chests stood against one wall. Robert waved an expansive arm. "My spacious quarters. I share them with four others, so do not think me too far above my station. Here. Try the black tunic first."

Luc caught the tossed garment, but draped it over the table near the door. "I brought suitable garments with me. I just wanted to talk to you where we would not be overheard. Tell me what has happened in my absence. I need to know William's mood."

Robert shrugged, and hooking a stool with one foot, pulled it to him and straddled it. "The Danes have gone back to their ships in the Humber River, and Earls Edgar and Cospatric are with King Malcolm and the Scots. William is intent on harrying and destroying all he can so that there will be few uprisings in the future. St. Peter was plundered and destroyed, but William has focused all his energies on rebuilding castles instead of churches. His mood is—most determined."

"When has William ever been less?" Luc rubbed a hand over his jaw. "How fares the situation with Sweyn?"

"The king sent Count Robert de Mortain and Count Robert de Eu to the Humber to guard the river and the land around it. If the Danes form another assault, we will know."

"There is no way to get at Sweyn's forces?"

Robert shook his head. "No. Their fleet lies in the river, but they are bound by winter as we will be."

"And Stafford?"

"Is secure and held in William's name. I do not think it will be overrun again." Robert placed both hands on his knees and leaned forward, his spurs clinking slightly against the wooden rungs of the stool. "Now tell me of this Saxon woman, and how she has come to be with you. Is she hostage?"

"She is the old lord's daughter."

"And the old lord?" Robert prompted. "Where is he?"

"Dead."

"Ah. Killed in battle. Too bad. William wished to deal with him as a lesson for any other upstart rebels."

Luc grimaced. "Lord Balfour has been dead near four months."

Silence fell. Robert stared at him. "Then who—? No. Not the maid! That fair damsel is the rebel leader?"

"You are much more clever than you have a right to be. How did you guess?"

Robert's dark eyes danced with suppressed mirth, which was just as irritating as his unctuous manner. "I am not so clever as you must be, my lord, to have defeated such a dread warrior in battle. And then to bring the hostage draped in chains—a dangerous feat which will be well rewarded, I am certain."

"Damn you, Robert." It was said without rancor.

Sympathetic now, Robert sighed. "The king will not be pleased."

"That was my thought as well." Luc's mouth twisted in a

wry grimace. "It will not sit well with him at all that Sir Simon was slain at the behest of a young maid."

"She could not do it alone. What of her housecarls? Her captains?"

"Those who were not slain have sworn fealty to me and to William. The lady took full responsibility for the rebellion, so it is her that I brought to William." He paused, frowning. "One of Sir Simon's own men told me that she tried to negotiate, but was refused. Her messenger's ears were returned as a reply from Sir Simon."

"Ah."

Luc glanced up, annoyed. "That information should earn a more appropriate reaction."

"Such as?"

"Outrage."

"I am properly incensed. Look you, Luc," Robert said, rising from the stool, "it is not to me you need tell this tale, but the king."

"I know that, Robert. I wanted to see how it sounded spoken aloud. It is not very believable."

"And you fear for the maid."

Luc hesitated. "In her place," he said slowly, "I might very well have done the same. She was assailed on all sides by Danes, Scots, and even Saxon earls. There was no one she could trust. Sir Simon betrayed his intentions by slaying her messenger, a boy of only fifteen years, so what was she to think?"

"The worst," Robert said succinctly. "In her place, I would have given control to the first capable man and then retreated to a safe corner."

"There are no safe corners in England. Surely you have learned that by now." Luc's mouth tightened. "There have never been safe corners in England, not as long as I have lived here."

Robert made no reply to that, but remarked instead on his intention to call for meat and wine. "And your baggage. You stink of horse and mud. Did you bring your squire?"

"No. He is left to tend Wulfridge in my absence."

"Then I will lend you mine." Robert paused at the door and turned back to look at Luc. "What of Lady Amélie?"

"What of her?"

"She thinks to bind you to her now that you are titled. But I suppose you are aware of that."

Luc grinned. "Her greeting left me in little doubt of her intentions. But it was not too long ago that she told me she could not waste herself on a man with no future, so I am not overly impressed by her sudden change of heart."

"Perhaps I should not worry about you unduly, after all. There was a time . . ."

His grin faded. "Yes, there was a time when I might have been fooled. But that was long ago, Robert, when I had more trust in words spoken by those who professed affection. I have learned better."

Robert leaned against the door frame, his gaze dark and searching. "Will you go home again?"

"Wulfridge will be my home."

"Once I would never have thought you would call England home again. Not after—"

"No, not after being disowned. There are times Fate must laugh at us all, Robert."

A sudden noise outside snared their attention, and Robert observed that the king must have returned from his hunt. "He will be advised of your arrival, so you had best make haste."

Luc rose and began to unbuckle his sword belt. "Send hot water first. You're right. I smell of horse and mud."

"It is not you who should worry about impressing the king, but the Saxon lady. I will assure that she has what is needed."

Luc wasn't at all certain it would help her with the king, but it could not hurt to be presentable. Perhaps her youth and gender would do more than anything else to earn mercy.

Robert's squire arrived shortly, bringing scented water and thick cloths. Stripped down to just his linen hose, Luc splashed hot water on his hair and face and scrubbed vigorously. There was need for haste, for he must retrieve the documents he had prepared for the king as well, then find the right words to tell him about Sir Simon. The squire held out a pot of soap for him, and Luc used it liberally. The water was soon brown with dislodged mud.

Soap lather stung his eyes, and he fumbled for a cloth to dry his face. It was thrust into his hand, and he mumbled appreciation to the squire.

Soft laughter greeted his thanks, and he opened one eye to peer at the source.

Lady Amélie de Vescy stood beside him, wreathed in smiles. Aggravated, he stared at her. Her green eyes were glowing and her lovely oval face lit with a welcome that fairly dripped honey. What a calculating little tart she had become. His sudden and fortuitous rise from mere knight to baron charmed her when he had not.

Amélie slid her hand into the crook of his elbow, her long, pale fingers squeezing gently. "You rogue, to leave me like you did, without even a farewell! You have no shame, to treat me that way after all we have meant to one another."

He removed her hand with controlled precision, lifting a brow. "Your memory serves you better than mine does me, my lady. What did we mean to one another?"

Her voice lowered, and her smile deepened. "Do you not recall that night in Winchester? When you spoke of longing for me?"

"I recall it very well. Longing was not the word I used, however."

She shrugged daintily. "Longing, desire, they both mean the same thing, Luc."

"And you rejected both the word and my attentions, if I

recall correctly." He dragged the cloth over his face and throat, then his chest, eyeing her with cynical amusement. "Am I to believe that you did not mean it when you informed me I was unworthy of you?"

"That was then. Now, you are more than worthy." She affected a sighing lisp. "You must know that I only intended to inspire you, to rouse you to action on your own behalf."

"I was already roused to action, but you did not choose to bestow your favors on me that night." Luc tossed the cloth to the table beside the bowl of water. Ignoring Amélie's pout, he moved to where the squire had laid out his clean clothing, and she followed.

"Ah, Luc, if I were to fall into your arms every time you asked, you would soon tire of me. I want to keep your interest." She ran a hand up his bare back, fingers stroking softly as she whispered in a sultry murmur, "But my heart still races when I remember our first night together, and how you swept me away with your passion."

He pulled a fine linen sherte over his head and laced it at the throat, then reached for the elegant black tunic trimmed in red braid and emblazoned with the image of a wolf. Young wolf—Louvat. It was a name he would bear with pride now, instead of the jest it had first been. Fitting, as William had said, that he won the lands of Wulfridge. A mental image of the white wolf flickered in his mind for a moment, quickly followed by the more vivid image of Ceara. Two she-wolves.

"Luc?"

Reaching for his belt, he frowned at Amélie when she demanded to know if he was listening to her. "No, I am not. I have an audience with the king. I do not have time to listen to a woman's prattle."

Amélie gasped with outrage, but quickly stifled it. She may be the queen's cousin and the widow of a Norman baron, but the lady put far too much worth on her rank, and even more on her beauty. It wasn't her fault, for men oft told her how lovely she was, and she had heard it so long, she believed her beauty could make up for a fickle heart. To him she had been only a casual conquest, and her refusal of his further advances had caused him no great concern. There were many willing women of equal fairness, with softer tongues and less vanity.

"I came to you at the wrong time, I see," Amélie said stiffly. "Later, we will have time for more talk, and . . ." She smiled. "Other things."

There was no advantage to being deliberately cruel when it was not required. He shrugged. "I do not have long in York. I must return swiftly to Wulfridge to hold my new lands."

"Of course. I understand." She moved to the door and turned, one hand smoothing the green folds of her gown in a restless motion. "I count it fortunate that the king saw fit to introduce us last year, Luc. Do you think he had ulterior motives in doing so?"

"No. You are his wife's cousin, and William is too courteous to ignore either of us. Attach no importance to that, Amélie, for it was naught but pure chance."

She laughed throatily. "Nothing is pure chance, Luc. There will be a banquet tonight. I will seek you there."

Luc did not reply, and after a moment, she eased out the door. Her perfume lingered, smelling of strong spice. But it only reminded him of the gentle, arousing scent of lavender on soft flesh, and he shook his head. He was becoming too engrossed with Ceara.

Hefting his sword, he buckled it around his waist and finished dressing. William would be waiting for his report. By nightfall, he would officially be the new lord of Wulfridge. It would be his by law as well as deed, a Norman holding instead of Saxon.

Ceara's image swam before his eyes again, and he swore softly as he quit the chamber and strode down the corridor toward the great hall where William waited. Why should he feel responsible for what another had done? His sense of honor demanded that he present her defense to William, but if she chose not to accept his aid or to be foolishly obstinate, he could do nothing else for her. She would have to save herself.

Chapter Nine

SHE HAD TO save herself. Fighting her apprehension, Ceara wound her hands tightly into the folds of the borrowed gown. It was too short, the hem not even reaching the tops of her ankle boots, so she had been given a long mantle of ivory wool to wear over it.

Only her insistence that Lord Luc had bade her wear it kept her mother's necklace from being taken away, as none dared to take what he had allowed her to keep. It hung from her neck, a solid weight between her breasts that reminded her fiercely of what she had already lost, and what she may yet lose.

Drawing in a deep breath as her guard told her in rough English to kneel in the presence of the king, Ceara did so blindly. Where was Luc? She saw only a blur of faces, none familiar to her. Had he decided not to attend after all? Her heart beat faster; her throat was tight and her mouth dry. If he did not attend, she might not be able to do what she must. . . .

Then she heard him, his familiar voice rising above the clamor of whispers from curious onlookers, and her head lifted. Garbed all in black, Luc stood at the foot of the dais below what could only be the king, who was seated on a straight-backed chair. She had a brief impression of a broad-shouldered man with a stern visage before she was told to rise, and she did so with thankfully steady grace.

Luc interpreted the king's French, so that she did not have to betray her knowledge of their tongue, though she understood William perfectly: "Louvat tells me a most interesting tale, Lady Ceara. I would hear your version of it before I make my decision."

Louvat? She blinked in confusion, then saw Luc's faint smile and realized 'twas he the king meant. Louvat—young wolf. How fitting. Her chin lifted, and she hid her trembling hands in the wool folds of the mantle as she met the king's dark, steady gaze. She answered in English while Luc performed the translation.

"With your permission, sire, I ask your patience. It has been a most trying experience that has left me uncertain as to the exact nature of your demands. Pray, clarify for me what you wish to know, and I will answer with the truth, for I know that is what you require."

"In all things, my lady. Untruths are dangerous in my court." Steepling his fingers, he studied her over their tips with nerve-racking shrewdness. "Tell me and the court what happened when Sir Simon came to survey Wulfridge."

Ceara chose her reply carefully. "Sir Simon arrived hard on the heels of other invaders, and announced he had been sent by the king to secure my lands. He demanded I open the gates and yield all to his inspection without delay. I asked for time to consider his request. It was denied." Her voice faltered slightly, but she steadied herself, somewhat strengthened by Luc's faultless translation. "Sir Simon's reply was to return to me my young messenger's ears in a cloth bag. From that, I deduced he did not want a gentle surrender. I gave that unworthy knight what he wanted."

At the periphery of her vision she could see Luc flinch, but the words were out. Luc repeated them verbatim though he did so in a mild tone. The silence drew out, so that her heartbeat sounded loudly in her ears. Her knees weakened, and she began to think the king would order her slain right there in the hall.

"You speak boldly, my lady," the king finally remarked. "I see that you are quite capable of leading men to battle if you think it necessary."

"I did what I thought would best serve my interests and those of my people. If I have erred, sire, it is because I value life and liberty."

William's brow lifted, but his expression remained the same, betraying nothing. "We all value life and liberty. What I command is for the good of all. I am not a harsh man when my demands are met. As he disobeyed my orders, I shall not require blood penance for the life of Sir Simon. He earned his fate by his feckless defiance. As you rebelled against a man sworn to me, your lands are forfeit. From this day forward, Wulfridge and the title of earl belongs to Sir Luc Louvat, who has served me faithfully and well. I reward those of my subjects who are loyal."

Leaning forward as Luc's translation ended, the king held her gaze, his hoarse voice stern as he demanded, "Do you swear fealty to me as your overlord and king?"

For a heartbeat, Ceara wavered. But she knew the consequences too well, and would not lose all for the sake of pride. Her father had been right. She briefly bowed her head in assent.

"Yea, sire, I swear to you as my overlord and king."

Luc shifted slightly, and his sword clinked against stone, but she did not look at him as he repeated her vow in grave tones. Her gaze fastened on the king, who sat back in his chair with a satisfied expression.

"You are as wise as you are lovely, my lady. It is my understanding that you are unwed. I propose to find you a suitable husband, and settle on you a small dowry as a restitution for the wrong done you by Sir Simon."

"Sire—I am aware of the favor you show me, and am not

ungrateful. You are well known for your swift justice and sense of honor." She took a deep breath for courage, not allowing her gaze to move for even an instant to Luc though she was well aware of his sudden wariness. "It is your renowned justice that allows me to protest a wrong done me, a personal wrong greater than even that of Sir Simon."

"Another wrong, my lady?" William's brow lowered over his piercing eyes. "Tell me of this wrong that is so great."

"Sire, I was a maid when I left Wulfridge, but am no longer. I protest the loss of my virginity and seek a retribution of my own choosing."

Luc took a step forward. "Do you know what you do?" he demanded harshly of her in English. "Am I to repeat that to the king?"

She did not look at him, did not waver in her resolve, though her nails dug fiercely into her palms. "Yea, my lord. If I am to be sold as a milch cow, the king should know my worth. Tell him what I have said, and do not change a word."

"You little fool, this will not help—"

"My lord Luc," William interrupted in a steely tone, "do you finish the translation. *Exactly* as it is said."

A muscle leaped in Luc's jaw as he turned to the king and bowed. "Yes, sire. The lady wishes me to inform you that she was virgin when she left Wulfridge, but is no longer. She protests the loss and asks retribution of her own choosing."

The great hall was so quiet Ceara could hear the shuffling of feet on the stone floor, the gasps of those near enough to hear, and the murmurs of others as the words were repeated. William's face did not change.

"Was she forced?"

Ceara answered hard on the heels of Luc's terse translation. "I was offered the choice of my surrender or the life of my loyal companion. I am nobly born, and have lost much. I did not wish to lose all."

Stonily, not looking at her, Luc repeated her words and William scowled.

"Did she name the man who took her virginity?"

"No, sire. She did not need to do so. I am that man."

Ceara glanced at Luc sharply. She'd not expected him to offer the information. A muscle leaped in his cheek, and the faint scar along his jawline was white with tension as he turned to face the king.

Before he could speak, William put up a hand to stop him. "We will discuss this further in private, Louvat. Bring the lady to my antechamber."

Luc bowed. As William rose to dismiss those in attendance, Ceara dared a glance at the king. He was very tall, but it was his harsh visage and forceful nature that intimidated those around him. Luc was right. The king was not a man easily swayed.

When the doors to the antechamber closed behind them, Ceara glanced at Luc. He stood stiffly, his off-hand on the hilt of his sword as he regarded William. A small flutter of disquiet stirred in her breast. She did not want to harm Luc, only keep what was hers. But how did she tell him that? He would not listen. In fact, he would not so much as glance in her direction now, but kept his dark gaze bent on the king.

A wall tapestry shifted in a cool draft. The king moved to a small table bearing a silver bowl of fruit and a flagon of new wine. A frown crowded his eyes, and his mouth was a taut line that gave him as even more forbidding presence.

Abruptly William demanded an explanation. "Tell me the way of it, Louvat. Does she speak the truth?"

"Yes, sire. She was virgin when I took her."

"And your reason for doing so?"

Luc flushed, a dull red color that swept up his neck to his face. "She was widowed. I did not think her to be virgin still."

A wry smile touched William's mouth. "That is not quite what I meant, Louvat, though I find myself intrigued by that marvel. Granted, she is lovely, but she is a rebel and my hostage.

Her father was a baron. She is no low-born wench used to sharing her favors with all who ask. Maid, widow, or matron, if she did not wish to be bedded, you should not have forced her."

"No, sire." Luc offered no more explanation, though there was an undercurrent of bitter resignation to his words.

Ceara shifted uneasily. She had not expected Luc to offer no defense. Indeed, she had thought he would protest her words and his innocence, would malign his accuser with harsh truths. For that, she had been prepared, but this? It was unexpected, and for a moment she regretted her decision to force the issue in this way. True, Luc had threatened to harm her pet if she refused to disrobe, but had she not tempted him at Wulfridge? She had wanted the very reaction he gave her, had rejoiced in his taking of her for it gave her a weapon to use against him. Yet now he had blunted that weapon with his lack of defense.

William sat down in a chair, his long legs sprawled in front of him, his gaze dark as he regarded Luc. "You have put me in an awkward situation, Louvat. I thought better of you. I need you in the north to help control the rebels, and to secure the coast. Lord Robert de Comines is dead, and Northumbria needs strong hands to hold it. Only a few of the Saxon barons of the north have sworn fealty to me. Though I am overrun with Normans eager to accept lands and titles, I must choose carefully." He tapped his fingers against the arm of the chair. "You were born in England. You speak their language, yet you are Norman. You are a man who can deal with both sides. You are just the man to hold Wulfridge and the coast. King Sweyn is likely to ravage again when good weather permits, and Norway and the Scots are waiting to plunder England's borders. But once I am secure, all will bow to me or feel the heel of my boot."

Ceara kept her eyes down to conceal her shock at the revelation of Luc's birthplace. It explained his familiarity with the Saxon tongue, but not his allegiance to William. With growing anger and alarm, she listened to the king's rebuke and Luc's passive response.

"I would not risk a hide of your land for my actions, sire. Perhaps Wulfridge would be best given to another man to hold."

William slammed his hand down on the arm of his chair and Ceara jumped, though Luc gave no sign of alarm. "No, by the Holy Rood, it would not be best! You have the best chance of bringing together Norman and Saxon—mayhap you need a wife, Louvat. A Saxon wife."

Luc's hand tightened around the hilt of his sword. He drew in a deep breath, his tone ironic. "I suppose you have decided upon the choice, sire."

"You are astute, Louvat. Too bad you did not choose such wisdom with the maid a few nights past." William stroked his bare chin with one hand, eyeing Ceara and his new baron with a faint smile. "The idea has merit. Obviously you find the maid to your liking. Your marriage would bind you to Northumbria by blood. Think you it will be restitution enough to the Saxon barons for her to be lady of Wulfridge?"

Through his teeth, Luc agreed, though Ceara could almost feel his fury. "It should be more than enough restitution, sire."

"Marriage is not so grim a business, Louvat." William rose, his temper restored now that he had decided upon a course of action, his mood almost friendly as he went to Luc to put an arm around his shoulders in comradely fashion. "Now that you have lands and a title, you need sons. Lawful sons who will hold the lands after you."

"While that is true, sire, we have not asked the lady how she feels about bearing those sons."

Ceara's hands were dug deep into the folds of her skirt, and she held tightly to the tattered remnants of her resolve so it would not become rebellion. She was still being discussed as if she were a cow or block of wood instead of a woman, and even though her goal was within her grasp, she could not help a surge of resentment. William's reply did not soften that hostility.

"She is a woman and my hostage. I offer her not dishonor but one of my best knights, and an earl to boot. I do not think her foolish enough to refuse, when the alternative could be much more unpleasant than a babe in her belly." The king paused, and Ceara met his gaze with trembling anger. William blinked, and his eyes narrowed. "Speak to her of it, Louvat. If she is bold enough to hold off an entire troop of Norman knights for near a fortnight, I do not think she will quail at taking a Norman to husband."

"It is not her refusal that concerns me," Luc muttered, "but her acceptance. I have been at the point of her sword or dagger more than once."

William grinned, looking less like a fearsome monarch. "It was told to me that there was some resistance, and that you found yourself in an awkward position."

"As I feared, bad news travels far more swiftly than good." Luc's smile was stiff.

"The measure of any household is the swiftness of its servants in repeating gossip. So what say you, Luc Louvat? Will you wed the wench to make her an honest wife and avoid more Saxon rebellion?"

Luc hesitated, then bowed slightly. "Never have I been able to refuse you anything, sire, and I cannot refuse you this, as I have caused my own troubles. I will wed her at your pleasure."

"Excellent. Now come, speak to the lady and tell her of her good fortune. Shall I leave you alone?"

"It would be best coming from you, sire."

"Very well. Tell her of my decision. And, Louvat—make it plain I will suffer no dispute."

"Yes, sire."

It was easy to pretend ignorance, for Ceara's anger was choking her to silence, a lump of resentment blocking the words she wanted to fling at them. Luc eyed her warily, as if sensing her rage, and the hand he put upon her arm was heavy as he spoke in English.

"My lady, the king wishes you to know he has your best welfare in mind." Dark eyes studied her from beneath his thick black lashes, a little distrustful at her silence. His fingers tightened around her wrist like steel bands. "Your wish to return to Wulfridge has been granted. But let it be made clear to you that even if you should disagree with the manner, the king will brook no argument in the matter."

"Why should I argue about returning to Wulfridge?" The words came out in a husky rasp, and she cleared her throat. "So tell me the rest, my lord, and quickly before I lose interest."

Luc's eyes narrowed slightly, and his mouth thinned. "William has decided you shall be wed." He paused as if loath to finish, and there was a pinched look about his mouth.

Did he hate the thought so much? Was she that repugnant to him? Or was it the loss of his precious Lady Amélie that grieved him? Piqued by the knowledge that he cared nothing for her, she did not resist the urge to goad him.

"I do not mind wedding, as long as the man is not you. Forgive me for speaking my mind, my lord."

"I share your sentiments, but it is not to be. Your plea for retribution has been answered in the truest sense. You are to be my wife."

"And mistress of Wulfridge?" She smiled. "Perhaps it is not I who am being punished, but you."

"So it seems." Luc released her arm and stepped back, hostility in his eyes. "Apparently, you are not as surprised by this event as was expected."

"It would have been clear to a mole that the king was not pleased by my request or your actions. No, I cannot say I am completely surprised. Nor am I completely displeased. I belong at Wulfridge."

Stepping close to her again, Luc said softly, "You may regret the manner in which you return, my lady. As my wife, you will belong to me, not to Wulfridge. Once we wed, no man may stand between us, not even the king."

A chill ran through her as she saw the fierce black anger

burning in the depths of his eyes. Had she wagered all just to once more taste defeat?

"MY LADY?"

Ceara looked up, lifting her head from atop her drawn-up knees when she recognized her visitor. He spoke rough English, heavily accented but comprehensible, and she rose from the narrow bed in her small room—cell—to greet him.

"You were in the bailey when we arrived."

A grin flashed across his swarthy face, and he nodded. "Yes. I am Robert de Brionne."

"What do you here, Robert of Brionne?" She swept out an arm to indicate her tiny chamber. "It is hardly a very comfortable room for conversation and merriment. Do you play a lute, perhaps?"

Robert edged into the room and shut the door behind him, but Ceara glimpsed the armed guard standing just outside. "I do not play well. My efforts make dogs howl and children flee."

She smiled a little. Some of her tension eased, and she smoothed the folds of her gown and gestured for him to be seated on the one stool the chamber boasted. "Then we would be a likely pair, for my singing has the same effect. Why are you here?"

"You do not bandy words, my lady." Robert's smile was wry. "I came because I am Luc's friend."

"And you think to talk me out of wedding him?" She shook her head. "Speak to the king instead. It was his decision."

"But one that serves you well, I think. Wait—" Robert put up a hand when she stiffened. "Do not mistake me, Ceara de Wulfridge. I do not disapprove. Indeed, I think it well met that Luc is to wed. He will need heirs one day, now that he has lands and title for them to inherit."

Ceara stared at him suspiciously. "What do you want with me?"

Robert shook his head. "Naught, my lady, I swear it. I just thought to meet the woman brave enough to put a sword to Luc's throat, and resourceful enough to keep her life afterward. Is that your wolf down in the kennels?"

"You have seen her? How does she fare?"

"The wolf fares well. The hounds are nervous, and the stable lads swear most foully that the horses will bolt, but the wolf seems content. A bit restless, perhaps."

She sighed. "Sheba is not meant for a cage. Nor am I."

Robert studied her a moment in the light afforded by the single lamp and a tiny window high overhead. "I find you to be an unusual woman, my lady. Word of your deeds has run rampant through the castle, until there are those who swear you are King Harold returned in female form, and others who would swear you are a . . . ah, *une putain* who seeks only to escape justice."

"The last man who used that word to me bled for near two miles," Ceara said mildly, and saw Robert's surprise. Then he grinned.

"Parlez-vous français?"

"I do not have to speak French in order to know a few words here and there." She turned, and began to pace in short steps across the wood floor. "I have not seen Luc since our audience with the king last week."

Robert remained silent. She turned to look at him, and he was watching her with his head tilted to one side, a faint smile curving his mouth. He shrugged at her regard.

"Luc is . . . unhappy."

"No, Luc is angry."

Robert grinned. "Furious. Outraged. I have not often seen him so angry."

She eyed him curiously. "How long have you known Luc?"

"Since he first came to Normandy when we were boys. He was sent as page to my father's house, and being older than I by only two years, we became friends. We belong to the same group of knights in William's service."

"So you are good friends."

"In Normandy, knights bond in groups of twenty-five, and are together for life. We have ridden together a long time now." Robert rubbed a thumb along the underside of his jaw, his gaze keen. "I wanted to meet the woman who is to be Luc's wife, and discover for myself if the rumors are true."

Her chin lifted. "And have you?"

"Perhaps." He rose from the stool, his tall, lean presence not intimidating, but making the chamber seem much smaller. "An odd turn of events, I think, that leads you to ride into York in chains, yet leave a Norman baron's wife."

"I rode into York a *Saxon* baron's daughter, sir, so I do not feel that the change is entirely to my advantage."

Robert laughed appreciatively. "A quick tongue, my lady, as Luc said. You will hold your own with him, I think. As long as you do not try to rule him."

"If that is meant to be a warning, it is unnecessary. I have no desire to rule Luc. I just want to go home."

She hadn't meant the last to sound so wistful, but saw from Robert's sympathetic smile that it had. She turned away, angry with herself for displaying emotion. "I am told the wedding is to be in a fortnight."

"The king wishes the festivities to be complete before the calends of December. The bishop of St. Peter will conduct the ceremony, I am told."

"A Norman bishop."

"As are most now, save a few who follow the church's old precepts."

"While William plunders the churches? I am surprised the pope countenances it."

Robert frowned. "The king does not wantonly burn churches, my lady, no matter what you have been told. St. Peter was in the path of the fire that raged out of control and it could not be helped. The Danes have long looted the churches with total disregard, but not the king. William is no fool. He knows he must have the church's approval and the pope behind him to successfully hold this land."

Waving an impatient hand, Ceara shook her head. "This has naught to do with me. I am here as prisoner until my wedding day, I presume, or until the king's whim dictates some other entertainment."

"William is not a man prone to whims. More like, firm convictions. You will be wed, my lady, make no mistake about it. Unless a reason is found for the marriage to be denied, you will be wed to Luc soon enough." He paused, then added softly, "I think you will find it not so grim a fate, no matter your feelings at this moment."

Ceara did not reply. Was this not all her fault? She had worked for this very thing, yet now that it was to be, she was afraid. She would return to Wulfridge, but would it be worth the price she would pay?

Luc was furious. She had known he would be when she began, but discounted the extent of his anger. Not until he had escorted her to this cell had she begun to see the full range of his fury. She still shuddered to recall his terse reminder that what she had wrought, she would bear.

Catching her face between his thumb and fingers, he'd held her head still to add softly, "I will wed you because the king commands it, but you will know no joy of it."

She had not seen him since, and been glad of it. Save for the servants who brought clean garments and food, she had seen no one but the guard until Robert's visit.

Robert was looking at her with an enigmatic expression on his face when the door opened. The guard was alert as Robert stepped into the hallway. Turning back to her, Robert said softly, "You have great strength. Use it. He will respect nothing else."

Then the door closed with a solid bang, English oak against English oak, a heavy sound that reverberated through the tiny room almost like a physical blow. The smell of lamp oil made the room stuffy, and the high window over the narrow bed let in only thin bars of light and very little air. Dimly, she could hear the sounds of life going on outside her prison. She shivered, curling her arms around herself.

It was cold. English winters always were. She wished she were at home, in Wulfridge's great hall, with familiar faces around her, the smell of the sea surrounding her instead of this stifling gloom. This world was so different, more than she had thought it could be while yet on England's shores. How had William made an English town seem so Norman? All around her were striking differences, not just in the language spoken, but the dress, the furniture, the food. Nothing was the same. Even Luc was different from the savage warrior she had first met, garbed now in fine clothing and expensive linen.

Yet there was still that spark of feral beast in him, glimpsed at the audience with the king, the fierce stare he had bent upon her both a promise and a threat. Beneath his rich tunic and careful manners still lurked the ruthless man she had first met.

Ah, Luc. Would he never come? Did he hate her for being forced into a marriage he did not want? She pulled a rough blanket around her legs and feet. No matter. It was not her ideal either. Yet she did what she had to do, just as he would, just as most did to survive. It was the way of things. If she let herself dwell on the objectionable aspects, she might lose sight of her goal. That, she could not do. She would not do. There was too much at stake.

Yet she wondered, as she watched the bars of light dim and fade into night, why Luc had not told the king the truth of it. She'd expected him to deny her claim, to tell William that she had tempted him, as indeed she had. Why had he not done so?

Why had he not told the king how, in truth, she had gone willingly into his arms?

Leaning her head back against the wall, she thought of Wulfridge and the sweet sea air brushing through tall grass and over familiar, beloved stone walls. Yes. It would all be worth it.

Chapter Ten

LUC LAY AWAKE, staring at the high ceiling draped with cobwebs and listening to the others snore. The past few weeks he had spent in energetic activity intended to keep him too busy to think. Days he left early on patrol to scour the countryside and lay waste to pockets of rebellion, driving those who defied William's rule from their lands. The king brooked no further opposition.

But the nights . . . ah, the nights. He should have fallen into exhausted slumber, for he drove himself hard during the day. Yet too often he found himself lying awake and thinking of the girl who was soon to be his wife. His moods swung from fury to grim resignation with alarming speed. Never had he been a man to lose sight of his goals because of a woman. None had been able to tempt him from his hard-held purpose. Yet, Ceara de Wulfridge had done so with astonishing speed. It still amazed him. Worse, he still wanted her—in his bed, if not to wife. He'd not been able to put from his mind the softness of her skin, the faint scent of lavender that clung to her, her sweetly yielding curves.

This night, it became unbearable. Restless and unsettled, he rose from his cot—tucked between two others filled with snoring men—and went out into the cold, clear moonlight. He wandered aimlessly, then found himself at the kennels, where the wolf was kept in her cage away from the hounds. The beast looked up when he approached, her lips curling into a faint snarl, but her tail thumping warily. A tame wolf. The term seemed contradictory. Especially now. With some meat on her bones from regular feeding, she looked more like a predator than before. He moved closer. The deep, gold-brown eyes regarded him without blinking, fringed by white lashes and unafraid.

It could not help but remind him of Ceara, that same steady regard, the lift of the head as if to ask what he intended. They were like, the Saxon wolf and the Saxon girl. Wary and waiting.

"I gave my word I would not harm you," he muttered to the wolf, and was awarded with another thump of the tail. Sheba whined, then put back her head and howled, a long, vibrating expression of misery that he felt like echoing.

"Would that I could howl my displeasure as do you," he murmured in English. Sheba put her great head between her paws and moaned. Luc put out a hand to stroke the head. But after a few moments he felt foolish for talking to a wolf, and left before someone found him. It would do him no good to have it said around the castle that he consorted with wolves on moonlit nights.

The next day, he went to visit Ceara. She watched him just as warily as Sheba had, though there was no welcome in any form, only a silent detachment that grated on his temper.

"We are to be wed in a sennight, Ceara."

"So I understand." She did not rise from the bed, but sat still and stiff. "Have you come to kill me?"

Unwillingly, he smiled a little at that. "No. Not that the thought has not occurred to me. I fear the king would disapprove."

She shrugged. "He may want you to wait until after the

wedding, so there is no outcry. I have no relatives alive, no one will take it amiss if I die after we are wed."

There was an odd monotony to her words that made him frown. "I do not slay unarmed females. You are safe enough for now."

Looking up, a faint smile curved her mouth, and for a moment he glimpsed the spirit that had first intrigued him. Then she shrugged again, and looked down at her lap where her hands toyed with a length of frayed material. He realized it was a crude rosary, the prayer beads knotted into the strip of linen.

"Do you pray for release from the marriage, my lady? You should have thought of that before you went to such lengths to arrange it."

"It was your king who arranged it, not I. And no, I do not pray for release, for after all, I will get what I want from it." A strange smile played about her lips. "Wulfridge has been my home all my life. It will be my home when I die, and I can expect no more."

"A melancholy mood, my lady?" He caught her hand in his and held it, not harshly, but hard enough to crush the rosary in her fist. "Pray you that it is worth it to you, for I shall not make it easy."

He meant it, and he saw that she understood. Her face paled a little, but her chin remained stubbornly lifted with defiance. Prompted by the same obscure emotion that had brought him to her room, he pulled her to him abruptly, his hand moving to tangle in her hair, his mouth seeking hers. Her hands were caught between them, pushing at him with steady resistance, but he ignored her efforts. Curse her, did she think to taunt him this way and escape? She would not . . . she haunted his waking moments, even his dreams, and he was weary of the struggle.

Forcing her backward until the edge of the cot was against her legs, he used his weight as leverage and pushed her down to the hard surface of the bed. She twisted in his grip, but he held her fast, driven by need and anger and the constant thrum of desire. *Jésu,* she was so soft, so warm, her skin heated ivory beneath his hands, tempting him to pull away her tunic and caress the smooth globes beneath, tease the taut peaks of her nipples into rosettes with his tongue . . . there was the sound of rending cloth, soft gasps, and his own harsh pants for air, but no protests other than the mute resistance of her hands against his chest.

Aching from the pressure of his need, Luc wedged his body between her thighs, heedless of the ominous creaking of the rope cot, lacing his hands in hers to pull them up and over her head. Her breath came in swift inhalations that lifted her chest, and her lips were drawn back from her small white teeth in a faint wolfish snarl.

"Is this how Normans woo their ladies to wife, my lord? What it lacks in charm, it makes up for in impatience."

Angry, he stared down at her, at the blue eyes filled with golden glints of mockery. "A rough wooing, to be certain, but one of your own making. I did not set out to pursue you, but find that this plight is of your doing. Am I to yield? I think not. Yielding to William is one matter, to a woman is quite another."

"Yet you expect me to yield to you."

"Aye, my fine lady, I do. You have yielded once for your own gain. The next yielding will be for mine."

Transferring her wrists to one hand, he held her while he moved his other hand with slow deliberation over her bared breasts, caressing, teasing, watching her through his lashes as she bit her lower lip between her teeth and closed her eyes. Yet her body betrayed her with small tremors, with the rapid rise and fall of her breasts, and the thrumming of the pulse in the hollow of her pale throat. He bent to kiss the shadowed dip, then moved lower, his tongue tracing tiny circles over her quivering flesh while his own need grew to aching tension.

Curving his hand around her breast, he blew softly on the

beaded nipple, then took it gently into his mouth, hot and cold, sweet skin and rousing solicitude lavished on first one, then the other. He rocked forward, pressing his hard length into the vee of her thighs so that she would know the full range of his desire, watching her as she moaned softly and shuddered involuntarily. There was something intensely erotic about lying with her like this, his clothes a barrier between them, yet caressing the bare skin of her breasts and thighs.

It was arousing and unnerving that he could lose himself like this in her, to the point of forgetting everything but being inside her. The memory of the night on the old Roman road was etched sharply in his mind. Yet if he took her now, it would tell her that little mattered but the easing of his need for her. It was too risky. That knowledge would be far too powerful a weapon for her to use against him.

Lifting his body from hers, he gazed down at her flushed face and moist mouth, struggling for the strength to refrain from taking her. He released her hands and pushed up from the bed, leaving her lying in a half-clothed sprawl on the thin mattress. She did not move to cover herself, but lay as he had left her, pale white thighs gleaming with sweet temptation in the dim light, her bared breasts still bearing the faint prints of his hands on her.

Luc straightened his tunic, then turned away to stride to the door and pull it open. Pausing in the opening, he surveyed her slender form. "You are not the first woman to betray me, but I swear that you will not do so again. I will give you no quarter. Think on that whilst you make your wedding preparations, my lady."

He slammed the door hard behind him, ignoring the wary scuttling of the guard to one side as he stalked down the dimly lit corridor. Never had he thought to be so unsettled by one small maid. She had done to him what none other had yet managed, and he had somehow allowed it to happen. But not again, as he had told her. She would not fool him again.

• • •

MUSIC FILLED THE air, and a festive atmosphere pervaded York and the castle. Streets were crowded with those come to the wedding of England's newest earl and his Saxon bride. The service held on the steps of St. Peter church for all to see was over. The workmen had paused in their rebuilding as the priest performed the ceremony.

With William observing the proceedings, Luc helped Ceara onto a white palfrey, then mounted his own steed. Someone had woven garlands of dried flowers in the manes and tails of both animals, and Drago snorted at the indignity as they wound through the city streets.

Despite the cold, spectators lined the narrow roads to see the Saxon lady who had become a Norman baron's wife. One would think no Norman had ever wed a Saxon before, Luc thought grimly. But perhaps it was because of the rumors that flew thick as crows through York that this marriage was one of Saxon benefit instead of Norman. After all, Ceara of Wulfridge was one of their own, and the king had bade his earl wed her to remedy the wrong that had been done her.

It was not a situation likely to improve Luc's temper. By all rights, he should have told William the truth, but he had not. It would have been too embarrassing to admit that a mere maid had managed to tempt him as she had done, then use that very seduction against him. Ceara had planned well.

A banquet was held in the great hall. Unfinished walls were covered with woven tapestries, and hundreds of candles gave off a bright, warm light. As guests of honor, Luc and Ceara were seated at the *table dormant*, a heavy oaken slab that stretched almost entirely across the dais at the head of the hall, reserved for use of the king and important barons. Trestle tables had been set up perpendicular to the dais, with benches for knights and guests. Delicate dishes were served: appulmoy, curlews in sauce, and exotic fish baked in pasties or stewed in pungent spices, jellies dyed with the juice of crushed columbine flowers. Marchpane subtleties garnished with feathers and leaves were borne proudly into the hall by pages, supervised by anxious cooks awaiting the king's praise. Silver nefs filled with condiments decorated even the lower tables, with gold-gilded cellars of salt set in the center of each table. Carved chairs had been set up for the honored guests, and cloths of fine embroidered linen from Ypres draped the tables. Even utensils were provided, wrought-silver handles decorating the spoons at the high table.

Several Saxon barons had been invited to witness the ceremony and partake of the sumptuous banquet afterward. The king had decided to display his willingness to be lenient to those who swore to him, as well as a warning of his intentions to bind Norman and Saxon into one nation. For most, it was a point well taken.

Knights from Luc's troop feted him with toasts and merriment, the men he had ridden with for a dozen years making ribald jests at his expense and not seeming to notice his forced courtesy. Ceara sat stiffly at his side without looking at him, her posture tense and wary, as if she expected him to take his dagger to her at any moment.

On his other side sat William, the monarch appearing serene and satisfied with the day's work, oblivious to the undercurrents between the bride and groom. Indeed, the king commented on how happy the new couple seemed.

"A new title and a new bride all in the same month, Louvat. You are fortunate indeed, to be so blessed."

"Yes, sire." Luc forced a smile. "I had not thought to be so fortunate."

"No doubt." William's dry words earned a sharp glance from Luc, but the king's face revealed nothing. He lifted his silver cup in a silent toast to Luc, then indicated the lady at his side. "Tell her that she makes a very beautiful countess, Louvat. And that her people will be most pleased to have her home again. A wise move, I think, to allow her to return to her father's land. See you, that yon Saxon barons have accepted this gesture most happily."

It was to be a gentle reminder to Ceara that her marriage to Luc was not of her choosing, but the king's. Luc repeated the king's words as he had said them.

Ceara looked up, a small frown knitting her brows, and Luc clenched his teeth. By all that was holy, if she provoked the king again, there would be no need for William to respond, for he would castigate her unmercifully himself.

"Sire," she said softly, "while once I would not have chosen this manner in which to return to my people, I am grateful that your justice has prevailed. But I pray you temper your decrees with mercy, so that more of my people will accept the edicts you force upon them."

Luc glared at her. William's gaze bent to him, then back to Ceara when Luc repeated her words through clenched teeth. The king stroked his chin, and displeasure darkened his eyes.

"Tell your lady wife that her people answer only to you in matters of judgment, for my northern barons are distant and must rule their lands absolutely in order to keep them. For myself, I do not give justice or mercy where it is not earned. If order is not kept in Wulfridge, she may yet find herself without a home."

Keeping his temper in check, Luc repeated William's words, adding his own harshly: "If you have anything else to say to the king, you had best think long and hard on the content, for you may find that your husband has no scruples about beating an errant wife."

Ceara looked full at him for the first time that day. He'd forgotten how blue her eyes were, with tiny gold flecks in them, and long lashes that curved in a graceful sweep. She lifted those lashes now as if amazed.

"My lord husband, I am at your mercy."

"Yea," he said softly, "you are. 'Tis best you remember that before you speak unwisely again."

Lowering her lashes, Ceara studied the untouched goblet in her hands, spinning it between her fingers steadily. The jewels around the cup glittered in the candlelight. "It is not possible for me to forget for even a moment how my very life depends upon the idle whim of another." She lifted the goblet and her voice. "Nay, I am not like to forget how you so graciously spared my life, only to dangle it before me like a hard-won prize. Was it so hard for you, my lord, to best a mere women in combat? Will you e'er forgive me for holding your life in my hands? Or do you dare admit how close you came to having a Saxon blade in your throat that day—"

"Enough," Luc warned.

Defiant, she tilted the goblet in her mouth and drained the wine, then set the jewel-encrusted vessel on the table with a thud. "Yea, my lord husband, 'tis quite enough, I think. Should you ever lay a harsh hand on me, you will have to kill me, for I will not suffer it idly."

Beyond her, Robert de Brionne sat with his mouth open, his eyes riveted on them both when Luc did not react.

But in truth, short of dragging her from the hall, there was little Luc could do at that moment unless he wanted to translate her comments to the king. The Saxon barons were ever watchful, and would take it amiss if he dealt harshly with his new wife at their wedding banquet. It might destroy William's efforts to consolidate Norman and Saxon.

Luc contented himself with putting a hand on her arm as if to caress her, but his fingers dug deeply into the tender skin of her wrist until she flinched.

"I told you once that I weary of hearing how you held your sword at my throat. I do not make a habit of repeating myself, but this one time I will—do not speak of it again, Ceara. 'Tis done. It would be your mistake to think that I will misjudge you again. By now, I know full well how capable you are of any word or deed."

Into the silence that fell between them, Sir Robert interjected in his rough English: "Is it true that Wulfridge lies on the northern coast? I understand it is lovely there."

Emotion flickered in Ceara's eyes, and it was she who answered Robert. "Yea, Sir Robert, it is a most lovely and fertile land, with fresh water and broad moors, and forests abounding with game. You would be welcome should you decide to visit, as you are my lord's companion and friend."

Neatly done, Luc thought grimly, as if she had every right to extend invitations in his name. He released her wrist. "Sir Robert is well aware that he is welcome in my home."

It sounded churlish even to his ears, and he saw that it did not pass Robert's notice as his friend grinned.

"There have been times in our past, Luc, that I was not so certain of a welcome at your hands, you may recall."

"I recall."

Another abrupt, surly reply that this time engaged the king's interest. Luc felt foolish as William asked if all was well.

"Yes, sire. A surfeit of natural strain from the day's events, is all."

"Then perhaps you should ease your strain with merrymaking instead of serious discussion. The minstrels play. Do you ask your lady to dance, Louvat. It will set the mood for us all."

Luc had his doubts about that. Those who were inclined were well on their way to being merry, and those who were sullen would not be cheered. But there was no use in saying that to the king, so he stood and held out his hand.

"My lady, do me the honor of a dance, if you will."

Ceara flashed him a quick upward glance. Consternation replaced defiance as she lifted her shoulders in a slight shrug. "My lord, I do not know your Norman dances."

"Then the minstrels will play a Saxon melody. That should

please you, as I am certain you will dance better than I, and thus shame me in front of all present."

It was apparently just the promise to convince her, for a smile curved her mouth and she placed her fingers in his outstretched palm. "Then of course I accept."

"I thought you might not be able to resist a challenge like this."

"I am dismayed that you know me so well, my lord." Her smile deepened, and she swung gracefully into the space cleared for the dancers, allowing him to continue holding her hand. Then she surprised him by affecting a deep, charming gesture of courtesy, bowing slightly with one foot forward and knees bending, the movement so effortless that one could see she had been born to it.

"When you are ready, my lord husband."

Fey creature, a changeling that swept him from anger to admiration with the blink of an eye, a woman as lovely to look at as she was capricious. Luc expelled a deep breath, and glanced toward the musicians.

Robert stood at the alcove where they played. He intercepted Luc's signal, and the musicians began to play a lively Saxon tune, the melody a bit halting as they were unfamiliar with it, but recognizable enough that some of the Saxon barons rose to join the dancers.

The mood in the hall grew gay and lively, as even some Normans joined in the unaccustomed steps of the Saxon dance. Ceara moved effortlessly, her skirts swinging about her slim ankles, her steps precise as she taught Luc. He did not tell her that as a boy he had been familiar with these dances, but allowed her to tutor him as if he had never pranced around the fire on a midsummer night.

"You learn quickly, my lord," she said once, glancing up at him, and he accepted her compliment with a shrug.

"All dances are similar."

"'Yea, so I have heard." She swung past him to the next partner, then skipped down the line before passing him again.

Robert had joined the dancers, and he grinned as he took Ceara's hands in his, obviously enjoying the moment. Sweeping her past Luc, he whispered loudly in English, "No need to look so black, my lord. She'll be returned to you soon enough."

Luc scowled. Even in jest, Robert need not foster any hope in Ceara that her husband cared for her. For he did not. He had wed her because his king requested it. If he desired her at all, it was not for any reason other than the usual reason a man desired a woman.

The steps of the dance took him in a pattern that required the frequent changing of partners, so that he was not often paired with Ceara. Yet he found himself watching her, seeking out the deep blue gown and tall, slender woman with the bright hair. Flowers had been woven into her loose curls, dainty white and blue and pink, trailing from a woven coronet of ribbons. The gown was lovely—as well it should be, for it had cost him a goodly portion to have it made for her in time for the wedding. The seamstress had done well, for the rich material was fitted to her waist, where a girdle of finely wrought gold links rode her slim hips. Intricate embroidery of golden thread trimmed the hem and long trailing cuffs of the sleeves.

As she swept gracefully past him, her eyes alight and her face flushed with exertion and enjoyment, Luc realized she was truly beautiful. He had never seen her thus, without a guarded expression or eyes full of contempt, and it rankled that she could so quickly forget her perfidy in lying to the king. And it was even more annoying that she could enjoy herself with such ease.

"My lord Luc," a breathless female voice implored, and he turned toward Lady Amélie's smiling invitation, "do me the favor of escorting me to the bailey for some fresh air. I find it most stifling in here."

Luc hesitated. He had assiduously avoided Amélie these past weeks, successfully evading her furious questions after she had learned of his betrothal to Ceara. Now, it seemed harmless enough, as the wedding was done and the widow would surely realize the futility of further pursuit. He bowed.

"I am at your disposal, Lady Amélie. A few moments of air that does not smell of smoke would benefit us both, I think."

He escorted her from the hall, allowing her to place her hand on his bent arm and walk beside him. A cold November wind blew as they left the shelter of the castle and walked along the ramparts. Torches sputtered in iron holders on the walls, casting flickering pools of light across the ground. Ever-vigilant guards glanced at them, then away. Amélie snuggled closer to him, shivering.

"It is colder out here than I had thought. Let us step into an alcove. There, we could share privacy and—anything that comes to your mind."

Luc paused to look down at her. "Amélie, you must know I am wed now."

"Of course I know. Do you think me blind and deaf?" She struck him lightly on the arm, shaking her pretty head. "But I also know it was not of your choosing. Everyone knows that the king commanded it. . . . Luc, why did you not come to me? Do you not find me desirable?"

"Yes, you know I do. If I remember aright, it was you who did not find me so desirable not too long ago."

"Foolish man. I have told you my reasons." She sighed and turned away. "If I had any idea you would have taken it so amiss, I would never have sought to inspire you to throw yourself into the arms of danger with my ploy. Oh, Luc, you must know that I care deeply for you. . . ."

He took a step back, frowning down at her. Torchlight wavered rosily over her lovely features, and her green eyes glinted with a moist sheen. His frown deepened, and he put out a hand to touch her wet cheek. "Tears, Amélie?"

She choked slightly and bent her head from his touch. "Why have you avoided me this past fortnight?"

Cynically amused by her show, Luc shrugged. "There was no point in seeing you. William bade me marry Ceara, and there was nothing else to say to you."

A steely note crept into her tone. "If you had only replied to my messages, I could have saved you from being wed to that Saxon chit."

"I doubt that. Once William has set his mind on a course, it is easier to change the direction of the wind than his decision."

Amélie frowned, her dainty brows puckering over the straight line of her nose. "Certainly, but as the king's wife is my cousin, I could have saved you if only you had come to me in time. Now, you are in a travesty of a marriage with little hope of escape."

Impatient now, Luc cupped her elbow in his palm and turned her back toward the castle doors. "It is growing late and we may have been missed. We need to return before the king wonders where I have gone during my own wedding feast."

"Oh, Luc—" Amélie turned and pressed her face against his chest. "I regret being so tardy in declaring my feelings for you. Can you ever forgive me, and . . . and think kindly of me?"

"I think kindly of you now, Amélie." Feeling a little awkward, Luc put his arms loosely around her body and held her. "But even had the king not decided I should wed Ceara, I do not think you and I would be suited to one another."

Her head tilted back, and even in the dim light he could see the sparks of anger in her eyes. "You do not mean that, Luc Louvat. You know you do not. You wanted me. You threw your heart at my feet in Winchester, and I spurned you so that you would renew your efforts to win lands and a title. You did that—you did it for me, so I would accept your suit. . . ."

"Amélie, what I have done, I have done for myself. You are lovely, it is true, and I did want you, but not in the way you so plainly think. There is a vast difference between bedding a woman, and wedding a woman."

It was as blunt and kind a refusal as he could make it. His

patience was wearing thin, and if the situation was not so irritating, it would have been amusing. But he was not so big a fool as to believe Amélie's vows of affection. What she desired most was a man's purse, not his heart. Her last husband had been elderly and frail when she wed him, unable to increase his holdings through merit, so had left his young widow with a title and not much else. Since then debts and heirs had taken most, leaving Amélie to make her own way.

Now she looked up at him with a pale face and flashing eyes, and he felt a twinge of regret for being so plain-spoken. He cupped her chin in his palm and said softly, "You are very beautiful. I remember fondly our times together, but it is not to be again. My liege lord bade me wed, and that I have done. I will make the best of it, just as you made the best of your lot when your father wed you to Lord de Vescy. Now let us go inside, each to our own lives."

Her anger was clear on her face, but she shrugged. "I am already on with my new life, Luc, though you might not care to hear of my plans. Once, they included you, but now . . . I can only say that you will always be in my life."

He frowned. "As you will always be in my past, Amélie. There is no room for you in my life now."

Amazingly, Amélie did not rail at him as he expected, but threw her arms around his neck and lifted to her toes to press a fervent kiss on his mouth. He did not push her away at once, but let the kiss linger a moment before gently taking her wrists in his hands to disengage himself.

A discreet cough was his first hint that they were not alone, and he drew down Amélie's arms and turned, expecting to find one of the guards. Instead, it was Robert and Ceara who stood there, Robert looking chagrined, and Ceara looking furious.

To make matters worse, Amélie cooed, "Why, Luc, we have been found out, it seems. I knew we should have gone to my chamber instead."

Releasing Amélie's arms, Luc shook his head. "There is

nothing we would have said there that could not be said here in plain view of all. Robert, what do you here?"

Robert gave a half shrug. "You were missed, and your lady wife and I were sent to search for you. The king wishes to toast your health, and has missed your presence."

Worse and worse. Luc moved forward, intending to take Ceara by the arm, but she jerked free of his attempt. Her eyes glinted blue fire in the dim light.

"Knave! I will not suffer your touch when you have just been holding another! Get you away from me. . . ."

He grabbed her arm before she could elude him again, and walked her several steps from Robert and Amélie. "This is not what you think, Ceara. Do not act the witless wife already. We have not been wed a full day yet."

" 'Tis not I who have forgotten that, my lord. Go back to your whore. She awaits you with your kiss still wet on her mouth—free my arm. Free my arm or I shall set up such a howl, all in York will come running to see the cause."

There was no doubt she meant what she said, and Luc released her arm with an oath. "*Sacré croix,* Ceara. Do you think me so unaware of my duty that I would woo another woman the same night I wed you?"

"The proof is before my eyes." Ceara shot a dark look toward Amélie. "Perhaps you should tell the king that he wed you to the wrong woman. It is obvious you have a favorite."

Luc's mouth set in a taut line. "I am in no mood to argue the truth. As I detest those who lie, I do not lie. If you would believe me, do so. If not, 'tis your own folly. But hear this—I will not suffer your ill temper because you choose wrongly. You will not lesson me with this, Ceara."

"Do you think I want the world to know of your false vow? I do not. All know already that we are forced to wed. I will not take on further shame because you choose to play the lecherous goat."

Luc stared after her angrily when she turned and walked

away. Curse her, he would not give her the satisfaction of running behind her like a love-sotted youth. Let her think what she willed. If she believed him no better than to make an assignation on the same night he was wed, then he could say nothing that would convince her differently.

"Luc. . . ." Robert stood at his side, his voice low. "I did not think we would find you in so awkward a situation. The guard said you walked outside to the ramparts, but did not mention that you were with a lady."

Luc glanced at him. Remorse settled on Robert's dark features. "It is of no matter. I cannot school my every deed or word so that it is not misunderstood. If Ceara chooses to believe me false, it is her burden. Now come. If William has summoned, I had best return."

He turned to Amélie. The expression on her face was as contented as a well-fed cat's, and he couldn't help a rueful smile. "Well you should look so smug, my lady. You have stirred a hornet's nest. It should provide you with much entertainment."

"Not as entertaining as it could have been had you come to my chamber, but it will do for now, Luc." She laughed. "If only you could have seen your face when your lady wife railed at you so meanly. I see that marriage will not always be agreeable for you, my love."

Still laughing, she accepted Robert's arm, and the three of them returned to the hall. Loud music and the acrid smell of smoke greeted them when the doors opened, and Luc blinked at the stinging haze. Tumblers were performing, leaping and rolling about the middle of the hall floor to capture the interest of the guests.

Yet Luc was well aware of interest diverting to him, from the king as well as Ceara. It did not help that he felt guilty, and it angered him that he should. He had done nothing wrong. He should not be made to feel as if he had. Nor would he, not even by William.

But the king said nothing beyond a courteous remark that

the acrobats were quite amazing, and Luc agreed. Ceara sat rigidly in her chair, eyes riveted on the rope dancer that balanced precariously on the narrow width of cord stretched high over the castle floor.

In that moment, Luc felt much the same as the rope dancer must, balanced high above hazards that awaited him. If he swayed too far to either side, he would plummet to the cold stone.

Ceara shot him a narrowed glance from beneath her lashes, and he was suddenly impatient to have it all behind him. The night, the consummation that would legalize their wedding—all of it weighed heavily. He wanted it done, so that he could leave York.

Rising to his feet, Luc signaled the king that he was ready to end his participation in the wedding feast, and William smiled assent.

"Ah, it is time for the wedding night to begin, I see. You have our blessing, Lord Louvat, you and the lady."

William rose to his feet and offered a toast to the bride and groom, and England's blessing upon them. The toast was echoed by many others, finally ending with a jocular toast from Robert de Brionne, who wished them healthy sons and beautiful daughters to grace their old age.

"And may they all look like the lady, instead of their homely sire," he ended to the accompaniment of much laughter from the guests.

But when Luc turned to Ceara, he was surprised by the stricken panic in her wide blue eyes as she realized the moment was at hand. Curse her, the worst had been done. What could she possibly fear from him now?

Chapter Eleven

A DRAFT STIRRED the wall hangings and made the candle flames dance. Shadows undulated across the walls and over the high, wide bed against the far wall. Ceara did not move. She would break into pieces if she dared move a muscle. All about were smiling faces, the Saxon and Norman barons who had come to witness the ceremonial bedding of the newly married couple.

It was a formality only, a ritual intended to complete the legal binding of the newly wedded couple. As she was widowed—and the events preceding the marriage were dubious—there would be no humiliating rite of public undressing and showing of the sheets afterward. All that was, thankfully, unnecessary.

Yet still, even this, the crowding into the chamber by barons and king, was fraught with tension for her. She did not want to look at Luc, much less lie beside him in the huge bed heavy with draperies. Nor did she wish to suffer the excited attentions of the giggling serving women who had removed her wedding garments and now garbed her in a soft flowing gown of fine linen embroidered with delicate stitchery and tiny pearls. It was a travesty. A mockery of all it should have been. Did no one else see it? Was she the only one to recognize that the king's efforts to gently bind Saxon and Norman were for naught?

Yes, and yes. Luc was aware of it. It was in his eyes, in his voice and his taut posture. How did he speak with their well-wishers as if they would soon return to Wulfridge and marital harmony? Yet she had heard him plainly, the regret in his voice when he told Lady Amélie: *"My liege lord bade me wed, and that I have done . . . I will make the best of it, just as you made the best of your lot when your father wed you to Lord de Vescy. Now let us go inside, each to our own lives. . . ."*

Her fingernails dug into her palms, but she allowed two serving women to guide her to the bed, where she stepped up the wooden assist to the high, thick mattress. Amid much laughter and bawdy jokes—she blushed to hear them and for once truly wished she did not understand their language—she was tucked beneath the coverings and her gown duly removed. A brief spurt of rebellion flared, but the image of being forcibly parted from her garments rose up to taunt her and she submitted silently. The lovely gown was laid over the end of the bed as she held the bedclothes up to her chin and waited in a stew of apprehension.

Luc was escorted to the bed by a much rowdier pair of gentlemen, one of them being Sir Robert. She averted her eyes when Luc was stripped of his clothing with none of the restraint that had been given her, then fairly tossed into the bed. More jests were made, then the king demanded that all depart and leave the couple in peace to begin their married lives.

A candle was placed atop a table near the bed, and in a few moments the chamber was empty of all save Luc and Ceara. As the door slammed shut, the echoes sounded much too loud in the sudden stillness.

It was cool, even beneath the warm coverings, and the bed hangings shifted in the room's drafts. Ceara shivered. The mattress dipped beneath his weight as Luc turned toward her, and his voice betrayed nothing of what he felt.

"We are to consummate in order to be bound legally."

"I know that."

Silence fell again, thick and freighted with tension. Luc's breathing seemed overloud, and the heat of his body seemed much too close though there was a good foot of empty space between them. He lay back upon the fat feather pillows and stared up at the canopy overhead.

"This is of your own making, Ceara," he said into the thick silence. "If you did not want this, you should not have provoked William. I tried to warn you. As seems usual for you, you did not listen to wiser heads."

She turned toward him angrily. "I wanted to go home. To *my* home. Wulfridge is mine, not yours, no matter how many dead Saxons you had to walk over to get it."

He sat up again, the covers falling down from his chest as he faced her, tension scoring grooves on each side of his mouth. "Pray tell me, gentle mistress, how many dead men do you think your father walked over to keep Wulfridge? And his father before him? And before him? How many were slain to take the lands from those who held them first? That castle is Roman in origin. Do you not think that your ancestors took it by force? Do you think the only blood spilled there is innocent? Nay, do not prate to me of such foolish things, for I know the ways of war far better than do you."

"You should. You wage it often enough." She drew a deep, painful breath, shaking with emotion. Honesty demanded that she recognize the truth of his claim. Sorrow reminded her that he wanted another woman in his bed.

"Yea," Luc said softly, "I do wage war often. It is the only life I have known since I was but a lad. Unlike you, who took it up as a caprice, war is my profession. I was trained to it from the time I was old enough to heft a wooden sword in my hands, since I was old enough to learn that one does not suffer blows without striking back. Do not think to lesson me on war, milady, for you are a poor pupil trying to teach a master."

"And yet—"

"Do not say it."

His soft warning held a wealth of menace, and she paused. To remind him again of how she had bested him might provoke him too greatly. After a moment, she looked away, brushing angrily at the tears in her eyes. It was all so hopeless, and any tenderness she had once thought to find in him was only an illusion. She had gravely erred if she thought this man felt any kindness toward her. He was just as he seemed—savage and warlike. A true Norman.

And she had seen him hold another woman in his arms, a woman he had freely chosen. How he must hate her for coming between them.

They lay there quietly for a time, staring up at the bed canopy and listening to the muffled noise of merriment that drifted from the great hall. York castle was unfinished yet, so sound traveled through the thin walls easily. She could hear the melodies of lute and lyre, accompanied by the thin sweet tune of a flute. It was a Saxon ballad like those she had heard as a child, and she closed her eyes, suddenly grieving for all that had been lost to her.

"It will do you no good to weep, Ceara," Luc said after a time. "What is done is done."

"What would you know of it?" Her throat ached from holding back sobs, and her eyes were hot and scratchy with suppressed tears. "You have won all. It is not your home that is lost to you."

"Yet I know that grief."

Opening her eyes, she turned her head to glare at him. "Do not think to ply me with empty words when you know nothing of what I feel!"

Luc turned on his side, propping his head on his palm to gaze at her with narrowed eyes. "Do you think you are the only one to ever lose your home? At least it was through no fault save that of greater arms."

"I suppose you want me to be grateful that my home was lost to you instead of to the Scots or the Danes. I see little difference between you. You are all predators, rapacious and greedy. Why should I care if Wulfridge is lost through war or wit? Do not make light of it."

"I do not make light of it. But you should think for a moment. You are not the only one to suffer loss. Is the world to stand still for you, Ceara de Wulfridge?" His voice was angry, and the hand he placed on the mattress between them was fisted. "No, do not talk to me of your loss when you have your life and honor left to you."

"Honor? To be forced to wed you to keep my home from being ravaged by Normans?" Her laugh sounded brittle even to her own ears. "I have no honor left. It is all over York and most likely England by now that I gave myself to a Norman on the old Roman road."

"That was your choice and your trick. Do not complain if it is not as you wished. What did you expect? That the king would deed you Wulfridge for the loss of your maidenhead? As I told you before, you put too great a value on it, Ceara. Maidens all over England have lost much more than you."

He was right, and she knew it, but it did not make her loss any easier to bear. Holding the covers to her chin, she sat up. In the shadows, he looked lean and predatory, almost wolfish. She closed her eyes briefly, then steeled herself.

"I cannot restore the losses of others. I must deal with my loss as best I can. If I have deceived you, it was a deception you happily submitted to. I have not yet heard of a woman being able to force a man to come to her bed. As I recall, you did not need much coaxing from me, for you had already made up your mind what you desired. Am I right, my lord? Or do you wish to call me liar on that as well as everything else? You did not listen when I told you I was virgin—why would you listen now?"

Breathless from her tirade, Ceara paused, trembling. Luc had not spoken, nor had he taken his eyes from her.

"No, I will not call you liar on that. It is true. I wanted you. I still want you. Whether you tempted me or not, my acts were of my own free will. I do not deny that. But you cannot deny that you did not loathe my touch, Ceara. I am not inexperienced. I can tell when a woman responds."

She flushed with indignant denial. "I only pretended interest so that you—"

"No." He reached out to cup her chin in his palm. "Do not bother with a lie that is so easily seen. You did not invent your response when I touched you here . . . and here." His hand shifted to move downward, gently shoving away the covers to caress her breast and the tight peak of her nipple. She shuddered, despite her best efforts not to react, and he smiled. "Nor can you hide your feelings now, though they are not as obvious as mine. It is a man's lot to always have his desire known, while a woman may yet hide hers. But there are ways to tell the truth of it, Ceara, and you cannot deny that your flesh likes my touch even if your heart will not admit it."

"Leave my heart out of this . . . and stop that."

She tried to push his hand away from her breast, but stopped with her fingers wrapped loosely around his wrist. He held still, his fingers warm and gentle against her skin. His voice lowered, becoming thick and husky.

"You have won what you desired, *ma belle.* Now yield me my desire."

Quivering beneath his caress and the warm, intimate tone of his voice, she tried not to let him see how he affected her. "I . . . cannot."

"Yea, you can. And you will, though you may not know why."

The enigmatic remark spurred her resistance, and she edged away from him. "You speak foolishly."

"And you, *ma chérie,* lightly ply a maiden's fancy if you think I will be stayed this night. You wanted to be my wife and lady of Wulfridge, and so you are. I wanted you in my bed—and so you are."

"Does it not matter to you that I do not want you?"

"Should it?" He took hold of her wrist as she let go of him, turning her arm over and lifting it to his mouth. His lips pressed against the thin skin of her wrist, her inner elbow, then higher, his mouth hot and soft and demanding, sending shivers through her entire body. "Did it not matter to you that I did not want to wed, *chérie?* I do not think so. Yet we are wed, and I want you, and for me, it is enough waiting."

"And if I refuse you?"

"I will take you anyway." He rubbed his thumb over her collarbone in a slow circle. "It is your choice, but make no mistake—this marriage will be consummated tonight."

Still holding her arm, he rose to his knees, a dark silhouette against the glowing light from the candle, a hard-muscled promise of change and danger. He was too close. Too overpowering. He seemed to fill not only the bed, but the entire chamber with his presence, and she thought wildly that she had been fool indeed to ever think she could manipulate this man.

"My lord—"

"Luc." His fingers tightened slightly on her arm. "My name is Luc. I have never heard you say my name, and would hear it on your lips. Luc Louvat—my name and now one shared with you. Say it, Ceara."

She tensed. It felt strange on her tongue, especially if she said it as he did. *Lewk Lew-vah.* So French. So alien, for all that it was now so familiar to her. But he waited, his hand a firm, unyielding pressure. And a reminder that though she may resist, he would force her to yield to his stronger will.

"Luc Louvat." She deliberately mispronounced it *Look Loovat,* and saw him wince. Her mouth set into a stubborn line when he started to correct her, and he paused with a shrug.

"One day I shall teach you to speak proper French, but for

now, that will do. There are other, more important things you must learn this night, *chérie.*"

She trembled when his hand slid up her arm in a lingering caress to her shoulder, his palm holding her steady as his other hand moved to cup her chin. Why did he stare at her so intently, as if he were trying to pierce her very soul?

His hands were so warm on her, searing wherever they touched. She wanted to move away, to flee from the bed and the chamber, but her limbs were leaden and uncooperative, so that she could only shiver helplessly under his caresses. On his knees, with the light behind him so that his face was in shadow, he loomed ruthless and predatory, relentlessly touching her wherever he pleased. His fingers skimmed her throat, her breasts, over her ribs to her belly and then lower, to touch her between her legs, a feathery caress that ignited a fierce ache.

"I did not give you the right to touch me," she began in a strangled tone that sounded foolish even as she said it, and Luc laughed softly as he caught the hand she put against his chest.

"Yea, *chérie,* you gave me rights when you spoke your vows in front of the priest this morning."

"Not to own me!"

"Ah, but I do own you. It is the way of things. But this is not about ownership. This, what we do, is sharing."

"And if I do not want to share?"

"That is not your choice." His faint smile barely lessened the sting of his reply, and he held her tightly when she tried to twist away. "But I do not think you mean what you say. The first time was not as it should have been. This time . . . this time can be what passion is supposed to be, *ma belle.* If I had known before that you were untried, I would have been more gentle."

While he talked, he stroked her quaking body, his hands admittedly gentle, fondling her with slow, careful movements that created shivering responses. Even the air felt warm now—almost stifling.

It was inevitable, and while she did not want to yield, Luc's caresses were smothering her resistance. And she had not forgotten that night on the old Roman road when she had been oblivious to everything but the mindless need he had ignited. While she could privately acknowledge the desire he roused in her, she dared not let him know the power he held over her body or her emotions.

But how did she counter his demanding kisses? The sweet touch of his hands that kindled such exquisite tremors? He seemed to instinctively know every vulnerability of her body, and use it against her.

His skin was hot, firm, and lightly furred beneath her palms as she pressed her hands against his chest, unable to admit surrender. He took her wrist and pulled her arm downward, so that her hand smoothed over the taut muscles of his chest and belly. Still holding her wrist, he muttered something in guttural French that she did not understand, and looked up at her. His expression was fiercely intent, his thick-lashed eyes dark and glittering.

Ceara's fingers trembled, and she shook her head when he pulled her hand lower. "No, Luc . . ."

"Are you afraid, *chérie?* You?"

Yes. Of you. Of me. Of what this will mean to me and will not mean to you. . . .

Aloud she said, "No. I am not afraid, just—unwilling."

"You will not always be unwilling," he said softly, and she remembered he'd said something very similar earlier.

Closing her eyes, Ceara tried to dismiss his soft words, the endearments in husky French and hoarse English that sifted between them, muttered with lingering kisses on her closed eyelids, earlobe, and mouth. His lips sought the drumming pulse in her throat, then moved lower to the cushioned swell of her breast, tasting and teasing until she writhed with breathless urgency. She could not fight him, not in this, not when she was so vulnerable to the unfamiliar pleasures he summoned from her quivering body. Insanity to allow it, but helpless to resist it, she could not hold back soft moans of mounting excitement.

As if he had been waiting for just that response, Luc shifted. He sat back, gazing down at her until she flushed with embarrassment and tried to cover herself with the heavy embroidered coverlet. He caught her hand.

"Ah no, beauty. Do not hide such a beautiful body. It would be a crime to cover this . . . or this . . . did you know your breasts are perfect? So round and firm . . . and your nipples are like tight rosebuds begging for my touch. . . ." He bent, taking a nipple into his mouth with a soft inhalation that made her gasp. Against her breast, he murmured, "You smell like lavender. Sweet. Tempting. *Bon Dieu,* you could drive a man to reckless idiocy—as you did me."

He looked up at her with wry amusement slanting his mouth. "Your vengeance must be sweet, *chérie.* You have maneuvered me exactly as you wanted to do."

"I never"—she halted, flushing a little when his brow lifted in mockery—"meant it to come to this, anyway," she finished irritably, and he laughed.

"That I can believe. We are both caught in this trap, it seems, but must make the best of it. And in truth, it may be worth the price to have you in my bed of a night."

There was no answer she could give to that, none that would sound as if she was not willing, or worse—remind him of Lady Amélie, so she kept her silence. Luc continued his exploration, hands stroking and caressing, fingers dipping into curves and hollows with breathtaking results. She quivered. His weight was heavy against her, the pressure of his hip and thigh against her bare flesh hot and arousing. Half lying on his side, his gaze skimmed over her as lightly as his hands, over the swell of her belly and lower, to tangle his fingers in the silky nest of her mound.

"Soft," he murmured, and stroked his thumb over the very center of her to spark an exquisite tremor that made her ache.

Immediately she clamped her thighs together to trap his hand. He glanced up. "Open for me, *ma chérie.*"

Ceara's entire body was aflame with a mixture of shame and arousal. She could not . . . but there was no need to make the decision, for he was gently pushing apart her thighs with his hands, his fingers making slow circles on her bare flesh, brushing inexorably toward the fiery center he had just touched. She could not bring herself to look away as his lashes lowered in a curved shadow on his dark cheeks and he gazed down at her.

And then he was caressing her there, thumbs raking over her sensitive flesh until she arched upward with shuddering moans, her hands reaching out to push him away but instead holding on to his hard-muscled arms. The heat spread upward and outward in fierce spirals, engulfing her, leaving her shaking and breathless and writhing beneath his hands.

When she moved into his caress blindly, clutching at him urgently, he slid his leg over her thighs to wedge his knee between them. Gently, he settled between her legs, and now there was a new pressure against her, a smooth heat that nudged with searing intimacy between her thighs. It caught her off guard, this hot, hard thrust that pushed against the aching center of her.

She looked up, breathless, uncertain, and he stared back down at her as his hips moved forward in a slow excursion into her damp curls. He slid just inside her, an oddly taut, exquisite invasion that hovered between pain and pleasure. With his head bent, he cupped his hands beneath her hips to lift her, and moved again, slowly penetrating with heavy fullness. She shuddered, and he paused.

"Am I hurting you, *chérie?*"

His voice was so odd, so hoarse and thick, and she shook her head, the words sticking in her throat so that they came out in a rasp. "No, it does not . . . hurt."

His chest rose and fell with harsh, quick breaths, and his arms quivered with strain as he held her to him. It felt so odd, his body just inside hers, soft yet so hard, a heated length that seemed much too large to fit. Yet it had fit before, she knew, but so briefly and so piercingly that if not for the bright blood on his blankets, she would not have been certain she'd lost her virginity.

But there was no mistaking it now, as Luc gave a sudden hard push that caught her by surprise as he sheathed his length inside her. She cried out with shock and he bent to kiss her, his mouth lingering on hers until her taut muscles relaxed and she kissed him back. As her body accepted his, he began to move again, in slow, luscious slides that summoned shuddering responses from her.

Now there was only the soaring sensation of excitement, a hovering goal just out of her reach. Whimpering, her hips driving up to meet his thrusts, her body clamored for the mysterious satisfaction that eluded her grasp.

"Luc . . . please," she whispered, "please. . . ." She didn't know what she wanted, what she asked for, but it didn't matter. He would know.

His head lifted, and he gave her a long look that seared her like fire. Dark hair tumbled over his forehead and into his eyes, and the fine white scar along his jawline looked vivid against his dark skin. His chest rose and fell in labored pants as he withdrew, hovered for a moment, then thrust again, heightening the excitement to near torture as he slammed into her body with exquisite force. She was only vaguely aware of anything but Luc, his muscled shoulders and hard body, the glistening arc of his throat and dark features above her—nothing mattered now, nothing but reaching that elusive peak that waited just beyond her reach.

And then, suddenly, she was there, the frenzy exploding into a whirling shock of ecstatic waves that dragged her into a void where there was nothing but discovery and wonder.

Dimly, she heard Luc groan, the sound muffled by layers of shuddering bliss, and his arms grew tight around her as his body went stiff and still. She felt a peculiar throb, a shudder, then he relaxed, and his mouth found her lips briefly before he shifted his weight to one side, still holding her.

She felt boneless, almost too weak to lift her head, and glanced at him with unaccustomed shyness. In the dim light, he stretched with unconcerned nudity beside her, his long body dark against the stark white of the bed linens. A faint smile lifted one corner of his mouth, and candlelight reflected in his dark eyes.

"Now, *chérie,*" he murmured, tracing his fingertip over the passion-bruised, swollen outline of her mouth, "you are truly my wife. And when I want you, you will come to me."

She shivered at the arrogance in his voice and eyes, and prayed that she would not lose her heart as well as her liberty to this man.

PART II

Chapter Twelve

SEA WINDS SWEPT over the tall grasses, bending them to the ground, howling over wave-lashed rocks at the foot of the promontory where Wulfridge castle stood sentinel. A seabird wheeled overhead, its cry sifting through cloud and wind. It was a raw day, with heavy gray skies and a steady drizzle that made man and beast alike miserable.

Through shifting fog and low-lying cloud, the gray stones of the castle were barely visible across the inlet. Luc could feel Ceara's rising excitement, and shot her a quick glance.

Mounted atop a snow-white palfrey, a wedding gift from William, Ceara wore a hooded cloak that covered her bright hair with crimson wool trimmed in ermine. It was a truly magnificent cloak, purchased with Luc's hard-won coin, and worth it to his mind, for it set off her fair coloring like a rich jewel. Before leaving York, he'd purchased an entire wardrobe for her. He had not expected nor wanted thanks, but she had come to him with bright eyes and an almost shy smile, and pressed a silent kiss against his cheek.

At that moment, he'd felt like an awkward youth again, clumsy and uncomfortable, but it had quickly passed. There was too much else to distract him, and he was swift to take advantage of her agreeable mood in the time-honored way husbands had with their wives.

Even now the memory of her soft body and eager caresses stirred him, and he shifted uncomfortably in his saddle and looked away from her across the choppy inlet toward the castle. He should not let a woman affect him like this, but somehow, Ceara crept into his thoughts with increasing frequency. At odd moments when he should be thinking of plans for fortifying the castle, or how many men he would need to garrison and how to strengthen his border positions, he would think instead of lavender-scented skin and hair the color of summer wheat.

It was as unnerving as it was arousing.

Luc urged Drago into a trot as they reached the road rounding the inlet. Cold wind burned his ears, stung his skin and eyes, smelling of snow and sea. Steam rose from Drago's hide, and the destrier snorted eagerly as if sensing the end of the journey was near, a reaction echoed by the other horses. The jangle of metal bridle bits and creak of leather was almost drowned out by the roar of the surf crashing against rocks and sandy tussocks. At the end of the line of mounted men came the baggage carts and the cart bearing the caged wolf. From Sheba, a howl rose into the air, barely audible above the sounds of the sea but still causing the horses to whicker uneasily.

Some of the men cursed and had to struggle to keep their mounts on the narrow road, portions of which had washed away and been replaced with a new bridge made of rough-hewn logs. Deep mud made rough work out of the last of the steep road leading into the castle, and a greeting was shouted down from the walls when Luc's standard came into view.

Remy came running out to meet them as the gates swung open, still buckling on his sword. Wind snarled his hair and curled his short cloak around him as the captain halted outside the castle and waited.

"I see you have taken great care of the castle, Captain

Remy." Luc dismounted inside the small bailey, glancing about him at the well-tended grounds. Crumbled stone walls had been repaired, and the rubbish that had been strewn about was gone.

"I have tried, my lord. When the weather clears, we will repair the road again." Remy glanced past Luc to the woman seated atop the elegant white palfrey, and his eyes widened. He cleared his throat and looked back at Luc. "I received your message, my lord, and have made ready the chamber you requested for your new bride."

Remy's curiosity was obvious, and Luc indicated Ceara with a tilt of his head. "The lady is weary, and will no doubt wish to go to our chamber at once. Where is Paul? Drago needs to be unsaddled and tended, as do the other horses—ah, Paul, here you are. I think Drago missed you."

Paul's weathered face creased with delight. "As I did him, my lord. We are much alike, in that we appreciate our old friends." Taking the destrier's reins, Paul murmured soothing words that earned a twitch of an ear and a welcoming nudge from the great head. "Come, meet a new friend, old fellow. Hardred will treat you most kindly."

Luc moved past the horse steward, Remy at his side, to where Ceara perched atop her palfrey. She glanced at him, then to Paul, frowning. "My lord, please release my wolf from her cage. I do not want her in the stables. Sheba has been imprisoned so long she no doubt cannot use her limbs by now, and must be exercised."

"One day without exercise will not harm her too greatly." Luc's mouth tightened when Ceara shook her head, and before she could argue, he stated his position more firmly. "I cannot just free the beast among my men."

"Sheba roamed this castle long before Normans came, and will not leave unless I bid her to do so. Ask, if you do not trust me to be truthful. Any man here who knows the wolf knows that she is tame, and would not harm a beast or man unless she is provoked."

Luc eyed her, and without replying, reached up to lift her down from the palfrey. Her hands flew to his shoulders for balance, and her body tensed beneath his hands as he deliberately held her above the ground. Blond hair tumbled from beneath the hood to frame her face, and her fingers dug into the mail over his shoulders. Her strong scent of lavender wafted over him, stirring him so that he set her on her feet and released her. It would never do to act as if he was besotted with her in front of his men.

"I will consider your request, and most likely allow Sheba to roam if it is proven that she is harmless. But tonight, I think it best the wolf remain safely in her cage, until I have had the opportunity to advise my men of her harmless nature."

Ceara smiled slightly. "I did not say she was harmless, only that she will not attack unless I allow it."

Luc's brow lifted. "Then I will think on it a long time before I make my decision." Switching back to French, he turned to Captain Remy. "I trust there is ample food for the evening meal, as we have ridden long and hard this day to reach Wulfridge before dark."

Remy nodded, and glanced toward the doors of the castle uneasily. "My lord, perhaps you are unaware, but you have guests."

"Guests?" Luc was surprised. "Who has come so swiftly that they arrive before I have?"

Coughing, Remy looked uncomfortable, but Luc had only a moment's apprehension before his captain replied, "It is your brother, my lord."

Luc's jaw set tensely, and his words came out in a low growl. "Jean-Paul is here?"

Remy nodded unhappily. "He arrived only yesterday. I did not know your wishes, so have allowed him to stay. I hope I have not erred, my lord."

"No. It is not your place to refuse entry to him. It is mine."

Tugging at his mail gauntlets, Luc strode toward the castle without waiting for Ceara. How could Jean-Paul arrive as if nothing had happened between them, as if there had been no fierce rivalry? And now, now that he had earned title and lands, Jean-Paul just appeared on his doorstep as if it had been yesterday instead of five years since they had seen one another.

But this time, it was not Luc who was the cast-off son, disinherited with nothing but his sword and an adopted name. It was Jean-Paul who had lost all but his life, although he was luckier than their father, for both had dealt treacherously with William and few men survived that.

Torches lit the short corridor leading to the hall, and armed guards straightened to attention when Luc stalked past them. A fire blazed in the center of the hall, huge logs crackling, smoke curling upward to blacken the rafters and ceiling.

Jean-Paul sat at the main table, talking with a woman and two other men. Reflected torchlight glinted in his blond hair. The hall fell silent as Luc entered and made his way past trestle tables set up for knights and soldiers, and finally the quiet caught Jean-Paul's attention so that he paused and glanced up. His face paled slightly, and he set down his wine goblet as Luc approached.

"Greetings, brother," Jean-Paul said when Luc reached the table. "I trust your journey was uneventful."

"What do you here, Jean-Paul?"

It was a demand more than a question. Jean-Paul's mouth turned down at the corner as he regarded Luc. "I came to beg succor."

"Did you. Why now? Why not last year? Two years past?" Luc stepped onto the dais and moved to the end of the table, watching narrowly as his brother rose to his feet to turn and face him.

Slowly holding his arms out to his sides to show that he wore no weapon, Jean-Paul said quietly, "I came now for I have nowhere else to go, Luc. I am bereft of all! Home. Land. Name. Family. You are all that is left to me."

"A bitter day for you, then, I warrant."

"Bitter indeed." Jean-Paul's blue eyes lowered under Luc's relentless gaze. "Once, you said if ever I needed you, you would come."

"That was a long time ago, Jean-Paul. Much has happened since then. Much of your own making."

"True enough. Yet I am here now, and I humble myself to you." He looked up, the blue eyes that Luc remembered from their childhood beseeching, reminding him of times that were not so bad, boring into him with hopeful regard. "Do not turn me out, Luc. No one else will take me in."

"Perhaps you should have chosen your former companions more carefully then." Luc drew in a deep breath that tasted of smoke and bitterness. "I will not turn you out this eve. We will talk on the morrow, once I have rested and thought on the matter."

It was a compromise of sorts, if not a victory, and Jean-Paul brightened immediately. "You will not be sorry, Luc. I will—"

"Who are your companions?"

Luc's abrupt query cut short his brother's promises, which always came much too easily and lacked sincerity, and Jean-Paul turned toward the woman and two men at the table.

"Friendless wanderers like myself. They mean no harm, Luc, but seek only shelter and your kindness."

Luc swept them with a critical glance. A disreputable lot, to be sure. Mercenaries oft came to England with high hopes but no merit, and were soon disappointed.

"My hospitality is extended to your companions for this night only. On the morrow, I will have my steward give them a coin and food, and they will be on their way."

Jean-Paul looked chagrined, and the woman's eyes grew wide with dismay, but Luc turned away. He had enough to do without providing charity to those unwilling to work.

As he left the hall, he saw Ceara. She stood just inside the outer door, an odd expression on her face. He halted beside her.

"There are guests in the hall. They will be on their way by the morrow. If you do not care to share the table with them, I will have Alain bring food to you in our chamber."

"Nay, that is not necessary." Her quick reply was followed by a light shrug. "I would see to Sheba before I eat, as she will be hungry and miserable."

"Curse that wolf—would you have her eat at the table as well?"

"Once, she ate where she pleased, but no, my lord. I would not ask you to do anything that made you uneasy."

His mouth tightened. "I do not fear the wolf, but my men are not as accepting."

"Yea, my lord. I understand."

Hard on the heels of Jean-Paul's unfamiliar humility, Ceara's mockery was more than he could stomach. He swore again, harshly this time, a vile French curse that caused one of the guards to glance at him with apprehension. Luc took Ceara's arm just above the elbow, and walked her several steps away. Though she was stiff with resistance, she offered no struggle when he turned her toward him.

"Take the wolf to your chamber. Be certain there is no trouble because of it, or she will be caged again. Keep her with you."

She gazed up at him a moment. The rebellion in her eyes faded, and a faint frown creased her brow. "Do you expect trouble, my lord? I mean—danger?"

"No." He released her arm, feeling suddenly foolish. She was more astute than he'd thought. And he had no reason to think of danger. Yet he knew his brother, knew him to be capable of great treachery, and would take no chances. Had he not been betrayed before? Taken in the night when he slept, before he could reach his weapon and defend himself? He would not chance it again.

Shrugging, his reply was brusque. "If you question my decision, leave the wolf in her cage. I do not care, but I am weary of your harping on the subject."

He pivoted and walked away before she could speak again, but he felt her gaze follow him. The homecoming he had anticipated was not as he had wished. But he should have expected trouble. When had it ever avoided him?

Luc was in the small room off the solar that he was to share with Ceara when Alain found him, sidling in the door in his customary way, a smile of welcome on his face.

"Welcome back, my lord. Your return is most timely, for it has begun to snow quite heavily."

Luc looked up with a faint smile. "I thought it would be soon, for the air smelled of snow. Have we stores enough for the winter?"

"Enough, I think. The harvest was in, but was not plentiful, as Sir Simon's arrival interrupted the gathering of crops. Now, much wheat has rotted in the fields, but I was able to save enough wheat and corn to last if we are frugal. Fatted pigs and kine have been salted down, and should the supply grow too low, wild game abounds aplenty in the forests, if the king's laws will permit our hunting."

"The king has granted me complete sovereignty over these lands, as we are so remote. I have only to hold them against the Scots and Danes, and any Saxon outlaws who would take them from me."

Alain looked a bit surprised as he glanced up from gathering Luc's armor. "I had not thought William so trusting as to lend complete sovereignty to any man, my lord."

"Nor did I. Yet Northumbria rumbles with the threat of rebellion, and is so near the land of the Scots that he has little choice but to give his earls free rein to hold the border as best they can." Luc bent a keen gaze on the squire. "Do you fear I will fail, Alain?"

"Fail? No, no, you misunderstand, my lord. Not for a moment do I think you will fail. You have won over all odds, have you not? And you have won all, my lord."

"No. I have not won all." Jean-Paul's arrival dredged up the old memories, the old hurts, and made raw the wounds he had thought healed. But it was his father who had done the worst, caused the damage of soul and body that would never heal. No matter where he went or what he achieved, he would never be able to forget his father's contempt, the words and deeds that had seared him so deeply.

"My lord?" Alain looked at him curiously, and Luc rose abruptly to his feet.

"My brother has arrived with guests. Jean-Paul may stay, but his companions are to be sent on their way in the morning with food and a gold coin apiece. Point them toward Malcolm, if you like." He paused, frowning. "And, Alain, see you that my brother has his needs met, but is not left to his own ends. He may roam the castle freely, but I want him watched. He is not to leave without my permission. Is that understood?"

"Of course, my lord. I will see to it at once."

"Good." Luc rubbed the back of his neck with one hand. "Your hard work in my absence will be rewarded well, Alain. Much has been restored, it seems. On the morrow, we will survey the castle and set about repairing the broached ramparts that are not yet mended. I have in mind a new wall to be built about the whole of it, like those in Spain and Normandy."

"With battlements?" Alain nodded approval. "A garrison could hold off an entire army with such strong defenses, my lord. I hope we do not soon need such a wall."

"I do not anticipate it, but neither would I be such a fool to think myself secure enough to let down my guard. King Sweyn of Denmark lies now in the Humber River for the winter, and Earls Cospatric and Edgar are just over the border with King Malcolm. Those ravening vultures would like nothing better than to get a foothold on William's lands, and Wulfridge lies near both those enemies. I must be ever vigilant. How many men are left to tend knight service?"

"Besides the six vassals who swore to you before you left for York, there are three who did not answer the call to arms, but are bound to Wulfridge."

"Send for them. I would hear their oaths of fealty or pledge of war, and know where I stand." He paused. "Are there preparations made for Christmas?"

"None yet, my lord. It is so near, and we knew not when you would return."

"Make plans. Invite those three barons, as well as the others who have sworn to me."

"But, so many, seignior! Our stores may not last if we dole out too plentifully—"

"As you said, Alain, there is plenty of game in the forests. Take you huntsmen and bring back boar and deer, as well as as many fowl as you can provide. We have the sea at our very door teeming with fish for the table, and I warrant there are many here who earn their livelihood that way. Offer coin. That will be more than enough incentive."

Alain goggled at him. "*Pay* for what is yours by right of sovereignty, my lord? That would be foolish, and set a dangerous precedent. Indeed, it would be best to send armed men to demand our full share, and then they would be—"

"Send armed men, if you like, but with purses of coin to pay for what we need." Luc's cool tone penetrated the squire's indignation, and he paused to stare at his lord with eyes still wide. "I will not beggar my own people to provide feasts for men already fat with plenty. Starving serfs make poor labor. And while I think on it, provide free materials for repair of their homes, and a measure of free wood for their fires. List beside each man's name how much he required, and explain that it will be portioned out now, but next year they will pay for it with tender of crops and beasts for my storehouses. If any should be hungry, he is to come to me for food, and he will be given what is needed for these lean times. In times of plenty, they will give generously in return to replenish the stores against the coming winter months."

Alain looked stunned. His mouth opened and shut, and finally he nodded, a short jerk of his chin that plainly told of his opposition. "As you will it, my lord. But I must state again that it is a dangerous precedent."

"No doubt. But well-fed, content serfs are unlikely to offer aid to outlaws seeking to stir rebellion, and much more likely to inform their lord of such attempts." He smiled slightly. "I will deal fairly with all who deal fairly with me. And I will destroy those who do not. See that my offers are made, Alain. But now, send to my chamber food and wine, as I have not eaten this eve. Nor has my lady."

Alain hesitated, then said stiffly. "My congratulations on your marriage, my lord. The lady is as lovely as she is brave."

"Yes. I recall well her bravery. And her temper. Tell me, Alain, what you know of the man you set to guard her. Giles."

"Giles . . . ah yes. He was one of Sir Simon's men. Did he displease you, seignior?"

"He displeased the lady. When I reached York and questioned him on it, he claimed he was bade by you to see to her welfare, and to offer her your kind regards should she be pleased to accept them."

Alain paled a little, but nodded. "Yes, my lord, so I did. I admit—I was taken with her. I thought—as you may recall—that if she should be given as wife, the king might look with favor on my suit if the lady was willing."

"The lady was not."

"No, my lord. And as it has happened, she chose the better man by far. Forgive me if I have displeased you."

Luc studied him a moment, the flushed face and fair hair tumbling into his eyes, hands clasped nervously around Luc's chain mail hauberk. He shrugged. "I am not displeased, but would remind you that I did warn you the lady was not for you."

"Yes, my lord. If I had known you wanted her, I would never have—"

"That is not it at all. I had no designs on the lady, only her father's lands." He paused, realizing how foolish he sounded in light of all that had happened, then shrugged again. "She is beautiful and any man would be tempted, but the king's will mattered above all. It pleased William to wed her to me to bind Saxon and Norman together."

An expression of contempt creased Alain's face. "Saxons will never be as Normans. All know the English breed an inferior race."

"So I have heard it said. Yet I was born near Oxford, and spent the first years of my life on English soil, so I would have a differing opinion."

Alain swallowed hard. "I had forgotten, my lord."

"Have my supper sent to me in my chamber. Enough for two. And a slab of beef or mutton joint as well."

The squire did not question the last, though he gave Luc another odd look before he departed, shutting the door softly behind him. The sudden draft made the candle flame dance wildly, and Luc stared at it for some time before rousing from his reverie.

It was late and he was bone-weary. The morrow would come soon enough with its problems and challenges. Not the least of which was his brother. Discretion bade him send Jean-Paul away, yet the memory of another time intruded to remind him that this was still his brother. Half brother, but his own blood. Should he yield to the appeal in Jean-Paul's eyes? Once, he would not have. But hatred destroyed the vessel in which it was carried, and he had learned to let go of that useless emotion years ago, before it ruined him.

A muffled yelp drew his attention, and his head jerked up at a sudden commotion in the hallway. Shouts in French and English rose into the air, mixed with snarls of bestial rage. Luc strode at once to the door and jerked it open, then came to an abrupt halt at the scene that met his eyes.

Backed against the stone wall of the corridor, a dagger in one fist, Jean-Paul glared at Ceara. The white wolf crouched low at Ceara's feet, hackles raised, curved teeth gleaming in the dim light of a wall torch. Only Ceara's hand held back the wolf.

Ceara glanced at Luc, her voice cool. "Give me but the word, and this knave will do for Sheba's supper, my lord."

Luc motioned impatiently. "Call off your wolf, Ceara. What is the cause of this? I told you that this beast might be too dangerous to allow inside—"

"If the beast you refer to is yon quaking knave, then I do agree with you, my lord. He needs be taught a lesson in manners, and Sheba thought only to school him well."

Luc's gaze shifted to Jean-Paul, who shrugged sullenly. "I thought her a serving wench." He gestured at Ceara with his dagger, which earned more snarls from the wolf. "Hold the cursed beast, for the love of God," Jean-Paul pleaded. "Luc—bid this silly bitch control her wolf. I will not accost her again, I swear it."

"The silly bitch you speak of is my wife, Jean-Paul."

Luc's soft, deadly tone penetrated his brother's fear, and he looked toward him with sudden consternation. "I did not know, I swear it. But look at her, garbed like a peasant—how was I to know?"

Indeed, Ceara wore none of the finery he had purchased for her in York, but one of her shortened tunics, well worn and barely covering her long legs. His mouth tightened with irritation, but reproofs for Ceara would be done in private, not in front of his brother.

"You have no leave to accost any woman on these lands, Jean-Paul, whether she be serf or lady. If I should hear of it, you will deal with me, and I do not think you want that."

Drawing himself up, Jean-Paul sheathed his dagger. "You have grown more like our father than you would like, Luc."

Fury rattled him so that for a moment Luc could not speak. Then he said, "You may be my brother, but liken me to our father again and you will regret it."

Silence fell heavily, with only the labored pants of the wolf filling the air between them. Finally Jean-Paul looked away, nodding his head, his voice a low mutter.

"I meant nothing by it, Luc. Pray, pardon me."

"Ask the lady's pardon for your rough treatment. She might be willing to give it."

Another silence stretched between them before Jean-Paul drew in a deep breath and turned to Ceara, bowing stiffly in her direction. "I crave your pardon for offending you, my lady. It was a mistake."

"Speak to her in English, Jean-Paul."

He repeated it in English, his voice sullen, and Ceara lifted a brow. "Indeed it was a mistake if you think you can force your attentions on any woman. Count yourself fortunate you are not a tasty morsel for my pet, nor are you yet bereft of what little manhood you may possess."

Jean-Paul's eyes flared with anger. "You have a sharp tongue, my lady."

"Aye, and a sharper dagger. Mark it well—should you think to lay hand on any woman here, I will know of it, and I will see that you pay dearly."

"Enough." Luc stepped between them. In English, he bade them both go their own ways, and added to his brother, "In the morn, we will meet after we break our fast, and discuss the future."

Putting a hand on Ceara's arm, he steered her to the antechamber he had just left, holding tightly when she tried to pull away. "Our supper is growing cold, my lady. Bring the wolf."

She shot him a quick glance, then shrugged. "Sheba, to me."

The wolf backed away from Jean-Paul, hackles up and ears

flattened. A savage expression on the animal's face made Luc doubt his wife's assurances that this wolf was tame, and he gazed at Sheba dubiously as she finally turned to heel at her mistress's side.

As if reading his thoughts, Ceara said softly, "She is very protective of me, my lord."

Luc shut the chamber door behind them. "So it seems. She will need to be if you insist upon wearing such attire about the halls, for few men would not think it an open invitation."

"I had not intended to wear it about the halls. Rudd had brought me warm water for a bath. I was already in the tub when I realized he had forgotten soap. I sought to call him back, and that was when I was accosted. In the privacy of my own chamber, it should not matter what I wear."

"Yet you were not in your chamber." He crossed his arms over his chest, frowning at the obstinate set of her mouth. "You are no longer just a Saxon baron's daughter, Ceara, but an earl's wife."

"What is that to me? Do you suggest that I am more now than I once was?" Danger glinted in her eyes and her tone, and her small hands curled into fists at her sides.

Irritated, Luc shook his head. "I mean only that if you dress like a serf, you will be treated as one."

"Ah, I see. Only Normans are moral. Saxons are wanton, and therefore welcome to advances. Is that it, my lord?"

"No. You twist my words."

"Do I? Yet I am chastised and the man who accosted me goes free with only an insincere apology."

"Heed me well, Ceara. If any man should touch you, he will answer to me most harshly. I do not allow that which is mine to be mishandled. But you will come to me with your complaint, and not put yourself in danger by tempting men to do as that one did."

It was the wrong thing to say. He knew it as soon as it was out, but the words were spoken and could not be recalled.

Bright flags of rage stained Ceara's cheeks like crimson banners, and her blue eyes sparked furiously.

"You Norman swine," she hissed so venomously that the hackles rose again on the wolf's back. "How dare you speak to me as if I am a child? I told you how it came to be that I was garbed so, but hear this—when this was Lord Balfour's hall, no man would dare touch me whether I was covered in wool from chin to foot, or in naught but a smile. If you cannot control your own, how do you expect to hold Wulfridge against those who would wrest it from you?"

"That will not be your concern."

"Will it not? Once my father said almost the same words to me, yet he died and it was left to me to hold this land against invaders. Can you swear it will never happen again, my lord? Can you promise me that Wulfridge will never be my concern again?"

Angry now, he crossed to the table and splashed wine into a goblet. Twisting the goblet stem between his fingers, he glanced up at her. Her shortened tunic clung to her in places, damply, as if she had just bathed. Warrior maid, golden hair tumbling over her shoulders and around her face, the wary wolf at her feet . . . she was a more impressive sight than she knew. How had she managed so well when her father died? It still amazed him that she had the courage to try, for it would be daunting for a trained warrior to go against such odds, much less a girl of such a tender age. Not even with experienced advisers at hand would there be much chance of success, yet she had held out for three months against superior forces.

His anger drained away and he set his untouched wine down on the table. Surprising himself, he shook his head. "No, I cannot promise you will never face such danger again, Ceara. But I can pledge that I will secure Wulfridge well while I live. In my life, I have also known defeat, and it set as ill with me as it does you. I do not intend to suffer it again, nor allow my own to suffer such a fate."

"And I am your own." Her mouth twisted with wry sarcasm, and he lifted his brows.

"Yea, you are my own, Ceara de Wulfridge. The day you swore your vows to me, you became mine. Never again will you know want while I live, nor even when I am gone. If it costs me my life, you will be safe."

She stared at him, her eyes growing wide and dark with shadows. Her lips trembled slightly, and when she lifted an arm to brush the hair from her eyes, her hand shook.

"Be wary, my lord, or I shall think you mean that."

"I mean it." His voice hardened. "I mean it most heartily. I keep what is mine, and none shall take it from me, nor abuse what I cherish."

A long silence stretched between them. The wolf lay down at Ceara's feet and put her great head between splayed paws. The candle flame flickered in a sudden draft of wind.

Finally Ceara moved, and there was an odd note to her voice when she said, "Long has Wulfridge needed a man of your strength." She lifted the goblet of wine in one hand, and held it out to him. Over the brimming cup she said softly, "If my land had to be won by Normans, it is well that you are the one to take it."

It was the closest she had ever come to an honest admission of defeat and offer of genuine goodwill, and he took the cup, curling his fingers around her hand to hold her. He lifted the wine to his lips, holding Ceara's hand around the stem, feeling suddenly awkward, almost tongue-tied.

Looking deep into her eyes, feeling as if he were drowning in their blue depths, he drank the wine without really tasting it. There was a new intimacy between them now, a bond that had not been there before, but he had no notion how it had happened. It was unplanned, and so fragile he wasn't certain it wouldn't shatter at the first sign of trouble. But it was there. And to his surprise, he found himself hoping nothing would destroy it.

This woman, this warrior maiden with the turbulent nature and honest eyes, had somehow wormed into the small part of his heart that was still vulnerable. Because even as he was vowing to protect her, the fear that he might fail near paralyzed him with apprehension. Never before had he felt so about a woman, as if he would dare anything to keep her.

It was a new and most illuminating discovery about himself.

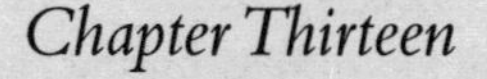

Chapter Thirteen

TREMBLING WITH UNCERTAINTY and raw hope, Ceara allowed Luc to pour wine for her. She sipped it from the cup as if they were truly lovers instead of strangers who shared a bed and intimacies. He surprised her, this man who was her husband. And frightened her, for she knew he truly meant what he said. He would allow no man to take away her home again. There was an inner strength in him that was more daunting than even his physical strength, and it was that virtue that would keep them all safe.

Yet it was all still novel and unfamiliar, and as fragile as a new-laid egg. So she trod cautiously, hopeful but not yet completely believing.

Luc smiled at her over the rim of the goblet, his dark eyes luminous with some secret concern. She managed a faint smile in return, though it felt wobbly. How did she react to him when all her previous responses were so different to what she felt now? Suddenly she was so unsure of herself, of him, of what he was and what he wanted.

"My lord . . ." The words came out too soft, too husky, an

invitation more than a question, and Luc took the wine from her and set it atop the table.

This response she recognized, for she had seen it often since their wedding, the quick flare in his eyes, the heat that radiated from him when he touched her. She started to retreat, but he grabbed her by the hand and pulled her toward the door to their chamber, not giving her a chance to speak as his mouth found hers in a hot, fierce kiss that left her in no doubt as to his mood or intentions.

The wide bed was still strewn with new garments she had unpacked from the trunk, and Luc shoved them carelessly aside as he lifted her to the bed, using his weight to pin her to the mattress. Excitement flared in her as he pulled roughly at her tunic, shoving up the hem to her waist, his hands impatient with the short garment.

Half leaning on her, half on the bed, Luc kissed her mouth, her cheek, the sensitive spot below her ear, his lips searing a fiery trail over her skin. There was the sound of rending material, and she jerked her mouth from his to protest the ruin of her tunic, but it was too late. Cool air whisked over her, and he rose to his knees, gazing down at her with satisfaction.

"You are very beautiful, my beauty," he said in husky French, and glancing up at her face, repeated it in English. She lay still while he touched her, his hands skimming over her bare breasts, belly, and lower, and then she closed her eyes.

Her breath came more swiftly now as he stroked her hot, moist center with his fingers, teasing her, summoning little moans that she could not hold back. Nor could she halt the arch of her hips into his hand, her fists pressing into the mattress, her heels pushing mounds into the thick coverlet spread over the bed.

Luc bent over her again, capturing her lips, his tongue mimicking the sex act with heated thrusts inside her open mouth while his hand coaxed a shivering response from her. She was quivering, excitement growing higher and hotter, sweeping her toward the brink of fulfillment.

Then he stopped, and she caught at his hand, pulling it back toward her, whimpering for him to continue. "Easy, beauty," he muttered thickly, and draped her legs on each side of his waist. He wrenched off his sherte and sat back with his legs folded beneath him to tug at the straps that held up his linen leggings.

With his dark head bent, she saw only the fall of his black hair and width of his bare shoulders until he looked up at her again. The open, naked need in his eyes was as arousing as his touch, and she caught her breath at the force of it.

Then he was leaning over her, the light furring of hair on his chest scraping erotically over her bare breasts as he stretched his length atop her, catching her hands in his and pulling them up to press into the mattress on each side of her head. A faint smile curved his mouth.

"Do you want me, *chérie*?"

"Ye—yes, Luc."

Her stammered whisper lingered in the air between them, soft and husky and filled with the longing she found so hard to articulate. But it was not going to be enough this night, for he pressed her for more.

"Tell me, *ma chérie,* tell me just how you want me. Tell me you want me as I want you. . . ."

Biting her lower lip between her teeth, she arched up into him in a silent effort to bring him closer. He laughed softly, and bent to lavish kisses along her throat and down to her breasts, teasing her with his tongue until she was panting for breath.

"Tell me," he murmured against her skin, his tongue circling her nipple in erotic strokes, "tell me. . . ."

"Luc . . . please. . . ."

Propping his weight on his hands, his fingers still laced with hers in a light clasp, he arched his hips forward to drag his swollen length over the arching center of her, creating a fiery sensation. Pressing forward, he moved in teasing strokes up and down between her thighs, until she writhed beneath him with urgent moans. He did not enter her yet, but slid over skin damp with anticipation, his every stroke sparking her, making her shiver.

Curving into his dragging strokes, her back arched and her thighs spread wider to receive him, to take him into her aching entrance. Yet still he held back, moving faster but not penetrating. Dazed with passion and filled with a rampant hunger for him, Ceara tilted her hips sharply, and his next stroke slid just inside her.

Luc's breath came in tortured pants. His arms were unsteady, and he lifted his head to look into her eyes, his lashes half lowered, his face sharp with desire.

"Tell me, *chérie*. . . ."

"Luc, I need you inside me . . . please. . . ." She turned her head, kissed his forearm, tasted the salt of him on her tongue, and whispered again, "Please, Luc . . . I want you . . . I want you inside me. . . ."

With a groan, his next stroke slid deep inside her, filling her, creating a new, sharp sensation that made her cry out. Urgency filled both of them with exquisite pleasure, his thrusts deep and hard inside her until she was holding him, half sobbing, her nails raking down his shoulders and back as the tension tightened almost unbearably. And then the pressure snapped, exploding into a shower of sparks that overwhelmed her, dragged her under into a dark tide of spinning release that left her weak and clinging to him, her cheeks wet with tears.

Slowly, Luc's taut body relaxed, and he shifted to one side, still holding her, still inside her, nipping lightly at the skin of her shoulder and throat with his teeth.

In that moment, with him drowsily holding her against his chest, his arms a warm shelter around her, she felt safer than she had ever felt in her life. It was as welcome as it was unexpected, and she prayed that it would never end.

She must have fallen asleep, for she was jerked awake by

Sheba's growl, and lifted her head. Then she flushed with embarrassment, for standing in the open door of the chamber and looking frozen with panic was Luc's squire.

"My lord," Alain said, his quavering voice soft and terrified, "is this the tame wolf?"

Luc had already sat up, one hand on his dagger and his eyes alert. "Yes. What do you here, Alain?"

"I brought the food you requested. Do I leave it in the antechamber for you?"

Shifting, Luc dragged the coverlet up over her, while Ceara nestled beneath it quickly. He flung her an amused glance, and tucked the coverlet around her before he rose from the bed and reached casually for his linen leggings.

"Leave the food in there, Alain. And if you wish to make a friend, toss the mutton joint to the wolf."

Alain made an inarticulate sound, then squeaked in alarm as Sheba caught the huge mutton joint in her jaws with a growl of satisfaction. Trotting past the squire, she came back into the chamber to curl up by the bed and gnaw her supper. Luc watched curiously, then glanced back at Alain with a grin as he laced his leggings around his waist.

"She would make a brave man quail, I think."

"Yes, my lord." Alain swallowed hard. His grin was weak. "I would not want to face the wolf without a weapon."

Ceara held back the tart words on the tip of her tongue. Soon, she would tell Luc that she could speak his language, and truthfully, she was not sure why she had not yet done so. Caution, perhaps, that bade her wait until she was certain she could trust him. A laugh caught in her throat. Foolish, to not trust him enough to speak his tongue, but allow him access to her body and her emotions.

When Alain left, she rose from the bed and followed Luc into the antechamber, the coverlet wrapped around her body and dragging along the floor. He eyed her with a lifted brow but did not comment except to say there was food and wine.

Warm meat and a round of cheese lay next to a trencher of white bread, and she picked at the bread, tearing off tiny portions to chew slowly while she poured wine. It was new wine, sweet and not heavy, tasting of summer grapes from across the Channel. A musty flavor filled her mouth as she drank, and she watched Luc over the rim of her goblet while he used his dagger to slice off generous slabs of boiled beef.

His bare chest gleamed in the lamplight, a rich golden sheen that made her think of summer days when the sun would darken her skin so that she had to wear long sleeves to keep from being as brown as a peasant. Yet on Luc, the bronze burnish of his muscled skin was attractive.

Ceara perched atop a stool. Her heart clutched at the knowledge that he had become much too important to her. Why had she allowed herself to care about him? To think about him at odd moments during the day, becoming as dreamy-eyed as a serving wench over a stable lad?

Never had she thought to lose herself this way. Not even with Wulfric had she been so moon-eyed, watching for him around every corner and waiting for the sound of his voice. Somehow their physical closeness had bound her to Luc. It had to be that. There was no other reason for her powerless slide into this ridiculous fascination. It left her uneasy, and she frowned as she wondered if he regretted leaving behind the Lady Amélie. Did he think of his lost love often? Did he wish that it was Amélie he had wed instead of her?

It was a question that tormented her at unexpected moments. Never had he indicated his loss, yet she could not forget that scene at York, when he had expressed regret for being forced to wed another, and held the lady so tenderly in his arms. *Amélie.* She hated even the name, resented being a substitute for another woman.

Glancing up at Luc, Ceara fought an odd sense of betrayal. Had he forgotten Lady Amélie?

She stuffed a wedge of cheese into her mouth, and realized

that she was starving. The day had been long and the journey rough, for Luc had pushed them hard to reach Wulfridge before dark and cold overtook them. But at least now they were here, and Sheba was safe, and away from danger. It would never have done to leave her in the stables, for though Paul seemed kind, his new Saxon assistant was Hardred, who had never liked Ceara or the wolf. She was grateful Luc had relented.

Chewing, she looked up at him again, and thought of the man he had called his brother. Was it for Jean-Paul that he had hurried back to Wulfridge? But no—she had the distinct impression that his brother's arrival was a surprise, and an unpleasant one. But why? She knew so little about Luc, other than the few things Robert of Brionne had told her—a fount of useful information if he was approached the right way. Yet when she had asked Sir Robert directly about Luc's family, he had evaded her questions with a skill that did not fool her for an instant.

With one foot tucked beneath her, she swung her other foot idly, reaching for a piece of cheese from the wooden platter as she asked, "Luc, who was that man in the hall?"

Luc paused in pouring wine, then shrugged as he lifted the goblet and drank. When he set it down again, he answered, his voice curt, "My brother."

"You never mentioned you have a brother." She ran a finger over the scarred wood of the table, an old one that should have been repaired long ago. It wobbled badly when leaned against, as she was doing now. "Is he here to stay?"

"Jean-Paul will not dare accost you again. Not even my reckless brother would push me that far."

She looked up at him, curious at the bitterness in his eyes and tone. "You have no love for him?"

Luc drew in a deep breath and turned away. "I have not seen him since he left Normandy."

The tone of his voice did not invite more questions, but Ceara could not help asking, "Why is there enmity between you? Was there trouble with an inheritance?"

Luc's brows lifted, and his mouth twisted in a grimace that held no humor. He snarled, "No, he inherited what he deserved from our father, while I was given the off side of their hands. Now, he bemoans the fate he earned, and would have me do what he would not do years ago."

When Ceara would have questioned him more, Luc turned to her with a ferocity she had not seen of late, and bade her not ask him anything more. "I will not ruin my night with more thought of Jean-Paul. If you have questions, ask him. He will be more than glad to give you answers, though I doubt they will have the ring of truth to them."

Unwilling to destroy their growing closeness, she bent her head and nodded. She intended to do just what he suggested. On the morrow, she would ask her questions. If there was to be trouble at Wulfridge, she would know it as soon as possible. And there were few more certain methods of finding out answers than asking the right person. She smiled slightly, and reached for another wedge of cheese.

Alain would know. Squires were usually privy to all manner of secrets, and from what she had seen of this one, he would have the information she wanted.

IT WAS A week before Ceara found the opportunity to query Alain, and he was not at all disposed to reply. His look was cool, and he only shrugged when she approached him in the outer hall and asked how much English he could speak.

Frowning, she worried her bottom lip with her teeth, then affected a winning smile. "Come now, Alain, you must know enough English to deal with the servants here. I think you just do not wish to talk to me. But I understand."

Alain's hazel eyes were hostile, and there was no suggestion of a thaw. He crossed his arms over his chest and lifted his shoulders in an expressive shrug. *"J'ai perdu, vous avez l'avantage, comtesse."*

"Advantage?" She picked out the only word that sounded the same in English and in French, and deliberately misunderstood him. "No, no, Alain. I have not taken advantage of you, if that is what you mean. Your offer of friendship came at a time when I trusted no one Norman, especially those who had invaded my home. Surely you can understand that. Giles was—shall we say—insistent that I yield. He was most unpleasant, and in the end, it would not have mattered to either of us if I trusted you. The king's command is ours to obey, it seems."

"Il faut lui rendre compte de tout."

Ceara smiled. "Now, perhaps you will be more at ease if I tell you that I appreciate your former offer of friendship. In these times, a true friend is better than gold."

Some of Alain's hostility faded, and there was a flicker of wary sympathy in his eyes. *"Les amis sont comme le melon, il faut en essayer plusieurs pour en trouver un bon. . . ."*

He was not as susceptible as she'd hoped, quoting the proverb that one should not trust a new friend or an old enemy, but she sensed that he had begun to soften toward her a little. She took a small risk.

"On connaît les amis au besoin. . . . An old proverb, but one that is still true, Alain. And a friend in need is what I am."

Alain's brows lifted at her French quote and clumsy accent, and now he smiled broadly. *"Parlez-vous Français!"*

"*Un peu.* A little. Not well, but I think you speak English well, do you not?"

Now Alain shrugged expansively, and said in thickly accented English, "Enough to give commands." He frowned then, shaking his head. "I admired you, *comtesse.* If you thought I meant more, Giles misled you."

This was not the time to debate the truth, and so she simply smiled. "Giles had his own ends in mind, I think, but he was sorely disappointed if he thought to undo me. I had the best of him long before we reached York, and had only to sit back and watch him destroy himself."

Lifting his shoulders again, Alain looked down at the ledgers he held. "He has disappointed me. I thought better of him."

Ceara did not comment on Alain's sudden command of excellent English, but said instead, "I fear that our visitor is much of the same cloth as Giles. He has his own goals, I think, and it worries me."

Alain looked a little surprised. "Do you mean the earl's brother?"

"His name is Jean-Paul. He confronted me in the corridor outside my chamber, and I am afraid our first meeting did not go well."

A faint smile touched Alain's mouth. "So I have heard. Servants gossip, and the boy Rudd is no exception."

"Rudd is a good boy, and quick for his age and size." She paused, wondering how far she could go to get the information she desired. It was apparent he knew much more than he betrayed, and yet he was still obviously wary of her.

"Rudd is quick enough," Alain conceded, "and obedient most of the time. As I must be, and Lord Luc has requested these ledgers to be brought to him."

Alain bowed slightly and moved away, and Ceara asked softly, "Is it true that you are privy to everything of importance that happens here, Alain?"

Her query stopped him and he turned back to face her. "Most of it. I am much more than just squire, but have become vital to the earl." A flicker of spite flared in his eyes, and he smiled. "Women can be displaced, but a squire who is scribe and steward and valet is hard to replace."

"No doubt." Ceara bit back the tart reply on the tip of her tongue, and managed an admiring comment instead. "It is obvious you are a man of consequence. You are most like privy even to personal details that none other would know."

"Sans doute."

"That is what I told Captain Remy, but of course, he has

no such good opinion of your position." She had done nothing of the sort, though she had long suspected a rivalry between the captain and the squire, and when Alain's eyes flashed with outrage and his face reddened, she was certain of it.

"Sacré bleu, je m'en fiche de le capitaine. . . ." He paused and drew in a deep breath, then blew it out again. Stepping close, he said softly, "The good captain had best watch his back, for he is not in the earl's best graces after allowing his men to slaughter helpless servants. No, not yet has he won back Lord Luc's respect, so he should look to his own instead of belittling my influence. If not for me, the earl's own brother might at this very moment be cast outside the castle with his companions instead of sitting comfortably by a fire."

"Poor Jean-Paul. But no doubt he deserves his brother's anger, is that not so?"

Alain shrugged. "Perhaps."

"But you would have no way of knowing about that, I am certain. . . ."

"Si fait." He lowered his voice, stepping even closer to her, so that his breath was warm against her cheek, smelling of wine. "I know that the earl's brother betrayed him years ago, and if not for the fact that he also betrayed William, Lord Luc would most like be dead by now."

"Luc betrayed the king?"

"No, no, it was the earl's father and brother who were accused of treason. Jean-Luc de Montfort lost his head for it, but his son, Jean-Paul, fled to King Malcolm in the north and survived William's wrath. William was only duke then, and not king, but he made Lord Luc's father pay dearly for the betrayal." Shrugging, Alain added, "It was rumored at the time that Luc was involved, and that it was he who convinced his father to fight for King Harold's side, but it was not true. Sir Luc had been disinherited by his father and sent to Normandy and France, away from his home in England."

"Disinherited? Why?"

"Some say this, and some say that."

Ceara kept her tone casual. "And what do you say?"

He laughed. "I agree with them, *comtesse.* Now I must go to Lord Luc, or he will think I am not doing my job."

She did not try to delay him again, but watched thoughtfully as Alain hurried down the corridor to the antechamber where Luc preferred meeting with his scribe. A most intriguing conversation. It explained much, but not all. Why would Luc allow his brother close enough to risk betrayal again? If Jean-Paul had betrayed him once, he would most certainly do it again if he thought it profitable.

And this time it might cost Luc more than just a bitter betrayal—for now he risked Wulfridge and possibly even his life.

Ceara's mouth thinned into a taut line, and she glanced toward the hall entrance. Perhaps it was time she took Luc's suggestion and talked to his brother herself. Then she could form her own opinion of his intentions.

But her only contact with Jean-Paul had been their meeting in the corridor outside her chamber, and one other brief encounter in the great hall when she had chosen to ignore him, and by tacit consent, he had done the same.

Yet she had often glimpsed him near Luc, at times with one hand on the hilt of the dagger at his waist, a speculative gleam in his eyes that worried her. Luc would not be amenable to anything she might suggest about his brother, for he refused to discuss him at all with her. Perhaps it would not be so troublesome if strange occurrences had not set her on edge.

A stone from the wall top had nearly fallen on Luc, and if his reflexes had not been so sharp, he would have been killed or at the least gravely injured. Another time, a chance arrow had been loosed, barely missing him. No one admitted loosing the shaft, nor could anyone be found with a similarly marked arrow in their possession. Stranger, and stranger still, the unexplained flagon of tainted wine set on the table Luc used to study his ledgers. If not for the chance of young Rudd spilling it so that a castle hound lapped the spillage and went into convulsions, Luc might have drank it unawares and sickened.

Yet all these things did Luc ignore, citing simple explanations for them. A man frequently risked life and limb in battle, and a careless arrow was hardly cause for alarm. Nor was a thoughtless worker. And from what he had seen of Wulfridge's store of wine, it was a wonder all of them had not sickened and died from the mere taste of it. Saxons should stick to ale and mead.

All simple explanations.

Thoughtfully, Ceara wrapped herself in her hooded cloak and took Sheba for a walk in the outer courtyard. It was easier to think out here, away from the hall that bore the strong stamp of Norman decorations. She hardly recognized it, even in the single week since their return it had changed much. Instead of the Saxon *wahrift* that once covered the walls, stiffly woven tapestries had been hung, and the horn panels in one of the windows had been replaced with glazed crystal that diffused rare winter sunlight and made it brighter. Scattered mats of elaborate patterns covered the stone floors in places, but thankfully, the beautiful tile patterns were still left visible for the most part.

Ah, God, everything was so different—including herself. Now she accepted without comment the rash of servants that crowded Wulfridge: pages, seneschals, stewards, and scribes, a different man for every post, it seemed. The sound of construction filled the days, and new structures had sprung up almost overnight in the courtyards to house men and beasts. York had been chaotic; here, at least, the sea winds and fresh air swept away the sounds of bickering servants and the tensions of the day.

Ceara paused beside the still-dry fountain in the outer bailey, letting the wind tangle her hair as she considered her options. The wolf cavorted in the cold air, gleeful at being free and blithely ignoring the soldiers who scuttled from her path with quick glances of trepidation.

One of the old Wulfridge hounds ambled outside, and Sheba gave a sharp yip of excitement, gamboling about the dog, proffering an obvious invitation to play. When the old dog showed his preference for a kind word and pat from Ceara, the wolf clawed at him with a huge front paw. She scolded the wolf, "Leave him be, Sheba. Can you not see he has grown too old and sedate to frolic with you?"

Sheba threw back her head and howled. Immediately, other howls resounded through the brisk air, stirring the domestic animals into a frenzy. Even the old dog began to whine, while Sheba sat back on her haunches and put up her head again, her eyes closed and her white muzzle skyward as she yowled in a long shuddering cry.

Ceara knelt beside the wolf, clutching her by the shaggy scruff of her neck to shake her gently. "You'll have all the castle in an uproar, silly cony," she muttered, and tugged at Sheba until she rose to her feet. Urging the animal along, she hurried to the postern gate before someone came to chasten her for setting the domestic beasts into turmoil, and slid back the iron bolt to slip through.

It wasn't until she had descended the steep slope to the sandy hummocks that rolled toward the sea that she considered what might be said if she was discovered to be gone. But no one would look for her until time for the evening meal, and she had not ventured from Wulfridge since she had returned. This was her first taste of freedom in almost two months.

Oddly, she still felt like a prisoner, for all that she was called lady and granted the respect due her position. None had dared by word or deed offer anything other than deference to the earl's wife. She had expected no different from those who once served Balfour, but had been a little surprised that not even one Norman had indicated in any way that they remembered how Luc had made her his captive after winning the castle. It was a measure of their respect for Luc, she knew, but it still surprised her that only Jean-Paul had offered her even the remotest insult, and that only because of an error in judgment.

Jean-Paul, Jean-Paul . . . Luc's brother seemed subdued, but after learning of his past betrayal, she found it incredible that Luc would allow him to stay even a moment at Wulfridge. There was an old saying that a dog that once developed a taste for chicken eggs would ever after be watching the henhouse, and she was certain of it. How could Luc be so reckless? He had not only himself to think of now, but the people of Wulfridge who trusted him to keep them safe.

A gust of wind tugged at the dragging hem of her kirtle and she thought longingly of the shorter costumes that were more suitable for trudging the sand hills and slopes. It could not be a coincidence that all her former garments were gone, leaving behind only the new clothes that Luc had purchased for her in York. They had been missing since the first night, when she had worn her short tunic into the hallway. She did not intend to give Luc the satisfaction of asking about them, but had made a mental note to quietly acquire more comfortable garb for her needs. He could regulate certain aspects of her life, but not all.

Just ahead of her, Sheba danced madly though the tall waving grasses, until only the tip of her plumed tail could be seen, a white banner streaking through the brown wands of sea grass. Snow still nestled in cracks and crevices of the rocks where the gray light of day did not reach, but had melted over most of the ground. Yet there was a sharp bite to the air that promised more snow, and in the wind that struck her cheeks she could feel icy pellets.

At low tide, the small barrier that was normally underwater provided a thin bridge to the mainland, tufted with bunches of reeds in places, and near invisible to those who did not know of it. It was just another path, but one she had been accustomed to using since she was a small child playing happily in the shadow of the castle. There were dozens of shallow inlet pools in the area, and other pools that were deep and treacherous with quicksand.

She knew them all, and stepped adroitly over the narrow strip of sandy ground to the mainland. Here the grass was thicker, and trees lined the shore in a steady clacking of leafless branches in the wind. Birds called, and overhead a hawk hunted, wings spread wide as it glided through the air on swift currents. Sea waves roared loudly, a whooshing froth of salty water and wind spit that peppered her face with damp sand. It was as exhilarating as it was familiar, and she realized that she had greatly missed the days when she could roam freely with her wolf. But that had been so long ago, before the Normans had come—while Wulfric was still alive.

Already she had seen many changes on the journey to York and back, the ruined villages, ravaged fields, and even burned monasteries and churches. The Danes had oft visited such destruction, but not on so wide a scale as had William. Those barons who did not proffer an oath of allegiance had their lands confiscated, their people scattered. The king was thorough. Few barons had lands large enough to raise up an army against William. The northern barons were the only ones given the power of absolute authority, and that only until William was secure on his throne, she suspected.

Luc spoke very little of business matters to her, turning her attempts to gain details into impromptu lovemaking sessions that usually eliminated any questions she had for him. For by the time she thought of them again, he was gone.

He had been busy. In the week since their return, there was a new air of prosperity that surprised and chagrined her. New walls, full storehouses, repaired buildings and roofs, all the things that had fallen into disrepair during her father's long illness and her futile attempts to hold on to the land with few resources. Wulfridge would once again be prosperous. Luc had the coin and the mettle to get the work done, and the men and courage to keep the lands against invasion.

It was what she had always wanted. So why was she so unsettled? Miserable at times? Was it because she felt herself falling in love with the man who had conquered her home?

She kicked idly at a stone, and it rolled down a thick tussock to a stretch of wet sand. Sheba had disappeared again, in search of rabbits, no doubt, or other lively game. The wolf was a quiet hunter, with none of the excited yelping or barking of the hunting dogs.

A gust of wind blew icy rain into her eyes, and she paused, turning her face to the sky. Clouds were low and gray and heavy with the promise of snow. She had come much farther than she had planned, and the air was very cold.

Pulling up the hood to her cloak, she felt icy trickles down the back of her neck and on her cheek. She shivered, and peered about the landscape for Sheba. No plumed tail was seen, nor even the shudder of tall grasses where the wolf might be stalking prey. Ceara called for her, then whistled, a shrill sound that usually worked. Still no Sheba. Nor was there any sign of her along the path she had just trod.

Ceara rubbed her hands together for warmth and trudged up the hill made slick with frozen rain and patches of ice. Her feet slipped slightly, and she grabbed at a patch of brittle brown reeds to keep from falling. Again she called, breathless from her exertions and the cutting bite of the wind against her face and throat. The cold had made her clumsy, and she stumbled as she climbed the sandy hill. Just ahead lay the road from the mainland, an easier trek than the way she had come down the back slopes.

With her hands tucked into her sleeves to keep her fingers from freezing, she hunched her back against the wind and moved toward the frozen tracks of the narrow road that led to Wulfridge castle. Thick weeds and slender saplings lined the road, making it easier to find, and she wobbled onto the ruts with relief.

A dry rustling in the tall weeds caught her attention and she turned, cheered to see Sheba bounding toward her with huge hops and tongue lolling from one side of her mouth. Her gold-brown eyes were alight with adventure as she trotted toward Ceara.

Pausing to wait, Ceara felt rather than saw the riders coming, for the ground vibrated slightly under the thud of many hooves. She glanced up and past the approaching wolf, as around a bend in the road, a dozen mounted men appeared.

One of them saw her, for he raised the alarm and spurred his horse forward. It was then Ceara realized that he meant to slay Sheba, for he leaned low from the side of his saddle, his naked sword glinting in the dull gray light as he pounded toward the loping wolf.

A scream locked in her throat. She tried to signal but her arms were caught beneath the cloak and her feet were slow with cold. She stumbled forward, but Sheba came to a halt, her great head turned with mild curiosity toward the pursuing rider. Ceara's heart lurched. She would never reach her in time, and Sheba was so used to soldiers that she would not know of the danger until it was too late.

Finally a scream burst from Ceara's throat, whipping Sheba's head toward her, the ears snapping forward in surprise. Too late, too late . . . the soldier was upon the animal, his sword swinging down in a lethal slice. . . .

A loud yelp rent the air, hooves sounding like thunder and crimson blood splashing, and Ceara was running, numb feet somehow stumbling over deep ruts and through ice-crusted puddles, and someone was screaming so loudly that it was hard to hear even the wind and the pounding roar of the surf over nearby rocks . . . and then a deep familiar voice cut through it all, calling her name and telling her to stop.

But she couldn't, not when Sheba was hurt, when the man on the horse had dismounted and was reeling to his knees, and blood splattered on the white-frosted ruts all around him.

The thunder grew louder, and then she was swept up from behind, and Luc's familiar voice snarled in her ear. *"Fais gaffe, tu vas te foutre!"*

"No, I won't fall." She dangled from his left arm, legs bumping against the side of his horse. Half sobbing, she struggled to get free of his grip. "Let me down! I won't fall—Sheba . . . she's hurt. . . ."

"You little fool, your bloody wolf is fine. Look at her. *Look* at her, Ceara."

Urgently, Luc pulled her up in front of him onto the horse, and turned to face the men who had ridden up behind their companion. They came to a halt several feet away, reining in their horses and furiously demanding an explanation.

Controlling his destrier with his knees, Luc gestured with the tip of his sword. "Your man is hurt."

"So I see," replied the front rider in a tight, angry voice. "How did you do it? And why?"

"I did not see the wolf until too late. I thought he was after the lady, and threw my dagger."

By now the injured man was on his feet, his face sullen and marked with pain, his sword lying by the side of the road in a puddle of icy water. Ceara gripped the pommel of Luc's saddle with both hands, suddenly weak. Her muscles ached with strain and cold, and even with Luc's left arm around her middle, holding her atop the horse, she felt as if at any moment she would pitch from the saddle to the hard ground.

"Please," she croaked, "it is my fault."

Luc's arm tightened. "Yes," he growled in her ear, "but be quiet for now."

Ceara glanced toward Sheba, and the wolf moved in an anxious circle, whining fitfully with her ears splayed out. She paced back and forth, out of reach of the soldiers, eyes returning again and again to Ceara.

But as Luc was talking to the men, Ceara realized that these were her father's vassals, the men who had not come to his standard when she called them, and her attention shifted to the conversation. She sat up straight, eyes narrowed as the man in front said harshly that he had come only because he did not want his villages burned, as others had been.

"All about me are ruined lands. Does William think dead serfs will still labor?"

"This is not a matter to be discussed here," Luc returned coolly. "I invited you to receive my hospitality. Tend your man, then join me in the hall for hot food by the fire. This misunderstanding can be rectified if you are willing."

Still obviously angry, the man considered, then gave a short jerk of his head. "I will listen. Do I have your safe conduct?"

"You were given my safe conduct to come, and you shall have my safe conduct to return to your home."

"I see the welcome you prepared," the man said in a disgruntled tone, but some of his anger was gone as he regarded Luc and Ceara. "Do you greet all your invited guests with wolves and daggers?"

"Only those worthy enough to pass the test," Luc returned easily, and the man grinned.

"Aye, then we should be welcome indeed into your hall, for poor Rudrick has borne the brunt of your reception."

"And borne it well. He shall have all the ale he can drink."

In a much lighter mood now, the men continued along the rutted road that led up to the castle. Ceara was held closely against Luc's broad chest.

"Please, let me call Sheba to me, Luc."

"There's been enough trouble. I will send Paul out for her later if she does not return on her own." His arm tightened around her, his voice low against her ear. "Little fool, what did you think to do out here in the wind and snow?"

She pushed angrily at his arm, but it was immovable. "Am I a prisoner, to be held inside a stifling chamber all day? I wanted to walk, and to let Sheba run. We can neither of us bear being shut up like caged birds."

Luc did not reply, but neither did he loosen his hold on her. It did not help that behind them, Sheba began to howl, shivering wails that pierced the whine of the wind and clatter of horses' hooves against hard frozen ground, a desolate sound that followed them into the castle grounds.

Chapter Fourteen

"Is it true that a knight's fee is five hides, Lord Luc?"

Luc eyed the speaker, Lord Oswald, for a moment, then shrugged. "It is my understanding that knights' services vary from fief to fief. I have not yet set my fees, for I do not know the strength of those who will serve me, or the currency they can bear."

Oswald snorted. "Rest assured that William knows. He had made it his business to know every knight, every vassal, every cow in England since he set foot in Pevensey."

"The king is thorough and just. He will not tax a man what he cannot pay, nor pay a man what he is not worth. But neither will he suffer refusal of his requests without redress."

Lord Oswald flashed him a quick, frowning glance. It was obvious the point had been noted, and Luc let his attention shift to Ceara. Her face was as pale as the snow that now lay in deep drifts outside, save for two bright spots of color on her cheeks that made her blue eyes glitter like brilliant jewels. She had not yet forgiven him for leaving her wolf, nor for following her. He wasn't certain which made her more angry, for she had railed at him furiously as soon as she was thawed enough to find her voice.

It had not been a pleasant scene, ended only by his insistence that she join him willingly in the hall or be forcibly dragged there.

"Your presence is important, Ceara. These are Saxon barons, and if they think you reluctant, so they might be."

"Let them be! That knave Oswald, when I called up his knight service he did not come . . . what do I care if he risks his neck now? I hope you burn down his castle with him inside it."

No, it had not been pleasant.

If he had not been so unsettled by the sharp bite of fear he'd felt at thinking her about to be run down by Oswald's man, he might have been more lenient about the wolf. But all he could think was that she had imperiled her own life for that of her pet. His blood still ran cold at the thought of her being hurt. Nor had he forgotten how she had answered him when he'd spoken in French. Now he wondered just how much French she could understand. Then, the moment had been chaotic, and since, she had not seemed to comprehend the language. Still . . .

Now she sat like a sullen lump in her chair, staring straight ahead and replying politely but curtly to any pleasantries from Lord Oswald or the others, Leofric and Eadwine, former vassals to Balfour. It must rankle her that they had not answered Ceara's call to arms, but they would have made little difference in the outcome. Luc would have won the day if their forces had been added or naught, as he had told her.

"My lord," Oswald said, turning to Luc and snaring his attention once more, "it is said that you were born in England. How came you to be aligned with the Norman cause?"

Luc's brow lifted. An unwise question to ask in front of all. Was Oswald that foolish? To be so bold and insolent at the table?

Leaning forward, Luc toyed with the stem of his jeweled goblet as his eyes caught and held Oswald's gaze. "If you have heard that I was born here, then you no doubt heard that my parents were Norman by birth."

Beyond Oswald, Jean-Paul laughed shortly. "Yea, but if a man is born in a kennel, it does not necessarily follow that he is a dog, I warrant."

Luc's gaze shifted to his brother. Wine flush had heightened Jean-Paul's color, and his eyes were fever-bright. "You choose an unflattering comparison, Jean-Paul. Do you suggest that my mother slept in kennels?"

Silence fell. Jean-Paul looked down at his empty wine goblet. "No, of course not. As you said, an unflattering comparison. It was unwise of me to speak thusly, and I beg pardon for any offense."

Oswald and Leofric exchanged glances, a gesture Luc noted well. This was not the impression he wanted to make on these visiting Saxon barons, and he turned again to Oswald in an attempt to smooth over any dissension.

"Lord Oswald, my father was granted lands in England by your own king, Edward, many years ago. He held them long and well, and until he broke with William, was still Norman in his thinking. If he had not betrayed the duke, he might still hold those lands, but his loyalties were withheld from William and given first to Edward, then to King Harold."

From Oswald's nod, Luc knew that the baron was well aware of all this, and most like, the entire truth behind Jean-Luc de Montfort's fall from ducal grace. At a time when men's loyalties were being tested, Jean-Luc had made the decision he considered best for his future, and that of his son and heir, Jean-Paul.

And he had betrayed his oldest son for not following him, for choosing Duke William over the Saxon king.

It had been a decision both father and son would come to regret, though for far different reasons.

"There were rumors, of course," Oswald murmured, and his eyes focused on the jeweled goblet instead of his host. "In these times, one never knows what to believe, for much is said that is not true."

"Hear this, Oswald de Paxton, for I tell you only the truth—William of Normandy has taken firm hold of England, and will deal fairly with all who deal fairly with him. If a man swears an oath, it will be expected that he hold to his sworn word. We have all seen that the church frowns on men who forswear oaths, even when a kingdom is at stake."

The unsubtle reminder of how King Harold had lost the church's favor in his claim to England still had the power to sting, and Luc saw it in Oswald's narrowed eyes. But it was the truth, however unpleasant, and there were men who needed to be reminded of what brought them to this point.

An ugly flush stained Oswald's cheeks. His voice was tight. "William tricked Harold into swearing an oath over the bones of saints."

"Yea, but Harold was willing to swear to an oath he did not mean to keep. Listen well, Oswald—William will not be stayed. If he must resort to trickery, he will do it to have his way. Yet he will not lie, and if he makes a promise, he keeps it. Never have I known him to renege on his sworn word, whether to prince or peasant, and if he promises you will keep your lands if you are loyal to him, then that is how it will be. Think on it."

Leofric, Oswald's boon companion and a man of the same age, studied Luc through hooded eyes as he absorbed the grave implications of the discussion. He was a handsome man, with a florid face and the bright gold hair of the Saxons, his manner bluff and hearty, but his clear blue eyes shrewd. He had spoken of little but trivial things, remaining silent during this exchange, but now cleared his throat.

"It is said that few Saxons have kept their lands since William was crowned. How know we that he will allow us to hold our ancestral estates?"

"Since Hastings, those Saxon barons who have gone home

and not taken up their swords against the king have lost nothing. Those who have joined with outlaw earls have been deseisined of lands and titles, and sometimes their lives. It is a brutal choice, but a simple one. Swear fealty to William as your rightful king and live on your lands in peace and prosperity." His voice hardened, and he saw Ceara turn toward him with pensive eyes as he said, "Take up sword against him, and he will destroy you."

"And you, Lord Luc, will you destroy those who defy you?"

"Yes."

It was a swift answer, meant to convince them of his determination, and he saw another quick exchange of glances. Between the three barons, Oswald, Leofric, and Eadwine, only Oswald seemed disinclined. Leofric nodded, and Eadwine, a spare man with nervous gestures and thinning hair, said gruffly that he was willing to offer allegiance to William if his lands would be left alone.

"I am old now, my lord, and not so quick to offer fight when the outcome is uncertain." Eadwine smiled, and glanced at Ceara. "Already, I have seen Normans and Saxons mingle their blood, and have come to realize that William is here to stay. With all of England united under one ruler, it may be that we can keep the Scots and Welsh at bay, instead of wasting time and lives and money waging petty battles at our borders."

"Fie on you," Oswald said angrily, his hand fisting atop the table, "you speak as a sniveling coward, Eadwine."

Eadwine drew himself up with dignity, his voice cold and steadier than yet Luc had heard it. "It is not cowardice to mislike watching serfs starve in their huts for want of food, or to walk fallow fields that will bear no yield for lack of seed and men to work them—no, and no, I say. I am weary of war. I would have peace, and William offers us what none other has yet attempted—a united kingdom."

"Well put, Lord Eadwine." Luc smiled a little, but knew that the baron's words would not convince Oswald. "But this is a conversation for another place. Now there are other things to think on, more pleasant subjects to discuss. My steward has planned entertainments for your amusement. Let us deal as companions this eve. Later, as men of judgment, we will come to terms on what is best for us all."

The next day, the six vassals who had already sworn to Luc arrived to accept his invitation, and Wulfridge was near to bursting with knights, barons, and their retinue. There were not enough chambers, and those who lagged behind ended up sleeping in rolled blankets on the hall floor, lining the corridors at night, and lying under stairwells and in alcoves. During the day, hunts were arranged, with barons ranging out into the forest to bring back game for the tables. A festive atmosphere prevailed for the most part, though there were several tense moments when quarrels broke out.

Through it all, Ceara remained aloof and remote. She had still not forgiven him for leaving her wolf behind. Nor had the beast come back, though four days had passed since he had plucked her from the road and the wolf had run away. Snow lay deep and thick on ground and road, and loud winds had lashed the castle for three days. Paul had not been able to find Sheba, though it was no wonder as the white wolf would most like blend in with the snowy slopes.

Every morning, Ceara would trudge through the snow to the postern gate and call. She repeated this at noon, and again before dusk, but there was no answering howl, no wolf bounding toward the castle to gladden her.

Luc intercepted her on the third Monday of Advent, when the hall was rowdy with merriment, and acrobats and tumblers entertained the guests. He followed her to the gate and caught her by one arm when she would have pushed past him.

"The wolf will return when she is ready, Ceara."

Pushing at his hand, she flashed him a hot look. "Leave me be. Go to your guests. Play the perfect host and leave me to my own."

"Own what?" He grabbed her by the shoulders, turning her to face him. Beyond the castle the setting sun painted the sky rose and lavender, making dark lace out of silhouetted tree branches and deepening the flush on Ceara's angry face. He shook her a little when she refused to look at him. "Own what, by all that is holy! This is your own, Ceara. Look about you. Wulfridge is yet yours, and it is habited by Saxon and Norman alike. If you feel apart, it is of your doing, for my intentions are to have us all as one people here."

"But we are not one people, Luc. For the love of God, can you not see that? You cannot force people to be what they are not, and there is yet too much enmity between our races to ignore. You are Norman. I am Saxon. We are separate. We will always be separate."

"You are wrong." He drew in a deep breath of cold air. "One day all of England will be united. If it is not, it will crumble into too many pieces to resist invaders. If we do not bind together, the Danes will come, and the Scots, and even the Welsh will seize portions of this country and chew them to bits. War will be constant, with neighbor against neighbor, none knowing who to trust. Every baron will have his own country, always holed up in his castle and afraid to leave for fear of being vulnerable. Is that what you want? Think on it, Ceara, for that is where England was headed until William came."

"That is not true."

Her answer was swift, but lacked conviction, and his grip on her shoulders eased. "Yes, it is. Even Harold's own brother Tostig fought against him, bringing King Hardrada of Norway to England to seize the crown. Listen to me, Ceara. William will hold England united under one ruler. The barons may still rebel and war against each other, but with a strong king, it will amount to little more than children's squabbles."

Ceara's taut muscles loosened beneath his hands, and she looked up at him finally, her eyes clear and direct. "I know what you say is true. It is just hard to hear."

"Yea, it would be. But know that William has England's welfare at his heart, for it is his chosen land."

"Even over Normandy?" Her gaze was mocking now, her mouth curled slightly. "It is Normandy he favors over all."

"He was born there."

"And so? You were born here, yet I do not hear your praise of your native land, only all things Norman."

It was a piercing barb, and true. He scowled. "It is not the same with me. William has no ill feelings toward England, only a sense of responsibility. My dislike is personal."

"You blame a country for what was done to you by a man, Lord Luc?"

Her mockery angered him, and he glared down at her with fierce resentment. "I do not blame fields and fens, no. Yet my demons are my own to conquer, and will not be discussed with you so that you may taunt me with them later."

"I would never taunt you with what you had not caused, my lord. You mistake me."

"Do I? I do not think so."

Ceara pulled away, agitated, her brow furrowed and her mouth tight. "I am not a fool. I may be stubborn, and at rare times mistaken, but I am not fool enough to think you the kind of man to knowingly choose folly over logic. You have proven otherwise in your brief tenure at Wulfridge."

"Unexpected praise from an unlikely source, madam."

"Curse you, Luc Louvat." She flashed him an angry look. "You must know that I cannot help but approve most of what you have done here. Needed repairs are made, more stores saved against lean times, and though you may have the hall looking more like the inside of a goat's stomach than the once austere beauty I admired, I must admit that you have taken great care and effort to better the castle."

Luc stared at her, anger warring with amusement. Rosy light still bathed her face and glinted in her eyes. She lowered her lashes to hide the sudden blue shimmer, and his anger faded. "So you do not approve of Norman furnishings."

"They are garish."

"Garish." His brow lifted in amusement. "By the cross, madam, those hangings cover up shabby walls and crude paintings that look as if someone dipped a dog's tail in paint and set it loose in the hall."

"Better that than excessive display and overweening pride! Who do you hope to impress? Oswald?" She snorted. "That fat baron would not be impressed by the pope's gold scepter. It may not have occurred to you, my lord, but Saxons are more impressed with an abundance of good food and drink in the stead of gold plate and embroidered hunting scenes. If you thought to sway Oswald with a display of wealth, you should have roasted an entire ox in every hearth and set out great tubs of ale for his consumption."

Luc gestured impatiently. "Oswald is not the only baron here. And I did not display gold and tapestry to impress, but to civilize crude lodgings. Hear me, Ceara," he said harshly when she turned toward him with fire in her eyes, "I may have been born in England, but I am Norman to the bone. Do not think to change me, or that my leanings to Norman ways are only temporary in nature. My father was born in Normandy, and my mother was born in Normandy, and the first eight years of my life were all that I spent on English soil until I became a man full grown. My allegiance is to King William. I owe everything to Normandy. England gave me nothing but pain, and I have no love for the country itself."

"Yet you force us to your standard, and threaten good Saxons with eviction or death? If you do not love England, then leave it to those who do."

She was trembling, her eyes wide with angry shadows and her lips quivering between tightly clenched teeth. Pale hair framed her face with gold curls that shone softly in the fading sunlight. Luc shook his head.

"You still do not understand, Ceara. England and Normandy are one now. What I love about Normandy, I will love about England. It takes more than trees and hills to make a country. There is beauty here, just as there is in Normandy, France, and Spain. Yet it is not beauty that bids a man risk his life and honor to hold his home." He reached out and cupped her chin in his palm, a little surprised that she did not jerk away from him. "You are beauteous, yet it is not your fair face and winsome smile that bids me risk my life to keep you. It is the inherent qualities that you possess that summon me to hold you safely."

Her eyes widened, lashes shadowing her cheeks as she stared at him. Funny little stick, with her furry brows like the markings of an inquisitive rabbit, endearing and vexing at the same time, a curious blend of child and woman that caught at his heart with unnerving tenacity. But he could not tell her that, could not betray the tenderness he oft felt for her, for it would be his undoing. Had he not erred by even mentioning to Amélie that he wanted her? She had leaped at once to the wrong conclusion, as women were prone to do, and he dared not risk shattering the fragile alliance he had with Ceara by saying the wrong thing.

"My lord. . . ." She inhaled audibly, then shrugged with a soft laugh. "You undo me."

As you do me, my beauty, as you do me. . . .

He smiled wryly. "No doubt, the barons are drunk as friars by now, and my stores you think me so proud of have dwindled to dry lentils and empty corn husks while we stand out here in the snow and cold air to shout at one another. If you think we are done for the evening, my lady, I will escort you inside to the hall."

"I make no promises about being done shouting, but I will go with you inside if you will allow me to call for Sheba one more time first."

"S'il arrive que vous avez besoin de moi . . . c'est ici."

She stared up at him oddly, and there was a faint tremor at

the corners of her mouth. Then she looked away, and gave a little shrug. "I do not understand. . . ."

"No matter. I will wait here." He released her chin and watched as she moved gracefully to the postern gate and slid back the bolt. Perhaps he was wrong, but there were moments he was certain she understood. Why would she lie to him? Was she yet unwilling to trust him? Or still willing to betray him? Neither were pleasant thoughts.

Dark shadows filled the courtyard now, flickering over the dry fountain and bare trees, casting the buildings and ground into gloom. It was quiet this night, with no howling wind to drown out the rhythmic murmur of the surf against rocks.

Stars overhead shimmered in the darkened sky, bright against deep blue, tiny beacons of light that reminded him how small were the things in this world. In contrast, he was an infinitesimal speck on a land peopled with others like himself. He thought of the comet-star that had been seen over England during the last week of April in 1066. Some had named it an omen, for it shone brightly with its long trailer of fire for the whole week before disappearing again. And that year William had invaded England, another omen like the comet-star.

But unlike the comet-star, William's duration would be long. Monks had noted the comet-star, just as they had noted the other bright stars of heaven, and so they would note William of Normandy. Luc had made the right choice, for all that it had cost him. There was no other choice he could have made, none other that would endure.

Like others, he was groping for the right way, hoping for a star to show him the path. William had long been his star, flawed, perhaps, but his very determination a bright beacon. He believed in William, believed in England's future, and believed in himself. Could he believe in his wife as well?

Iron hinges creaked, and he looked toward the postern gate to see Ceara coming toward him, her shoulders slumping with weary disappointment, no wolf at her heels. Luc went to her and put an arm around her to hold her against his side, steadying her as they made their way across the slick patches of ice in the courtyard.

"Sheba must be dead." Ceara's voice was toneless, but betrayed the deep hurt beneath her words. "Never has she stayed away this long."

"The wolf is not dead. Where did you leave her before? Perhaps she has gone back there."

Ceara glanced up at him, hope shining in her eyes. "I had not thought of that. I left her in the woods with an old huntsman. She might have gone to Sighere. On the morrow, I will—"

"Hold. The snow is too deep. I will send Paul."

"Sighere will tell nothing to a Norman, my lord." Her voice was tart. "He is old, and not as trusting as some of us."

Luc laughed at that. "God help us all, then. Wait, *ma chérie.* I will think of another way to find Sheba. Do not despair, for it is my notion that she has gone far afield hunting fat winter hares and does not care to return. When she is hungry enough and cold enough, she will come to you."

"I hope so." Ceara sounded forlorn. "She has been with me since she was a pup, and though it may be odd to you, she has been my only friend these past years. None other did I dare trust."

Luc envisioned a wary maid, her nature prickly to keep away those who might hurt her, and to keep from growing close to those who might die or leave her behind. He knew well the emotions that attended those fears, for he had fought them himself: alone in a strange land, sent away because of a woman's hatred, spurned by his father. Yes, he knew well how she had felt.

"I will find Sheba for you," he said softly, and pulled her under a vaulted stairwell to take her face between his cold palms. She stared up at him and nodded.

"If you set out to do it, my lord, it will be done."

Her faith shattered him, and he bent his head and kissed

her, almost fiercely, needing to feel her warmth and her surrender, needing the intimacy. This time it was not the urges of the body that drove him, but the urges of the heart.

Until Ceara put her arms around his neck to kiss him back, and his control splintered. He held her hard against him, his hands moving beneath her heavy cloak to scrub over her curves, palms sliding over the layers of her clothing with impatience. Hidden in the dusky shadows of the stairwell, he leaned against her, pressing her back against the wall with his weight, kissing her hungrily, needing to feel her around him, her softness and heat and the small excited noises she made when he entered her. . . .

"Luc—what are you . . . here?"

He had the hem of her skirts up, bunching them around her waist, then his hands moved to untie the straps of his linen chausses enough to release the fierce pressure. Ceara gave a shocked gasp when he lifted her legs to wrap around his waist and lunged forward, his length sliding inside her with exquisite friction. Sweet torment, the scrape of her bare thighs against his sides, the pressure of her velvet heat around his shaft, and the soft, panting breaths against his throat as she clung to him.

It was madness, ecstasy, searing pleasure and rising tension that made him forget everything around him, forget all but the lady in his arms. He rocked against her with driving thrusts, and she answered him with fervent arches of her hips, taking all of him, moaning his name in breathless sobs that filled the steamy space between them. The tautness stretched out almost unbearably, release trembling just out of reach, another thrust, another drag of his body that radiated heat and exquisite sensation down his spine, and he held tight to his control until he heard her spiraling cry in his ear, felt her body grow taut with tension and shudder. Then, gripping her hard by the waist, he slammed into her with a final thrust that drained him of everything. Groaning, his mouth pressed into the sweetly scented curve of her neck and shoulder, he held her still against the wall for several moments as he tried to gather the strength to move.

Her hand fumbled for him in the dark, fingers stroking through his hair to cup the back of his neck in her curved palm. Her whisper was soft and replete. "Soon it will be Christmas, Luc."

"Joyeux Noël, ma petite choute."

Unable to see through the thick shadows that shrouded them, he stroked her cheek and shifted his weight to keep from hurting her. Her legs were still clasped tightly around his waist, her cloak draped over them but a chill breeze that he had not noticed before cooled their damp, naked flesh.

As he circled her waist with his hands to free her from him, he heard a sudden noise behind them and swore softly, cursing himself for being so foolish as to lose awareness of his surroundings. Lowering Ceara to the ground, he slid his hand to the hilt of his dagger and half turned, putting her behind him.

A single shadow detached from the deeper ones under the stairwell and moved into a wavering pool of light cast by a wall torch. A dry voice said with droll inflection, "What a novel way to celebrate Advent, Luc. Won't they let you in your own hall to fornicate?"

Robert. And beside him stood Amélie, her green cat's eyes shining in the dim light with glittering sharpness.

Chapter Fifteen

"YOU DID INVITE me to come anytime, you know, Luc." Robert eyed his host with amusement, rather enjoying Luc's embarrassed hostility. It was not often he had been able to truly surprise Luc, and this was a moment to cherish.

"Yes," Luc snapped, "but it did not occur to me you would arrive at so inconvenient a moment, bringing trouble on your arm."

"Trouble? Do you refer to the Lady Amélie?" Robert flinched at the look in Luc's eyes, and shrugged, spreading his hands helplessly. "It was not my idea, Luc, I swear it."

"Then you should have spared yourself the pain of having to cut short your visit, and left her behind."

"Will you allow her to come between us, Luc? After all our years together?" Robert studied Luc, noting the lines of tension around his mouth. He rose to his feet, contrite. "I am certain your lady wife did not mean what she said. She will reflect, and once I explain to her that Lady Amélie is to wed another, I do not think she will feel so . . . harsh toward her."

"Amélie is to wed?"

"Yes. The king has set into motion the agreement that will

bind her to Malcolm's cousin. He hopes that it will form ties between the Scots and England."

Luc flung one leg over the corner of the table and rested his weight on it. "I still do not see why you brought her here, Robert. Especially knowing the enmity Ceara feels toward her."

Unhappily, Robert nodded. "It was not to be helped, Luc. Do you think I wanted to travel the goat tracks that pass for roads in this weather? The king celebrates the season in York, tucked warmly into his castle with fine food and amusements, while I have been stuck with a complaining shrew." He rose from his chair and moved to the brass brazier, putting out his hands to warm them over the hot coals. "It has been hellish."

"No doubt. I recall Amélie's fondness for her comfort." Luc scraped a hand through his hair, fingering locks that looked to have been recently shorn. Always worn a bit longer than most Normans, now his hair was neatly trimmed below his ears and on the nape of his neck. He frowned at Robert. "How long have these negotiations been discussed?"

Robert shrugged. "Awhile, I think, but you know how secretive the king can be about arrangements. Only Lady Amélie knew and, of course, the king's advisers and Malcolm. It may yet work, though often these arranged marriages never reach the altar."

"True." Luc glanced toward the closed door of the solar he shared with Ceara. There had been the distinctive sound of metal grating against metal that indicated it had also been bolted. Not a good sign, Robert knew, and he could hardly blame her for being angry.

Not only had she been embarrassed at being caught in so indelicate a situation, but Amélie worsened it with a laughing reminder to Luc of how they had once been caught in just that position in Winchester.

"Of course it was warmer weather then," she added, putting her hand lightly on Luc's arm and smiling at Ceara's flushed chagrin, "but most exciting, as well. Do you not recall, Luc?"

It was hardly the sort of thing a man should be reminded of in front of his wife, and quite obvious that Luc had no recollection of it. He shot Amélie a furious look that should have made her quail, and shook loose her hand. Turning protectively to Ceara, he offered in English to see her to their chamber.

Ceara rudely rejected his efforts, shoving him away and snapping that he need not escort her anywhere. "Stay and see to your guests. I have duties to tend, and do not want your company."

If she had planned it, Robert thought, it could not have worked out better for Amélie. There were moments on the journey he'd wondered if she even cared about her betrothal, for she spoke mostly of Luc, lamenting that Malcolm's cousin was not an earl like Luc, nor was he Norman.

But he dared not mention that now. There was trouble enough without stirring more.

"Tell me about Jean-Paul, Luc. Why is he here?"

"He has no other refuge, I am told." Luc's smile was wry. "Not long ago, I would not have cared. I am not at all certain I should let him stay now, save to watch him."

"Does William know he is here?"

"I sent a messenger to York with the news. I have not yet heard back."

"And what will you do if the king demands Jean-Paul be delivered to him?"

"Take him." Luc shrugged. "I do not think William will demand that, for he granted him his life and set him free after he paid the ransom."

"You mean Montfort."

Luc nodded. "Yes. A small price to pay for treason, I vow."

"Yet everything when it is a man's home." Robert watched Luc closely, but there was no sign of regret in his face. "Do you ever wonder why Montfort was not given to you for your service to William?"

Luc's lip curled. "It was offered. I refused."

Astounded, Robert stared at him. "You refused the home where you were born?"

"It was not mine, but my father's and his wife's. I did not have happy memories of it, Robert, as you must know."

"Yes. I know. But still, it is a grand estate, with a tidy income."

"Nothing would induce me to live there again. And it has been burned, I heard, so there is nothing left of the house, only the lands."

"Now you have this." Robert waved a hand to indicate the stone walls. "It puts me in mind of ancient ruins I saw in Italy."

"Roman influence. There are odd little chambers everywhere, some dug into the ground that seem to have no purpose. And in the kitchens, there is a tile oven that rises all the way to the ceiling, with several openings for cooking and for wood, and a place to set pots. Very clever, and it still works efficiently." Luc rose from his perch on the edge of the table, glancing again toward the closed solar door. "Her family has lived on these lands since the Romans were here, I think. She knows nothing else."

Robert watched keenly. There was a softness in Luc's eyes when he spoke of Ceara that had not been there in York. The attraction had been there, the angry refusal to admit that he wanted her, but not this tenderness. Perhaps the Saxon maid had actually managed to touch his heart. It would be a wonder. After the way Luc had suffered at the hands of his father's wife, he had come away with a strong dislike for the fairer sex. He was honest in his dealings with women, never lying about his feelings or hinting that there would be anything other than a physical relationship between them, but neither did he like them very much.

To Robert, who had been reared with four loving sisters, it

had been troubling. He liked all women, tall or short, plump or thin, pretty or not so pretty. It was one of his chief failings, for he could never decide on one woman to take to wife. They were all too tempting.

"Where shall I sleep, Luc? I do not care to invade your chamber, as you and your lady may need to, ah, discuss plans for the morrow."

Luc grinned. "You are just afraid of being caught in the middle. I'll have Alain bring you straw for a pallet in here. It's warmer, and besides, there is no room elsewhere. All the available space in hall and under stairs has been taken—do not say what you are about to say concerning stairwells, Robert de Brionne, or I will lesson you with the blade of my dagger, I swear it."

Feigning innocence, Robert laughed. "You wrong me, Luc. I have no remarks about stairwells or those who use them for dissolute purposes."

"Curse you, Robert." Luc moved to the door and sent for his squire, then glanced back over his shoulder. "Keep the lady Amélie out of my path, and Ceara's, if you can. It will ease my days if I do not have to deal with sharp tongues and cat fights."

"I will do my best, Luc, but women have minds of their own, I fear."

It was a sentiment that Robert was to recall with dismay in the following days.

"WHY DO YOU not ride with Luc, my lady?"

Ceara glanced over her shoulder. She stood atop the wall near the front gate, looking over the twisted road that fell steeply away from the castle. "Lord Luc bade me wait for him here, Sir Robert."

"Ah." Robert of Brionne climbed the ragged stones that formed the wall, slipping slightly on a patch of ice. "He is afraid you will be harmed, no doubt."

"No doubt, but hardly likely. I was born here, and grew up running these hills and moors as I pleased. I know every blade of grass and stretch of bog. He does not."

"Do you worry Luc will be harmed?"

"I worry he will fail to find Sheba." She turned away to stare over the landscape again, flinching as the wind whipped a strand of hair into her eyes.

Robert sighed. "Will you forgive him, my lady?"

"Forgive him for what?" She eyed Robert with a growing irritation that did not lessen when he did not meet her gaze. "What has my lord done that he should be forgiven?"

"Nothing." Robert looked up at her, a sheepish glance. "It was not Luc who erred, it was I who committed the folly of intruding on such a . . . a . . ."

"Pray, do *not* go on, sir."

"No." Robert looked relieved. "Of course not. But I did err in bringing Lady Amélie here, I think, as her presence seems to have distressed you."

Ceara frowned. "I am not distressed. Annoyed, perhaps, as the lady is rude and demanding. Already, she has ensconced herself in the most comfortable chamber, evicting the guests who had been given it, and has done nothing but command this and that from servants who are already overworked and tired. And she has in her retinue a man Luc dismissed from his employ."

"You mean Giles."

"Yea, I do. The man was insolent and rude, and thus dismissed in York. Now he is here again, a most unpleasant reminder to me of his audacity."

"Yet he must be employed somewhere, my lady. It was not meant as an insult to you when Lady Amélie hired him as a man-at-arms. She knew only that he had been dismissed from Luc's service."

"Perhaps. See that he is kept clear of me, for I find his attitude most unpleasing, as well as that of your lady."

"Yea, I agree most heartily. Will you forgive me for bringing her here? It was not my advice that brought her, but the king's—I suppose you know of the coming nuptials for Lady Amélie."

"Yea. Luc told me." She did not mention that Luc had grown furious with her for suggesting that the lady had prospects in mind other than a Scottish husband. They had quarreled heatedly, until she'd felt close to tears of rage and frustration at his blindness. Of course, he did not know that she had understood quite well Amélie's reminder in French of their earlier tryst, and so did not know the real cause of her anger. But she had seen Amélie's hand on Luc's arm, seen the triumphant flare of light in her green cat's eyes, and heard her purring satisfaction at provoking a quarrel between them.

She should not have allowed Amélie to see her distress, but the moment had been awkward and disconcerting. Later, she had been more angry at herself than Luc—until he had turned from concerned husband to cornered animal. Then he had informed her coldly that she was behaving foolishly, and inventing reasons to keep him at bay.

That comment had evolved into a furious argument, ending with Luc slamming from their chamber and spending the night elsewhere. She did not even want to think about where he had gone to sleep. It was all so absurd, her anger and his, that she wished she could start over again.

"My lady?" Robert was looking at her curiously, snow powdering his hair with tiny flakes. He looked up at the sky, then back at her, his brow lifted questioningly.

She managed a smile, some of her resentment easing at his obvious repentance. "Forgiveness does not come without penance, Sir Robert."

He looked pained, but nodded. "So I have been told too many times to number. But you will pardon my blunder?"

"As it was not entirely your fault, I will take it under consideration." She turned from the wall, blinking at the blowing snow clogging her lashes. "However, you must make amends."

Robert took her arm, solicitous in helping her down, so she refrained from telling him that she was used to running along the top of this wall since she was but a child.

"I will most gladly make amends, my lady. Just name the penance."

Allowing him to guide her across the courtyard with his palm cupping her elbow, Ceara waited until they were inside the hall, shed of cloaks and capes and seated on a bolstered bench before she pronounced her terms.

"I would know more about my lord Luc, Sir Robert. And you shall answer my questions forthrightly, or you shall not be absolved of your transgression."

Robert's eyes widened, and expectant amusement faded from his face. "My lady, Luc would not forgive me for idle gossip about him. I fear you must name another penance."

"No." Servants were still clearing the hall, stacking trestle tables against the wall by the benches. She beckoned a page to her to pour wine for them, and eyed Robert's discomfiture with speculation. "You are his friend, and will not tell untruths or half truths about him. I do not wish to know of former lovers, if that is what is distressing you. That is of no consequence to me. No, not even Lady Amélie, save that she seeks to drive a wedge between us for some unknown reason. Her, I can deal with in my own way. It is the farther past that concerns me, the reasons Luc will not give me for his enmity with his brother."

"Ah, the real meat." Robert shook his head with a faint smile. "Again, Luc would not thank me for idle gossip."

"I do not want gossip, Sir Robert." Her sharp tone brought his eyes back to her with surprise. "I want the truth. Can Jean-Paul be trusted not to betray his brother again?"

A long silence stretched between them. Several soldiers who were gathered by the central fire talked quietly among themselves, and two of the castle dogs broke into a fight over spilled scraps of food from the morning meal. A cold draft fluttered a tapestry on the wall behind them, and gray light streamed through the glazed window to brighten the hall. Robert cleared his throat, and looked down at his fingers locked around the wine goblet.

"It is not likely he can be trusted, no. Yet men do change, my lady," he added, looking up at her, "and it may well be that Jean-Paul has seen the error of his ways. That I do not know, as I have talked with him only briefly since my arrival."

"Do you think he has changed?"

"My lady . . ." Robert looked around helplessly. "Do me the favor of asking your husband these questions. I fear I am not the one to query."

Robert's already accented English had grown thicker, and she smiled a little at his agitation. She took a sip of wine, giving him time to compose himself before murmuring, "He refuses to discuss it with me. You must tell me all."

"Mon Dieu! C'est impossible. . . ."

"Impossible or not, there is no one else I trust to tell me the truth."

"Why must you know?" Rather cross now, Robert downed his wine in a single gulp. "It will avail nothing."

"On the contrary, Robert of Brionne. If any man thinks to betray Luc, I will see him stopped."

"Do you think Luc so easily duped that he will allow his brother to betray him again?" Robert shook his head. "You do not know him as you think if you believe that. Luc is no fool."

"No, but he has granted sanctuary to a viper. How long before he is bitten?"

"My lady, you wear me down." Robert's smile was ironic. "Will you not give me peace on this?"

"Yea, as soon as I have heard the truth."

Robert groaned. "You are inflexible. *Très bien*. What is it you wish to know?"

"As I said, I wish to know the truth behind the rumors."

Sighing, Robert gazed down into his empty wine goblet, twisting it back and forth between his fingers distractedly. "It began so long ago, before Luc came to Normandy and my father's house as squire. He was a boy of only eight years when he came to us, but by then, he had been declared bastard by his father in favor of his younger son, Jean-Paul. It was at the urging of his wife, Jean-Paul's mother, that he repudiated Luc's claim to Montfort. It had to be done through the church, since Luc's mother had been a Norman, while Jean-Luc's new wife was a Saxon."

"Where is Luc's mother now?"

"Dead. She died of a fever when Luc was still in swaddling. Then Jean-Luc wed again, to form an alliance between Saxon and Norman, King Edward said."

Ceara's throat tightened. "So Luc's father put him aside in favor of his new son?"

Robert nodded. "He had the church declare his first marriage unlawful on grounds of consanguinity due to the fact that Luc's mother had been related by marriage to his uncle. That meant that Jean-Paul, born in England of a Saxon mother, would inherit English lands. Jean-Luc sent Luc away."

Sent him away . . . the vision of a young boy, confused and motherless, was a haunting one. How could a father do that to his own son?

The question must have been in her eyes, for Robert put out a hand to touch her arm, saying gently, "It was better that he was sent away, for his new mother was a cruel one. When he came to my father's house, he still bore marks of beatings, and the scars remain yet, though more inward then outward."

True enough. She had seen the scars on him, trophies of battle, she had assumed, as so many fighting men bore. She sipped her wine, gathering her composure.

"Tell me, Sir Robert, what happened to his father and stepmother."

"Ah, that becomes more difficult. By then, Luc was a man full-grown, and we were separated by circumstance for a time."

"You once told me that Norman knights form groups for life. How is it he was not with you?"

Robert's smile was wry. "Your memory is too long and too good. Yes, it is true, but knight service is only required by our overlord for forty days a year. During the rest of the year, we are free to pursue other interests. Luc had been called to England by his father. That was when William was still duke, and King Edward still alive, though the king was deranged at times."

"He was religious, not deranged."

Robert's shoulders lifted in a shrug that indicated his disagreement, and she glared at him. "Tell me the rest."

"Ah, lady . . . set me free. Grant me peace and let me slink off to lick my wounds. This is grave business, the telling of secrets that are not mine."

"It is not secret when half the world whispers of it, Sir Robert."

"Yea, but if Luc wanted you to know, he would tell you himself."

"Must I go to his brother to seek the answers I crave?"

Robert's groan was heartfelt. "You do me an injury by suggesting it. But hear this, my lady, what I tell you next is all that I know of it, and that from Luc himself." He paused and drew in a deep breath, and Ceara signaled to the page for more wine to be brought. Robert gave her a grateful glance, and sipped freely before setting down the cup and clearing his throat. "Luc was summoned to England by his father. By then, Harold was back in England after having been shipwrecked on the shores of Ponthieu and given into William's waiting hands. Before he would release him, the duke forced Harold to swear an oath that he would aid William in his quest to be king. When Luc arrived in England, Jean-Luc told him that as King Edward was near dying, the barons had chosen Harold to be king. Luc was most disturbed to hear of this treachery. He warned his father that if Harold broke his oath to William, it would cause conflict between Normandy and England, but Jean-Luc demanded that Luc choose one or the other. He reminded him how he had paid for Luc's knight's training and service, and swore that if Luc would yet lend his sword to Harold's cause, he would share Montfort with his brother.

"When Jean-Paul heard of this offer, he was furious. He did not intend to share Montfort. Jean-Paul was so angry, he involved the wrong man in his scheming. Between them, Tostig and Jean-Paul arranged for Duke William to learn of Luc's intent to betray him and to fight for Harold. It was a lie, of course, but Tostig had William's ear, for he was wed to the duke's sister-in-law."

"And William believed him?"

Robert smiled. "William knew his man—both of them. Tostig had already asked for William's aid in taking England once King Edward died, fool that he was to go to the very man who coveted the crown for himself. So the duke believed not what he was told, but the man he knew was honorable. Not everyone was so kind." He paused. "Jean-Luc had sworn an oath of fealty to Duke William as his overlord, and still owed him knight service. The duke called him up."

"And Jean-Luc refused."

"No. He went, but he betrayed the duke's plans to the Saxons. If not for a fortuitous wind that delayed William's arrival in England, it might very well have turned out differently. Jean-Luc was found out, and he lost his head for it. Jean-Paul barely escaped with his life, and forfeited Montfort as ransom."

"And Luc—"

"Was disgraced. Humiliated. There were those who believed him as guilty as his father. Only William did not, and kept Luc in his service. No man dared say aloud what he thought, for the king was no more tolerant of gossip as king than he had been as duke."

Ceara picked at the embroidery on the cuff of her long

sleeve, reflecting on Robert's tale. Then she looked up at him. "What happened to Luc's stepmother?"

"Gone. Dead, most like. She fled when William won the day and her husband lost his head. She has not been missed, I assure you."

"Not even by her only son?"

Robert looked startled. "I do not know."

"It might be wise to think of such things." Ceara rose to her feet and set her barely touched goblet of wine on the bench. "If the cruel lady is still alive, might she not blame Luc for her fall?"

"It is possible, but not likely that she would be able to do him ill. Lady Ceara, no one has seen or heard of the widow in years."

"Yet her son arrives at Wulfridge before Luc returns from York. Someone has watched him closely enough. Has anyone thought to ask Jean-Paul how he knew where to come?"

"No, I assumed—all of England knew that Luc Louvat had won an earldom. It was no secret. News flies swiftly."

"Not just to England, it seems." She smiled at Robert's perplexed frown. "I am told Jean-Paul fled to the land of the Scots for shelter from William's wrath."

"Yes, but that means nothing. North, south, news does travel, my lady."

"Sir Robert, I do not mean to impugn your intelligence, but think for a moment why would Jean-Paul leave a land where he is safe to come to one where he may be at risk?"

"Lady, you do raise some interesting questions."

"It has been on my mind since we returned from York. I do not want to seem presumptuous, but it does seem that Luc should have considered this himself."

"He has not discussed his brother with me, my lady. It is still a sore subject with him."

"It will be sorer still if he is betrayed again. He might think on that."

Glancing up, she saw at the entrance to the hall Lady Amélie, who spied them and turned her steps toward the bench where they stood. "Sir Robert, forgive me, but I have just recalled important duties that cannot wait."

Robert followed her gaze, and grinned. "Do not leave me alone with the dragon, my lady. She frightens me."

"Good. Perhaps next time you will think on't before you bring a dragon to Wulfridge. Good day, sir."

Robert's soft laughter followed her as she left the hall, nodding coolly to Lady Amélie as she passed.

Chapter Sixteen

SWEARING, LUC SLASHED at the tall reeds with the flat of his sword. His feet were wet, his horse limping, and he was freezing. All for a wolf. Tame or not, he was ready to slay the beast if he had to wade through slush and bog much longer.

He knelt, studying a snowbank. Brown reeds thrust up through the snow in clumps, rustling slightly in the wind, and huge paw prints could be seen in the wet whiteness. Ice formed tiny crystals in the indentations, indicating that it had been some time since these were made.

Glancing up with a frown, he scrutinized the barren land around him. The boundaries of Wulfridge stretched all the way from the seacoast west to the priory on the River Coquet, then south in a ragged line to the bay, forming a rough three-sided parcel. Moors covered much of it inland, with great bands of ancient forest sheltering the slopes and providing abundant game. Not far from where he now stood, the river flowed eastward to the sea. But the wolf could not have crossed the swift current, and would have avoided the desolate land that lay seaward.

The wolf could be anywhere. A hawk soared overhead, a

faint shadow flickering over the white slopes of snow, and a keening cry broke the stillness.

Rising to his feet, he slapped his reins against his palm irritably. Curse the beast. He should not have promised Ceara he would return with the wolf. It was more than a matter of pride should he fail; he did not want to see the sorrow in her eyes, the fear that her pet was dead. Yet, all things died, and if Sheba were gone, it was a verity she must accept—though she had certainly been acquainted with those truths well enough already.

His horse snorted, ears pricking forward and front hooves stamping nervously in the snow. Luc turned to soothe it. No Drago this time, but a handsome bay gelding less prone to fits of temper. After all, destriers were meant to be used in war, not as pack animals or workhorses.

The bay sidled away from his outstretched hand, nostrils flaring, and Luc paused. The smell of smoke drifted to him on the wind, sharp and acrid. Metal bridle bits and curb chains clanked as the bay tossed its head with another nervous snort.

Luc mounted and followed the smell of smoke until he saw a thin gray curl rise above the snowy slopes. It came from a grove of ancient trees, bare now in the winter, hoary trunks gray with age and weather. He moved closer. Or more precisely, it came from a rough structure squatting beneath the trees, built of stone and wood, the smoke rising from a hole in the thatched roof.

Halting his horse on the narrow slope overlooking the grove, Luc assessed the possible danger. It was a crude hut, with no sign of trouble, but he was wary. Long ago he had learned not to trust appearances. Drifts of snow spilled over a low stone fence and climbed against an arbor made of willow branches and festooned with withered brown vines.

The smoke made long streamers in the wind, white-gray and drifting through the tops of the trees. A flash of white smoke caught his attention—and then he realized it was not smoke, but a shaggy beast that had streaked along the ground waving a plumed tail. Sheba.

Luc nudged his horse down the slope, and the bay snorted again, ears pricked forward as it picked its way over dead grass and fallen limbs. Hooves made crunching sounds in the wet snow, and Luc noticed the flicker at the unshuttered window of the hut. He had been seen.

He halted the gelding near the hut. White frost clouds blew from the agitated bay's nostrils, and it shifted nervously in a small circle.

" 'Tis the wolf you seek."

The strange voice was deep, Saxon words spoken with authority, emanating from a hidden source. Luc's eyes narrowed.

"Show yourself."

"Aye, as soon as I know your intentions. Who comes to my door?"

"Luc Louvat, lord de Wulfridge and your overlord as well. This cottage is on my land."

Laughter greeted his words. "I have heard of you, Luc Louvat. Your fame has spread far, and 'tis said that you are a fierce fighter but new at lordship."

"Show yourself. I do not care to speak to the wind."

Leather creaked as Luc shifted in his saddle, and after a moment a figure stepped from behind a clump of bushes near the hut. Limping, the man approached, wrapped in animal skins with furry heads and feet still dangling. Long matted hair of reddish-gray straggled to his shoulders, and a thick beard reached to the middle of his chest.

"You are Sighere," Luc said, and the man nodded.

"Yea. I am. You have heard of me as well."

"Lady Ceara has spoken of you."

"She sent you for Sheba."

Luc nodded. "Yea. Will the wolf come to you?"

"Sooner than to you, my fine Norman friend." A dry cackle accompanied that comment, and Sighere beckoned to Luc to dismount. "Come. There is a hot stew in the pot, with rabbit and barley broth."

Without waiting to see if Luc accepted his hospitality, Sighere turned and limped back to the hut, dragging one leg through the snow and supporting himself with the aid of a gnarled crutch. Luc dismounted and sheltered the bay beneath the sloped roof of a small lean-to built against the side of the cottage.

He had to duck to enter the low doorway, and was at once struck with an assortment of pungent scents. Animal skins lay everywhere. Rows of bared teeth greeted him from cluttered shelves and hooks over the door and window, tiny creatures long dead and staring out with empty eye sockets. A huge cauldron bubbled over an open fire, with smoke rising up to the large vent hole in the thatched roof. A cup was thrust into his hand, smelling strongly of honey and spices.

"Mead," the old man said shortly. "Our Saxon wine."

Sighere dipped a goodly portion of stew into a wooden bowl and held it out, and Luc accepted it with a murmur of thanks. A chunk of brown bread was proffered, and then Sighere lowered his weight onto a stool without the courtesy of waiting for permission or offering a chair to his lord. He glanced up at Luc expectantly.

"Tell me of my lady. It has been overlong since I have seen her. Is she well? Does she speak often of Sighere?"

Luc looked about him, and in the dim light of fire and badly smoking candle, found a stool for his use. He pulled it to him with his foot, and seated himself. Sighere was eating the stew with his fingers and bread as utensils. Luc looked down at his bowl.

"Your lady is well. But she misses her wolf."

"And you came to find it for her." Sighere smacked his lips, eyeing Luc over his bowl. "Why did she not come for herself?"

Luc dunked his bread into the steaming stew and scooped

up a mouthful. He ate several bites before replying. "I bade her stay at the castle."

"Ah."

After several moments, when Sighere made no other comment, Luc said, "The snow is deep. It can be treacherous to the unwary."

Sighere nodded, his concentration bent on the stew and not Luc. They ate in silence, and Luc began to grow impatient. The old man was toying with him.

"Can you call the wolf, Sighere? I would get her back to Wulfridge before dark."

"How?"

Luc stared at him. Sighere met his gaze, fingers dripping with gravy as he regarded him with lifted brows. "I brought a rope," Luc said.

"Do you intend to drag the wolf?"

"If need be. The wolf knows me."

"Ah, and that is why she came to you so freely." Setting down his bowl, Sighere wiped his greasy mouth on his sleeve. "Sheba is tame when it suits her. Like your lady."

Luc smiled at that, if a little ruefully. "I think you are right. If I must bind the wolf, so be it. I swore to find the beast for Ceara, and I will keep that promise."

"There are promises and promises, my lord. Most of them are made by men who seek only their own ends."

Luc's mouth tightened. "If I never saw the wolf again, I would not care. But it would please my lady to have her back. Do you help or not?"

"Ah, a great Norman lord asking for help from a Saxon churl? I can die happy now, for having heard that."

"Lest I am tempted to hasten that happiness, lend me your aid in summoning the wolf. Ceara says the beast knows you."

"Aye. She does. If I call her, she will come. But do I call her to her own grief? The wolf trusts me. I do not wish to betray that trust."

Leaning forward, Luc fixed the old man with a stern eye. "Neither do I wish to betray a trust. My lady wants her pet returned to her, and I swore to do so. Would I harm the animal after plowing through snow and field to find her?"

Sighere did not reply for a moment, but surveyed Luc from beneath the tangled shelf of his bushy brows. Then he nodded. "I wondered as to the kind of man you be. Some say you are just, but Kerwin bought his life from you for an oath, so I did not know whether he spoke from truth or fear. You have offered peace, but also given strife. Your king is a dread lord. No man who thwarts him lives long. And you, Lord Luc of Wulfridge? What do you offer the people of your lands?"

It was insolent. Another lord might have slain the old man right there, but Luc had spent too long among peasants not to recognize stiff pride and the promise of unyielding loyalty. To win over a man like Sighere would be worth ten barons like Oswald.

Luc held Sighere's gaze and answered softly: "I offer peace and prosperity. It will not come without a price, but that is the way of things. Those who rally to me will have my sword and my protection. What is mine, I keep. I allow no other to abuse those who belong to me."

"And those who oppose you? Who refuse your protection?"

"Will be dealt with accordingly. In these times, a man who is not a master must choose a master. I chose mine, and I chose well. William is a strong lord, and will hold what he has taken. Just as I will."

Sighere leaned back on his stool and pulled his crutch to him. He rose with the aid of the gnarled branch and took a limping step forward. Then he slowly knelt and put out his hands, palms together in the same gesture of fealty the barons swore.

"Once I was a young, strong man, a master-at-arms for my lord, his housecarl, then his loyal huntsman when I could no longer fight. My station is low, but I am not without pride. My honor comes from serving an honorable master. We Saxons are a proud people, used to being our own masters in ways that Normans do not understand. Yet I see the way the wind blows from Normandy, and have seen with mine own eyes the honor of men who are not Saxon. You are a fierce man, my lord, but a just one. I swear to serve you, if not with a sword, with my honor and my life."

Luc gravely covered the old man's hands with his own and accepted his oath. "Now rise, Sighere. You are welcome at Wulfridge and in my hall."

Sighere rose clumsily to his feet and stood proudly a moment, swaying a bit with the crutch under his arm but his body held stiffly straight. Then he smiled. "The wolf will go with you, my lord."

CEARA PACED THE floor of the solar with growing concern. Dark had fallen, and still Luc had not returned. The fool—he did not know this land as she did. He should not have been so determined to go alone, and if not her, at least taken another who was familiar with the bogs and forest.

Candles flickered on the table, and a draft swept across the chamber to stir wall hangings and bed curtains. Ceara paused. She stood stiff and still, listening with rising tension. Were those hoofbeats in the courtyard? No, of course she would not hear them, not here in the solar when the hall was so thick with people.

But she held her breath when there came a muffled sound from the corridor outside the solar, and moved slowly to the door that led to the antechamber. It was quiet—until the door was flung open, and Luc filled the portal, smelling of wind and snow. Her throat tightened, and as glad as she was to see him, there was no wolf at his feet.

"My lord . . . were you—"

A yelp rent the air, and a brown and white mass of matted

fur pushed past Luc. Ceara knelt, her legs too weak to hold her erect any longer, and Sheba bounded across the floor to reach her in almost a single hop. A wet tongue raked her face from chin to brows, smearing tears of gladness and relief. Ceara grabbed Sheba around the neck, pressing her face into fur that smelled of mud and smoke. Her voice broke a little as she murmured, "Oh, Sheba, silly cony . . . where have you been?"

Luc watched, leaning against the door frame with his arms folded over his chest, his voice dry. "I warrant that I would not rate such a welcome were I to be gone near a week from you."

Between swipes of wet wolf tongue and ecstatic yips, Ceara managed to say, "You underestimate yourself, my lord."

He smiled as she looked up at him from the floor, trying futilely to calm the excited wolf. "I met a friend of yours, Ceara. He sent you his regards."

"A friend?"

"Sighere."

"So that was where she went." Ceara shook Sheba with hands curled into the thick ruff of her neck, scolding her without much firmness. "You did not come when I called, wicked wolf. Shame on you for being so willful."

Sheba flopped onto her belly and put her head between her paws, but there was no real remorse in the gold-brown eyes. Fringed white lashes flickered briefly, then she put out a paw in a gesture of conciliation. Ceara took the paw in her hands and turned it over. Mud and ice crusted the thick white hair between the black pads of her paws, forming hard little balls. She bent to the task of working them free, and when she glanced up again, Luc was gone.

His silent departure left her feeling suddenly bereft, and despite her joy at having Sheba back, she could not help a pang of sadness. There were moments when she thought she had touched him in some way, when perhaps he felt fondness for her. Was she more to him than just a possession? He claimed he held what was his, but had said nothing about love. He had gone after Sheba, but was it because he had sworn to retrieve what he considered his, or because he wanted to please her?

Sir Robert's tale had explained much. But he had not touched on how Luc felt about her. And she did not know how to discover the truth for herself.

Never had she accepted defeat well, and it was no different now.

Sheba nudged her, cold nose digging into the cup of her palm, and Ceara stroked the great head, sighing softly. It should be enough that she was lady of Wulfridge and had her beloved pet back. But she knew it was not enough anymore. Unless she could win Luc's heart as he had won hers, nothing would ever be enough.

"Still sitting on the floor, wife?"

Her head jerked up, and Luc was there, looking weary but indulgent. He wagged a mutton joint, and Sheba sat up abruptly to stare at the treat with intense interest. A low warbling moan began low in her throat, escalating into a full howl, with head thrown back and eyes slitted, the black lips of her muzzle folded over her curved teeth.

Pushing away from the door, Luc tossed the mutton and Sheba leaped agilely to catch it in her great jaws, teeth chomping down on the meat with relish. Then she trotted to the far side of the chamber and sprawled on the stone with the mutton held between her paws.

Ceara glanced up at Luc, and he grinned. "I felt I had a better chance winning the wolf from you than you from the wolf."

"Perhaps you did not try the right inducement."

"Perhaps." The smile still lingered on Luc's mouth as he crossed to her and held out his hand, and she put her fingers into his open palm and allowed him to pull her to her feet. "Do you not wish to know about Sighere?"

"Is that your inducement? I had thought you more inventive, my lord. Jewels, or fine cloth from the East."

Luc swung her about, catching her around the waist with

one arm. His smile faded, and there was an intensity to his gaze to equal that of Sheba's. "I kept my promise, Ceara."

"Yea, lord." She put her palms lightly against his chest, her voice soft. "I had no doubt you would succeed."

Some of his tension eased, and he swept up a hand to cup her chin in his palm. "Liar."

She laughed. "Yea, lord, so I am at times. You should punish me for my willful ways."

"You jest, but do not think I have not considered it, especially when I was knee-deep in snowdrifts."

She kissed the underside of his jaw, along the faint, jagged scar that marked his skin. Dark beard stubble tickled her lips. "If you had not gone, you would not have met Sighere. Did you like him?"

His arms curved around her. "He was not what I expected from a former huntsman."

"He is a Saxon. Once, there were not class distinctions here as there are in Normandy. It was only when Normans brought pride of position to England that it became the mode to say one man was better than the next."

"I do not agree. There were Saxon kings, earls, and thegns."

"Yea, but the gulf between was not as wide then." She laid her face against his chest, feeling the strong beat of his heart under her cheek. Then she smiled, and tilted her head back to look up at him. "You smell sheepish, my lord husband. Do you wish to wash away the scent, or is it your preference to sleep in the stable?"

Luc grimaced. "I slept there last night. One of my men suggested I seek other lodging this night, for my temper disturbed the horses."

"Cheeky wretch."

"I could not chastise him. He was right." Luc peered at her with a gleam in his eyes. "If I am to be forced to bathe, I demand assistance."

"I am certain we can arrange that." Ceara spread her hand

against his chest, pushing him away from her. "I will send for Rudd to bring a tub and soap, and buckets of hot water."

He caught her hand when she stepped away, holding her. "And you to wash my back."

Contentment bubbled inside her as she promised, and she thought as she moved to the door that if he had not yet said he loved her, he felt it. Soon, he would say the words, would give her his heart as well as his name, and then her world would be complete. Soon.

Chapter Seventeen

JANUARY PASSED, AND the calends of February was fast approaching. Winter had gripped the land in icy talons and prevented Robert and Amélie from continuing their northward journey. Evenings were spent in the great hall with music, minstrels, and games of chess or backgammon, long lazy nights when the best spot was by the blazing fire. Even a short distance from the flames it was cold, with icy drafts whistling around corners and seeping between layers of clothing to chill flesh and spirit.

Robert de Brionne was impatient to be on his way, to be rid of the lady he was to escort to Malcolm's court. "It is wearing to hear her constant complaints in my ear, Luc. How did you ever bear her harping?"

"It was not her art of conversation that attracted me," Luc responded dryly, and Robert had to laugh.

"Admittedly, she is passing fair, but for her sharp tongue. Ah, Luc, would that I had accepted the king's first offer to court glory in Normandy. Then I would not be here with fair Amélie and your lady wife looking daggers at one another every meal."

Luc shrugged. "Ceara has little patience with Amélie's demands."

"No, she has little patience with Amélie's attempts to gain more than just your attention." Robert gave a grunt of irritation. "I vow, the lady liked you less when you were still vying for her favors than she does now."

"Ah, Robert, do you really not know that that is the way of some women? There are those who will flee at the slightest hint of rejection, and those whose appetites are only whetted by being spurned. If a man wants to win the heart of fair Amélie, he would do better to show her his back than his smile."

Robert looked up from the flames dancing on the hearth and regarded Luc thoughtfully for a moment, before he nodded his agreement. Juggling the dice in his hand, he tossed them to the game board without glancing to see how they fell. "She is a proud dame. I pity Malcolm's cousin, for he will not find in her the comfort you have found in your lady."

"There are those men who prefer constant challenge to harmony." Luc picked up the dice, rolling them in his palm with an idle motion. He glanced toward the end of the hall where Ceara stood with one of the young Saxon servants.

Robert followed his gaze. The wolf lay at Ceara's feet, returned again from a fortnight's disappearance. No one knew how the animal had left the castle, but she had suddenly vanished one morning, and as suddenly reappeared without explanation two weeks later. Ceara had feared that one of the soldiers had harmed the beast, but now Sheba was back, although still wary when armored soldiers hove into view. Natural enough, Robert supposed, since the wolf had near been run down by Oswald's man before Christmas. He turned back to Luc.

"What news of Oswald?"

"None." Luc frowned and rolled the dice against his palm with his thumb. "He swore no oath, to me or to William. But I did not expect it."

"What do you expect?"

Glancing up, Luc tossed the dice to the game board. "I expect that when the weather eases, Oswald will announce his intentions with a sword."

"What precautions do you take?"

"Wulfridge is strong. I have a network of loyal churls on the perimeters who will give the alarm should there be trouble."

"Can you count on churls to risk their own safety to give warning?" Skeptical, Robert shook his head. "My past experience has been that they look solely to their own."

"Only if they have not been convinced of the greater good in trusting an overlord to give them succor against the coming of invaders."

"And the peasants of Wulfridge trust you in so short a time?"

"Not me." Luc indicated Ceara with a tilt of his head. "It is her they trust. They fought for her before, with pitchforks and scythes, standing alongside veterans who should have been at home in front of fires instead of facing soldiers and knights. Balfour's vassals have sworn to me, save for Oswald, and the peasantry have been united by Balfour's old master-at-arms. If needed, they will come, though I think my garrison is well manned enough."

"You have experienced soldiers that even William envies, I think." Robert glanced down at the backgammon board and frowned. "Whose turn is it?"

Luc rose, stretching. "Yours. I have in mind another game to pass the night."

As he turned in the direction of his wife, Robert called after him, "Then you must forfeit our game."

Luc laughed and replied that it was of little matter to him, and Robert poured himself more wine, slumping onto the bench next to the abandoned game. There were moments he envied Luc, not for his lands or title, but for the promise of contentment within his grasp. Perhaps it was time he left his carefree ways behind and took a wife as well. A fair woman to enliven his nights and inhabit a home with female things. He thought of his estate in Normandy, empty save for servants and a widowed sister. It was not grand, but comfortable, with broad fields and healthy vines that made excellent wine. Long had he been too restless to remain there, preferring to use his sword in William's service, whether in France, Normandy, Flanders, or England, wherever there was strife that needed strength of arms. It paid him good coin, but did not lend to a long future.

"Must you sprawl all over the bench like a common churl, Sir Robert?"

Robert sighed, and looked up at Lady Amélie, who stood beside him with pinched mouth and narrowed eyes. Her arms were crossed over her chest, and her gaze shifted from Robert down the length of the hall. He did not have to look to know that she was watching Luc and Ceara.

"Your spite is showing, my lady."

Amélie's gaze jerked back to him. "Knave. What would you know of anything?"

"Enough to see what everyone else here sees." His fingers tightened around the pewter stem of the wine goblet. "If you do not mind being the butt of poor jests, pray continue with your covetous ways. But do not expect much sympathy from me when Lady Ceara takes her eating dagger to your lily-white throat, madam, for you will have earned her wrath with your clumsy attempts to win Luc's affection."

Amélie's pale skin had gone the color of ash. She did not speak for a moment, but stared at him with green eyes burning like emerald fires. "You know nothing of which you speak, varlet! Do you judge all by your sluttish ways? I am only conscious of the past friendship between Luc and myself, not—"

Surging to his feet, suddenly angry, Robert grasped her by the wrist, startling a gasp from her. "Do not use me as a dupe, madam, for I am not. Do you think I do not know why you asked the king for *my* escort north? Why you insisted upon coming at a time of year when the roads are at their worst?" He released her wrist with a slight shove, heedless of curious stares from others in the hall, his voice a low growl of warning. "I would not advise that you continue to view me as a witless fool, for I have known all along your game."

Amélie retrieved her dignity with a lifted chin and cool gaze. "You have spilled your wine on my gown."

"I crave your pardon most heartily." Robert lifted his goblet and drained the last of his wine, then with a tight glance at Amélie, pushed past her and left the hall. It was even colder in the corridor, drafts blowing in between the cracks of the huge double doors guarded by armed soldiers. Luc left little to chance. Sentries were posted on walls and at the outer gates of Wulfridge as well.

Still, he could not help an oppressive feeling of impending doom. It had lain on him heavily the past week. Irritable and restless, smarting from the contempt with which Amélie regarded him, he wandered down the long corridor aimlessly. A shadow flickered at the far end of the corridor where recent repairs had been abandoned because of inclement weather. Wooden partitions had been hastily constructed until stonemasons could be brought to Wulfridge. When a soft thunk caught his attention, as if something had fallen, he moved in the direction of the sound.

Glancing down, Robert shoved at a loose board with the toe of his boot, and was surprised when it shifted to one side. Beneath it, a gaping hole loomed black in the floor, and he knelt beside it, frowning. It was not just a hole, but a chamber of some kind, vast and dank with a musty smell that made him think of the sea. An oubliette? He peered into it, with the brisk whisper of clammy air chilling his face. A board creaked somewhere behind him and he glanced up, but saw only a vague shadow before something hard struck the side of his head. A flash of white lights spun in front of his eyes, and he pitched forward into empty air, trying to catch himself but failing as the black shadows swallowed him.

• • •

LUC COAXED CEARA into an alcove off the corridor leading from the hall, his hands as insolent as his wicked suggestions. Sternly, she put her palm against his chest, schooling the laughter from her lips as she bade him be more politic.

"The halls are yet peopled, my lord. Can you not wait until we reach the solar?"

"You lesson me greatly with modesty, but I know you too well, lady fair." He skimmed his fingers along the line of her throat to her covered bosom, grinning at her indignant protest. "What does it matter, here or there? There is little enough privacy for our pleasure."

"Then perhaps we should command a table in the hall for your display of affection," Ceara returned tartly, and Luc's soft laughter warmed her cheek. She tried to maneuver him to one side, but he used his weight as leverage, leaning against her with a mocking grin that let her know he thought her efforts amusing. She bit back her laughter and managed a convincing scowl, poking him in the middle of his chest. "You do not set a proper example for the others in your hall, Luc Louvat."

"Ah, but I do. They should all be wedded and bedded." Blocking her flight, he put his hands on her shoulders and pushed her into the wall with gentle force, leaning into her to hold her, his hands busied with the side laces of her gown.

A low growl emanated from the edge of the alcove, and Luc glanced over his shoulder, muttering about interruptions as he bade Sheba be still. Yet the wolf would not be quiet, and the snarling warning penetrated Luc's interest in Ceara's gown enough to turn him around.

Ceara pushed past him, frowning at her pet. "What is it, Sheba?"

Agitated, the wolf flicked white-tufted ears forward, hackles lifted on her shoulder blades, her body tensed as if stalking prey. The huge paws moved across the floor with slow deliberation, her sharp eyes intent on the far end of the corridor where repairs were being made.

"She sees something, Luc."

"Shadows." He grasped her by the arm. "Come. We will go to the solar, if you insist."

"No, Luc. There is something that disturbs Sheba."

"Since Oswald, every soldier she sees disturbs her." He did not release his grip. Impatience edged his words. "There are guards stationed all about the castle, Ceara. If there was trouble, I would have been informed. Now come, before—"

"Luc, I heard something."

Swearing softly, Luc blew out an exasperated breath, resignation in his tone now as he said, "Let us go see what has so alarmed your wolf that you would refuse your husband his needs."

She shot him a reproving glance. "Desire and need are different things."

"Not always, fair lady, not always."

But he was moving down the corridor, his strides long and determined next to the wolf's stalking gait. Ceara was not really frightened, for as Luc had said, guards were all about the grounds, but she *had* heard something that sounded alien, despairing, perhaps.

Several steps behind Luc, she did not see the cause when he stopped suddenly and knelt on the floor, exclaiming loudly. Sheba whined, then put back her head and howled, pawing at the floor.

"*Jésu,* the floor must have given way—Ceara, bring me a torch and fetch Alain. I think someone has fallen in a hole left by the workmen. Curse them for their carelessness—go swiftly, for the wolf seems to agree with me."

Ceara did not wait to hear more, but ran swiftly to fetch Alain and some guards. They gathered rope and torches before returning, and when they reached Luc, he looked up with a grim face.

"It is Robert. Make haste. Give me a length of rope. Light this area—Ceara, move back. You are only in the way. I need some men to lower me down there—by the love of God, I will soon discover what fool left this hole open."

Ceara moved back, a little indignant that she was so summarily dismissed, but too worried about Robert to protest Luc's brusque commands. Several men took hold of the end of the rope, bracing themselves as Luc wrapped the other end around his waist and slid over the edge of the hole into darkness.

Leaning back against the wall, she waited tensely, while the men strained against Luc's weight and torches flickered eerily over the gaping hole.

"What new diversion is this?" Amélie's familiar, caustic voice intruded on Ceara's absorption as she paused to observe the activity. "Is your husband trying to flee your loving arms again?"

Ceara clamped her lips together to keep from saying the words on the tip of her tongue, and held to the pretense that she did not understand Amélie's French taunts.

"Do not be so smug, my fine Saxon peasant. If not for the king, Luc would be in my arms instead of yours. In fact, he may yet be there. He'll tire of you soon. I know him. Never has he stayed long with a woman. Your vows will mean nothing when he wearies of living like a crude peasant—"

Pushing away from the wall, Ceara strode away before she yielded to the overwhelming temptation to do great damage to the haughty Lady Amélie. It was beyond her comprehension how Luc could ever have been interested in such a vain creature, or why Robert watched her with such intent eyes. She was lovely, yea, but mean-spirited. Yet she could not say so to Robert, for he would only think her jealous, as did Luc.

But now there were more important things to concern her, for there was a deep cavern under the castle that had been there since the time of the Romans. She prayed that Robert was not badly injured.

Amélie ambled over to one of the guards holding a torch aloft, and asked the cause of the commotion. When she was told Sir Robert had fallen, she gave a soft cry of real concern. A little surprised, Ceara watched as the widow stumbled back out of the way and clung anxiously to a post to watch as the rescue continued.

Panting from exertion, the guards began to haul on the rope, backing slowly across the floor so as not to break it with sudden tension. Robert's head appeared in the opening, blood on his forehead and matting his hair. They laid him carefully to one side, and Amélie knelt by him at once, murmuring soft assurances.

Ceara watched stoically as the rope was once more cast down to Luc, and only when his dark head thrust up from the yawning cavity did she relax. She knelt then, and put her arms around Sheba, rubbing the soft fur between her hands as Luc moved to his friend's side.

"Someone hit me," Robert mumbled groggily, trying to sit up.

"You fell into the hole, Robert." Luc pushed him back down on the floor, gently but firmly, his hands moving over Robert's limbs to check for breaks. A broken leg could oft kill a man if not tended properly, and sometimes even with the best of care, corruption set in and resulted in the loss of a limb. Luc sat back after a moment and grinned. "You are still whole, save for your cracked head."

Robert blinked, his eyes shifting from Luc to Amélie and back. "Someone hit me."

"Someone should hit you," Amélie said tartly. "You are an idiot to wander about like a child. Have you no sense? I can hardly go on to Scotland without my envoy. My position demands that I be properly attended, and you may very well have set my marriage back another month with this ridiculous incaution."

A frown flickered on Robert's bloodied brow, and he grimaced. "Amélie—" He paused to lick his lips and struggle to a sitting position, then pushed his face close to hers, startling her into drawing back a bit. "Cease your shrewish railing. You put me in mind of a fishwife."

Ceara clapped a hand over her mouth to smother her laughter. Amélie's features expressed both shock and amazement, and Luc had to turn his head to hide a grin. Amélie's face went crimson, then white, and she stumbled to her feet with an indignant gasp. Robert blinked crossly, and demanded that Luc help him to his feet. Luc refused.

"You shall rest this night, old friend."

Before Robert could protest, Luc bent and slung him over his shoulder, carrying him down the corridor to the antechamber outside the solar. The Norman knight was not a small man, but Luc carried him as easily as if he had been a child, and Ceara hurried behind to see that a pallet was laid for Robert's comfort.

But even when Robert's head was bandaged and he was laid upon a pallet of straw and fine linen, he was fretful and insistent that he had been struck.

"I tell you, Luc, I was hit. Do you think me witless enough to just tumble into a hole?"

"Calm yourself, Robert. Who here at Wulfridge would have cause to harm you? Have you done anyone here an ill?"

"No, of course not." He paused, frowning. "I did beat Remy at chess twice, but he does not seem the kind who would take it so amiss to lose a few coins on a friendly wager."

Luc exchanged an amused glance with Ceara. "No, Remy has never exhibited a tendency to deplore the loss of an honest wager. Rest now. On the morrow, we shall seek answers to your concerns."

Laying his head back, Robert closed his eyes, but a faint smile touched the corners of his mouth and he muttered, "You will be heartened to know you are right on occasion, Luc."

"About what?"

Robert did not reply, but turned his head toward the wall and expelled a long sigh of weariness. In a moment he was snoring softly.

Shoving a hand through his hair, Luc looked at Ceara with a frown. "Do you think him addled by the fall?"

"No. I think someone must have hit him."

"Good God, not you as well." Irritation lined his brow, and he gave an impatient gesture. "Danger in every shadow, Ceara?"

"It is a possibility, my lord. You have taken a castle that many have coveted. Do you not think others may resent your achievement?"

"It was not I who fell into a hole."

"Nay, but Robert is your loyal companion. Perhaps he saw something he was not meant to see."

Luc muttered a curse, but there was a speculative gleam in his eyes.

The gleam sharpened when Jean-Paul appeared at the door to ask after Robert's health. Shrugging at Luc's lifted brow, he answered his brother's unspoken question. "I was dicing with your captain in his quarters when one of the men-at-arms told us of it. How was he harmed?"

Crossing his arms over his chest, Luc regarded Jean-Paul as if waiting for him to make an expected announcement.

"We are not certain how he came by his injury, Jean-Paul. He was found in the hole at the end of the corridor."

"A hole?" Jean-Paul's blue eyes narrowed a bit. "You have a hole in the floor big enough for a man to fall through?"

"There is a chamber beneath. An old chamber, sealed but for this hole made by the workmen."

Ceara studied Jean-Paul. He did not seem disturbed, more curious than concerned. Many times she had searched for traces of resemblance to his half-brother, but found little, save for the way his eyes narrowed when he was irritated, or his mouth thinned into a taut line that formed deep grooves on his cheeks.

Where Luc's hair was a gleaming black, thick and shining and almost blue in the sunlight, Jean-Paul had fair hair, dark blond with streaks of brown. He was tall, but not as tall as Luc, and the strong determination that marked his brother's face was absent from his. Same father, different mother, Norman and Saxon combined. Was this what Luc wanted? What the king wanted? A Norman and Saxon alliance that would be ever-conflicted?

She sighed, and moved to the table to pour wine. Holding out a goblet to Jean-Paul, she saw surprise reflected in his face at her offer. He accepted the wine with a swift glance at Luc, as if expecting to be rebuked.

"Jean-Paul," she said, diverting his attention, "a long time ago, Romans built on this site. Most of the buildings are gone now, but traces remain. The tile designs in the great hall were done by the Romans, and according to my father, there were stoke holes built beneath the original building to provide heat through vents in the floor. On occasion, animals managed to get in, crawling in to die until Balfour ordered it sealed. No doubt, the hole the workmen uncovered was one of those."

" 'Tis a deep pit for a stoke hole," Luc observed. "It is twice my height or more."

"Time has eroded much of what was once here, as you are discovering, my lord."

Luc nodded. "My dwindling purse tells me that swiftly enough. But when I am done, Wulfridge will be able to withstand siege and assault."

"Do you expect such?" Jean-Paul stared at Luc over the rim of his goblet. "Do you expect assault here?"

"Mayhaps." Luc bent an assessing glance on him. "There are those barons who have yet to swear, as you know, and there is still Malcolm to the north."

Jean-Paul looked down. "Earls Edgar and Cospatric seek to stir rebellion there and gain aid from Malcolm. You are wise to prepare."

"I would be a fool not to know traitors can lurk in any corner," Luc said softly, and his brother's hands shook as he lifted the wine to his mouth.

He drank, and clenching the goblet tightly, gave Luc a searing look. "It was long ago, Luc. I was overyoung and overproud."

"Not that long ago. And you are still young, though youth is no excuse for treachery." Luc spoke in French now, a soft snarl of accusation.

"No." Jean-Paul sucked in a deep breath and answered in that language. "It is no excuse. I thought myself strong enough and wise enough to seize that which I wanted, to keep that which was mine. I wanted vengeance when our father offered you half of Montfort. I vowed never to let another usurp my rights, whatever it cost me. I did not want to lose what I held dear."

"Yet it is I who has the most to lose now, so do not think to betray me again."

Jean-Paul gave him a bitter glance. "You have the most to lose, perhaps, but it is because you *have* the most."

Ceara stared at him. Like an echo of the past, she heard her own cries of defiance to her father, heard her vow not to allow any to take what was hers. And she heard her father's reply, his weary admonition that there were ofttimes difficult choices to be made, and vengeance had no place in a wise decision. Balfour had been right, and there were times she wished she could tell him his daughter had finally come to that realization.

Before Luc, she had harbored so much hatred in her heart that is was near impossible to see past it. But since their return to Wulfridge, as she had watched him building not just new structures but allegiance in the people her father had tried so desperately to protect, those emotions had faded. There were depths to this Norman lord that she had never considered, facets of his character that were as noble as any Saxon she had ever known.

It had begun the night of their return, when he had vowed to keep safe that which was his—to keep *her* safe. It had been years since she had felt safe, years since she had felt hope for the morrow. Luc had given her that security, not just with words, but with his strength. When he had gone out in search of Sheba, and brought her back as he had promised, she'd known then that this man would do whatever he swore to do. Her faith grew every day, with every stone that was laid in the walls, with every strategy he provided for the defense of Wulfridge.

But until now, when Jean-Paul had echoed her words with such clarity, she had not really understood the reasons she had changed.

Luc was still staring harshly at his brother, his eyes flinty and cold as he told him this discussion could wait.

Bitterly, Jean-Paul set down his wine goblet and faced him. "You will never accept my repentance, will you, Luc? It is easier to hate me than it is to forgive me."

"I do not hate you, Jean-Paul. Neither do I trust you. If you want forgiveness, see a priest. I allow you to stay here only to govern your movements. Not for any other reason. It should not surprise you."

"It does not surprise me." Jean-Paul gave him a dark look. "You are truly more like our father than I had ever remembered."

A snarl like that of the wolf's lifted Luc's lips, and his hand lashed out to strike his brother across the face, sending him reeling. As Jean-Paul stumbled to his knees, Sheba leaped to her feet, crouched and wary. Ceara called to her, and knelt beside the animal to hold her, looking up at Luc with alarm.

"Luc, do not do this. It will solve nothing."

But his gaze remained on his brother, his words curt: "Go to the solar, Ceara. This is not for your eyes or ears. And take that cursed wolf with you."

"Do you forget your friend lies wounded on that pallet? Would you have all in an uproar for a quarrel with your brother? Let it be, Luc. Whatever is between you tonight will be there on the morrow."

Jean-Paul wiped blood from the corner of his mouth with the back of his hand, his voice quiet. "With your leave, Luc, I will take myself from your protection."

"This is not sanctuary, Jean-Paul. This is your prison. You will go nowhere I do not allow you to go."

Ceara stared at her husband helplessly. There was no softness in him now, no mercy, just a hard, ruthless intent that was as frightening as it was sorrowful. Yet she understood it. Had felt it herself after Wulfric died, when all that was left to her was danger and betrayal. And she could not say Luc was wrong, for had she not been suspicious of Jean-Paul herself?

Silently, Ceara rose to her feet and coaxed Sheba with her, moving to the solar she shared with Luc and shutting the door behind her. Always, there were two sides to a matter, and decisions must be carefully weighed.

At times, she did not know who to trust.

TENSION STILL SEPARATED Luc and his brother when Robert and Amélie prepared to leave for Scotland a sennight before the calends of March. The weather had let up, with snow melting but cold winds still prevailing.

Ceara went out to bid Robert farewell, sad that he was leaving, as he had provided much merriment in the time he had been at Wulfridge. She smiled at him as he stood waiting by his caparisoned horse.

"You will come again, Sir Robert?"

Grinning, Robert flicked a glance toward Luc. "If your fierce lord husband will allow it. I fear I have overstayed my welcome."

"You always do, Robert." Luc returned his grin. "But I will kill the fatted calf when I see your approach, so be assured that in your absence, I will no doubt forget how annoying you can be."

"For which, I am grateful. In your dotage, you have become almost even-tempered. Take care of your lovely lady, Luc."

"Do not doubt it for a moment." Luc's gaze shifted to Lady Amélie, who sat her horse swathed in rich furs and robes, gazing at them with uncomprehending hauteur, as she understood not a word of English. In French, he bid her a cordial farewell, and she beckoned him close.

Ceara stiffened slightly, but did not otherwise betray that she detested Amélie's overtures. He moved to the lady, his height so great that Amélie had only to bend a little to reach him from atop her mount. She caressed his face, her dainty, gloved hand lingering on his jaw, and her soft whisper carried even to Ceara.

"You have made the best of a bad business, Luc, and I admire you for it. Your pledge to honor your vows is worthy of the greatest knight, but I will not give up all hope that one day it will be possible for us to be together."

Luc clasped Amélie's hand with his, his voice flat. "You harbor a hope that is vain, my lady. I am wed, and my lady wife is not like to be put aside."

Sighing, Amélie's beautiful mouth curved into a pensive smile. "Honorable knight, I hold you in such esteem, and know that but for my foolish play, you might be happy with me. Words cannot express my regret for how I cast you aside, and I can only plead now that you know it was not for lack of affection, but for excess that I endeavored to inspire you to deeds worthy of great gain. It grieves me to see you caught in a loveless marriage, when you might have had happiness with me."

Ceara stood frozen, as if she did not see or hear, but was aware of Robert's quick, frowning glance toward her. If he knew that she understood their conversation, he did not betray her, and she was grateful.

"You dream the impossible, Amélie." Luc's voice was rough, but whether with emotion or irritation Ceara could not tell. He deliberately removed her hand from his face, and took a backward step. "I wish you well on your journey, and pray that your marriage will be agreeable to you. It is not likely that we will meet again."

A slight smile curved Amélie's mouth. "You may see me before you think, handsome knight, so do not be forlorn."

As Luc stepped back and turned to Robert, Amélie glanced at Ceara with an expression of triumph that was as unmistakable as it was perplexing. Ceara did not look away, but held the lady's gaze with a matched arrogance, until it was Amélie who looked away, frowning a little now as she gathered up the reins to her palfrey and turned the animal toward the gate.

Luc moved to Robert's side, glancing up with a wry smile. "Deliver the lady safely to Malcolm's court, Robert."

"I will guard her well. My honor rests upon the success of completing my obligation." Robert's mouth twisted. "Nor do I wish to endure her wrath should obstacles delay our purpose much longer. Already, she has berated me most heartily for being foolish enough to crack my head in your hallway."

Luc frowned. "The workmen swear it was well covered, Robert. I still do not know how it came about that you were injured."

Shrugging, Robert looked back at Ceara. "It is behind me, and I am hale now. Farewell, beautiful countess. Do you resist your husband with zealous vigor when he attempts to tyrannize you. He is a dreadful overlord when he is in a temper."

"I know well how to bear his temper, Sir Robert." She managed a smile. "If I go far from him, it does not bother me."

Robert laughed at that, and took up the reins to his horse. Chain mail clicked softly, and his sword clattered against the saddle as he mounted. He gave them a salute of farewell, and turned the caravan through the open gates.

It was a bittersweet moment for Ceara, for though she would truly miss Robert, she was glad to see the last of Lady Amélie. She had refused to give Amélie the satisfaction of being the cause of a quarrel between her and Luc, though several times she had come close to losing her temper with them both. Could Luc not see how the lady maneuvered him?

He certainly gave no indication that he did, but neither did he betray any feelings for her. It was a situation that left Ceara uneasy with too many questions and no answers.

Thankfully, other pressing matters distracted her. Soon Lenten season would end, and fields would be planted. It was her duty as chatelaine to bring the castle to its full potential as a working manor.

Luc came to her as Robert and Amélie disappeared from sight into the forest, smiling slightly. "I thought they would never leave."

She lifted her brows. "Nor I, my lord, but not for the same reason, I think."

"No doubt." He caught her by the hand. "Now come. With all their retinue quit of my hall, there should be peaceful corners wherever we look."

"Have you forgotten the workmen?"

"Nay, sweet lady, but I know their haunts." Lifting her hand to his lips, Luc held her eyes with a heated gaze that promised pleasure.

Her heart lurched. There was undisguised passion in his eyes that was not diluted with any secret longing for another lady. Could it be that the interest was only on the lady's side? Common sense bade her think so, but fear that she might lose him intruded at the most awkward times to prick her with doubt. Yet she would not allow him to guess her fears, would not betray the worry that he had wed her when he still loved another.

Ceara did not withdraw her hand from Luc's clasp, but went with him willingly, forgetting anything but the pressing desire to please him, to please herself, and to taste for a while the sweetness of love. The most pleasurable distraction of all.

Luc's impatient desire swept her up, and she did not protest when he pulled her into the soft, dark shadows of a hayrick spiced with the musty scent of old hay. Hazy chaff spiraled up when he stretched his length upon a sweet mound and pulled her down with him, his eyes wicked with laughter and hot with need.

"Shall we linger awhile, *chérie*?"

"Here? Wallowing in a donkey's breakfast?" She put a hand against his chest, unable to keep a smile from her lips as he took her hand and pressed his mouth to her palm.

"Aye. 'Tis a most agreeable place, as the donkeys do not mind and the stable lads are far afield this day." His mouth moved from her palm to her wrist, pushing aside the long embroidered cuff of her gown. "There is never enough privacy here. While I do not mind others knowing that I enjoy my wife, I do not relish displaying my talents"—he quirked a glance up at her—"or lack of them, to all who care to listen."

"Talent, my lord?" She swallowed a bubble of laughter. "Do you mean your precocious way with my laces?"

"Among other things." The tight sleeve of the gunna she wore under her kirtle frustrated him for a moment, and he plucked at it with a frown. "I think I prefer the way you once dressed. I regret discarding your brief garments."

Ceara watched smiling as he began to untie the laces at her sides, tugging them free with an impatience that betrayed his need. He glanced up at her.

"You could help, my lady."

"Yea, but then you would have your desire too easily. 'Tis my thought that a man should have to work for that which he wants, or he does not fully appreciate it when it is his."

"You"—he pressed a kiss on her bare shoulder as he pulled aside her kirtle—"are wiser than"—the kirtle slipped over her head and sailed through the air—"any woman I have"—now the gunna slid free, and she lay on the straw cushioned by linen and sweet grass as he moved his hands over her body with a hunger he could not hide—"ever known, *ma biche*."

She closed her eyes. A shudder made her flesh quiver as his hot mouth found the spot beneath her ear that drew shivering responses from her. *Ma biche* . . . my doe. A tender endearment, as were the others he used. But did he love her? Or did he only love loving her? She wished she knew, wished he would indicate that he thought of her as more than a possession, that he loved her. Ah, God, she knew she loved him, with heart and body and soul, and every breath she took. She kept as tight a rein on it as she could. If he did not love her, she could never admit her feelings for him. It would only put an awkwardness between them, for then he would be compelled to acknowledge his feelings—or lack of them.

No, it was best this way, to lose herself in the passion and not allow emotion to shatter their fragile new contentment. After all, Lady Amélie had not been able to draw Luc away from her, though the lady had certainly tried. He had honor, and he would stay with her even if he did not love her. She would always have that. Perhaps one day he would learn to love her for more than her lands and his vow to the king.

Luc lifted himself to his knees over her, his dark eyes glittering with sharp desire, his mouth taut with need. His sherte and tunic were gone, his bare chest gleaming bronze in the dusty light of the stable as his hands moved to the laces of his linen leggings. Her gaze did not waver; she relished the sight of him, this magnificent man who was her husband, this knight with taut bands of muscle on his chest and belly, and the raging evidence of his desire before her. Ah, he was so fine, so beautiful in his potent masculinity, and she ached with such swelling love for him that she had to close her eyes so he would not see.

Skimming his hands up her bare thighs, Luc parted them with urgent gentleness. His fingers trailed caresses from her knees to the silky mound between her legs, and when her legs began to tremble he caught them up and pulled forward. Startled, her eyes flew open as he held her with her legs draped over his shoulders, his mouth pressing kisses where his hands had just been, his tongue a flame that seared her quivering flesh. She cried out but he held her firm, scraping his morning beard against her tender thighs in an erotic abrasion.

Shocked and at the same time throbbing with need, she drew in breaths of liquid heat that turned her blood to molten fire. Luc's hands moved to her breasts, caressing her, his thumbs raking over her taut nipples as his tongue darted over that aching center of excitement. She made a fervent sound, incoherent, but he seemed to understand what she wanted when she did not.

Never had she dreamed of such exquisite sensations, and there was something so arousingly dangerous about this, lying naked in the straw with Luc above her, his chest bare and his leggings opened so that his rampant maleness was uncovered in an open display of his desire. Moaning and twisting beneath his tongue and hands, she tried to clutch at the queer singing excitement that coursed through her body but it eluded her. A growing frenzy filled her with increasing anxiety, and then it all exploded into a starburst of fire like a comet trailing sparks. Gasping his name, curling fists full of straw as she heaved upward, she felt the fierce heat spin through her in a tidal wave of release. It was overpowering, exhausting, and depleted her of strength and thought.

Barely, she was aware of Luc lowering her to the straw and moving over her, his body a hard pressure against her, his lips at her ear as he murmured sweet words. And then he was inside her, his hard body sliding into her with exquisite tremors, thrusting, slowly then more swiftly until the pressure began to build again and she soared to match his thrusts. Her hands moved to hold him, to curve around the taut muscles of his arms as he levered his body over hers to drive powerfully, taking her up and over again—and again, until he collapsed atop her in the straw, damp and exhausted and weak with satisfaction.

It seemed like hours before he stirred, moving from between her thighs with a sigh of regret and pushing the damp hair from her eyes so that she opened them and looked up at him. A haze of repletion lit his face and curved his mouth into a smile.

"You content me, *ma chérie*."

For now, it was enough.

Chapter Eighteen

"LUC, YOU CANNOT do this!"

Ceara stared at him, her lovely face white with anger. A startled page scuttled to duck behind trestle tables stacked against the wall of the hall and avoid being caught in their dispute. April light streamed in through the glazed window high up on the wall, hazy with dust motes. Luc propped his booted foot on the bench between them. His voice was tight.

"I can do it. I will. They were given a choice, Ceara. They have made theirs, now I will make mine."

"But to destroy homes . . . crops and livestock—you cannot mean to do that, Luc. Tell me that you will not be so cruel."

His mouth tightened. Why must she look at him like that? Shadows filled her wide blue eyes like clouds in a summer sky, as if he were some monster dredged up to ravage the land. He struggled for a way to make her understand. It was not his choice. It was Oswald's. She should see that if he allowed one man to defy him, he would never have control of his lands. He had observed well at William's side, and seen the effectiveness of his methods. It was cruel, yes, but necessary if Northumbria was ever to be conquered. Half the region now lay smoking and charred, rubble where once new green fields had been, bones where once sheep and cattle had grazed. But the rebel barons were yielding. Without land and food and shelter, they could not offer an organized resistance.

"It is not a matter we can discuss, Ceara," he said at length. "You will not understand it no matter how many times I tell it. My views have not changed."

Trembling, her voice was shaky with grief and fury. "If you do this, I swear I will not forgive it."

He looked at her dispassionately. "Then so be it."

Ceara gave him a look of utter disbelief, then spun on her heel and fled the hall. Her butter-yellow skirts whirled up around her ankles. Curse her. She should try to understand his position. He had made a stand. If he veered from it, none of his vassals would respect him. Without respect, he would not be able to hold so much as a single hide of land.

A slight, embarrassed cough caught his attention, and he looked around to see Captain Remy standing not far from him. It was obvious Remy had heard their argument, for he could not look directly at his lord.

"The men await, my lord."

"I will be there anon." Reaching for his sword, he buckled it around his waist and over his hauberk. His spurs clinked softly as he walked past Remy, his strides long and determined. She may hate him for this, but by God, she was still his wife.

Ceara was not in the solar, nor in the antechamber where he expected to find her, and Luc's temper was not improved at the prospect of playing the chastened husband seeking out his angry wife. With each empty chamber, his temper grew hotter, so that by the time he found her, his irritation had swelled to anger.

It did not help that she was sitting on a flat stone by the cairn that held her parents' bodies. Just beyond beneath a tall beech lay the grave of Wulfric, her first husband and boon companion, always a hero in her eyes. But Wulfric was a hero who had lost all, and he did not intend to do the same.

Hugging her knees to her chest, Ceara stared straight ahead and did not even glance at him when he said her name. A breeze lifted a strand of her hair that had come loose from a long blond plait to curl over her shoulder. It was still cool, though April at Wulfridge was warmer, and yet she wore no cloak around her slender shoulders.

"Ceara," he repeated more forcefully. "You must abide by my commands when I am gone." No reply. "Antoine le Bec is to be master-of-arms in my absence. His orders are to not allow you to leave Wulfridge for any reason. This means that you must not walk your wolf, nor seek out herbs and roots in the forest, nor visit Sighere. If there is need to leave the castle, send another."

She turned at last, blue eyes scornful beneath the puckered twist of her brows. "I am not so fragile a flower that I will wilt at the first sign of your anger, my lord."

"Well I know that. Yet what I command, I do for your best interests. Oswald knows that I would not countenance his defiance long. Now that Lent is ended and Easter past, he will be waiting and watching for my forces. I will have your vow that you will not leave Wulfridge, Ceara."

"You will have *my* promise when I have yours that you will not carry out this destruction you have planned."

He bent and plucked her from her rock, hand curled so tightly around her arm that she flinched. With his other hand, he shoved up her chin so that she had to look into his eyes. "Do not try to lesson me, Ceara. This is not a time for dissension. It is important that you understand. You must not risk being taken hostage."

"God forbid that you should part with coin for—"

His hand tightened until he could see red marks on the creamy skin of her jaw and cheeks. "It is not the coin I care about. Your life might very well be a prize to some who begrudge me what I have won. Do not think yourself able to elude capture. One mistake might be all it would take to bring down disaster on your head. Now swear to me that you will not leave Wulfridge."

"What will you do if I do not swear? Slay my wolf as you once threatened to?" Bright tears sparkled in her eyes, but whether from sorrow or rage, he could not tell.

"No. I would never slay your wolf to wring your acquiescence from you."

"Not true, my lord. Perhaps you have forgotten, but I have not, how you swore to slay Sheba if I did not disrobe for you."

"I never threatened to slay the beast. No—think back. I said it would be a shame if the wolf were to have to pay for your sins, and so it would have been. But I never meant to harm an innocent beast just to gain your cooperation. It would have been far too easy to disrobe you myself."

She shook back the loose hair from her eyes and set her jaw in a familiar line of defiance. It had been a while since this obdurate expression had settled on her fair features, and he was sorry to see it now.

But her words belied her expression as she gave a shrug of her shoulders and said, "You do not mind playing me false, I see. Very well. If you must have my vow, I give it to you."

"The words, Ceara."

"I swear I will not abandon Wulfridge."

"No, swear you will not leave the castle."

"My lord, I must be allowed to go to the stables, or to the storehouse to—"

His grip tightened on her arm. "You must know my meaning. All that is encompassed here within these walls is safe. It is outside the walls that is dangerous. I cannot be distracted with worry for you when I am pursuing rebel barons on their own ground, so you had best swear to me now before I am tempted to leave you in chains."

Her gaze lowered and he tried not to notice the slight quiver of her lips. A pulse beat madly in her throat, and her skin was ashen. After a moment she looked up at him again.

"I vow to remain here, my lord, as you command."

He studied her. She did not look away, but gazed at him steadily, pale but defiant. Uncertain, he tried to judge her temper. Did he dare trust her? *Jésu,* he wasn't even certain she was honest with him about her lack of French—would she keep her sworn word? Reluctantly, he released her arm and nodded.

"It is for the best, Ceara."

"Yea, lord, if you say it, it must be true."

Irritated, he started to turn and walk away, but halted and reached for her. Jerking her into his arms, he held her hard against him and kissed her fiercely. He kissed her until her lips parted, and he felt her stiffened spine relax beneath his hands. Releasing her, he cupped her face in his palms to gaze down at her.

"I will keep you safe if you allow it, *chérie*."

Bright tears spangled her curved lashes, and she curled her fingers around his wrist and sighed. "Keep yourself safe, Luc. For me."

"Yea, fair lady, for you I will return." The smile on her lips was a little wobbly, and he brushed away a dewy tear from her cheek with his thumb. It was enough that she knew he wanted only to protect her from those who may cause her harm. He kissed her again, gently this time, a light brush of his lips against her mouth, then left her there in the grove of young trees that guarded the burial cairn.

Remy and the mounted soldiers were waiting. Paul held Drago on a tight rein, as the destrier had already worked into a lather, with steam rising from his heated hide. Frost clouds blew from scarlet nostrils, and tack chains rattled as the animal shook its massive head.

Luc mounted, and they rode from Wulfridge with his banner raised, the standard-bearer riding close by. The weak April sun glinted on frosted grass at the roadside. Wind blew sea waves into frothy lace caps on the surface of the inlet and bent long supple reeds as they headed for Rothbury.

It was a grim business, and not one he liked, but it must be done. Oswald must yield.

They followed the Coquet River until they reached the priory at Brinkburn, and rested there before moving on. The weather held, though it shifted to a slight drizzle that wet the roads. Night was cold, but not freezing, and did not disturb the sleep of soldiers used to harsh marching conditions.

On the second day they arrived at the edge of Rothbury Forest. It was a thick wood, studded with crags and streams swollen by the runoff of spring thaw. The river was too swift to ford under cover of darkness, but no doubt Oswald had already heard of their approach.

Luc was right in that assumption, and when they reached the fortress high atop an earthen mound, it was shut up tight against them, gates locked and manned with archers and spearmen posted along the walls. Luc sent a messenger with an offer of clemency for all save Oswald if the stronghold was yielded to him. The reply was a volley of arrows and defiant yells, as he had anticipated.

Luc settled in to besiege Oswald, instructing his men to build cats to shelter their assault on the wooden walls and ordering arrows to be dipped in pitch. He did not expect a long siege, for Oswald's palisades were of wooden construction, and vulnerable to fire. While his men were obeying these commands, Luc sent out forces to ravage villages and fields, to take what plunder they willed, to destroy Oswald's resources and bring his people to their knees. It was not a part of war that he relished, but he knew well that to allow the rebel baron any support would only lengthen the conflict.

Along with his command to ravage, he had also given the stern edict to Remy that women and children were to be spared, that rape would be viewed in the harshest light, and any man who disobeyed would be put to the sword. Captain Remy, reminded of Luc's wrath when unarmed servants were slain in the taking of Wulfridge, relayed these orders in the bluntest of terms.

Luc expected these people to bend the knee to him, and while he intended to instill respect and fear, he did not wish to earn unyielding hatred as a cruel Norman overlord. Mercy would be given to those who surrendered, so Oswald would be viewed as the cause of their losses. It was a tactic he had seen stand William in good stead, earning him loyalty from those he conquered. Whether from fear or respect, it did not matter.

What did matter to Luc was Ceara's regard. She would not forgive the rampant slaughter of Saxons. Even had he not desired to avoid shedding the blood of those who owed him service, he desired even less the enmity of the Saxon maid who had become his wife. It was she he thought about in odd moments, watching as his men built the portable wooden shelters with which to storm Oswald's walls, thinking instead of Ceara's soft skin. He had stormed her citadel with passion and determination, and the spirited surrenders he had won left him aching for even more. Yet she guarded her heart so well that he was still uncertain of her. When he thought perhaps she felt more than a passing fondness for him, she turned, eyes flashing and head lifted with defiance, her tongue sharp enough to flay him to the bone.

War was more certain than a woman's mind, he thought with annoyance. In battle, he knew what to do. With his wife, he was too often at a loss. She turned from yielding sweetness to hissing defiance in the blink of an eye. It was enough to unnerve a man at times.

ROBERT DE BRIONNE was uneasy. Their acceptance by King Malcolm's vassal was cordial, his hospitality abundant, but as of yet, there was no sign of the king's seal on the terms of marriage for

Amélie. He fretted at the delay, but his requests for explanation were deftly turned aside by Lord Niall, who bent smiles and wiles on him that were intended to soothe his misgivings.

When the second fortnight passed with no word from the king of the Scots, nor sign of nuptials, Robert announced his intention to depart with the lady unless he was shown proof of their good intentions.

Niall, stroking his chin thoughtfully, regarded Robert with a lifted brow and slight smile. "I would not do that, were I you, Sir Robert. It might be misunderstood."

"There is no misunderstanding." Robert eyed the men who quietly came to flank Niall with a sudden qualm. "You have not kept your bargain. The Lady Amélie was to be wed with the king's sanction, yet I see no envoy from Malcolm, nor yet a bridegroom."

"He is unaccountably delayed, Sir Robert, as you have been told more than once." Niall's eyes narrowed with sly hostility. "Do you think us reluctant to wed our vassal with a lady of William's choosing?"

Robert drew in a deep breath. "Yea, I do. The negotiations were said to be complete, yet there is now too much delay, to my mind."

"How unfortunate."

"Perhaps the lady and I should depart, and when the king wishes to secure the pact, we will return."

"Ah, that would not be wise, Sir Robert. You are our honored guests here, and we would take it amiss were you to attempt to leave our hospitality. Do you not care for the food? Or our diversions? Not a Norman court, perhaps, with a surfeit of silk and comfits, but we are more civilized in our way. And we know how to honor guests."

"I feel more prisoner than guest," Robert said quite bluntly, and knew from Niall's casual shrug that he was right. His muscles tightened. It was a trick, as he had begun to suspect. "What is expected from us, Lord Niall?"

"Nothing more than your cooperation, my friend." Niall smiled. "We know that the new earl of Wulfridge has mounted an assault on our ally, Oswald of Paxton. We would have you send word to him that if he wishes to keep his own, he will withdraw from Northumbria."

It was a cryptic suggestion that had grave import. Robert paused before replying. If Oswald were allied with Malcolm, that left Wulfridge in grave danger, for Luc's forces would be divided, the castle vulnerable.

"And if he does not withdraw, Lord Niall?"

Shrugging, the old lord sat back in his chair and put his hands together, fingertips against fingertips. "Then his lady wife will not be returned to him."

Robert stared at Niall with mounting anxiety. "Where is his lady now?"

Niall smiled. "She is now, or soon will be, in Oswald's custody. But do not fear for her. I have agreed to accept her as my guest until we are assured that Northumbria is secure in our hands. It is your part in this, Lord Robert, to persuade Luc Louvat that he must accept our demands."

"And if I refuse?"

"You will not. Your own life you might risk, but not that of fair Amélie. It would hardly be chivalrous of you, and it is well known how you Normans pride yourselves on feats of chivalry."

Scorn underscored his words, and Robert stiffened. If Malcolm supported this insurrection, then nothing could avert war, for William would not suffer it. He looked at Niall. "Does King Malcolm involve himself in this?"

Niall shrugged. "The king has other concerns at the moment, but if we succeed, he will support us."

"You fool. Malcolm is not in a position to defy William. Why would he?"

"Why, for the rewards, of course. As do I. By the by, Sir Robert, have you met my lady wife?"

Robert stared at him warily. "Nay, I have not."

"She is known to you, I think. And most certainly known to Lord Luc."

Once, Robert would have been astonished, but now it was only further proof of the suspected treachery when Lady Adela entered the chamber, her expression triumphant.

"Robert of Brionne, it has been a long time since I have seen you. Tell me, how is my son?"

"If you mean Jean-Paul, he was well when last I saw him."

"No, I meant my *other* son—my bastard stepson, Luc. Does he fare well also?"

"Madam, I have a feeling you know the answer to that far better than I do." Robert fought his rising frustration. "Did you send Jean-Paul to Wulfridge? Bones of God, you have a lot to answer for, madam!"

Laughter greeted his furious demand, and Lady Adela exchanged a long glance with her husband before Niall turned back to Robert. "Well, Sir Robert? What have you decided?"

After a moment Robert nodded, his heart heavy and his voice gruff. "I will send a man to Lord Luc with your damned message."

Niall nodded in satisfaction. "Excellent. And since you are staying with us awhile longer, Sir Robert, you and the lady may continue to enjoy our pleasant pastimes."

"I do not enjoy being hostage," Robert snapped.

"Hostage? No, you mistake me. You are merely our guests for a time, until Lord Luc is convinced that to wage war on Northumbria is most unwise."

"You have chosen a wolf to make into a lapdog, I fear, Lord Niall. I do not think you will like its bite."

"I do not fear the bite of a mongrel. Our borders are besieged, and we will do what must be done to secure them."

"Then take care you do not earn the wrath of the lion as well as the wolf, for William will not swallow this insult without retaliation."

Niall smiled blandly. "William is far away, and must concern himself with unrest in other areas. Here, where Saxon earls align with Scots, lies much land that we have long considered our own. We do not yield it gladly."

"It is not yours to yield. There will be bitter battle done for this, Lord Niall, mistake it not."

"I do not think so. Luc of Wulfridge is one man."

"You forget Leofric and Eadwine."

"Pah! Eadwine is old and Leofric wavering. If Oswald triumphs, Leofric will sway his forces to our side and the wolf will be overrun. We might have had the lands already if not for Luc Louvat. Had we known they were held by only a maid and her grizzled commander, we would have taken them long before he arrived.

"Yet the maid held them against you successfully, I hear."

Niall rose abruptly. "It is of no matter now. You are here, and when Lord Luc receives our offer, he will make his decision. Pray you that it is in our favor, or you will rue this day, Sir Robert."

Outraged but outnumbered, Robert could only keep his own counsel as he was shown to the chamber he had occupied since arriving. The old fox had maneuvered slyly and now Luc must make the next move. Did he risk his childhood friend, or his wife and lands? Robert's heart was heavy, and as he summoned to him a man from the retinue he had traveled here with, he knew with grim certainty what he would do were he Luc. Therefore, it would behoove him to think of a way to extract himself and Lady Amélie from what was certain to be a dangerous position—and thus free Luc from having to decide.

The messenger arrived, nervous but alert. "Yes, Sir Robert, you summoned me."

Robert nodded. "Giles, though I know there was strife between you and Lord Luc, you must put that behind you. He will recognize you and my seal. Deliver to him this message and my ring. . . ."

• • •

It was near dusk. Purple and crimson shadows stained the horizon, reflected in the shimmering waves of the inlet cradling Wulfridge castle. Ceara stood atop the wall clutching her arms to her body, gazing across the water. The wind tugged at the hem of her blue kirtle and blew her loose hair about her face. Luc had been gone over a week, long days and nights had passed since he set out to lay siege to Oswald. Only one message had come, and that soon after Luc's departure, the weary courier covered with mud and flecks of lather from his horse as he relayed the news that Luc had laid siege and sent his assurances that he was well.

There had also been a personal note from him, and she had read his neat penned words with a little difficulty, as her training was scant. Still, she knew enough to make out his message to her, and had tucked the wrinkled parchment with his seal beneath her pillow that night.

He thought of her often. He hoped she heeded his command and her vow, and was safe in the confines of the castle. It had been signed with a flourish, *Luc Louvat, earl of Wulfridge.*

Arrogant, perhaps, but the essence of the man was there in the sanded ink and the wax seal imprinted with his ring. The signet depicted a wolf's head, familiar and defiant. Odd, that a man so named had come to take her lands. It was almost as if her father had sent him to her, for Lord Balfour had said that Wulfridge needed a man who is as fierce as a wolf to hold it, not a she-wolf. At the time, she had been furious. Now, she knew he was right.

Beside her, Sheba began to pace, huge paws padding along the top of the wall as the animal picked a path over the jagged stones. Ceara followed the wolf's gaze over the battlement and saw in the distance faint plumes of smoke rising above treetops to smudge the dusky sky. Her throat tightened. Surely Luc would not lay waste to his own lands. Not even if churls defied him or the villagers closed their shop doors against him would he destroy his own resources. Would he?

She shifted uneasily. In the courtyard below came the rumble of soldiers, and she glanced down uneasily as men began to scurry back and forth with hasty purpose. An air of grim preparation clothed their movements, as cauldrons were dragged from storehouses, leather hides pulled out, and the smell of heating pitch rose into the air. By the time she reached the bailey, the activity was fevered, chaotic.

She sought out Lieutenant le Bec, castellan in Luc's absence, charged with keeping the castle safe. He spoke rough English, but was too hurried to do more than tell her that news had come of an army's approach.

"Men from the north, my lady, from what we know," he added, then moved away before she could ask more questions.

Men from the north? Danes? Or Scots? She hurried to the castle, and found the hall in an uproar. The room was being stripped of valuables which would be hidden in one of the underground vaults Luc had restored. Servants took care to remove everything down to the fragile glazing from the window.

It was an organized procedure, carried out under the swift, capable direction of the squire, Alain. She found him in the corridor outside the hall.

"Alain, tell me, what do you know?"

"Little more than you, most like. Here, boy—Rudd. Do not bother with that tapestry, but take instead the gold and silver vessels to the vault."

Ceara grabbed the squire's arm when he would have pushed past, too agitated to care about property. "Curse you, Alain of Montbray, tell me what word has come to your ears before I flay you for disobedience!"

That halted the squire, and he looked at her with cold eyes. "I owe allegiance to my lord, not you, with all pardon for my bluntness, Lady Ceara."

"Yea, but I am one of Lord Luc's prized possessions, so do not be so insolent that you allow me to be lost in the confusion."

Her veiled threat convinced him, and he sighed impatiently. "The Scots approach. They are garbed for war. It is a great force, and with only a single troop left to defend our walls, Lieutenant le Bec has sent out an urgent message to Lord Luc that we are under attack. I do not think we will be overrun, as our defenses are stout, but it might be difficult for the earl to relieve us if he is in the midst of besieging Oswald."

Fear skipped along her spine, but she nodded. "I am not unaccustomed to assault, you may recall. I have experience with this. Have our vassals been summoned?"

"Messengers have gone out to Leofric and Eadwine. The towns have been warned to shut their gates, those that have walls, and the villagers cautioned to take cover against the invaders. The coastal towns are advised to move all merchant ships from their harbors. That is all that can be done for the moment."

"It is enough. We will hold the castle until my lord arrives to defend us."

Alain gave her an odd look, a little smile at one corner of his mouth. "You seem confident he will come, my lady."

"He will come."

"And if he is delayed by Oswald? What then?"

"Do you seek out worries, Alain?"

"Not when there are worries aplenty without seeking." Alain shifted from one foot to the other, anxious to be gone. She did not delay him longer, and hurried to her own chamber, Sheba at her heels.

The wolf was uneasy with the armed men running to and fro, and let her distress be known by rumbling moans and brief howls. Ceara comforted her briefly, then moved to the wooden chest set against the far wall of the solar. Hidden in the bottom was the gladius that had long been hers, beneath what was left of the Roman armor. The leather straps of the armor were worn almost in two, as they had been for some time. She withdrew the short sword and hefted it in one hand with a smile of satisfaction. Much better than her dainty little eating dagger that was all Luc would allow her to wear, a pitiful weapon in her opinion. This old sword had endured through the ages, kept sharp at the grindstone, carefully cherished by many before her.

Now she strapped it around her waist, fastening the buckles that held it secure over her blue kirtle. At once, she felt better. If need be, she could defend herself.

Sheba put back her head and howled again, black lips dark against the white of her fur, eyes slitted. The wolf sensed danger, and reacted with restless anticipation.

"Shush, cony," Ceara soothed, stroking the thick white fur of Sheba's ruff. "There is naught to fear. We will hold until our lord comes, and together we shall drive out the invaders. This time, we fight together."

Sheba swept a tongue across Ceara's cheek, but did not cease her restive prowling about the chamber. It was likely to be a lengthy wait, and Ceara finally left the solar to join the others in the hall.

The wolf came behind her, a low whine in her throat as she followed Ceara through the corridor, now strangely empty of guards. All had been called to man the walls and gates. Dark shadows shrouded the far end of the passageway, where construction was still under way though the hole that had waylaid Robert had been well covered now.

The hall was empty of Luc's fine Norman furnishings. Little remained to indicate that woven tapestries had covered the bare walls, or gilt salt cellars and silver nefs had held spices for their food. Even the feather bolsters that cushioned chairs and benches were gone.

Alain was quite efficient, it seemed. She smiled a little, and moved to the far end of the hall where the *table dormant* remained in place, a huge, heavy oaken slab that had served her father and his father before him. Motifs of ancient Celtic deities were still etched into the sides and framework of the table, intri cate swirls and coils that resembled the ornamentation of he mother's pendant. At the thought, she put up a hand to touc the amber and silver necklace around her neck.

In the confusion, it might very well be lost—or taken. I should be in the vault with the other treasures, tucked safel away until danger had passed. Turning, she left the hall again Sheba a white shadow slinking behind her with hackles raise and eyes alert.

Below Wulfridge, in the deep chambers dug aeons befor by invaders long departed from England, Luc had chosen a single vault to hold valuables. An iron door had been fitted to th only entrance, and a lock secured the door with a thick hasp. I was a good-sized chamber, with walls chiseled of rock that were damp from the cold, musty air of the sea. Huge chests ranged along the walls, lined with spiced wood that had been treated with pitch to withstand the moisture and keep mold from the bolts of precious cloth.

The door was ajar, and a single torch lit the dank chamber with fitful light. Ceara drew off the pendant, and stood in front of one of the chests. The lid was heavy, as high as her waist and curved, a massive chest indeed.

With an effort, she managed to open it, straining at the weight of the lid. She was impatient to get back to the hall, and coiled the silver and amber pendant into a jewel-crusted chalice, then slowly lowered the lid, puffing with exertion.

When Sheba snarled, Ceara turned swiftly, letting the lid fall the last bit with a loud crash. The sound was muffled by thick stone, quickly smothered in the gloom. Torchlight flickered. The wolf crouched low, teeth bared, hackles stiff along the line of her back.

Invaders could not have breached the walls in the time it took for her to come down to the vault, Ceara reassured herself, and she moved toward Sheba with cautious steps.

"Who goes there?"

The sound of her demand faded quickly. Just outside the

door a shadow moved, and she put her hand on the hilt of her sword. Heart pounding, she cleared her throat and again demanded that they show themselves.

Still no reply, and Sheba's low snarls grew into violent rumbles. With a hand on the wolf's back and the other hand around her drawn sword, Ceara approached the vault door. No doubt the wolf just sensed an armed soldier beyond the door, still ever wary since the incident with Oswald's man.

It was quiet in the bowels of the castle. Her steps made an eerie shuffling sound over the stone floor, and she put out a hand to push the heavy door open wider. Everything happened so quickly that she had no time to think. Someone grabbed her wrist, there was a curse, snarling growls, and the flash of steel, and she was jabbing with her short sword at the shadowed figure of a man, vaguely aware of a white streak of fur before the man screamed. Sheba's fierce attack brought more curses and screams, and then another man was there, and a sword lifted high into the air, a silvery glitter in the dim light as it descended in a deadly arc.

Ceara screamed at the same time as the wolf, a high-pitched wail of terror and pain and hatred that bounced off the corbeled walls of the hall outside the vault in deafening echoes. A final yelp, then Sheba dropped, her white body spouting blood from a deep slash across her ribs. Ceara fought free of the man holding her, trying to reach the wolf, but she was dragged away. Turning, she lashed out with the sword, slicing it in a wicked gash that met with temporary resistance against vulnerable flesh and bone before wrenching free. The sound of mortal wounding rent the air, and one of the men staggered and slid to the floor near Sheba's body, his sword clattering uselessly on stone.

The other man held her fast, his arm around her neck though they were of like height, and Ceara grasped his forearm between her teeth and bit down hard. Grunting with pain, he slammed her hard against the wall. Lights exploded in front of her eyes like the brief flare of a thousand candles. The gladius went flying from her hand. Her head rang. Grief and rage choked her, and her hair tangled in front of her eyes so that she could hardly see. Slowly, he began to drag her back into the vault, though she still struggled weakly.

It occurred to her that the man's curses were in the Saxon tongue, panting and furious but familiar. This was no Norman enemy who dared slay her wolf and assault her, but another Saxon.

With a tremendous burst of strength fueled by fury, she threw off her assailant and sent him hard against the wall. She darted for the door, but he caught her and swung her around, slamming her into one of the heavy chests with a force hard enough to stun her for a moment. Panting, on her hands and knees, she peered up through the tangle of her hair as the man bent to retrieve her sword from the stones. Torchlight slid along the red-stained blade in runnels of reflected light.

"You have bloodied your sword on your own man, my fine lady," came the hoarse taunt, and Ceara's blood chilled. He laughed harshly. "Aye, your brave rescuer was cut down by the very one he sought to help."

Ceara threw a glance toward the still body on the floor, but his face was turned away. She glimpsed fair hair, and closed her eyes. Loathing and grief welled up in an overwhelming tide, and she fought the encroaching darkness that threatened to envelop her. She must be alert to thwart this enemy, for she had the sinking feeling that he could bring down not only Wulfridge, but Luc, as well. Why had she not sensed this threat from within?

Opening her eyes, she rallied enough to push herself upright and face the gloating man holding her sword. "Kill me and you will surely die."

"Ah, but, lady, your death is not what will bring the Norman wolf running to meet his own fate. . . ."

Chapter Nineteen

Luc mounted his destrier, grimly rejecting the town mayor's excuses that he had not seen Oswald. The siege had ended with assault, the successful breaching of the fortress walls and the taking of Oswald's holding. Yet Oswald had escaped. There was no sign of him. Nor could any of his men say where he had gone. The search had led them from Rothbury Forest north to Oswald's other holdings.

"Burn it," Luc ordered, casting a last brief look at the village that had harbored the rebel baron. Torches were lit and set to thatched roofs despite the wails of the occupants who tried to drag out what belongings they could before the flames consumed all. Luc watched dispassionately. He had spent near a week searching for Oswald. It had not taken long to effect the fall of the fortress, yet the search for the rebel baron had ranged far afield, through towns and villages like this last one that had set up a brief resistance. It had been quickly quelled with sword and fire. But no Oswald.

Captain Remy approached, face streaked with soot. Flames cast eerie shadows over them, crimson as blood and flickering wildly. "My lord, he was here, but fled before first light. A villager claims he rode north."

"Any farther north and we will be in Malcolm's lap," Luc retorted. The smell of smoke was thick and choking. It boiled up from the burning cottages in black clouds that blotted out the sunlight.

Turning Drago to the villagers clustered in a tight circle like frightened geese, he bent a stern eye on them. "Now hear this, you people of Oswald's fief, for what I say to you may well save your lives this winter when the winds blow cold and your storehouses loom empty. I have left you your lives and livestock. I have not killed your children, nor trampled your newly planted fields. But know this—if I find you harbor this rebel baron, I will come back. And I will lay waste to field and stores and beasts until there is nothing left. Your children will cry from empty bellies and the sky will be your only roof, for I will leave you nothing else. This is William's land now, and any man who defies me, defies the king. Heed my warning and I will show you mercy. Ignore it at your own peril."

Gaunt, terrified faces stared up at Luc from under shaggy manes of hair, and some of the men tugged at their forelocks in gestures of servility. He nudged Drago close to one of them, and pointed with the tip of his sword. "You. What know you of Oswald's whereabouts?"

Quaking, the man looked at his companions, but none offered comfort. A few sidled away, as if afraid to be too close to a man noticed by the earl. Mailed Norman soldiers surrounded them, riding back and forth to set fire to cottages and corn cribs. The man thus singled out swallowed hard, and his words were rough and halting.

"I know naught, m'lord, truly. He were here, they say. 'Tis all I know."

"But others here know. I will wait until one of you comes forward to tell me what I want to know, but I will not wait long. I charge you with yielding up this news. Do not fail."

Wrenching Drago around, Luc rode a short distance away and stopped beneath the sheltering branches of a huge oak. It was dirty work. But it was necessary. He had learned intimidation at William's side, and he had chosen the man he thought most likely to secure the information he wanted. Within the space of a few moments, the man came toward him, kneading his cap between his hands as he approached.

"Well?" Luc gazed down, expressionless, and the man bobbed his head.

"M'lord, 'twill not be news well come to ye—but it is said that Oswald rides south to the coast. To Wulfridge. . . ."

Luc stared at him. Oswald could not have many men with him. What could he hope to accomplish? Yet it was worrisome, and even as he granted the man mercy and spared the village, he puzzled over it. A sense of urgency rode him hard as they turned south toward Wulfridge. There was something wicked afoot.

They pushed their mounts hard, until foam lathered the animals' necks and sides and flecked the riders' legs with white specks. When they were within a few miles of Wulfridge, they saw the first sign of trouble: rising plumes of smoke from burned villages.

Grimly, Luc slowed his pace as they rode, taking in the evidence of ruined cottages, still smoldering under the meager April sun. The road was deserted, and he heard Remy swear harshly under his breath at the widespread destruction. It seemed as if all of Northumbria lay charred and smoking beneath the sky.

It was nearing dark when they rounded the inlet and Wulfridge at last came into sight. Across water that was as smooth as polished silver, the castle looked serene and untroubled, and Luc felt a moment's relief. No smoke rose above ruined ramparts to signal destruction such as he had seen. Ceara was safe.

Urging Drago faster, he pounded down the rutted road, the wind from his brutal pace whipping against his face and smelling of the sea. He was riding so swiftly that when a figure loomed in the road ahead, he missed a collision only narrowly. Cursing, he swerved to miss the man, and the unaccustomed jerk of the reins against Drago's neck made the destrier snort and rear, huge hooves pawing into the air with lethal power.

It took several moments for Luc to control the horse, and while he wrestled with the reins, Remy lunged forward, sword lifted to cut down the man in the road. Luc's harsh shout stopped the captain from completing his strike.

"Hold! I know him." Controlling Drago with a fierce effort, Luc looked down at the man lurching to his feet. "Do you seek me?"

Swathed in animal skins, red-gray hair tangled and streaming over his shoulders, Sighere muttered something under his breath as he brought his crutch under him again. "Yea, though 'tis a marvel that I still live." He gestured with the end of his crutch toward Wulfridge. "Traitors lurk in wait for you, my lord."

"Oswald?"

"Aye, but more than that, there are traitors within the castle." Leaning heavily on his crutch now, Sighere stumped forward, peering up at Luc in the fading light. "You have been betrayed, my lord."

Luc steeled himself. Thoughts of Ceara flickered briefly in his mind before he thrust them away. She would not—not even to take back her legacy. . . . "Who betrayed me?"

"The name is not known to me, but the traitor is fair of hair and face. A Saxon born, though 'tis bitter to admit."

Not Ceara. . . .

Luc looked toward Wulfridge lying serenely beneath the beautiful sunset, fading light gilding the high walls with gold and crimson. Perhaps his brother had lent himself to betrayal again.

Bitter news, but not as bitter as before. This time, he had almost expected it. He looked back down at Sighere. "Does Oswald hold the castle now?"

"Yea, my lord. It fell to him only this morning, right after the cock crowed. It did not take might, but deceit to win entry, and I fear for your lady."

"As do I, Sighere. As do I." Half-ashamed of his brief doubt of Ceara, he resolved to trust in her, now more than ever. Luc thought of his own trick in gaining entrance to Wulfridge, but he had since taken steps to prevent another from entering the same way. The door was guarded, and bolted securely from the inside. No simple lock now, but a hasp with the keys in possession of the castellan. How had it been done? Had someone let the traitor walk freely in?

Captain Remy nudged close. "Shall we lay siege, my lord?"

Luc shook his head, frowning. "It will do us little good, I fear. I planned well. Wulfridge is no wooden fortress vulnerable to fire, but made of stone and well stocked with supplies. No, Remy, we will have to find another way." He paused, rage swelling in him at the thought of Ceara coming to harm at Oswald's hands. Softly, through his clenched teeth, he said, "But I swear, if I have to raze my own castle stone by stone, I will find a way, and if Ceara has been harmed, not even hell will be able to hide Oswald from my vengeance."

Silence fell, with only the rasping of winded horses and jangling of chain mail and bridles to fill it. After a moment, Sighere limped forward. "Your people are behind you, my lord. Kerwin, Leofric, Eadwine. All of them."

Luc wrenched his gaze to the old huntsman. He could say nothing around the rage that still burned in his throat, but nodded curtly, and Sighere smiled.

"The villagers did just as you bade them. None were killed, for the warning spread more swiftly than Oswald's fires. They wait for you now, my lord, with pitchforks and scythes, or whatever weapons you choose for them to wield against the rebel who would seek to harm our lord."

"So, are Saxons then to avenge Normans, Sighere?"

"Nay, lord. Countrymen are to avenge countrymen."

Luc took a deep breath, ashamed at his caustic remark. "It is meet that it should be this way. Summon them to me, Sighere. I will devise a way for us to take back that which is ours."

"Yea, my lord. They will answer your summons."

Captain Remy watched as the old huntsman limped away, disappearing into the tall reeds by the road and then into the deep shadows of the forest beyond. "Do you think the Saxons will truly come, my lord?"

Luc turned Drago toward Wulfridge and nodded as he said with a conviction he did not feel, "They will come, Remy."

AMÉLIE'S PERFECT OVAL face was as serene as that of a child. Robert cleared his throat.

"Say that again, my lady."

"Oh, you heard me, Robert. Do not pretend ignorance. You have known all along what I wanted, so why feign innocence now?"

Clenching his hands behind his back to keep from striking her, Robert said calmly, "I have known you want what you cannot have. That is Luc Louvat."

"Pish. Luc will yet be mine."

"And your betrothal to Niall's son?"

"As false as the message you sent to Luc." She smiled. Tracing a finger over the smooth fur of a cony skin muff, she glanced up at him with assessing eyes. "Do not tell me—you really did not know."

"Know that I have betrayed my best friend? No, I did not know. But then, I am not as experienced in guile as you seem to be, Amélie."

She laughed as if he had paid her a lavish compliment. "It is all an illusion, Robert, as with the smoke and mirrors that wizards use at fairs. Nothing is real. My entire life has been spent living a lie." She slid him a secret smile. "Even my concern over your injury was a lie, if you would know it. You chanced upon us as we were discussing Oswald's capture of the castle, and before I could stop him, he struck you. You were not meant to fall down the hole, however."

"Who struck me—Oswald? He had gone from Wulfridge. I doubt me he would have slunk in unnoticed."

"Do not be a fool. Of course it was not Oswald. Do you think he can be in two places at once? There are those in the castle who do not like the lady, and would see her cast down from her position. See, Robert, I am not the only one who dislikes her."

"Curse you—" He took a deep breath to calm his temper. "Do you think the king will accept this tamely?"

"If I must annoy William with my little ruse, he will soon see that it is for the best. After all, it was the king who first sent me to Luc with the possibility of marriage."

"William is hardly a man to pander, Amélie. There would be no benefit to England or to Normandy for you to wed Luc Louvat. Your lands are small, your influence nil. If he sent you to Luc, it was not for the reason you think."

She shot him an annoyed frown. "Do not be so blind, Robert. Try to see beyond the moment to the future. Oswald wants Ceara. Niall wants Northumbria and William wants England. I want Luc. If I yield up Luc's crude Saxon wife to Oswald, she will be with her own people again. With her as hostage, the Saxon rebels will have leverage to demand peace and sovereignty over their own holdings, as Luc will not wish to endanger his wench. In time, Luc will realize she means nothing to him, but by then, Niall will have a firm hold on Northumbria once his ally, Oswald, has succeeded in securing his own lands. Luc will still have Wulfridge, and because of my influence with the king, I will have Luc. He will soon see the sense in allying with Niall instead. See how simply it works?"

"Why do you think you will have influence with William? His wife is your cousin, perhaps, but that is no guarantee that he will excuse your betrayal of his baron."

"You fool. That is the beauty—he will never know. Unless you are imbecile enough to tell him, but of course, you risk being implicated as well if you do. And I will be happy to tell him how you forced me to go along." She smiled then, and her eyes looked very green. "It could easily be pointed out that you insisted upon accompanying me to Scotland, and that you did not warn Luc—your best friend—that Niall meant to side with the Saxons. Everyone knows that you want me. It will be believed that you betrayed Luc and the king as well if you mention my part in it."

Robert could not help an angry laugh. "I stand amazed at the workings of your mind, Amélie, rather like the twisted tunnels of a rabbit's warren. Alas, there are so many holes in your scheme, you are doomed to failure."

Coldly, Amélie said, "I do not see how it can fail. Oswald will take Ceara and hold her while Niall negotiates terms with William. Luc will certainly influence the king and even after William cedes Northumbria to the rebels and the Scots, he will still hold Wulfridge. With his wife out of the way, I will flee to him for shelter and he will take me in. We will be together at last."

With growing fury, Robert shook his head. "You little fool, all you have done is endangered Luc's life as well as taken his lands and wife. Oswald is too clever to agree to your scheme, though he may well have told you how wonderful it is. He wants Wulfridge, not Ceara. And Niall wants all of Northumbria, not just Oswald's holdings, which he might just be able to seize if he holds enough border positions against the king. You have no doubt started a war you will not forget, and you will never have Luc. He does not want you. He wants Ceara."

"He wants *me*. And what would you know about it? You cannot tell the difference between love and loathing, or you would not follow me around like a dog, for I do loathe you."

Her sneering comment pricked Robert hard, and he drew in a sharp, angry breath. "You have used me just as you tried to use Luc. Did you think Luc cared for you? He never cared for you as anything but a passing whim. And you call me a fool . . . you are doomed to disappointment, for he would not give up the lady he loves for a light-skirt like you."

"You loathsome beast! You are so pathetic . . . do not dare walk away from me! I will see you dead, I swear it!"

Furious, Amélie lashed out, slapping Robert hard across the face. The blow, though slight, was hard enough to rock him back a step, and long years of war and training made him react with instinctive retaliation. Amélie's head snapped back on her slender neck and she flew backward into a heavy table before he could catch her. Then she slumped to the floor and lay still.

Robert stared down at her, breathing hard, his chest aching with suppressed rage. When Amélie did not move, he grew alarmed and moved to kneel at her side. There was no pulse in her throat. Shaken, he knelt there for a long moment.

He had killed her. Ah, God, he had slain a woman, and one he had wanted even if he did not love her. Proud dame, haughty lady—false lady. Robert pressed his palms over his eyes and shuddered.

How long he knelt there, he did not know. But when he regained awareness, it was growing dark. Light at the windows faded and grew dim. He lifted Amélie in his arms and carried her almost tenderly to the wide bed on the other side of the chamber. Placing her on the mattress, he drew up the coverlet to her chin, then stepped back and pulled the bed hangings closed around her still form.

With Amélie dead, he might well count his days on one finger in Niall's court. If he was to die, it might as well be fighting instead of as a bull awaiting slaughter. It was time to put his preparations for escape to use.

When night had fallen and the shadows were deep, Robert slipped from the window and leaped to the ground below. It was a steep drop, and he landed hard so that he had to catch his breath a moment. Then he rose to his feet and crept to the wild hedges that bordered the garden of Niall's rough manor. Since arriving, he had noted the timing of the sentry that patrolled, and now he waited in silence until he had passed. He knew he had little time to make good his escape, and when the sentry's shadow faded, he wriggled through the thorny hedge and sprinted across the field toward Northumbria.

NIGHT FIRES HAD been lit within sight of Wulfridge, beacons in the night to show Oswald that he had come. Luc leaned against the huge trunk of an old oak, staring at the castle with bitter thoughts. It still chafed him that Oswald had managed to elude capture and gather enough men to form an assault. Even with treachery, some men were needed to storm the walls, for Lieutenant le Bec would not yield up the gate without a fierce fight. But how? How had Oswald done it?

Were that many of his own people against him? Had none of the overtures he'd made since taking Wulfridge made any difference? The chasm between Saxon and Norman had never seemed wider, and Luc fought overpowering discouragement. A handful of faithful was comforting, but he would need more than a token few to hold these lands.

And God, he had sworn to Ceara that he would protect her with his life, yet she was held captive by Oswald while he was out here, chafing at the distance between them. He wanted to mount Drago and ride straight into Wulfridge, demand that Oswald come out to settle this in trial by combat. But he knew that would be a futile gesture, as Oswald had made plain he had no intention of fighting Luc, whether in single combat or in battle.

"Rider coming!"

Luc straightened, turning toward the road as one of his sentries challenged the mounted man. There was a brief exchange, and even as Luc was striding toward them, the rider dismounted and was brought to him, flanked by two soldiers.

"Giles." Luc's eyes narrowed. "What do you here? I thought you were with Lady Amélie and Sir Robert."

Giles went to one knee. Mud caked his boots and spurs, and he was breathing hard. "I was, my lord. I have been sent to you with a message."

"From Robert?"

Giles nodded, still breathless, his words coming out on a winded wheeze. "He asks that you lend him aid in his need, my lord."

"In need of what? Out with it, man!"

"He is being held hostage, he and the Lady Amélie, and they beg your aid." Fumbling in a pouch at his waist, Giles withdrew something and held it up. Light from a campfire reflected dully on gold, and Luc took it, slowly turning the ring to look at the familiar Brionne signet.

"Christ above!" Luc blew a harsh breath between his teeth. "Rise, Giles. Have wine and bread to calm yourself. Remy, bring a cloak for him and have his horse tended. Before God, I am in the mood to set fire to all of Northumbria, so let us hear this tale quickly."

IT WAS DARK. Torchlight had dwindled to a sputtering hiss, sparks settling on the floor of the vault and flickering out. Ceara flinched at the throbbing ache in her head. She wanted to shriek her anguish aloud at the painful vision of Sheba's bloody fur. But she could not exhibit weakness to the gloating man watching her with such satisfaction.

"You have long been a thorn in my side," he said in a grating voice. With one hand, he wiped blood from his cheek, a token of her fierce struggle against him. His eyes were glittering, mouth twisted with hatred. "Lord Balfour let you have your own way too often. He should have beat you daily, rather than coddle you."

Ceara gazed coolly at Hardred. "My father was a just man."

"Your *father*," Hardred mimicked, "was a fool. A weak fool. He allowed you to lead him by the nose when he should have wed you to a man able to hold these lands, not that useless cripple."

Rage burned hotly in Ceara's eyes. "Wulfric was more of a man than you could ever be!"

"A twisted waste of a man was what he was. All knew when Balfour allowed you to wed him that we were doomed. Yet we could do nothing but stand by helplessly and watch, when we knew that one day invaders would come who would not be stayed. That was before the Normans came, but the Scots and Danes were always harrying our borders until we were afraid to leave the shadows of the castle for fear we would be slaughtered like defenseless sheep. No more."

"Who is this *we* you speak of? I see only you, a warped Saxon slave who will die swiftly once Lord Luc returns."

Hardred laughed. He leveled her sword at her, gazing at her down the length of the blade as if judging where best to thrust it. "There are enough of us, I vow. Lord Oswald is inside the gates by now, and Wulfridge is Saxon once more."

"You opened the gates to him! Ah, you senseless fool. If Saxons could have triumphed, King Harold would still be on his throne. Yet even if Harold had won at Hastings, England would be lost to us. It was not just that one battle, not just that one man, but many who have tried to rend us asunder for far too long. It was destined that England would fall, and we should be glad that it was to William, who at least is capable of binding us into one nation instead of a hundred small kingdoms led by these quarrelsome earls with only their own interests to mind."

She drew in a shaky breath. It was true. She knew it was true. And now, honesty bade her admit it.

Furious, Hardred rose abruptly, and the lethal point of the Roman gladius grazed her chest as he ordered her to rise to her feet. She did so, slowly, and noted distractedly that her kirtle was shredded on one side, leaving her left leg bare almost to the waist. Hardred's eyes flicked down, then up to her face again, his lips curling into a sneer.

"Oswald is not a witless fool like Balfour, but strong in his own right. He holds not only you hostage, but the lord's brother. And he will not bend the knee to Normans, nay, nor let his sluttish daughters warm their beds as you have done. Oswald will retrieve Saxon glory and restore to us that which the Normans have stolen."

Eye level with the Saxon who held her sword, she gave him her most disdainful stare. "When Lord Luc arrives, you will rue this most heartily."

"Lord Luc has arrived, but cannot find his way into the castle." Hardred laughed harshly. "The wolf is at our door, but we will leash him well, so that he will roam no more in England."

Ceara flinched. "You will never do it, Hardred. He is too strong for you."

"He is caught between two forces, and will not escape us. For we have men here, and men behind, and while he waits and thinks to lay siege, we will slowly crush him between. And you, my lady, are the bait that keeps him here."

"You lie."

"Nay, 'tis no lie. He waits. He is too distracted to guess what fate awaits, and will not know until 'tis too late." Gesturing with the sword, Hardred backed her to the open door of the vault. "Come now, for Lord Oswald awaits above for the key to the wolf's heart."

Ceara stumbled as he pushed her forward, trying not to glance at the supine body of her wolf sprawled upon the stones. Grief clogged her throat as she was escorted from the echoing corridor outside the vault up the shallow steps to the main floor. Evidence of battle was everywhere, in lifeless bodies and broken doors, and in the distance she could still hear the faint clangs of resistance being waged. Then she was thrust before Lord Oswald, who peered at her with grim satisfaction.

"You have done well, Hardred. I did not think to have the mate of the Norman wolf snared so swiftly."

"I followed her, my liege. She thought to hide her treasure in the vault."

"Did she?" Lord Oswald smiled, and lifted his head to listen to the shouts from without the hall. "We are victors, yet must be wary of cunning, for all is not yet secure. Take her back to the vault, Hardred. She will gain us our ends, and must not be risked. When the hall and the woman are mine, the rest will be mine."

Ceara's chin lifted. "You are a fool if you think Luc Louvat will yield one hide of land, Oswald. Not for me, nor for any would he give up that which is his."

"Yea, lady, he will yield to keep you safe. For he knows that I will have no great reluctance to slay a traitor to the Saxons. And do it more easily than I would wed her to keep her from spreading her favors among Normans."

"Traitor? Not I, Oswald of Paxton, not I. My loyalty lies with the Saxon people so that I am loath to see them slaughtered in vengeance. What of you?"

Oswald gestured impatiently. "A few deaths are expected when men wage war. It is a small price to pay for freedom."

"There will be no freedom in this land until there is peace. And men like you love war more than peace."

"She is right, Oswald."

Ceara turned toward the voice, and her brows lifted as she saw Jean-Paul approach. Luc's brother barely glanced at her, but his manner was so casual she stiffened. There was no distress in him, no sign that he had offered resistance to the invaders. Her lip curled with contempt.

Oswald turned to Jean-Paul. "This is not a matter of who is right. That has been decided. Are you with us?"

"That depends."

Bushy brows swooped low over Oswald's eyes. "Depends on

what? You are Saxon, are you not? Your father died for Harold's cause."

"My father died for his own cause," Jean-Paul drawled with a laugh. "It was a simple mistake. He wagered on the wrong man winning. When he lost, he lost all."

"And you fled to Malcolm like a kicked cur."

Jean-Paul shrugged. "Yea, but a live cur. My head, you will notice, is still atop my shoulders."

"And you bide in a Norman stronghold, eating at the whim of a Norman."

"My brother's memory is long. I am more a hostage than guest." Jean-Paul's gaze flicked to Ceara. There was an odd light in his eyes. "Tell him, my lady, how well I am regarded by Luc."

"As well as any traitor, I think." She returned his gaze coldly.

"So you see, Oswald? You and I are like. We value our skins above all."

"Do not taint me with your brush, for I am no coward."

"Are you not? You did not linger at Paxton to receive Luc, I see. Could it be that the Norman wolf instills fear in you after all?"

"Which side do you claim?" Oswald growled. "You speak too boldly for my liking."

Again Jean-Paul shrugged. " 'Tis my way."

Uncertainty creased Oswald's brow as he regarded Jean-Paul with narrowed eyes. A clamor arose in the corridor outside the hall, and the Saxon lord glanced toward the doors as the sounds of the struggle grew loud. Sword blades clashed with metallic harshness, and he looked back at Ceara with sudden decision.

"The lady must be hidden well, Hardred."

"Are you afraid of me Oswald?" Ceara laughed softly. "But 'tis Luc Louvat who will rend you limb from limb when he comes—"

"Begone with you, shrewish bitch!" Oswald snarled, but

apprehension clouded his eyes. "You have been tainted by this Norman wolf who holds your lands, but will not be for much longer. As you are Louvat's treasure, my lady whore, so you will be kept safely with his other precious stores. Take her below, Hardred, and confine her in the vault until we take her north."

Ceara stiffened. North—to Malcolm? Oh, God, Luc would never be able to free her then. Not without fighting a war. . . .

"I will take her," Jean-Paul offered, but Oswald shook his head.

"Nay. You come with me, and lend aid with your sword. I need able warriors to withstand these men Louvat has left to guard his castle."

So Hardred dragged her below again, forcing her ahead of him with rough pressure until they reached the gaping door of the vault. She averted her gaze from the man's body still in front of the door, but saw that Sheba's body had been removed. No doubt, some man would soon wear a white wolf pelt on his back, a grievous thought that burned into her breast.

Then Hardred shoved her toward the wall lined with carved furniture. "Get into the chest."

Ceara's eyes widened. She glanced at the chest. It was massive, but confined. "I will smother."

"Nay, lady. There are holes on the side for air."

"No. . . ."

But Hardred was pushing her inexorably forward, the tip of the sword pressing into her skin until she could feel stinging blood ooze from a cut on her shoulder. Bolts of cloth filled the bottom of the chest, and Hardred flung them to one side, then gestured for her to climb in.

"Get in, or you will be tied on the battlements for Luc Louvat to see. That should bring him running hotfoot, do you not think?"

Reluctantly, Ceara climbed into the trunk, drawing her knees up and shuddering as the heavy lid was slammed down. Closeness and shadows surrounded her, smelling faintly of spices. She could hear the muffled clink of metal, and knew that he had fastened the hasp. It occurred to her as she huddled in the trunk that if Hardred was slain, no one would find her before she died of suffocation.

Packed into the darkness, she thought of Luc, and prayed that he would triumph over his enemies and rescue her. And when he did, she would exact a most terrible vengeance on the traitors.

LUC STARED INTO the dying embers of the fire. It would be light soon. He had not slept all night, mulling over his options long after Remy and the others had rolled into their blankets for sleep. With Oswald in front and Niall at his back, he was caught. The only smart move would be to retreat. But that would give the rebels undisputed control of Wulfridge. Niall and Adela had made it plain that unless he yielded up the castle, Robert and Amélie would remain hostages and perhaps come to harm. Yet Ceara was hostage now, held by Oswald as assurance that he would yield. If only she were free, he would be at liberty to defy Oswald. But until then, he risked her life.

Closing his eyes, Luc leaned his head back against the trunk of the tree that sheltered him. It was two days from the calends of May. Nights were still cool, but the days were warm and soft. He wore light mail, too tense to disarm, too restless to sleep. Round and round in his brain went the dread thought that his brother had once more betrayed him. This time, to Oswald and Adela. Before, to their father. God, why did he not merit love and loyalty from his own kin? There were times he thought himself cursed, for if not, his own father would not have disowned him in favor of another, would not have tried to betray him to William. And now Jean-Paul had taken the first chance to betray him again. Ceara was right. He should not have trusted him.

Now he was in a damnable position. If he did not discover

a way to free himself of this coil, he would be forced to retreat in order to save Ceara and Robert. But even then, there was no assurance that Oswald or Niall would not slay their hostages.

His hand curled into a fist on his knee. Curse it all, if only he had not worked so hard to make Wulfridge impervious to assault. It seemed that he had sealed his own fate, for now he could not take the castle. He had not guessed that one day he would find himself barred, and had secured every entrance. Not even a mole could get in. . . .

Luc sat up and opened his eyes. Ceara had said something not long ago, about the chambers beneath the castle. If animals had managed to get in, perhaps there was yet a way for men.

Rising, he moved swiftly to his men and kicked them gruffly awake. There was much to be done before light, and he could not waste a moment.

Groggily, Remy peered up at him, struggling to his feet. "I am awake, my lord."

"Arm yourselves. Do you recall how we were garbed when I first took Wulfridge? Don similar garb now, and prepare to come with me."

By the time they reached the slope beneath the castle, their feet and legs were wet from sloshing through tidal pools and high reeds. Surf crashed against the rocks. In the deep shadows, Luc searched for the pile of rubble he had cleared from one of the underground chambers. After Robert's fall, he had explored several of them, and one had stretched much farther than the others. Perhaps all the way inside.

"My lord," Remy muttered, stumbling over rocks, "is there a sign we should seek?"

"Most likely. But I do not know what it would be."

Kerwin, Ceara's former commander, suggested they search the lee side of the slope. "It is less steep there, my lord, and more likely to give us shelter from being seen."

"No, this is the side that leads to the underground chambers." Luc knelt, frustrated by the sudden sense of futility. How ould he find it when he did not know where to look? Time vas running out. Soon it would be light, and Oswald's men vould see them. Any hope of surprise would be lost. Where was hat cursed mist when he needed it? Sketchy moonlight poured hrough the ragged clouds overhead, far too revealing illumina-ion for their purposes, forcing them to keep close to the shad-ows so as not to alert Oswald's sentries on the ramparts above.

Crouched there in the dusky shadows, Luc strained his eyes o find anything that might indicate an opening. Then he blinked, for a shred of white fluttered for a moment in the fitful moonlight, and was gone. A trick of light. Yet his instincts led him in that direction, and he crept stealthily toward the brief licker. Thankfully, the wash of the surf drowned out the slight clink his sword made against stone.

Suddenly a faint but familiar sound arrested him, and he paused. High, feeble, it seeped through the other night sounds, a familiar whine like that of a dog. Or a wolf.

Kerwin heard it, too, and said cautiously that there was something ahead on the slope. Luc scrabbled over rocks, and the moon peeked briefly from behind a cloud to shine dully on a small patch of white. He moved more swiftly now, not quite daring to whistle. Not quite daring to hope.

But when he drew close he saw that it *was* Sheba. She crawled on her belly, panting, white hair matted with something dark. He knelt beside her, and put out a hand to encounter wet, sticky fur. Blood. He recognized the smell and the feel immedi-ately. Sheba whined, and he motioned for Remy and Kerwin, who stood looking gravely down at the animal.

"The wolf is wounded, my lord." Kerwin's voice was sober. "Does she still cling close to our lady?"

"Yes. She would never leave Ceara's side willingly."

"So they tried to slay her."

Sheba's wet tongue raked across Luc's hand, and his lips tightened. "They have almost succeeded."

"Do you think they threw her out here?"

"No, I think she managed to crawl this far. Now I know how she has been leaving the castle without us knowing it. She has found the hidden tunnel." He stroked Sheba's head, hating what he must ask of this valiant creature, but knowing no other way. "Ceara. Find her, Sheba. Ceara."

The English words brought the wolf struggling to her feet. Luc touched her side, saw that the wound was deep and she had lost much blood. To use her now might kill her. Yet he must. Talking softly, stroking the great head, he urged her with gentle words, and Sheba staggered in a tight circle, whining.

After a moment, when he thought perhaps she was too weak to manage, the wolf turned up the slope. Luc moved beside her, supporting the animal as best he could while she moved with stumbling determination. Then he saw it in a sliver of moonlight, the slight crevice that offered entry. It looked barely large enough for a man to squeeze through. Hurriedly, Luc shoved aside some stones and slid inside. Dank air greeted him, but it was clearly the beginning of a tunnel. He looked over his shoulder.

"Remy, send the wolf back to camp with one of the men. I dare not risk her more, for she is weak and might give away our presence."

One of the men held Sheba gingerly and Luc and the others crawled into the dark tunnel. They worked their way painfully up the steep, narrow incline, and several times Luc had to slide on his belly or pull himself along on his side to fit through.

It seemed to take much too long by his reckoning, so that he began to think the tunnel led nowhere and they had wasted valuable time. Then he saw a faint, thin splinter of light. It was dim, but a beacon nonetheless, and he crawled the rest of the way more quickly, holding his sword in his hands and sliding it over the jagged rocks to wriggle through the last narrow part. Behind him, he could hear the labored breathing of his men and knew they did the same. Remy was panting.

"M'lord . . . are we near? I fear me that . . . I cannot abide such . . . close quarters. . . ."

Luc laughed softly, exultant as he saw the clear shape of a wall sconce holding a torch. When he reached it, he paused to peer out cautiously. He recognized this as the corridor leading to the treasure vault, and it seemed to be empty. In a moment he was standing up again, relief at being free of confinement changing to grim determination now that he was once more in the castle. The worst was yet ahead of him. He must see how many of his loyal men still lived and free them, then open the gates before he dared look for Ceara. The castle must be secured.

Moving swiftly along the hallway, he kept close to the side and in the shadows, motioning his men to follow. They all knew what must be done. If God and fortune were with them, they would succeed.

Rounding a turn in the corridor, he saw a man's body sprawled on the stone floor in a spreading pool of blood. He started to pass with little more than a glance, then stopped and turned back. In the same instant as Remy, he recognized the man, and knelt beside him.

"Alain. . . ."

"He lives, my lord. Look you, he is breathing."

Alain's chest rose and fell in rapid gasps. His eyelids fluttered, and one hand moved slightly. Luc bent close to hear him. "Lady . . . danger. . . ."

"Is she alive, Alain?"

Licking his lips, Alain grimaced, bubbles flecking his mouth with traces of blood. "Yes . . . but they have . . . her."

"Where?" he demanded, but Alain had slipped back into unconsciousness.

Giving the squire into the care of one of the other men, Luc took the rest and continued down the corridor. Some of the torches had guttered, but enough were lit that he could see evidence of enemy occupation. His lips tightened with fury at the havoc they had wreaked in such a short time.

Remy took two soldiers and moved to the prison cells to free any of Luc's men kept there, while Luc took the other three and slipped toward the main hall. Just ahead loomed two guards, and he motioned silently. A moment later both guards had been dispatched, throats neatly slit from ear to ear. Luc looked up with a reckless grin.

Kerwin laughed softly. "The devil has been loosed again, my lord."

Pockets of fighting could be heard, and Luc advanced toward them. They must strike hard and swift, for now that the element of surprise was gone, the advantage would rest with those best armed and most able. If Remy could not manage to get the gates open for his men, they may well die in these halls.

Sword lifted and ready, Luc and his small band stormed down the hall, dispatching any enemy in their way, bellowing war cries at the top of their lungs.

The fiercest fighting took place at the entrance to the great hall, where six men swarmed to meet them with fire in their eyes. Luc and the three men with him fought savagely. Kerwin waged battle with fierce energy, laying low those who opposed him with a strength that bespoke the power of a much younger man instead of this grizzled veteran. He was not a Saxon fighting against Saxon, but a man fighting for his lord and lands, and Luc knew he would not doubt his loyalty again.

They fought their way into the hall, and Luc stood panting just inside the entrance, surveying the damaged chamber quickly. At the far end stood Oswald and Jean-Paul, and the bitterness in Luc's throat rose so hot and high that he thought for a moment he would choke on it. He held his bloody sword aloft, vengeance and hatred in his eyes as he approached the waiting men.

Oswald wore a faint smile that should have warned him, but Luc was unprepared for the two men who burst from behind the trestle tables stacked to one side. Still, he turned on the balls of his feet, sword slashing out in a wicked arc that caught one of the men broadside and folded him over Luc's blade. Sweeping the blade free, he swung again to catch the other man just below the shoulder. It happened swiftly, and was over.

Turning, Luc glanced at the dais, and halted. Jean-Paul held his sword in an almost negligent grip, the tip hard against Oswald's throat. "Loose your weapon, Oswald," he said softly, a faint smile curving his lips, "or you shall have two gaping mouths instead of one."

"Curse you," Oswald got out. "You are a traitor to your own kind!"

"Nay, Oswald. I am Saxon through and through, heedless of my father's birth. But I am also smart enough to have learned who is the better man. And that man is not you, nor the other outlaw earls. It is William, and it is men like my brother, who are strong enough to hold these lands against the Danes and the Scots. You must call Malcolm to you for strength, and that is worse than the Normans. Now drop your sword, and you will live to face my brother's justice."

Still cursing, Oswald held his blade out to one side, his eyes glittering with hatred. His fingers clenched and unclenched around the bloodied hilt, and Luc started forward, observing the intention in Oswald's eyes before Jean-Paul did.

Swinging hard, Oswald managed to catch Jean-Paul hard against the side, even as he dodged to elude the sword thrust at his throat. But he did not twist far enough, for Jean-Paul's blade sliced through the side of his neck in a clean sweep that spouted blood. As Oswald collapsed, his knees striking hard against the stone floor, Jean-Paul turned in a curiously graceful step and slowly sagged to his knees, hands slipping down the blade of his sword heedless of the sharp edge. Already, his eyes were glazing when Luc reached him, catching him as he pitched forward and the gaping wound in his side gushed torrents of blood over both of them.

"Ah, God, Jean-Paul. . . ."

Grimacing, his brother looked up. His hand caught at Luc's sleeve, gripping hard. "For . . . give me, Luc. . . ."

"Yea, Jean-Paul, you are forgiven all. But do not talk now. Save your strength until—"

"Nay." The fist in his sleeve tightened. "It is . . . in vain. Do not think . . . I mind. I do . . . not." He shuddered, and his lips formed faint words that Luc leaned close to hear. "Keep what . . . you have earned, brother." He drew in a wet, rasping breath and his eyelids fluttered. "Your lady is . . . in . . . the vault. I tried . . . to help her."

"She is safe, Jean-Paul. You have redeemed yourself most honorably. Now rest, brother, for you have earned it."

A faint smile quivered on Jean-Paul's lips, then his body contorted and he gave a gurgling sigh that was his last. Luc stared down at him, throat tight with emotion, and prayed that his brother would forgive him for his dark suspicions.

"My lord."

Luc glanced up. Kerwin stood breathing hard, his eyes filled with sympathy but his manner urgent.

"Yes, Kerwin?"

"Remy has opened the gates. Our men are inside, and carrying the day. What should we do with the traitors?"

Luc glanced down at Jean-Paul's lifeless body, and gently closed the sightlessly staring blue eyes with the edge of his palm. "Do not put them to the sword yet. There is always time for a man to offer penance. Those that swear fealty will be given another chance."

He rose to his feet, and turned to the entrance. "Find the man with the key to the vault and send him to me."

Chapter Twenty

CEARA TRIED NOT to breathe. She spaced her breaths, drawing air deep into her lungs before letting it out slowly again. But she felt dizzy. It was a test of endurance, she told herself, and she would wait. Luc would come for her. He had to come.

She closed her eyes. A sword cut on her side ached, but the blood had stopped flowing. Now, her gown was only damp with it and growing stiff as it dried. Time passed so slowly. Was it still night? Or had morning dawned? She thought of her wolf although she tried not to. The vision of Sheba sprawled lifelessly on the stones brought tears to her eyes, but she could not afford the luxury of weeping when air was so close.

Then she thought of Hardred, and the hatred he had nurtured for her all these years. He had been only a thrall in her father's service, and less than that for the Normans. And he could not abide that she had given all to Luc that truly mattered. For she had. It had happened slowly, so that she did not realize how much she had yielded until it was done. But she did not regret it. Luc was a worthy lord, and worthy of her heart.

She thought of the vow she had once made never to yield

willingly. In a way, she had kept that vow. It had been a reluctant surrender, but it was now complete—and willing. Since Luc had gone, she had thought much about what he had said, and knew that he was right. If he did not control the barons, he would lose everything. Oswald should have yielded, as had Leofric and Eadwine. It shamed her that she had protested Luc's seeming cruelty. He had known better than she what should be done.

Pressing her face against her drawn-up knees, she tried to envision Luc's face. The dark eyes fringed with black lashes, the often mocking curl of his mouth, the faint scar that stitched his jawline . . . she could almost feel him kiss her, feel his strong, sturdy body pressed against hers. . . .

It was so close, and she could not breathe. The chest seemed to grow smaller. It was crushing her, collapsing in on her until she wanted to scream but dared not use the air. Her hands curled into claws, and she drifted into a dreamless haze, anything to escape the confines of the chest.

There was a ringing in her ears, and her trapped breath whispered over her folded arms. She was dying. They would find her too late. Her air was almost gone, the holes in the chest were much too small. . . .

A loud noise rumbled. She could barely breathe. Only a little air now. So stuffy. Her lungs ached, and her chest began to hurt. She wanted to die quietly, but her body would not allow it. Deprived of air, she arched involuntarily, arms flinging outward, clawing at the walls of her tiny prison. The noise again, barely discernible now over the thundering beat of her heart. It pounded in her ears, a dreadful din, and she made awkward noises that hurt her throat. She pushed against the ceiling of her prison with both hands, desperate for air, and tried to hold on to her slipping awareness. She thought then of Luc, and tried to visualize his face. But it was growing so dim. . . .

• • •

THE KEY COULD not be found to unlock the vault. Luc stared at the solid iron door. It had been built with the hinges inward, so none could remove it from the outside. Heedless of the congealing blood on the floor, he paced in front of the vault while Remy and Kerwin searched for another key.

Finally, he ordered the door smashed, and men came with heavy staves and axes. The blows dented it heavily, but it did not yield. Remy sought to comfort him.

"There is air aplenty in the vault, my lord. She may be hungry and thirsty, but no harm will come to her."

Luc nodded grimly. He surveyed the door closely. Bolts held the iron strips overlaying wood. If all the bolts were undone, then the wood could be splintered or burned, and thus yield entrance. God in heaven, it would take so much time to accomplish, but as Remy had said, the vault was spacious.

A yelp rent the air behind him, and Luc turned, frowning when he saw a young Saxon being dragged toward them with blood streaming from his head and mouth.

It was Kerwin who thrust him forward brutally, a fist gripping the young man's collar. "This is Hardred, my lord. He betrayed you, I fear, by giving Oswald's men entrance to the gates. He has all the keys."

Hardred was pushed to his knees in front of Luc, his face white but still defiant. It was obvious he had received rough treatment, for one eye was swollen shut, and there were cuts etched on his face.

Luc eyed him without pity. "You have bought yourself a harsh death, Hardred."

Hatred gleamed in the Saxon's eyes. "Yea, I may well have done so, but the wolf will rule here without his mate."

Something in the man's face chilled Luc's blood, and when Kerwin cuffed the prisoner, Luc put up a hand to hold the next blow. "Is the lady in the vault, Hardred?"

"Aye, that she is. And there she will die."

Luc gazed at him dispassionately, though fear had spurted in his breast at the certainty in Hardred's voice. He gave a careless shrug as if disputing the claim. "There is air enough for her to survive until we break down the door. The vault is large."

"Yea, Norman, the vault is large."

Kerwin shook the man viciously. "Give us the key."

"I threw the key down the well."

When Kerwin drew back his fist, Luc halted him. "Wait. There is something he has not said. Tell me, Hardred, what you know."

Triumph settled on the battered face, and Hardred's lips drew back from his teeth in a snarl. "Your lady is indeed in the vault, as I said. She rests most comfortably in a prison of wood and iron."

Luc knelt in front of him, and there was hoarse menace in each word as he said softly, "Tell me the rest, or you will beg for death long before it releases you from your pain."

Their eyes were level, Hardred's one open eye a pale glitter as he smiled. "As your greatest treasure, I put her safely where you keep your finest silks. She is where no rain or damp can mold her, nor musty air tarnish her treacherous hide. . . ."

Luc looked up, and saw his own horror mirrored in Remy's eyes at the implication. He rose swiftly then, ignoring Hardred's wild shriek as Kerwin dragged him away.

"My lord," Remy began helplessly, "if she is in one of those chests—"

"Bring men to batter the door."

"My lord—"

"Curse you, Remy, bring them! Ah, God, if he has killed her I will flay him alive and wear his skin as a cape . . . no. Wait. Remy, bring me a small piece of metal. Perhaps . . . Ah, fool that I am for not thinking of it already. It must be slender and sturdy. Hurry, Remy, for every moment we waste is precious to her."

Marshaling all his concentration, Luc knelt in front of the dented door and took a deep breath. This was no simple lock such as those he was accustomed to picking as a boy. No, this vas a lock made of intricate tumblers that he had devised him-elf. Remy put into his open palm a slender wand of metal, and uc turned all his fierce attention to the lock.

Sweat stung his eyes, and twice he had to still his hand from rembling as he slowly maneuvered the steel pick into the lock, ingers aching with strain. A tumbler clicked softly with metallic rispness, and he paused, then moved the steel with painstaking lowness.

When another tumbler clicked, he tried the door, but it still ield. Slowly, his breath harsh in his throat, the rasping sound of t filling his ears, he moved the steel wand again. This time when ie tried the clasp and depressed the handle, the door creaked oudly on its hinges and swung outward. Luc stumbled back, re-gained his balance, and lurched to his feet.

Silks and linens were strewn on the floor, and he moved to first one chest, then another, calling Ceara's name. Remy and the others ranged behind him, flinging the chests open.

"This one is locked, my lord!"

Luc swung around and seized a heavy mallet from one of the men. One blow, two, and then the padlock sprang open. He grabbed the lid and flung it up, his heart in his throat as he saw the lifeless form curled in the bottom of the trunk.

Tenderly, he scooped her from the tiny prison and held her against him, hardly daring to hope that she was still alive. How long had she been in there?

Luc went to his knees on the stone floor and laid Ceara gently atop a pile of discarded silks. He felt for a pulse in her throat, then her wrist, and detected a faint flutter that heart-ened him.

"Wine, Remy. Bring wine. Stand back and give her air, for the love of God. Ah, Ceara, Ceara . . . what have I done to you?"

Her kirtle was torn to her waist, blue folds falling from her slender thighs, and her bright hair was matted beneath her head. Her face was so pale and still, her chewed lips bloody, and he

took her hand between his and rubbed, not knowing what els
to do.

Then a soft breath lifted her chest, and her long brow
lashes fluttered slightly. He slid an arm beneath her shoulders t
hold her up, and when Remy brought a goblet of wine, held i
to her lips. Red liquid cascaded over her mouth and down he
chin to her throat, bright as blood. He winced at the sight.

"Drink, *chérie*. Drink, my love, my heart. Ah, God, will you
ever forgive me?"

She coughed as he pressed the wine to her lips, and pushed i
feebly away. "No," she said in a cross voice, "not if you drown me."

Startled, Luc did not at once move the goblet. It was Remy
who reached over his shoulder and took it from his hand, murmuring that perhaps she needed air more than wine.

Ceara opened her eyes, blinking a little at the light and
faces around her. Then she turned her gaze to Luc, rasping, "It
was Hardred who locked me in here. Oh, Luc, he betrayed us
all!"

"I know. Shush, my heart. Do not worry about Hardred. I
have a notion that Kerwin will give him his just reward for what
he has done."

Her hand curled into the sleeve of his linen tunic, and she
shook her head weakly. "Nay, I want vengeance on him. He has
caused so much pain . . . he slew Sheba, Luc." Her voice broke
slightly. "He killed my beloved Sheba, and one of Oswald's men
has taken her to make into a pelt—"

"Do not distress yourself. The last time I saw the pelt it was
chewing with amazing vigor on the leather gauntlet of the man
I set to guard her. No doubt, when we next see your wolf, it will
be wearing poor Pierre as a pelt instead."

To his surprise, the glad tidings did not make her rejoice,
but undid her. She collapsed with shuddering sobs in his arms,
and he held her to him tightly, rocking her back and forth as if
she were a small child, crooning soft words to her in French and
English, endearments and words of love, wild promises that he

would always make the sun shine for her, he would never let it rain on her, and anything else he could think of to say to comfort her. It was not a familiar emotion to him, and he felt clumsy and awkward, but could not stop the spate of words that poured from his mouth and his heart.

It was several moments before he noticed that they were quite alone, Remy apparently having gathered the men and given them their privacy. He made a mental note of where such an elusive thing could be found, but doubted that Ceara would want to come here again after her close brush with death.

"Are you better, my heart?" he murmured when her sobs ceased and she clung to him quietly. She nodded.

"I have never been better. Luc, did you mean all that?"

He flinched, embarrassed and more than a little reluctant to confirm all the flowery phrases he had uttered. But he dragged in a deep breath and nodded, looking down at her as she lay in his arms.

"Yea, *chérie*, I meant every word. Save for the part about the sun and rain. I fear my influence does not extend to the heavens."

She laughed softly. "Oh, I would not be surprised if it did. But I meant the part about loving me. Do you?"

"Yea. I love you, Ceara. With all my heart and soul, and with every breath. I will not disappoint you again."

"You have never disappointed me, Luc. You are my rock, my strength, a man of honor who keeps his vows. Nay, you have never disappointed me, but I fear I have you."

He shrugged. "Annoyed me at times, but nothing worse. When you make a vow, you hold to it, and I know that well."

She smiled up at him, and he wiped away the traces of tears on her pale cheeks. After a moment he took a deep breath, and said regretfully, "Now that you are safe, I must leave you again, but it is necessary. I will leave you Remy and Kerwin as guards, and there will be none here who are not loyal."

"Leave—no, Luc!" Her fingers clenched around his wrist,

and her eyes were filled with panic. "Do not leave—are we no safe here?"

"Yea, *chérie*, more safe than ever you have been, for now w know who we can trust. But news was brought to me of Rober and Amélie. They are being held hostage by Niall and my step mother. They beg my aid."

"Your stepmother! Dear God. Niall lures you there to ki you, so he can take Wulfridge. Do not go—send word to th king, and he will—"

"Ceara. I cannot forsake Robert, for he has long been m friend. I must go."

She moaned softly then, and he held her close, a faint smil on his mouth that she would worry so for him. After a moment he rose, and carried Ceara to the solar they shared, staying just long enough to be certain she was well guarded and would rest.

Calling only a few trusted men to him, he mounted Drago and rode from Wulfridge to rally others to march on Niall and rescue Robert and Amélie. He only prayed that he was in time to save them.

CEARA FRETTED. LUC had been gone near a fortnight, with only one message from him, and that more for Remy than for her. Every morning she went up to the battlements to gaze past the inlet to the road where he would approach. She did not stay long, but returned often.

Sheba was so weak, but her strength was slowly coming back. She had been carrying pups when Hardred attacked her, and she had lost them. Now thin and frail, the wolf wanted to follow Ceara everywhere, and set up a great howl when she was forced to stay behind. Often, Remy would send a man to carry the wolf to the hall for her, as Sheba would drag herself there if left in the solar.

It was only when Ceara went to visit Alain, who had been all but invalided by the assault, that Sheba did not attempt to accompany her. A nagging sense of guilt in Ceara bade her seek out Alain on his sickbed, for he had come to her rescue and it had been her sword that near cost him a leg. But if he resented it, he did not show it. Instead, he amused himself by teaching her naughty epigrams in French and Latin.

"To impress your lord husband when he returns," Alain said with a sly grin that left her no doubt that Luc would be anything but impressed. Yet, still she learned them, more to keep her mind from the fact that Luc had not returned than anything else.

Wulfridge was secure again. Repairs were being made, and the sound of workmen filled the air most of the days. In the fields beyond, crops were planted and new green shoots filled the furrows with the promise of an excellent harvest. Men had been sent from the castle with supplies to help the burned villages rebuild, and the people responded with tributes of livestock and goods. As Wulfridge squatted on the very tip of a promontory thrust into the sea, it guarded the inlet that led to the burgeoning new city on the mainland. Prosperity loomed ahead, with the promise of peace once Northumbria was subdued.

Remy considered it near accomplished, for William had visited devastation upon most of the northern region. So wasted was the land, it would take years for the people to rebuild, or for forests to grow and crops to thrive. Yet here on the coast, Wulfridge was spared. These people were loyal to William, and loyal to their Norman overlord, and so lived quietly for the most part.

Ceara moved restlessly from the hall to the ramparts again, to gaze out over the walls and watch for Luc. It would all be for naught if he had been slain. What would she do without him? Their reunion had been so brief, and though heartened to know he loved her, it would yet be more bitter to lose him now.

Twilight cast faint pink and purple shadows on the land, softening the sharp ridge of trees, and out on the sea, she could see a mist rolling slowly in. When it dipped to blanket the ground in hazy shrouds that would hide any sign of approaching men, she gave up her watch. Dispirited, she moved away from the wall to the steep, winding steps that led downward. Below in the courtyard, men went about their business, tending domestic animals, drawing water from the wells, repairing harness, and cleaning armor. Then a shout went up. A dog yapped, and one of the hounds bayed as she was crossing the bailey toward the main building.

She glanced over her shoulder and paused, frowning as a man ran to the gates and began to haul on the chains of the windlass that swung open the heavy gates of iron and wood. Another man slid the bar out of its thick metal hasp, and it groaned a protest. Slowly, the gates began to open, and now Ceara heard the pounding thunder of hooves on the road outside the walls.

Mist dewed the air thickly, shining on metal and stone and forming hazy clouds around the sputtering wall torches. She clenched her hands into the folds of her kirtle, shivering though the night was not cold. Was it a messenger from Luc, perhaps?

But the noise was too great for just one horse, even muffled by the rolling fog. A "halloo" went up, and she saw through the pearly mist the familiar banner against the gray sky, scarlet and black, the wolf insignia that she had once thought Luc too quick to bear. It was his device, had been his symbol long before he had come to Wulfridge, and now it was most dear to her.

She stood still there near the fountain, where water splashed now from spouts shaped like fish to cascade into the pool where once Saxon blood had flowed. Sudden fear seized her, that he had been hurt—maimed, perhaps, like poor Alain, or that the Lady Amélie would ride pillion behind him, clinging to her rescuer with dainty hands that always made Ceara feel so big and clumsy—

Then Luc was there, riding at the head of the line by the standard-bearer, his familiar destrier churning up the damp earth with great hooves, chomping at the metal bit in his mouth and snorting fiercely. No less fierce was his lone rider, garbed in mud-caked armor and long Norman sword, his helmet gleaming wetly under the flickering light of torches.

Ceara watched as Paul ran forward to take the reins of the destrier and Luc dismounted in a clink of mail and weapons. He swept off his helmet and tucked it beneath his arm, and turned to look up at the rider next to him, saying something she could not hear.

It was Sir Robert, and he must have been injured for Luc was reaching up to take his arm as he dismounted much more slowly than he had once done. There was no sign of Lady Amélie, and Ceara was almost ashamed of the burst of relief she felt. She hoped the lady had remained in the land of the Scots. . . .

Moving forward, she halted just out of the wavering pool of torchlight, hungrily devouring Luc with her eyes, anxious that he was unharmed and still the same man she loved. And then at last he turned and saw her, and held out an arm with a smile. She went to him, giddy with delight and feeling faintly foolish at the same time, but unable to stop herself. His mail was wet and cold against her skin, but she didn't care as she was swept into his embrace. He smelled of leather and mud. He gripped her hands tightly and brought them to his lips, kissing her fingers.

Then he smiled down at her, and his voice was husky. *"Froides mains, chaudes amours. . . ."*

"Je t'aime . . . de tout mon coeur. . . ." Luc drew back and eyed her quizzically, and she shrugged. *"Je parle français, mon époux."*

"Yea, I hear you speaking French," Luc said in English, and glanced over his shoulder when Robert was rude enough to laugh. Then he looked back at her with a lazy grin. "It did occur to me on several occasions that you might know more than you betrayed. I should probably box your ears for you, saucy wench."

She smiled up at him. "I do not think you want to do that, my husband. I am still proficient with my dagger."

"Ah, and would no doubt use it." Luc sighed, and slid an arm around her shoulders. "I see that I shall have to stay home more often, for when I return you are most undisciplined. Now come, and tell me the news. Did Remy repair the door to the vault? I shall go at once to see it if he did, for I told him what must be done in that message I sent."

She pulled away from him, vexed that he cared more for the castle repairs than he did her, but when she glanced up, she saw the laughter in his eyes and knew he was teasing her.

"I do not see why you would care about the vault door," she said then, stepping back so that Luc could give Robert his arm to lean on as they walked across the courtyard. "It is peaceful here now."

"So I saw on my return. It was a much more peaceful ride than the one that took me to Niall."

She flashed him a quick glance, then looked at Robert. "Are you hurt badly, Sir Robert? Shall I run ahead and have a surgeon ready his instruments?"

Robert shook his head. "No, it is a small injury. I just had it lanced again, and now it has begun to heal, but it has left me sore and limping like a three-legged dog. Your husband is not the most gentle of surgeons."

"It was me or Sighere, and you see how he already limps," Luc retorted. "You might have ended up skinned, with your head displayed on his shelf like a grinning fox."

"Sighere went with you?" Ceara looked at them with surprise.

"No, but we were forced to stop at his cottage on our return, when Robert's leg worsened." Despite Robert's protest, Luc lifted him and carried him up the steep flight of steps to the entrance hall. Then he set him down and turned to Ceara. He held out his hand. "Robert can find his own way now, and we have much to discuss, wife. Come."

She put her hand in his, and went with him to the antechamber of the solar they shared, where she helped him remove his armor. It was crusted with mud and dark reddish stains that she did not want to examine closely, and she laid it aside for Rudd to clean. The boy had become quite proficient of late, taking up the duties that Alain was still too slow to do. One day, Alain had promised, Rudd might become a squire, and then a knight if he found a sponsor. It was an unlikely dream, but Ceara thought that many unlikely dreams had come true.

Warm water and a tub were brought, with pots of soap and thick cloths, and Ceara lovingly bathed Luc's back and washed his hair, her heart full as she performed duties she once would never have considered. Food had been brought to the chamber, and Sheba roused for her morsel, limping back to her bed of straw and rags in the corner to happily gnaw a meaty bone.

Then Luc rose from the tub, water splashing all about the floor, his body wet and gleaming in the soft light of candle and torch. Ceara's heart lurched, for she recognized the glitter in his eyes as he held out a hand.

Suddenly shy, she indicated the tray of food with a sweep of her arm. "My lord, your supper awaits."

"Let it. My hunger is great, but not for food. It has been overlong since we were together, and I find that I cannot wait."

"My lord. . . ."

But Luc moved to her in a single long stride, sweeping her up and ignoring her gasping protest that he was wet as he carried her from the antechamber into the solar. A fire burned in a brass brazier, and a single candle flickered in a tall stand on the small table near the bed. He lay her down and stretched across her, his damp skin heated and smelling of sandalwood. She buried her face in the curve of his neck and shoulder and breathed deeply.

He shifted to one side, smiling lazily at her as he traced an imaginary line around her mouth with one finger. "I dreamed of you at night, when I was lying on the cold ground listening to Robert or the other men snore. And I wanted nothing more than to be with you."

She caught his hand and turned it over to kiss his palm and calluses. "And now you are."

"Yea, *chérie*, now I am. And I intend to stay. This is my home and heart, and I am weary of war."

Ceara drew in a deep breath of happiness, then asked the question that had worried her since he had returned. "My lord, Sir Robert has returned, but I thought that the messenger said both he and Lady Amélie needed your aid."

Luc propped himself on one elbow, his long body sprawled beside her, and tucked a curl of her blond hair behind her ear. "Lady Amélie is dead, I fear."

"Dead? How?"

Silence spun between them, then Luc sighed and shook his head. " 'Tis a tale best told once, then forgotten. She betrayed us all, and for reasons that were spun out of air. In a . . . struggle . . . with Robert, she was killed. Robert was fortunate to escape Niall and Adela with his life, and he almost lost that on the road. If I had not come upon him when I did, he would now be dead as well. There was a fierce fight, but Niall has retreated. I do not think he and my stepmother will plan any more nefarious schemes for a while. This last one cost him dear." He smiled slightly. "William is in negotiations with King Malcolm for a truce. They barter back and forth as kings so often do, so that Niall may now find himself fighting both England and Scotland. Amélie's death will not please William, though no doubt he will not be as grieved once he learns of her betrayal. He is not a man to long bemoan the fate of traitors, as you may know. Nor is Malcolm pleased to offer sanctuary to rebel earls anymore, so Niall is losing all his allies."

He kissed her, brushing his mouth over her lips, his eyes half-veiled by a brush of his lashes that did not hide the sensual gleam. "But I weary of discussing rebel earls and clever kings. I prefer more pleasurable conversation. Tell me, my sweet, do you still make those breathless little sounds when I kiss you here . . . and here . . . or even—here?"

She gasped, her body arching when his roving mouth found a sensitive spot. Her skirts were up around her waist, his hands eliciting delicious shivers that went from her fingers to her toes, and she was only barely aware when she was as naked as he, lying in the warmth of his arms and the shelter of their bed, returning his caresses with an eagerness that betrayed her answering passion.

And when Luc slipped inside her, she rose to meet him, her arms around his neck and her love for him so great she thought she must shatter with it. Her hands tangled in his black hair, grown long again to cover his neck, and she held him still and kissed him with mounting need. Long had she yearned for him to be with her just like this, his hands on her breasts, her mouth, the fiery sweep of his tongue on flesh and quivering lips . . . it was over much too soon, but the tempest that swept over them left Luc resting against her with drowsy satisfaction. He lifted his head and kissed her mouth, then held her close to him as he slipped into weary slumber. Ceara smiled, content.

Later, when the excitement of his return had calmed and she had his full attention, she would tell him about the babe. It would be born before the calends of November, as she had been. And this child would be well loved, a child of parents who were not Saxon and Norman, but English. One country, one people. For all time, though it would not be easy. But one day, all would be bound together and there would be no more division.

Ceara thought that Balfour would be happy to know that Wulfridge would soon ring with the happy laughter of his heirs.

In the antechamber, Sheba lifted her head and howled, a warbling cry that reverberated through the chamber. A gift and a promise, Wulfric had told Ceara when he'd given her the wolf pup bought from Danish merchants. As long as Wulfridge was guarded by a wolf, it would be safe.

And then Ceara remembered the old crone down by the sea, and the words that had made no sense to a young, grieving girl:

"The wolf will bring great grief and strife to the land, but after there will come peace for a time, and with it—love. Great love, m'lady, and the lifelong loyalty of a wolf will be yours. . . ."

Yea, it was true. Wulfridge would be ever safe, for it offered a home for them all.

About the Author

Juliana Garnett is a bestselling author writing under a new name to indulge her passion for medieval history. Always fascinated by the romance of *knights in shining armor*, this Southern writer is now at liberty to focus on the pageantry and allure of days when chivalry was expected and there were plenty of damsels in distress.

Ms. Garnett has won numerous awards for her previous works, and hopes to entertain new readers who share her passion for valorous heroes and strong, beautiful heroines.

If you loved

THE VOW

Don't miss Juliana Garnett's next medieval romance, sure to wrap you up in the breathtaking passion and stirring pageantry of another time . . .

THE SCOTSMAN

a Bantam Fanfare title on sale in February 1998

(Read on for a sneak preview. . . .)

Chapter One

"THERE IT LIES, m'lord. Warfield Castle, home to the bloody earl himself."

Alexander Fraser peered through new leaves at the huge, gray stone castle squatting atop a distant ridge. It was silhouetted against a bright blue sky like the backbone of a gigantic dragon, pennants flapping atop the tallest turret. He slanted a wary glance at the English woodsman who leaned casually against a thick oak, and wondered if he could trust him.

"The earl must have done you a grave injustice for you to so gladly betray him."

"Aye." With open contempt creasing his craggy features, the woodsman spat on the ground. "As he has done injustice to all who fall to his uncertain mercy. If not for his value to the earl, yer brother would have met the same fate as Robert Bruce's cousin, I warrant."

"No doubt." Alex drew in a deep breath that smelled of forest and wet earth. "Adam de Brus's death at the earl's hands caused Robert Bruce much sorrow. 'Tis why I am come to barter with Warfield for my brother's freedom."

The woodsman gave a short bark of laughter. "Ye have not enough gold to barter with that one, m'lord. It's yer life he's after, not yer gold. Aye, he's a cruel Norman overlord who hates Saxon and Scot alike. Beware yer back."

"I always watch my back." Alex gestured, and Robbie MacLeod tossed the woodsman a small bag of coins. "For your trouble, Ham of Warfield."

But Ham shook his head. His hand lifted, cradling the leather pouch in his palm as he held it out. "Nay, m'lord. 'Tis not for gold that I lent ye aid. I am a poor man, and if 'twas seen that I had coin, there are some 'twould guess I had done ye a service. Vengeance shall be my payment."

"Yet 'tis not vengeance I have come to seek, but my brother's freedom."

"Aye, but ye are more likely to get a sword in yer gullet instead." Ham's craggy face was seamed with bitter sorrow. "These are harsh times for Saxon and Scot alike. The Border Watchdog shows mercy to none."

Alex nodded understanding, and turned in his saddle. His gray eyes narrowed as he gazed across the broad meadow scattered with bright yellow buttercups; it sloped down from the high ridge upon which Warfield Castle perched like a giant bird of prey. P'raps 'twas true what the woodsman said, but how else could he free Jamie from the earl's hold? Confrontation might be chancy, but 'twas the only choice he had left to him. Robert Bruce had exhausted all appeals and, indeed, was too caught up in the struggle for an entire country's freedom to spend much time on one rash lad who had defied his brother's orders to remain safely behind. That Jamie had had the misfortune to be taken captive in the company of Adam de Brus had near earned him death. And 'twas a mystery why the lad still lived, when those with him were now dead.

"Alex?" Robbie nudged his horse closer on the narrow path. Leafy branches dumped recent rain on his fair head as he leaned close to say softly, "We hae no' much time left tae us afore we are bound tae be seen. There is no cover tae hide our approach. Do we ride boldy in through the front gate, or sneak in by the postern door as yon woodsman counsels?"

"We do not have enough men with us to risk a fight. 'Twould only ensure Jamie's death, as well as our own capture. I will do as I intended, and barter with the earl."

Ham cleared his throat and with a frown looked up at Alex. "Ye will not succeed, not without the devil's own luck. 'Twould be best to go in disguise. I will lend ye my bundle of faggots to bear upon yer back, and with a leather jerkin instead of yon plaid ye are wearing, ye may have a chance."

Robbie's eyes brightened, and his grin was reckless. "Aye, and 'tis a fine plan indeed, woodsman! I will wear the faggots upon my back, Alex, while ye—"

"Nay." Alex ignored Robbie's crestfallen expression and muttered oath. "Warfield is too great a keep. I willna risk it."

"No' even for Jamie?"

Alex met Robbie's gaze steadily. "If I thought my

life would purchase my brother's, I would do it. But I cannot buy his life with yours or any other man's, Robbie. Do not ask it of me."

For several moments the sounds of muffled hooves on wet leaves and the brittle jangle of harnesses were all that broke the silence. Then Robbie swore softly, and nodded. "Bloody hell, Alex, 'tis no' a choice a man should hae tae make."

Tactfully, the woodsman inclined his head toward a narrow path. "Yonder lies the road to Warfield Keep, m'lord. I will go with ye as far as the main road."

"You have been a great help, Ham of Warfield, and I will not forget you."

A grin squared the woodsman's mouth. "Nay, nor will I forget ye so easy, m'lord. Ye have a wicked look about ye, though yer tongue speaks fairly."

Alex smiled, but his hand lifted to finger the rough scar that swooped along his left jaw. Token from an English sword. A little higher and it would have blinded him in that eye, so he was lucky enough.

"Och, dinna be vain, Alex!" Robbie laughed at his gesture. "I hae no' noticed a lack of female regard since ye earned tha' cut. The lasses seem tae love ye more fer it. Aye, an' I hae no' forgot how ye ha' one on each arm no' so long ago, so dinna be worrit aboot yer bonny face...."

Nudging his mount forward as Robbie began to expand his rhetoric, Alex turned his attention to the path ahead. It wound through the woods along a shallow burn, gurgling over flat rocks, hidden at times by towering trees and thick underbrush. The path took them out of sight of the castle, plunging them into shadowy forest gloom that muffled the noise of horse hooves and harnesses. It was quiet here, with the birds in the trees a gentle twitter overhead and the wind a soft sigh through leafy branches.

Yet despite the tranquillity, an alien sound intruded, catching his horse's attention so that the velvety ears pricked forward. Alex tensed. One hand went to the sword dangling at his left side and he turned in his saddle.

"Do you hear that, Robbie?"

Robbie swore softly, slapping at an annoying insect buzzing about his head. "Hear wha'? I dinna hear aught but these bloody English flies in my ears."

Alex halted and slid from his mount to the leaf-cushioned ground. Wet leaves rustled under his booted feet as he moved toward the source of the intrusive noise. When Robbie protested, he waved an admonishing hand. "Bide here with the others while I seek out the lay of the land."

Deeper into the thicket, muffled sounds like the clapping of hands drifted to him through the thick new leaves of the copse. The rush of water grew louder where the small burn twined its way down through the rocks. A perfect spot for thirsty men and beasts—and ambush. The hair on the back of his neck prickled.

"Whist! Alex . . ." Robbie loomed behind him, a soft voice against his shoulder. " 'Tis Warfield's men ye hear?"

"It could be."

A metallic whisk of sword being drawn from sheath sang softly in the still, dense air. "*A h-uile mac máther*—Och, I am ready enow tae kill a bluidy Sassenach."

Alex put out a warning hand. "Be still. Wait here for me." He pressed forward alone, moving on the balls of his feet, slipping through the bushes carefully so as not to alert any men beyond. His unsheathed sword was in his right hand, the wicked blade of the *skean dhu* he kept hidden in his boot top glittering in his left.

Above the cheerful rush of water from the melting of winter snows, he heard the same rhythmic slapping, and paused behind the prickly shelter of a towering fir. The pungent scent of the needles filled his nose, and an overhead branch dripped residue from a recent rain onto his bare head. The water was cold, sliding down his neck and beneath his collar, dampening his dark hair and the fine linen of his shirt.

Though April, the air was still brisk, and he wore his plaid slung over one shoulder and belted around his waist, his shirt open at the neck and the sleeves rolled up to his elbows. Sunlight filtered through high tree branches, slanting into his eyes so that he blinked against it and narrowed his eyes to dark gray slits.

Using the tip of his sword blade, Alex parted the fir branches slowly so that he could view the enemy beyond. To his surprise, he saw only a slender girl kneeling by the stream, scrubbing at a wad of cloth. No soldiers were in sight, but he would not have noticed if a full score of them ranged along the banks of the burn.

It was the maid who caught his immediate attention.

Sunlight shone bright on her, lending brilliance to loose waves of coppery hair that spread over her shoulders and back, framing a face of such exquisite beauty it took away his breath. Alex stood like a stone, watching as she held up the dripping material, frowned at the drenched folds of gown, then dunked it beneath the water again, scrubbing vigorously. He was close enough that he could see the slight mist of water spray moistening her cheeks, see the elegant straight line of her nose, and the luxuriant sweep of her lashes over wide, luminous eyes. Green? Blue? 'Twas impossible to tell from this distance.

She was graceful, slender, and completely oblivious to anything but the gown she was washing and the fine day. When she sat back with her face tilted up to the sun as she did now, resting on her heels, he saw that she wore only a thin shift that hid very little from his gaze. Ripe breasts pressed against the thin material, and because the shift was damp, he could see the faint dark circles of her nipples beneath. Her legs were long and bare, tucked beneath her, and when she stood up to wring out the gown, he caught a glimpse of the inward curve of her waist and flare of her slender hips.

His throat tightened. He hadn't expected this. He was primed for battle, not this sudden surge of pure lust that filled him with a heavy need.

Behind him, he heard Robbie expel a long breath as if he'd been holding it. "Sweet Jesus, Alex—d'ye see the lass . . . ?

"Yea, Robbie. I see her full well. . . ."

A moment of weighty silence fell again before Robbie muttered harshly, "Wha' the devil—d'ye think she's out here alone?"

"Mayhap I should find out." He glanced over his

shoulder. "I dinna suppose 'twould do me any good to tell you again to stay back, would it?"

"Nay." Robbie's grin was unabashed. "No' a bit. I ha' best go wi' ye. 'Tis most like an English trick, and ye will need me. And if 'tis no' a trick, the lass may need me."

Ignoring him, Alex pushed through the fragrant branches of fir and stepped onto the banks of the narrow burn. The maid's head flung up, and her eyes widened with alarm when she saw the two men. Alex was almost within arm's length of her now, close enough to see shadows of reaction flicker across her face and quiver on her lips. Blue—no, green eyes, stared at him, shaded by impossibly long lashes.

He'd seen the same kind of expression in the eyes of a startled young doe—fear mixed with curiosity. It held him immobile as he regarded the maid. She tightly gripped her dripping gown in front of her, pressed against her chest as if a shield. Lips parted, she darted a quick glance around her, then lifted her chin, a defensive gesture.

"Tell me what you do here on Warfield's land."

Whatever he'd anticipated, it wasn't this cool, imperative challenge delivered in the precise English of an aristocrat. A glance sufficed to show him that her garments were not those of a peasant, and her undergarment was of fine linen instead of coarse flax.

Alex lifted a brow and decided lying would best suit his ends: "I did not know 'twas Warfield's land, lass. Does he own all of this?"

Hesitation darkened her eyes when he waved a hand to encompass forest, fen, and distant keep. Then she shrugged, a light casual gesture.

“ ’Tis well-known to any but the dullest of men that this land belongs to the earl of Warfield.”

Alex laughed softly at her implied insult. “Ah, lass, you wound me with your sharp tongue. Do you always speak so harsh to gentle visitors?” As he took a casual step forward he smiled, a reassuring lift of his lips meant to convince her he meant her no harm. “I have heard of the earl. He wields much power, ’tis said.”

Water curled in bubbling froth around her feet as she dug bare toes into the muddy grass on the bank and stood her ground. “There are some who say he does.”

“And you, lass? What do you say?” He took another step forward, this time putting himself close enough to reach out and graze her cheek with his fingers, close enough to see that her eyes were a peculiar, riveting shade of blue-green. “Does the earl’s power reach even to this distant glen?”

Her breath came in shallow pants for air that drew his gaze to the rapid movement of her breasts beneath the thin, wet shift. For a long moment she stared at him. A hawk soared overhead with a high, keening cry that seemed to linger over tall tree spires and mingle with puffs of white cloud. Water made a cheerful, gurgling sound, and the wind rustled thick branches of fir and pine in a heavy whisper.

Sunlight cast long lash-shadows on her cheeks, and her lips were slightly parted, moist and tempting as she drew in a sharp breath. Her gaze shifted to the naked sword he held, and her pupils dilated. Another quickly indrawn breath stirred a tendril of hair at the side of her mouth, but her words were calm enough:

“Do you think to test the earl’s power whilst you

are so safely distant from his keep? 'Tis a coward's trick."

"Bold words from a wee lass, I vow." He sheathed his sword and moved even closer, smiling a little when she moved away from him. Taking a quick step to thwart her retreat, he lifted a brow. "Ah, lass, do you think you could run fast enough to get away from me?"

"Do you mean to chase me?"

"Aye, if you run."

Another step took him close enough to lift a slightly damp strand of coppery hair in his palm, and this time, she made no move to avoid him but stood still and quivering, staring up at him. A thin blue ribbon dangled from one of her curls, no longer holding it in what must have been a neat plait but was now disarrayed. He tugged the ribbon free, holding her gaze steadily while he wound the length of blue silk around his fist.

She sucked in a deep breath; her eyes were wide enough to trap sunlight in the dark centers like a deep green forest pool. A changeling, with eyes as inconstant as the wind. . . .

"What do you want?"

Her question was a trembling whisper, seeming to hang in the air between them. He looked past her to the line of trees and the quiet serenity of the towering forest beyond the burn. Nothing stirred but the wind and water. No one came roaring out of the trees to protect the maid; yet she was no peasant lass whiling away a pleasant day in the wood. She stood now and watched him warily, and though nothing seemed amiss, he was aware of a sense of urgency.

He smiled, and closed his fingers around the slender, fragile bones of the maid's wrist, pulling her to him.

"You should not be out here alone, lass. Let me see you safely away."

"I was safe enough until you came. Release me." She tugged, but he did not loose her. Her gaze flew upward to meet his. "Do you hold me against my will, sir?"

"Nay, I do but seek to keep you safe. Come. I shall see you home."

Doubt registered in her eyes again, and he sensed the conflict within her as she shook her head. "I am quite capable of seeing myself home, sir. 'Tis not far."

"Aye, but between here and Warfield Keep anything could happen. What would the earl say if you came to harm and I did naught to aid you?"

"Why do you think he would care?" She strained against his grip, a bit angrily now, with her eyes narrowed into jeweled slits. A deep flush rode her high cheekbones, and an erratic pulse beat in the hollow of her bare throat. "Set me free, knave, or—"

"Or?" he prompted when she halted. "Or do you intend to flee? Summon aid, mayhap?"

"Mayhap."

His eyes narrowed. The pugnacious tilt of her chin was far too determined—and arrogant. She was no miller's daughter, this lass, but a maid of importance, that was certain. Important to whom?

Beyond her, a sudden gust of wind shifted new green leaves, and he glanced toward the thick dark line of trees. His hand tightened on the hilt of his sheathed sword. It was possible men waited in the shadowed glen to fall upon them. It could be a trap—just as Robbie had warned earlier.

After a moment of tense silence, Alex gave a careless shrug designed to disguise his suspicions. "Nay, bonny lass, I think I shall escort you straight to the earl himself."

"Fool, you will earn your death should you meet with the earl. Even a Lowland Scot should know better."

Her disparaging tone and obvious scorn stung. His grip on her tightened. "I do not fear Warfield."

"Then you deserve your fate. Release me."

This time he allowed her to twist free. She rubbed at her wrist, watching him from narrowed eyes when he joined Robbie at the edge of the trees.

Robbie nudged him, voice lowered to a rolling mutter. "Ham knows her, Alex lad. The woodsman claims she is the earl's daughter."

"Warfield's *daughter*?"

"Aye . . . Alex, d'ye recall how ye said ye canna buy Jamie's life wi' yer own or any other man's? This is the earl's daughter—wha' d'ye reckon her worth wa'd be tae him?"

Alex nodded slowly. "P'raps we have more to barter with than I dared hope for, Robbie: a life for a life, after all."

He turned to look at the maid. She was watching them, her nostrils slightly flared as that of a cornered doe, eyes wary and turbulent with emotion. Yea, the earl would no doubt give him whatever he demanded to have the safe return of his daughter. For the first time in near two years, hope soared high.

Alex started toward her with long strides. The maid's eyes widened. By all that was holy, she was the loveliest thing he had ever seen in England, and he almost regretted that he must return her . . . almost.